Praise f

Avenger: The

"I am a huge fan of J.R.R Tolkien and Terry Goodkind and I seriously believe that these books, Defender and Avenger, could be another classic in the fantasy genre."
Reviewer Amy Sanders, Read To My Heart's Content Book Blog

"...I cannot wait for the next book in this series."
Reviewer Mindy Kleinfelter

I liked this one even more than the first...it is a joy to read some of the quips...some of them even made me laugh out loud. The story is filled with elements that a lover of fantasy will adore...I enjoyed the read and highly recommend it. —"
Reviewer Cheryl M.

I enjoyed this second book in the Sanctuary Series even more than the first (the first was good too!)
Reviewer Jen, Goodreads.com

Defender: The Sanctuary Series, Volume One

"This book is full of action, adventure, emotion and anticipation, so much so that I didn't want it to end!"
Reviewer Gina Hurteau-Jackson

"I have always been a fan of fantasy novels and this book rates way up there with "Lord of the Rings" and others...am so excited for the next in the series I can barely contain myself and please give this book a chance because it is really going to be one of the best of our time. Great author and great novel!"
Reviewer Amy Sanders, Read To My Heart's Content Book Blog

"The characters are well written and the dialog can be very witty...will gladly order the next book in the series."
Reviewer Jeremy/Andrea S.

"...despite my early reservations, I found myself wanting the next book in this series and I do recommend it to anyone looking for a fantasy with plenty of action and adventure!"
Reviewer Littleroonkanga2

"Cyrus leads a cast of wonderful characters and the character development is topnotch...I would highly recommend this book to anyone who loves to get "lost" in a fantasy world when they read."
Reviewer Marie C. Cordalis

CHAMPION

The Sanctuary Series

Robert J. Crane

CHAMPION
THE SANCTUARY SERIES: VOLUME THREE

2nd Edition

AUTHOR'S NOTE
This is a work of fiction. Names, characters, places, and incidents
either are the product of the author's imagination or are used
fictitiously, and any resemblance to actual persons, living or dead,
business establishments, events, or locales is entirely coincidental.

For information regarding permissions, please contact
cyrusdavidon@gmail.com.

Find Robert J. Crane online at
http://www.robertjcrane.com

Layout provided by **Everything Indie**
http://www.everything-indie.com

Acknowledgments

Here we are again, the third time around (this series, not counting short stories), and I again have a mountain of thanks to dispense. So let's get to it, shall we?

First, major gratitude to the inestimable Heather Rodefer. This time she not only fulfilled the function of first reader (again) but also was responsible for finding the cover art. For her extraordinary beyond-the-call-of-duty efforts, I hereby award her the designation of my Editor-In-Chief.

Next was the contributions of Shannon Garza, who once more contributed a weather eye (or two, she's not Alaric, after all) to finding errors that no one else seemed to find. She also helped me keep on track with the emotion of the story, letting me know when if I was resonating the way I wanted to be. Also, I owe her my apologies, because Niamh was based largely on her. Sorry, Red.

Last of the editing trio, thanks goes again to the knowledgeable and brilliant Debra Wesley whose wide breadth of knowledge about all things, from the mundane to the arcane, helped me create a better manuscript. Who else would keep me informed about the running abilities of horses and the growing patterns of grasses?

Also, thanks to Kari Layman, who may or may not have read this book at some point in time; I'm not really sure. Better safe than sorry, though, especially with her. She will cut you.

I'd like to thank Patrick Ashton, Trevor Norman, Sam Best and Brittany Scott for helping to get my books out there in one way or another. Much appreciated, folks.

The cover art was once again handled on the second edition by Karri Klawiter of artbykarri.com, who has quite a prodigious talent for making my books look pretty.

Editing, formatting, all the stuff that holds the book together, was done by the great Nicholas J. Ambrose, as always.

Last of all, I'd like to give my grateful thanks to my mom and dad, wife and kids. As always, it's all for you guys and because of you guys.

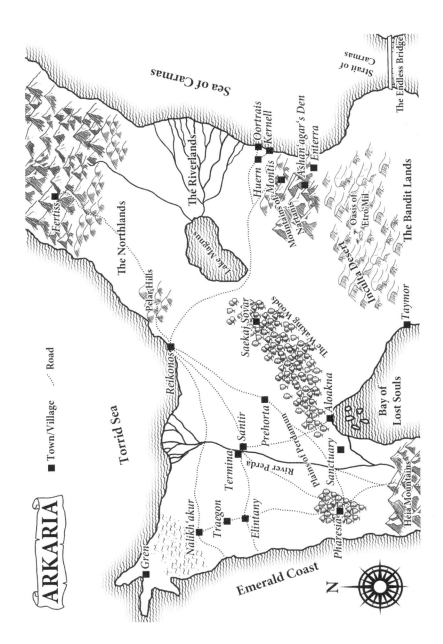

champion (*n.*) — a person who fights for or defends any person or cause

NOW

Prologue

Even at a time when all manner of hell had broken loose, bright spots were there to be found if one looked hard enough. Rain drenched the Plains of Perdamun as Cyrus Davidon sat in the archives of Sanctuary, a book across his lap. Outside the window, a single beam of light stretched down from the clouds and shone on the fields in the distance. Cyrus smiled, a small, grim one that contained only the smallest kernel of actual happiness.

The window was broken off its hinges, shattered glass littering the floor in front of it. The light in the archive came from torches burning on the wall and a fire in the hearth that kept the damp chill of the rain at bay. He stared at the painting that hung crooked above the fireplace, a simple old picture of a hut built in a style far different from those of Arkaria.

The weight of his armor was heavier than it had been in years. He reached down and grasped the hilt of his sword and felt the power it held course through him, giving him strength. He looked over the plains and thought with a rueful smile, *This is the perfect domain for me. Dark and gloomy, like my thoughts of late, with only the barest light for hope.* The smile faded.

He looked back to the book that was cradled in his hands. *The Journal of Vara*, it said inside the cover. *An Account of My Days With Sanctuary.* He had stopped reading as the rains swept in, pausing to admire the quiet fury of the storm. *Drenching, drowning rains*, he thought, *reshaping the landscape.* He recalled a stream he'd seen on the ride to Sanctuary that had carved its way across the plains, one he couldn't recall being there just a few years earlier.

Nothing stops the rains. Water runs its course, inevitable, and ploughs new pathways across the fields and the land. You can't fight it; it's a losing battle. He chuckled, again rueful. *I know a thing or two about fighting losing battles.* He stared back at the journal in his hands.

The words blurred as he refocused on them, and he realized that a droplet of water had fallen on the page. He looked around and realized the rest of the world had blurred as well. He sighed and removed his gauntlet, using the exposed sleeve of his undershirt to wipe his eyes. He wondered why he was bothering to read the next segment of the diary; after all, his memory was clear on what had happened.

Still, he blinked and focused on the words, the flowing script produced by the hand of Vara. He could picture her, sitting at the table in her quarters, long blond hair tucked in a ponytail that bounced as her hand moved up and down the page with the quill, laboring to produce the words he now read. *The best days of my life, I am convinced, are those when I knew exactly who I was, and what I was willing to fight for. Unfortunately, as I age, those days seem to have long since disappeared, and I even find myself wondering if some fights are worth fighting at all. Especially when it comes to arguing with the most pigheaded man walking the face of Arkaria...*

He laughed. "To be called pigheaded by her is an irony of the highest order," he told the empty room. "And likely a compliment." Her words went on, and Cyrus remembered the days Vara wrote about, as the feeble southern winter had settled in around Sanctuary. He remembered the night, the cold, the return from Purgatory, and all that had happened afterward. Inexplicably, another droplet of water appeared on the aged parchment...and another, until he could scarcely see the words that she had written.

6 YEARS EARLIER

Chapter 1

The light of a teleport spell faded around Cyrus Davidon. He looked across the Sanctuary foyer, from the massive balcony above the doors to the Great Hall to the open lounge, where already a celebration was taking place. The smell of the wood burning in the hearth filled his nose and gave him the warm feeling of home, taking the chill out of the early winter air.

"Keeps getting easier, doesn't it?" The voice of Andren, his oldest friend came from behind him. Andren was an elf, dark hair reaching down to his shoulders, his beard wild and unkempt. His look was a contrast to the usual for elven men who sported shorter locks and no facial hair. Light freckles dusted his complexion and his hair covered his elongated ears, leading some who met him to assume he was human based on personality alone.

Cyrus looked back at him. "I would hope so. We've gone through the Trials of Purgatory a good dozen times now; we'd be in trouble if it was getting tougher." He looked past Andren to see others talking, boasting and drinking all around them. Samwen Longwell, a dragoon who carried a lance as his weapon, stood in the corner of the Lounge talking with Thad Proelius, a warrior whose armor was red as raw meat.

"Aye." Andren smiled at him; then the elf shot a look at Larana Stillhet, Sanctuary's brewer and cook, who had teleported next to him. Her vivid green eyes looked out from underneath her black, tousled bangs. Her skin was dark – a surprise for someone who spent so much time in the kitchens, Cyrus had always thought. "Fresh kegs out in the lounge?"

She cast a brief glance at Cyrus, keeping her eyes low, not meeting his gaze. She nodded then shuffled toward the kitchen.

"Quiet one when you're around, isn't she?" Andren moved to stand shoulder to shoulder with Cyrus and watched the diminutive druid disappear into the Great Hall. The elf shot Cyrus a twisted smile. "Has some feelings for you, doesn't she?"

"It's unkind to insult her when she's not here to defend herself." The voice that came from behind them lashed at Andren with a sarcastic edge. Cyrus turned to see cold blue eyes staring him down from a lovely face. The speaker was tall, even for an elven woman, standing a few inches under six feet. Her armor was shined to a glaring silver sheen even though they had been traipsing through the Trials of Purgatory for the last several hours. Not a hair was out of place in her golden ponytail, which was still bound tight behind her.

"Vara," he said with a nod of his head.

"I didn't say anything unkind about Larana," Andren replied. "All I said was she gets quiet when Cyrus is around; thought maybe she had a little crush on him."

"Implying she would have such poor judgment as to find herself attracted to this oafish lout is insult enough for the issuance of a duel in most cultures." Vara's eyes narrowed but glittered in the dancing firelight of the torches and the hearth behind them.

A deep sigh was followed by a slump of Cyrus's shoulders. "I thought after all the work we've done planning these expeditions to Purgatory that you'd finally buried your need to belittle me."

A gleam in her eye matched the slightest tug at the corner of her mouth. "Perhaps I was making a joke."

Andren shook his head. "Impossible. You're far too serious for that."

Vara arched an eyebrow at the older elf then turned back to Cyrus. "Niamh just informed me that Alaric has called a Council meeting. I assumed," she said, "you would want to know." She brushed past them, running her shoulder into Cyrus's as she passed and casting him a look that was equal parts affection and annoyance.

"What was all that about?" Andren looked at Cyrus as Vara reached the stairs.

"The Ice Princess teases the warrior in black," came a voice from a grating below them.

"Fortin," Cyrus said, looking down into the grate, "we've talked about listening in on private conversations." Red eyes stared up at him from the darkness below. Fortin was a rock giant, half again as tall as most men, and more dangerous than any other warrior Cyrus had met. He lived in a dungeon room below the foyer.

"Yes, and if you want to keep them private, you wouldn't have them in public. But," the rock giant said with a hint of amusement, "I wouldn't be nearly so entertained."

Cyrus shook his head and turned back to Andren. "She's been

a lot kinder to me since Enterra." He caught a glimpse of Aisling Nightwind skulking at the edge of the room, a dark elf with a roguish bent, looking at him with sly eyes as she slipped up the staircase behind Vara. Once she was gone, he looked to his left and through the doors to the Great Hall. Tables were lined up for dinner and already occupied by a sea of unfamiliar faces, almost all of them human. Andren followed his gaze.

"More refugees?" Andren shook his head. "I didn't expect the dark elves would be ravaging your peoples' lands the way they have."

Cyrus shook his head, his spirits falling. "I don't think anyone anticipated that. The war has gone badly for the Human Confederation—I heard that the dark elves have sacked and are holding Prehorta now."

"Aye," Andren agreed. "I remember the last war—and the one before that—and..." He frowned. "I remember a lot of them. One of them, I was in a town that they sacked in a surprise offensive. Their army came in, all lined up in neat rows, and once they realized there wasn't anyone to defend the village, they just ran wild. Tore up everything in sight, killing the men—" his ruddy complexion whitened—"dragging away the women, burning everything and stealing what they could carry."

"You made it out alive, though."

"Clearly," Andren said. "Once I knew it was a lost cause, I used my return spell to scamper back to Pharesia." He swallowed, his eyes haunted, and he took a deep swig from his flask. "They're not kind to their prisoners, either."

Cyrus listened, thinking about what the dark elves might be doing in human towns even now. Andren was over two thousand years old, in spite of looking as though he was only in his thirties by human standards. "How many wars did you see between the Elven Kingdom and the Dark Elves?"

Andren shook his head. "Too many to count. They're a warlike people, you know."

"I'm sure they say the same thing about you."

"Bah!" Andren waved him off. "It's all about territory; they always infringed on ours."

"I don't know that they're a warlike people, but it would seem that the Sovereign of the Dark Elves has an affinity for war." Cyrus looked around to make sure he wasn't overheard. "Do you know anything about their Sovereign?"

"Mostly bullroar. He's a fearsome beast; eleventy feet tall, breathes fire, all that ruckus."

"You don't believe it?" Cyrus said with a smile that faded a moment later. "Do you think the Elves will intervene? If the Confederation keeps getting battered like this?"

Andren looked away. "I wouldn't bet on it. The King...he's unlikely to interfere if he can avoid it. The last war between the dark elves and the Elven Kingdom was a scarce hundred years ago, and the downside of us living so long is that we remember. We all remember the deaths of friends and loved ones, the cities burned, all that..." He looked at Cyrus. "Now that it's aimed at your people and not ours? The King won't order our soldiers to so much as look at them funny unless the dark elves cross our border at the river Perda."

Cyrus shook his head. "I thought not." He felt the pain, the punch in his stomach as the bile rose up, and he thought of villages being burned and ravaged. There was a bitter taste in the back of his mouth, and Cyrus took a deep breath. "It's not easy watching your homeland get pummeled while you stay out of the fight."

"Aye. Just remember your foolish Council of Twelve in Reikonos were the ones that wanted this war, not you or the other humans."

Reikonos was the human capital, where Cyrus had been born and raised. He had a brief flash of remembrance; childhood days spent playing in the city square, of splashing water from the fountain. "They may have started it, but they sit high in the Citadel in Reikonos while the people of the Confederation bear its effects." An image flashed through his mind of the city in flames, dark elves marching through the street with torches and swords, citizens screaming. "But if it comes to them invading Reikonos..." His words trailed off. He clapped Andren on the shoulder with more enthusiasm than he felt and walked toward the staircase.

"Don't Council for too long!" Andren called after him. "The victory celebration will have started by the time you get back!"

Cyrus didn't answer, mind still dwelling on the dark thoughts their conversation had stirred. *In spite of our successes in Sanctuary, it doesn't feel like victory because my homeland is in flames.* He felt a stir within him, deep inside, and the acrid taste in the back of his mouth grew stronger as the torches on the walls seemed to burn all the brighter, as if to give him a sense of what the flames of war were doing to the Confederation. *If the dark elves invade Reikonos*...he thought as he climbed. *...I don't think I can stay here and let my city burn.*

Chapter 2

"You'd have been proud, Alaric," Curatio said. "Another flawless run through the Trials." Curatio was the chief healer of Sanctuary, an elder elf with a constant gleam in his eye. He wore long, flowing robes with an ornamental sash wrapped around his shoulders that indicated his profession. His short-cropped hair contained just a touch of gray, giving his angular, regal features an air of distinguishment.

"I expected no less." Alaric Garaunt tilted his head in the direction of Cyrus and then Vara. Alaric's hair was peppered by far more gray than Curatio's, and extended to the back of his neck. His armor was weathered but still polished, and his eyes bore a fire. His fine, chiseled features were handsome, the only mark upon them the black leather patch that covered his missing left eye. He favored them all with a smile that was at odds with his nickname: "The Ghost of Sanctuary."

"We were in fine form," said Niamh. Her red hair flowed down her shoulders, her green eyes alight with the same excitement that ran through her voice. "I don't think I've ever seen the Gatekeeper any madder. We tore through the Trials in record time."

"Agreed." Vaste the troll spoke up. His green skin was flushed dark with victory. "He was so flustered he didn't insult us half as much as usual."

"At the rate, our people are getting mystical swords and better armor. We'll have the best equipped force in Arkaria before too much longer," Curatio said with a smile.

Cyrus looked around the Council Chambers. The room was centered on a large round table with eight seats. Behind Alaric was a set of double doors to the balcony, surrounded by windows that looked over the darkened Plains of Perdamun. On either side of the room stood fireplaces, crackling along with a dozen torches that burned without a hint of smoke. The brightness of Sanctuary at night had surprised Cyrus at first; it was unlike any place he had ever been.

"I hate to interrupt the circle of self-love," an annoyed voice interrupted. Cyrus's head swiveled to Terian Lepos, a weathered dark elf with a long nose and navy blue armor crowned with spikes jutting from his shoulder pauldrons. "Can we please focus on the meeting? I'd like to drink a little bit before I pass out from exhaustion."

Alaric's staid expression returned, the levity gone. "Of course. We have a few things to discuss..."

"War news," came the muttered voice of J'anda Aimant, Sanctuary's most skilled enchanter. Capable of creating illusions upon himself, this evening he wore the serene features of an aged elf.

"I would prefer you come to the Council in your true form, J'anda." Alaric's eyebrow twitched as he stared down the enchanter.

J'anda's chest heaved with a great sigh. "As you will." His hand waved in a lazy pattern and his illusion vanished. The enchanter was a dark elf with features so average that they were overshadowed by any illusion he cast, leaving Cyrus unable to picture the dark elf's face if he was not staring at it. "Now can we talk about the war?"

Alaric cleared his throat. "Another wave of human refugees has reached us, along with some new information. It is as we feared; Prehorta has fallen to the dark elven army and they have sacked and burned the town."

"That'll be a brutal end for a lot of men and a torturous experience for a great many women." J'anda shook his head, appalled. "The dark elven army are bestial when they sack a town; nothing is prohibited."

"And yet somehow they call your lot a civilization," Vara said.

Terian leaned back in his chair, focusing on Alaric. "Do you think that army will be moving south?"

Alaric put his hands on the table and interlaced the fingers of his gauntlets in front of him. "I doubt it, but it would be unwise to assume. Both you and J'anda," he said with a nod toward the enchanter, "have knowledge of the Sovereign of the Dark Elves; what do you believe his next move will be? Take the war here, to the Plains, or head west toward the river Perda and destroy the southern edge of Confederation territory?"

Terian shook his head. "I doubt he'll march west to the river. I think sacking Prehorta and leaving a garrison will do much to cut off Reikonos from the food supply of the Plains of Perdamun, increasing the hardship the Confederation will endure as the war grinds on. He'll likely move this army up to join the forces driving toward Reikonos."

"A wise strategic move," Curatio added. "Since the humans have been able to turn aside the dark elf attacks along a line south of Reikonos, it's keeping the Sovereign from laying siege to their capital. If he cuts off routes to the Plains of Perdamun, it'll help him weaken Reikonos when he does get around to moving his armies into siege positions."

"There are still human armies in the east and north that have yet to come into battle," Cyrus said. "If the Council of Twelve had anyone with brains planning this war they would have realized they had the dark elves damn near encircled at the start of the fight and would have moved to keep it that way."

J'anda and Terian laughed, the enchanter in soft tones, the dark knight in loud, discordant ones. Curatio and Alaric shared a knowing look.

Vara's eyes narrowed. "I would have agreed with the warrior's assessment, yet I get the feeling there is something that you're not sharing with us."

Terian laughed again, alone this time. "Unlike humans or elves, we have one major city – Saekaj Sovar. All the dark elves live there except for exiles and expatriates like us." He pointed to himself, then J'anda. "Saekaj is underground, with entrances and exits hundreds of miles in different directions. Good luck encircling it; you'd never find them all."

"So it's like Enterra?" Cyrus looked at Terian.

"No. Enterra was tunnels in a mountain; small, like a mine or an anthill. Saekaj is built into underground caves that are a hundred miles long and hundreds of feet deep."

Vara wheeled to favor Alaric and Curatio with a glare. "How did the two of you know this? Are foreigners not put to death in Saekaj Sovar?"

Curatio remained mute but Alaric smiled and answered, "If they are found, I am told that is true."

"Fascinating as this geography lesson is," Vaste spoke in his low, rumbling voice, "the fact remains that an unpredictable dark elven host remains on the march a few hundred miles north of us and more refugees stream out of human territory by the day, unable to find help anywhere but through us." The troll fingered the white crystal at the top of his staff, which rested against the edge of the table.

Alaric cleared his throat again and attention pivoted back to him. "We already have an overwhelming number of refugees passing through our halls, all seeking the relative safety of these lands. They arrive without food nor means to survive, and we will continue to help them as best we can. Those who come to us hungry will be fed, those who arrive naked will be clothed—"

"Unless they're pretty," Terian amended, "in which case they should be kept naked and sent to me."

A light laugh echoed through the room. Alaric wore a slight smile and shook his head in dismissal. "Other business?"

"Applicants," Curatio said. "In the past six months we've had a flood of them and Niamh and I are overwhelmed. Some of the refugees are even applying; merchants and farmers, people without proper experience." He held up a hand to forestall Cyrus, who had started to interrupt. "I know we accept folks without experience and I'm glad of it, especially to give some of these poor souls a better lot in life, but it is making our job more difficult."

"I've taken to falling asleep on a stack of parchment at night," Niamh said, her bright eyes more lined than usual. "I'm doing everything I can to sort through and learn the stories of all these people that have joined us, but even with members helping us vet them, we're backlogged evaluating all these potential guildmates."

"Is it my imagination, or has the median size of our applicants diminished since our Enterra expedition?" Terian said with a sly smile.

"I haven't noticed," Vaste said, easily a foot taller than Cyrus, who was six and a half feet in height. "You all look like ants to me."

"You're right, Terian," Niamh answered with a smile of her own. "Since we crushed the Goblin Imperium, we've had large numbers of goblin and gnomish applicants—gnomes because we knocked flat the Imperium, which was their biggest enemy, and goblins because we destroyed a hated government and brought freedom to their underclass and peace to their lands."

"One would think there might be tension between the goblin and gnomish applicants," Vaste said, a thoughtful expression pasted on his green face.

"Not thus far," Curatio said. "They seem to be getting on rather well."

"Pleased to hear it," Alaric said with a nod. "One final matter before us, and we will part for the evening. With the growth in our numbers, I think it would be prudent to add new officers to the Council—"

He was interrupted by the doors to the hallway blowing open with exaggerated violence. Cyrus turned to look as the doors banged against the wall and then slammed shut. He looked back to the faces around the table and found them as confused as his own. "What was that?"

Alaric was still, his eyes lit with concern. "Peculiar." The light in the room increased threefold as the fire of the torches blazed and the fireplaces burned with sudden force. Alaric's expression shifted to mild alarm. "Most peculiar. I suggest we adjourn; the enchantments on Sanctuary seem to be trying to call our attention to something unusual occurring within our walls. Let us sweep the halls for any sign of...trouble."

Chapter 3

"Never seen anything like that, and I've been here for two years," Cyrus said with a grunt as he reached the bottom of the stairs, Curatio, Niamh and Vaste in tow.

"Can't say I've seen it more than once myself." Vaste's long strides carried him into the foyer. "And that was quite some time ago."

"Same here," Niamh said, her red hair draped around her shoulders. "Curatio and I will sweep the Great Hall; you two check the foyer and the lounge."

"Sounds good," Cyrus said before turning to the front entrance doors, which blew open and slammed shut. The attention of everyone in the room was on them as the torches on the walls burned higher than the ones in the Council Chamber had and the fireplace belched forth a gout of flame that pushed bystanders back several feet.

Andren crossed from the lounge to join Cyrus and Vaste. "What the bloody hell is going on?" He looked at them askance. "There's no wind outside; it's like the doors and fires in this place have a mind of their own—and it's a crazy one."

Cyrus pointed to the doors, which slammed and opened again, making a thundering noise. "How long has this been going on?"

"A few minutes now," Andren said, taking a sip from his flagon. "What does it mean?"

"Trouble," Vaste replied. "Sanctuary carries enchantments that warn when someone has malicious intentions."

"Couldn't it find a quieter way of warning us?" Andren said with a pleading note. "I was carrying a keg of ale when it went off the first time. The entrance doors shut so loud I dropped it. Ruined a perfectly good run of Larana's dark...and then, as if that weren't bad enough, the fireplace exploded and I damned near ruined my pants..."

"Exploding fireplace?" Cyrus said.

"Not good," Vaste interrupted his thought. "I wonder if the strength of the warning is tied to the seriousness of the threat?"

"So if someone were planning to steal one of our kegs..." Cyrus let his voice trail off.

"The doors would perhaps clap shut once or twice. Minor

mischief. I've seen that a few times but never connected it."

"But if the fireplace explodes and the doors slam over and over..."

"Right," Vaste said. "Nothing good can come of this."

"Stealing a keg is not 'minor mischief,'" Andren said in a huff.

"Do the enchantments give us any clue as to where the trouble comes from?" Cyrus looked at Vaste with concern.

"The effects seem worse down here than in the Council Chambers." His hand stroked his green chin, puzzling it out. "The worse the effects, the closer you're getting to the disturbance?" Vaste wondered. "Since the entrance doors are slamming at the same rate as those of the Great Hall—" he pointed at the doors behind them—"if I'm right, it would follow that whatever is setting them off is in this room."

"Ack!" Andren said with a cry. "I left the kegs undefended!" He beat a hasty path back to the lounge.

"At some point you're going to have to deal with his overindulgence," Vaste said in a warning tone.

"Not now." Cyrus scanned the crowd for any sign of trouble. Refugees and new applicants were mixed with familiar faces, one of which was making its way toward him.

Aisling slinked down the stairs wearing a wicked smile that blended with her almost glowing white hair. She wore a red dress that clung to her figure and emphasized her womanly attributes; something much different than her usual apparel, loose fitting light leather armor that allowed her to move without making a sound. The daggers she wore in her belt were missing now, and Cyrus looked at her trim waistline for a moment too long, wondering if she had secreted them away on her person.

"I saw that," she said with a hint of glee. "I chose this dress hoping it would catch your attention, and it would appear I succeeded." She sashayed over, pressing herself against his armor. He felt one of her hands slide around to his back.

"Aisling," he said. "Do you have your daggers?"

The mirth left her eyes as her hand disappeared into the folds of her dress, reappearing with two small, elegant blades that were curved, razor sharp and as wicked as the smile of the woman who wielded them. "So you weren't looking at my figure?" Her voice went flat and her eyes flicked down, unable to hide her disappointment.

"Perhaps later. This thunderous racket," he breathed, her face still next to his, "is an enchantment warning us of someone with very bad intentions, and that person is here in the foyer."

She pulled back from him. "And you need to sort out who." Her hand withdrew from his back and she turned to the crowd, focused and seeming to sift through them, one by one. She stopped and pointed to a figure, a refugee. "Him."

Cyrus stared at the man, an elf, who was blond and had long hair in a ponytail. "How do you know?" Cyrus watched him as he awaited Aisling's answer, but something about the elf gave Cyrus a peculiar feeling; whether it was Aisling's warning or something else, he could not tell.

"We have over two thousand members and applicants and countless more refugees on our premises," Vaste said. "You picked him out of a crowd in a room of at least three hundred in about ten seconds. Please, explain." The troll folded his arms and favored the dark elf with an expectant look.

Aisling shrugged. "How is he dressed?"

Cyrus stared at the elf. "Like a refugee."

"Where are the refugees coming from?"

"The Human Confederation," Vaste answered, now impatient. "But there are plenty of elves, dark elves, gnomes and dwarves that live within their borders."

"Sure," Aisling said. "But the refugees are coming from small towns and villages. How many elves have you seen in rural areas of the Confederation?"

"Few," Vaste said, now ponderous. "But that still doesn't mean—"

The elf turned and Cyrus broke off his watch, but not before catching a glance of piercing eyes, absolutely at odds with the look of the elf's clothing. Far from seeming like a scared refugee, worried about the ruckus, the elf had a predatorial air. "I think she's right," Cyrus cut him off. "Everyone else is gawking at the doors and fireplace. He's scanning the room like he's looking for something."

"Being as there's nothing in this room, he's likely after *someone*." Aisling leaned close to Cyrus and whispered, "Any idea who?"

"Any idea who what?" An icy tone washed over Cyrus from behind and he turned so fast that only Aisling's catlike reflexes saved her from being knocked over. Vara stood silhouetted in the entry to the stairs, a cold glare focused on him and then Aisling in quick succession. "Any idea who is actually trying to sort out this threat? Because that's what you're supposed to be doing, not arranging a tryst."

Cyrus's cheeks reddened and he felt a twist in his stomach. "Aisling's figured out who's setting the enchantments off."

"Has she?" Vara's eyebrow shifted upward, but the rest of her expression did not change. "How convenient. May I wager that she believes the responsible party to be in your armor, and that if she can simply persuade you to remove it, she'll show you who it is? And you, ignorant, naïve and undersexed, will find out on the morrow how wrong you were, both by the burning in your loins and the absence of your coinpurse."

Aisling smiled, a deep, self-satisfied grin that bore no resemblance to actual joy. "Which would sting more? Me striking you down right now, or me bedding this man that you insult so frequently?"

"I daresay the striking down for me and the bedding for him."

"Ladies, we have no time for this—" Vaste began to speak but stopped. "Oh gods."

So focused was Cyrus on the rising tension between Vara and Aisling that he had not heard the clamor behind him die down. A scream brought his head around and he locked eyes with the elf that Aisling had pointed out. The man had moved and now had blades in his hands. His cloak was splayed out on the floor and he held a body tight against his, the red hair of his hostage standing out in contrast with the spotless white silk doublet he was wearing underneath his worn traveling cloak.

Niamh! Cyrus's mind raced as he pushed his way through the crowd, Vara, Aisling and Vaste behind him. The red-haired druid had a knife tight against her throat, blood already running into the small amount of cleavage revealed by her robes. The dagger stood out against the pale skin and red hair of Niamh; it was obsidian black, with a small octagonal pommel that bore a circular emblem Cyrus could not see from where he was.

"No one come near me!" The elf's voice was high and stressed, and Curatio stood closest to him, hands extended in a peaceful gesture. "Stay where you are and this one doesn't have to die!" Niamh, for her part, was expressionless, biting her lip and staring into the crowd. When she caught sight of Cyrus, her lips tugged upward in a seemingly involuntary motion, then returned to the lack of expression that had been there before.

"I can help you," Curatio said, maintaining his distance. "I'm an officer of Sanctuary. What do you want?"

"We can resurrect Niamh later if need be," Vaste muttered in Cyrus's ear.

"Let's avoid getting our fellow guildmate and officer killed if we can, yes?" Vara's eyes never left the elf that was holding Niamh prisoner.

"Something is wrong," Aisling said. Cyrus chanced to look back at her and saw the dark elf wore a puzzled expression, her eyes concentrating on the scene in front of her.

"You are not the most powerful spell in the book, are you?" Vara said in a biting voice. "One of our own is being held hostage at the point of a knife in our own guildhall; yes, something is very wrong —"

"The daggers!" Aisling hissed. "They're —"

She did not get a chance to finish. Niamh screamed, an agonizing, painful cry as the elf shoved her toward Curatio. Cyrus's hand was already on the hilt of his sword, Praelior, and it was halfway drawn when the floor of the foyer exploded in a burst of broken stone.

Chapter 4

The power of his sword flowed through Cyrus, enhancing his reflexes and sending strength coursing through his muscles. Pieces of stone and rock flew into the crowd; shrieks and cries drowned out Niamh's scream. Cyrus kept moving, realizing as the rock flew through the air that he would have to move quickly.

A long, craggy arm extended from the hole in the ground and grabbed the elven refugee around the waist. Stones moved aside as Fortin, the rock giant, pushed his way up from the dungeons below Sanctuary, a deafening howl of enmity drowning out all other noise. The rock giant lifted the elf above his head and pitched him with crushing force.

Cyrus watched the elf soar past, then the sound of crunching bone and flesh came from behind. He turned to look at the interloper, now a messy, broken heap, splintered against the wall near the doors to the Great Hall.

"Impeccable timing, Fortin," Vaste called out. "But next time, couldn't you restrain him?"

"Could have restrained him this time," the rock giant rumbled, his torso jutting from the hole he had made in the floor, "but he stabbed the red-haired elf. I like her. He needed to suffer."

Vara cuffed Cyrus on the shoulder. "Niamh."

"Right." Cyrus changed course, running to Niamh, who was lying in Curatio's arms. He slid to his knees, the plate mail on his greaves screeching against the stone. "Hey, Red," he said with a smile. She managed a weak one back at him, her white skin almost gray. "Curatio will have you healed in a second—" He looked up at Curatio, whose face was ashen, his head shaking from left to right.

"Knew you guys would save me..." Niamh's eyes were dazed, glassy, and they honed in on Cyrus. "Especially you. After all, who else would save your..." Her words drifted off and her body went slack in Curatio's arms, her eyes staring off into nothingness.

"What the hell, Curatio?" Andren's voice came from behind Cyrus as the elven healer pushed his way through the crowd to Cyrus's side. "Why didn't you heal her? Looking to practice your resurrection spell?"

Curatio looked up at Andren with an anguish Cyrus had never

seen from the healer. Cyrus turned to Andren, whose indignation had faded to uncertainty. Andren shook his head and bowed it, indistinguishable mutterings coming from under his breath as the healer began to cast a spell. With a flourish, he held his hands out and bluish white light filled the air around them; a resurrection spell sweeping from them to Niamh's body, encompassing the red-haired elf's corpse with a glow that could restore life...

...but didn't.

"What the..." Andren muttered a curse and began to cast again.

"It won't do any good," Curatio broke his silence, voice laden with a mournful sadness that Cyrus hadn't heard from the healer, ever. "She's been afflicted with the black lace...a poison that nullifies magic." The healer's numb gaze shifted to where the elven assailant had been thrown by Fortin. "He must have coated his blades with it. I couldn't heal her...and now she's dead and we can't bring her back..." His hand brushed against her cheek and came to rest in her red hair.

"Son of a..." Cyrus felt the rage overwhelming him, consuming him. He stood, and his vision swam as he pulled away from the druid's body, and suddenly she seemed far away, even though he stood only a few feet above her. He turned on his heel and pushed through the crowd, not caring who he knocked aside as he made his way toward the killer.

He broke through the small circle grouped around the elf and stopped. Her assailant was crushed; bones jutted from points around his body, his blood covering the floor.

"Someone heal this bastard," Cyrus seethed, "so I can do this to him again."

"No good." Vara spoke from his side. "We've already tried; it would appear he caught the blades of his own daggers when he landed."

"Serves him right," Cyrus said, a flush of white-hot rage upon him. "If he were still alive, I'd kill him myself."

A coughing, gagging sound from the elf caused a stir in those who encircled him. "It would appear you get your wish," came Fortin's dry rumble from nearby. "You might want to hurry; it would seem he's about to die of natural causes."

"Which part of being thrown against the wall by a rock giant is natural?" Vaste shot back.

"If someone kills one of my friends, it's natural that they will be next and that I will cause it," Fortin replied.

All thought of revenge forgotten, Cyrus dropped to his knees next to the elf, whose head was shaped unnaturally from the fracturing of his skull. "Why did you come here?" Cyrus asked, trying to meet the unsteady gaze of the killer's eyes.

"He's an assassin," Aisling said, handing Cyrus one of the daggers, its black blade gleaming in the light of a nearby torch. On the pommel was a snake eating its own tail. "An elven order by the name of Inta'yrakhir. I've only heard a whisper of them, once, and that was long ago. They're quiet, all shadows and mystery — the sort of group that you get nothing out of but a name."

Cyrus turned back to the assassin. "You had to know that you'd never get out of here alive. Who sent you? And who were you after?"

"My master ordered death...he will...receive death..." In a gasping, choking voice, the elf turned his head to look past Cyrus. "You will not see us...and we will keep coming...until you die."

Cyrus reached down, calmness masking a more furious rage than almost any he'd ever felt, and grabbed the elf by the remains of his once spotless doublet, now more red than white. "Who sent you...and who are you here for?"

"My master...is greater than any you know." The rasping of the assassin's voice got deeper, more guttural, and slower as his eyes crept past Cyrus's. "Your death is ordered...it shall be delivered...and we will not stop until you are dead..." He rasped, and his eyes fluttered as he looked over Cyrus's shoulder and uttered one more word before succumbing to his wounds.

"Shelas'akur."

Chapter 5

There was silence in the Council Chamber, the flames licking at the logs in the hearth, consuming them, sending shadows across everything. Cyrus sat in his chair, wondering how the room had become so veiled in shadow when it was bright only a short while earlier. Vaste had broken the news with a simple, "Niamh is dead."

"Then resurrect her," Terian said with a flat laugh. "We've got a meeting to finish."

"She's dead..." Vaste's voice trailed off. "Permanently."

"What?" The dark elf's complexion darkened as though clouds had rolled in to obscure the light from his face. "She hasn't been gone over an hour, so if she's dead you could still use a resurrection spell —"

J'anda looked at them, wary disbelief cutting through his human illusion. "Was...her body destroyed?"

"No," Vaste said. "Her body is still quite intact, unlike her assailant."

"I don't understand." Terian's voice rose, taking on a timbre and quality of madness. "If we still have her body, and it's been less than an hour, why isn't she being resurrected?"

Alaric spoke in a low, quiet voice filled with sufficient authority to silence the Council. "There are some curses and magics that can prevent healing from taking place." He raised his head, his lone eye fixed on Curatio, who sat to his right. "Am I to assume that Niamh fell victim to something of this sort?"

Curatio seemed to gather his thoughts before speaking. "It was a poison, I believe, rather than a curse, but yes. Neither healing nor resurrection magic took hold on her and now she is simply...gone." He choked on the last word.

Cyrus felt the grief and misery close in on him as he pictured Niamh, happy and carefree, her laugh like the twinkling of a crystal wind chime and her eyes as green as the grass of the plains in late spring. His eyes fell on her seat to his left, and he stared at the empty chair, the black leather skin glossy in the dim light, as if it was some amorphous, oily surface of despair that would devour anyone who sat in it.

With a choking feeling he remembered the times she had saved his life—or as she had put it, "saved his ass"—and wondered if, when he remembered her, it would be the thought of carrying her body through the foyer and Great Hall while their guildmates wept and cried out around him. It had been a long walk; maybe the longest he'd ever taken, and when he placed her in the iced room in the back of the kitchen, the freezing chill had come to rest in his bones, causing an ache that permeated through him, settling in his heart.

He had set her down with care, closing her eyes, the green in them faded to a dull sheen. Her cheeks were fair and white, and he took his gauntlet off to wipe a drop of blood from the pristine, snowy flesh and was amazed at how warm she still felt to his touch. He smoothed her flame-red tresses around her shoulders, feeling the fine hair slip between his fingers while Larana stared on from behind him in numb shock. As he left the kitchen, facing an audience of refugees and guildmates, silent in their respect for the fallen, the only noise he could hear was Larana's sobs behind him.

A loud curse from Terian broke his reverie, catapulting Cyrus back to the Council Chamber. "Who did this?"

"An assassin," Vaste replied. "From the Inta'yrakhir."

"You say that name like it's supposed to mean something to me." Terian's words slipped out in a long, uninterrupted stream, each flushed with the hotness of his anger. "The only thing it means is that every single person who is associated with this organization will die horribly, with their heads mounted on pikes as an example of what happens when you strike at Sanctuary." He looked around the table, his long nose and spiked pauldrons combining with the dark clouds to give him an almost demonic look. "Who's with me?"

"Hold," Alaric said. "I must first confess I am not familiar with the Inta'yrakhir. What is this...'Hand of Fear'?"

"'Hand of Fear'?" Cyrus asked, still waiting to feel something, anything.

"'Inta'yrakhir' is elvish for 'Hand of Fear'," Curatio said, features haggard and worn. "Aisling seemed to indicate that it was an order of elvish assassins."

"Why would an assassin want to kill Niamh?" Terian's fist hit the table, shaking it. "She was the sweetest of us..."

"They didn't." Vaste's words seemed to echo through the chamber more than Terian's rage. "They weren't after her at all."

"I'm sorry," J'anda said. "Who was the assassin after?"

"Vara." Vaste's reply was cool. "He said his order would not stop until the 'shelas'akur' was dead."

The pause was broken once more by Terian, now approaching the height of screeching as he swiveled to face the elven paladin. "What did you do to bring this down?"

Vara, who had remained silent and expressionless, now swelled as she turned to Terian, looking as though she were an adder about to strike. "What did I do to attract the death warrant of a band of assassins? I'm not quite certain." Her sarcasm hung thick. "Perhaps you could track them down and ask on my behalf. If they attempt to stab you in the face, let them; it's merely a ritual required for entrance to their good graces."

"I don't understand how this assassin could be after you without you knowing why. Have you offended someone... um... maybe done something to agitate... uh..." J'anda held up his hands in exasperation.

Vara's hand slapped onto the table, her hue crimson with rage. "Let me repeat this for those of you who may be struggling with substandard intellects: I...DO...NOT...KNOW! I have no idea whether this is some personal grudge or related to..." She reddened further but her voice faltered. "Other...aspects of my life."

She halted and Cyrus watched her lip quiver. "I don't know why that bloody bastard felt the need to kill Niamh rather than restrict his murderous activities to me. I am...sorry for it." Her face fell. "I would have preferred that if someone had to be caught on the end of that blade it be me instead of her." Her chin came up and she looked around the table. "But it wasn't. Please don't ask me to apologize for being alive."

"No one faults you for that, lass." Alaric's voice was soothing, filled with authority. "In our grief, we are trying to understand something that, without more facts—and possibly even with them—will be incomprehensible."

"Yes, well, let's try more facts," Terian said. "This assassin, he said he was after Vara?"

"No." Cyrus spoke up, ending his silence. "He said 'shelas'akur'." He had heard other elves refer to Vara by the name "shelas'akur" but none had ever been willing to discuss what it meant, not even Andren.

Terian stared Vara down. "And you can't tell us what that

means."

"We do not discuss it with offlanders — non-elves," she replied.

"It means 'last hope'," Cyrus said, drawing looks of surprise from Vara, Alaric and Curatio. He frowned and looked back at them. "What?"

"I was not aware you spoke elvish, brother," Alaric said.

"I don't know much," Cyrus replied.

"A point on which we can all agree," Vara said. "But regardless, it remains a matter of internal secrecy to the Elven Kingdom."

"Your matter of internal secrecy just cost the life of an elf, and while that wouldn't much trouble me if it happened inside your damned Kingdom," Terian replied, voice rising once again until he was yelling, "it happened here! In Sanctuary! To one of our officers! To our *friend*! *And I want to know why she's dead!*"

"I DON'T KNOW, YOU IGNORANT SODDING JACKASS!" Vara exploded at Terian, standing with such violence her chair flew back and broke into pieces on the floor.

"Perhaps," J'anda stood, cold fury radiating from his eyes but his voice as smooth as steel, "you could give us some idea of why an elvish assassin might want to kill the...shelas'akur."

"I DON'T KNOW! Are you deaf or merely addled by casting illusions on yourself so frequently that you can no longer remember who you are?"

"There is no good reason why an elvish assassin would want to kill Vara," Curatio said. The elf tried to smile but failed, grimacing instead. "She's a symbol to our people of...well, hope."

"Leaving the 'why' of that aside for now," Vaste said, "there are plenty of reasons that someone might want to kill a symbol of hope." He began to tick them off on his fingers. "They have a grudge against your government and want to send a message; they dislike something she stands for; they want to upset your entire race..."

The grimace remained on Curatio's face. "Without getting into much detail, Vara's never associated herself with the Kingdom's government in any way, so that doesn't fit — "

"Perhaps someone in the government is displeased with that?" J'anda raised his hands in a questioning manner.

"Seems a bit much, sending an assassin because she doesn't endorse the monarch," Curatio said with a shrug. "King Danay I has been in place for about four thousand years and he's not unpopular. The political situation in the Kingdom is stable; no major upheavals, no challenges to the powers that be..." He shrugged again. "I don't think that's it. The likelihood that someone is trying to dishearten the entire elvish race is much more likely...and rather sad."

"This is all bullshit," Terian said, seething. He pointed at Vara, hand shaking so hard it waved at her. "You should tell us everything. She trusted you, she died for you; the least you can do is give us the full facts so that we can find out what this is all about and slap this 'Hand of Fear' to a bloody pulp."

Vara stood silent at Terian's rebuke. Cyrus watched her, and for the first time he realized that she was trembling — ever so slightly, but there it was. "If Niamh were here, she wouldn't tell you," Cyrus said, drawing Terian's stinging glare. "She always refused to tell me about this 'shelas'akur' business."

Alaric folded his hands on the table in front of him. "In spite of having suffered a great loss we should remember that Vara is one of us and her loyalty to Sanctuary is unquestioned. Were she aware of any reason why these assassins were after her, I am certain she would tell us."

"I would," Vara affirmed, even though no one had looked at her. "I may not wish to discuss internal elven matters, but be assured, I would not put any of you in danger if it could be avoided." Her hand came up to her neck and rested there; to Cyrus's eyes it looked as though she were preparing to strangle herself.

"I do not wish to discuss this further until we have had time to settle," Alaric said with finality. "Nor will we argue any longer. This is a time to pull together, remembering the friend and officer we have lost. Niamh would not wish to see us divided; nor should our guildmates have to suffer from our distraction."

J'anda's eyes narrowed as he focused on Alaric. "What will we do about this threat?"

"The assassin was disguised as a refugee," Cyrus said. "We close the damned gates." He looked to Alaric for confirmation.

"Agreed," Alaric said with a deep sigh. "We will assign guard forces to watch the more sensitive areas of Sanctuary, and we will find a way to assist the refugees without compromising our security. Perhaps we can set up aid tents outside the walls."

"Before I came up here I tasked Aisling with finding some trustworthy guildmates to set up guard at the applicant, member and officer quarters," Cyrus said.

"Which means that by now all the good items will have been stolen," Vara said under her breath.

"We know nothing about these assassins," Cyrus went on, ignoring Vara's jab. "It seems unlikely that the Hand of Fear will send another assassin so soon after the failure of the first—"

"Unless they're already here," Terian said, his voice filled with disgust.

"—but it doesn't hurt to be prepared," Cyrus finished. "After all, we know next to nothing about them."

"Too true," Alaric said with a quiet exhalation. "Let us be the source of strength for our brothers and sisters in this sad hour."

"And when we track down these Hand of Fear bastards, let us be the hammer of bloody vengeance for our fallen comrade," Terian said, pushing away from the table, leaving without saying anything else.

"Alaric," Cyrus said. "Did you know the disturbances caused by the enchantments get worse the closer you get to the cause of the problem?"

Alaric's face remained impassive. "Alas, my friend—there are things about Sanctuary that remain a mystery even to me." He turned his head to face Curatio. "Old friend...we have matters to discuss. Go. I will wait for you in my quarters." The Ghost of Sanctuary stood while the rest of the officers filed out one by one. Alaric began to fade, his armor turning insubstantial as a thick white mist filled the room and then dissipated, leaving Cyrus alone.

How could this happen? he wondered. *Niamh was one of the first people I met from Sanctuary; the thought of her gone...*

He pulled to his feet, the weight of his grief making his armor seem like stones strapped to his body. He made his way to the door and past two sentries to the staircase leading up to the officer's quarters, high atop the center tower. The seams in the stone walls blurred together as he climbed, and he was almost in a world of his own, dazed, by the time he reached the top of the staircase and entered the hallway leading to the officer quarters.

A potion that nullifies magic? With a blade coated in black lace, no one would be safe, he thought. *All the rules that we've built our adventuring lives on change with something so simple and deadly as that.* He shuddered at the thought of real, permanent death.

He paused at the entrance to his quarters. A deep, unsettled feeling in his stomach gave him pause. *I'm going to be seeing trouble around every corner. In our own foyer, of all places!* He shook his head. *How are we supposed to feel safe here? How can we get things back to normal after watching...her...die like that?* A bitter unease filled him. *Things may never be normal again.*

A sound from one of the far rooms stopped him before he turned the handle. A long, rattling cacophony filled the hallway as every door shook with explosive force and the torches lit off in a burst of fire that stretched to the high ceilings. Cyrus sprang forward, sword in hand. He burst into the room two doors down from his own, not stopping to consider the privacy of its occupant. The door crashed, broken, and he collided with someone as he flew through the frame.

Two someones.

An elven male shrugged out of his traveling cloak as Cyrus grabbed him around the neck and slammed him against the wall. A thin length of chain whipped across Cyrus's face, freed from where it had been coiled around Vara's neck, followed by an obsidian dagger that raked him across the cheek, only missing his throat courtesy of the enhanced reflexes granted him by Praelior. His gaze caught the dagger and found the same insignia that had been on the weapon of the assassin that slew Niamh.

A scream cut through the night air from behind Cyrus and he glanced back to see Vara clutching her neck, a red mark creasing it all the way around. He brought his sword forward in time to block the dagger as the elf spun free of his grasp, dancing away from him through the broken door, blade in hand.

Cyrus followed, interposing himself between the assassin and Vara. She remained on the floor behind Cy, gasping for air after the garrotting that the elf had given her. He felt breath force its way between his teeth and realized he was livid with the elven assassin. The elf, for his part, smiled and twirled his dagger.

Doors began to open in the hall, and a scream of utmost fury echoed as Terian burst forth from his room, sandwiched between Cyrus and Vara's, a battle axe raised above his head. Before Cyrus could react, the dark knight brought his weapon down as the fleeing assassin tried to dodge away from both Cyrus and Terian and backed into another door opening behind him.

Vaste's staff lowered against the assassin's neck and the elf, almost a foot shorter than Cyrus, was lifted into the air by the troll. The assassin's black blade came down on Vaste's forearm, burying itself to the hilt and bringing forth no more than a grunt from the troll as he spun the elf about and rammed him into the wall thrice in rapid succession. When the assassin went limp in his arms, Vaste dropped him to the ground and stepped on the elf's chest.

"Vaste," Cyrus said with a quiet resignation, pointing at the dagger buried in the troll's forearm.

"Yes, it hurts," the troll said, plucking it out with nothing more than a grimace. The blade looked small next to his massive arm, like a black needle buried in a green ham.

"It probably had black lace on it." Cyrus looked up at the troll's dark eyes, feeling a rattling breath of exasperation leave his chest. *Not you too, Vaste...*

"Were I fatally injured, I might worry," Vaste replied with a look of greatest unconcern. "I can't heal it with a spell, but this wound won't kill me."

"I can bandage it; staunch the bleeding." Terian's axe was slung over his shoulder but his eyes were focused on the elf unconscious beneath Vaste's foot. "We need to get him to the dungeons and under guard." A flash of annoyance ran across the dark elf's features. "I don't know why there wasn't a guard on this hallway; it is the officer quarters—you know, the living space of this 'Hand of Fear's' supposed target."

Cyrus looked back at Vara, who had pulled herself to the bed and was rubbing her throat. Her hand glowed with the light of a spell, faint blue magics of healing wrapped around her neck.

"They were posted downstairs," Cyrus replied. "I didn't think about an assassin having already made their way up here—until the doors rattled and I heard noise from Vara's quarters—which turned out to be—"

"This fellow, doing his level best to keep me quiet until he could run me through. He must have wanted it to go quietly so he could escape afterward." She was on her feet now, and joined them in the hallway, although her hand still hovered around her thin neck. She looked at Cyrus, her eyes softer than usual. "Your timing was impeccable; another few moments and I would have been unconscious and I suspect, shortly thereafter, quite dead."

"Two assassins in two hours?" Cyrus shook his head. He looked from Vaste to Terian and finally his gaze came to rest on Vara, who did not meet his eyes.

"This does not bode well for your safety," Terian said to Vara, voice much gentler than it had been during the Council meeting. "If we can't protect you here..."

The words hung in the air as the four of them looked around, the shadows of the corridors deep in all directions. *If we can't protect her here,* Cyrus followed Terian's unfinished thought, *will she be safe anywhere in Sanctuary?*

Chapter 6

Cyrus sat, steeped in the early morning darkness of the lounge with only the small, flickering firelight of the hearth to keep him company. He watched the front entrance doors, bathed in shadow in both reality and thought.

They're going to keep coming for her until she's dead. Dark musings filled his mind, reminding him of a long ago revelation from J'anda's mesmerization spell. It had given him a vision of that which his heart desired most; Vara, coy and seductive, kissing him. The fact that he harbored deep feelings for her had thus far gone unstated. *They're going to keep coming for her until she's dead. And we are going to have to button this guildhall up so tight that even the applicants may have to sleep outside until this is settled.*

The torches had dimmed of their own accord sometime after midnight and the hearths with them. Only a trace of the smell of wood burning lingered, filling the giant foyer with the same scent that had earlier reminded him of home. Now it reminded him of Niamh, of death and loss.

A solitary figure moved through the room, a shadow stretching across the floor as they crept from the staircase toward the front doors. A slight smile creased Cyrus's lips. *Nice to know my predictive powers haven't atrophied,* he thought as the firelight glimmered off a shining silver breastplate.

"You didn't think you'd be able to slip out unnoticed, did you?" His words were scarcely above a whisper, but felt loud in the still quiet.

Vara froze, a half dozen paces from the doors, looking around in surprise until she saw him, at which point her eyes narrowed. "Seeing as two assassins have slipped through thus far tonight, I assumed that as an officer of this guild, I might be allowed to pass." She wore a satchel draped across her back and her sword was slung at her side. "Was I in error?"

He rose to meet her. "Yes. You were in error." He clapped his hands and a half dozen figures stepped out of the shadows, all members of Sanctuary that he had put on guard. "There are assassins out to kill you. I can't just let you leave."

Her face fell and her mouth wavered from its usual severe line. "May I speak with you in private? Perhaps just outside the doors?"

He looked around the assembled faces that were standing watch. "I'm going out. Keep guard." Extending a hand, he opened one of the doors to Vara and stepped out into the chill of the autumn evening.

Cyrus heard Longwell speak as he shut the door behind them. "But aren't we supposed to guard her?"

"You can't just leave," he said, preempting her as they walked down the front steps. "Assuming you manage to dodge these assassins as you make your escape, it's not as though they'll just stop coming after you—"

"I can't stay. Every moment I remain here, lives are in danger. The lives of my guildmates are far more important to me than the illusion of safety that Sanctuary brings."

He watched the emotions play across her face by the light of the moon. "Where would you go?"

"South," she said without hesitation. "Following the refugees."

"Bad idea." He shook his head in disapproval. "After you cross the river, you're penned in on two sides by the Heia Mountains and the Bay of Lost Souls. A party on horseback could run you down."

Air hissed between her lips. "You have a better suggestion? Run toward Pharesia, perhaps?"

"Doubtful that the elven capital would be the safest place to hide from an order of elvish assassins. I was thinking we could get one of the wizards—"

"I don't want to involve anyone from Sanctuary in this," Vara said with a shake of her head. "Wherever they took me, I think Alaric would send well-intentioned search parties to bring me back."

"Fine," Cyrus said. "Then the best bet is to go north through the villages in the plains until you run into a wizard or druid who will teleport for a fee—they do those kind of jobs all the time for travelers who can pay."

"And where should I go?" Vara's voice carried no hint of sarcasm, and her blue eyes glittered, deadly earnest.

"North," Cyrus said. "Either to Fertiss, the dwarven capital—there are enough outsiders there that non-dwarves are a common sight—or the Gnomish Dominions—Huern is a city built for them to trade with non-gnomes. Otherwise the Northlands or the Riverlands of the Confederation. They don't get many elven visitors but if you wore a cloak with a hood you could pass for human easily enough—"

"Marvelous."

"—if you'd speak with more humility. We don't have a class system in the Confederation, so rather than be labeled 'noble' you'd be known as a 'prissy wench'."

"'Prissy wench'?" Her nostrils flared. "I am not—"

"We need to leave now and ride at least until tomorrow morning to get us out of range of Alaric's good intentions."

She paused, eyeing him with suspicion. "We?"

He took a slow, deep breath before answering. "I can't let you go alone."

Vara looked around, her eyes cast to the curtain wall that surrounded Sanctuary. "I don't have a great deal of time; certainly not enough for you to pack or lay in provisions—"

"My horse is saddled and provisioned," he said. "I've left a note for Alaric and the Council in my room. Thad is in charge of the detachment manning the gate tonight; at my command, he'll let us pass through."

She looked at him, staring a great hole through him. "You knew I would be leaving."

"I suspected that you'd see what I see," he replied.

"And that is?

"Sanctuary is so large, and our security so porous, that it would take a long time to tighten it up enough to protect you—time we don't have, at the rate of two assassination attempts per day. But if we were to get away for a while," he said, leaning in toward her, "it would give Alaric and the Council time to weed out the assassins that have slipped in."

"How long do you expect that will take?"

"I don't know." He sighed. "I don't know that it can even be done. I just know that, right now, it's not safe for you here."

"I don't think it would be wise to take you away from Sanctuary at this critical juncture," she said. "You could stay, help them to get things under control and then find me when you know it's safe for me to return."

"No." His voice was quiet but emphatic as he stepped in closer and placed his hand upon her arm. "I know your pride recoils at the thought of me protecting you, but put it aside. These assassins are deadly, and they have no desire to best you in a fair fight; they will strike you down when you least expect it."

"I see." Her eyes flickered and her arms remained crossed. "If you come with me, what's to stop them from striking you down? I am leaving to remove myself from the responsibility of seeing others harmed for my sake. I cannot see how bringing you along will accomplish that."

"Because you need help, Vara." His gauntlet clanked against the metal of the bracer that protected her wrist. "Your whole life you've fought alone and you've come to a point where you need someone you can trust—at the very least someone to watch out for you while you sleep. Unless you plan to not sleep at all?" He looked at her with a questioning glare. "Even without the Hand of Fear, there are countless dangers on the road—bandits, highwaymen—"

"Packs of goblins. Yes, very well," she said with a shake of her head. "Do not dare slow me down or I shall leave you behind."

"I won't go any slower than you," he said. He led her to the stables, passing by the guards with a simple nod of his head. He mounted Windrider, his preferred horse, while Vara put a saddle and her bags on a black stallion that she herself owned. With murmured affections, she led her horse out of the stables and swung herself into the saddle. Cyrus, for his part, managed to keep up.

"Hail, Thad," Cyrus called into the darkness when they reached the gate. The wall that surrounded Sanctuary was massive, stretching forty feet into the air.

A helmeted head popped into view over the parapet and fired off a crisp salute. "Hail, General. How goes it?"

Cyrus tugged on Windrider's reins, bringing the horse to a halt. "Not bad. I need you to open the gate for me, just as we discussed."

The warrior atop the wall was clad in a red-painted armor that in the washed out light of the moon appeared to be more of a mauve. "All right." Thad's earnest face stared down at Cyrus, visible in the pale white glow from above. "Best of luck, General. See you...whenever I see you."

"Take care, Thad." Cyrus fired off a rough salute of his own as the portcullis began to rise.

"And he won't betray us by telling Alaric?" Vara's whisper was lost in the sound of the chains dragging the gates and portcullis open; the cowl of her traveling cloak was pulled over her head, casting all but her nose and mouth into impenetrable shadow. "Or anyone else?"

"He won't until tomorrow morning, when Alaric comes to him. I trust Thad," Cyrus replied, spurring Windrider through the gates as they opened, Vara a few paces behind him. "So the question is, do you trust me? Because if not, this is going to be a lot more difficult."

Vara brought her horse alongside Cyrus and they cantered along. "I trust you," she said at last, her face still shrouded by the darkness of the cowl. "But from this point, we trust no one else." She spurred her horse to a gallop, riding north, Cyrus behind her.

Chapter 7

They rode through the day, taking breaks only when the horses grew weary. Vara said little, leading them north along the road. They passed caravans, almost all made up of humans, most wretched, bedraggled and begging for food. Although she apologized as she passed, she did not stop.

Cyrus followed in her wake, repeating the same message over and over. "Keep going, a day's travel south. Sanctuary is not far from a fork in the road; they'll give you food and help you however they can."

By sundown, Cyrus could feel the pain that came from sitting on a horse all day, and the fatigue of being awake for two days also wore on him. Windrider whinnied, moving at a walk. "I think we're going to have to bed down for the night."

Vara gave no indication she had heard him. He urged Windrider alongside her. Her features were frozen in place, her eyelids shut, and she bobbed with the motion of the horse. "Vara," he said, and reached over to nudge her.

With a start she jerked awake, surprise in her eyes. Her gauntlets gripped the reins and she pulled back in a sudden, violent motion.

He held his arms up, openhanded. "You fell asleep. I think it's time to stop for the night."

She stared back, her wall of glacial reserve melting under the strain of fatigue. "Perhaps you're right. But not here." She pointed off the road toward a copse of trees a few hundred yards away. "Over there, out of sight. And no fire." Without waiting for him to respond she urged her horse off the road in the direction she'd indicated.

Cyrus followed, and caught her as she began to dismount. He cringed as he lifted himself off the saddle, feeling the sticky, painful prickle of skin peeling from his body. Vara busied herself unpacking her saddle bag and a bedroll from the side of the horse then spreading it on the ground. She pulled a small loaf of bread from the bag and began to nibble on it as she sat and stared into the trees.

"You seem to be the most tired," Cyrus said, breaking the silence. "I'll take first watch and wake you after midnight."

"All right." Her voice was hollow and far away. She turned to him. "The second assassin—you questioned him?"

A cool unrelated to the air caused Cyrus to shiver. "Yes."

"What did he say?"

"Not a thing," Cyrus replied. "Fortin offered to torture him but Alaric refused." He did not tell her the other thing he had noted from the interrogation; that the elf had the most soulless eyes Cyrus had ever seen.

"Probably for the best."

"Terian threatened to transform him into a female with his axe, and he still wouldn't talk—"

Vara blinked. "Did he?" She ran a hand across her bedroll, smoothing it. "He would do it, too."

"He started to. Alaric had Fortin pull him from the room." Cyrus frowned as he started to sit down but winced as the pain of his saddle soreness halted him.

A quiet murmuring filled the air around him and Cyrus looked to see Vara with her head bowed, muttered words on her lips. Faint light radiated from the tips of her fingers as she pointed a hand toward him. A soothing feeling coursed over his aching body as the raw spots his skin had developed in the last hour healed, leaving behind only a ghost of the pain he had been experiencing. "Thank you," he said.

"Forgive me for not doing it sooner; I forget that you lack the ability to heal yourself."

"Biggest drawback to being possessed of no magical talent," Cyrus remarked, a rueful smile on his lips. "If you get impaled, you can't save yourself."

"Yes, well, do try and avoid that—as a paladin, my abilities are somewhat limited compared to a healer and I doubt I'd be able to save you from a wound so grievous as that." She yawned. "In addition, I have no desire to clean up the significant mess that would leave on my boots."

Cyrus chuckled. "Yes, I imagine that with me bleeding from a gaping hole in the chest, your biggest concern would be keeping the shine on your boots." He stared at her feet, covered in the same metal plating as the rest of her body, a healthy sheen obvious even with the dust of travel still on them.

"Quite so," she said with only a trace of irony, lying back onto her bedroll. "I can't recall the last time I slept in my armor. Still, under the circumstances, I suppose it's the wisest course."

"I used to sleep in my armor all the time," Cyrus said. "Before I joined Sanctuary, the guild I led adventured in far off places and we were...uh...well, broke, so we didn't have the money to stay in local inns. We spent a lot of nights under the stars."

"The stars." Vara's eyes sprung open. "I've grown so accustomed to spending my nights in the halls of Sanctuary, I've forgotten what it's like to sleep under the stars."

"Did you do it a lot as a child?"

Her eyes looked into the darkening sky as though she expected them to already be out. "No. I was raised in Termina and my mother and father rarely ventured outside the city."

"I suppose that made them difficult to see." Cyrus stared up at the last rays of sunlight springing over the horizon. The sloping hills of the Plains of Perdamun made way for trees every so often, with farms and homesteads spread out over miles and miles of empty space. "I was raised in Reikonos and because of all the torches and fires I didn't see a sky full of stars until I was seven, with the Society of Arms on a wilderness survival course."

"How old were you when you went to the Society?" Her voice was fading, the sleep beginning to turn it lyrical.

"Six." He watched her as she stared into the darkening sky. "You must have had a similar experience, since you went to...uh..." He racked his brain, trying to remember the name of the League that trained paladins.

Her quiet words filled the distance between them. "The Holy Brethren. And no, I did not begin my training with them until I was fourteen; before that I had a steady stream of League-Certified private tutors, the best that were available in the Elven Kingdom." She stated it matter-of-factly, though Cyrus still caught a hint of pretension.

"Hm." Cyrus pondered her upbringing. "We had a few people that joined the Society late, but they were all from families like yours; those that could afford to pay tutors to train their kids so they didn't have to live in the barracks with us 'uncivilized' commoners, the orphans that were there from childhood." He chuckled. "You probably didn't have many of those in the Holy Brethren."

She sniffed and turned toward him with irritated intensity. "What are you implying? Magical talent is hardly restricted to those who are well to do."

"No, no!" He backpedaled. "I meant that because you don't

need magical talent, anyone can be trained to be a warrior, so they scoop orphans and truants off the streets of Reikonos and put them in the barracks at the Society or with the rangers at the Wanderers' Brotherhood."

"Ah." She shifted in her bedroll, returning to her back to stare up once more. "My experience was quite a bit different than yours." She paused. "What was it like, growing up in the Society?"

He thought about it before answering. "Tough. From day one, you learn that life as a warrior is about strength, and the whole Society reflects that. You start training with real weapons at eight or so and there are a lot of training accidents—"

"That's barbaric." Vara rolled toward him, a look of disgust plastered on her face.

Cyrus shrugged. "They kept a healer in the Society. Few of the injuries were permanent or maiming. Only the occasional death, followed by a resurrection spell. Maybe five to ten a year. Very few permanent deaths."

Vara's grimace had become an openmouthed stare of horror. "That's appalling. You were mere children!"

"Well, none of the deaths were of the young children; most of them were from the family fights with the older—"

"Family fights?" Outrage dripped from her words.

Cyrus nodded. "When you join the Society, there's a ritual in which you're assigned a blood family. There are two defined blood families in the Society—the Able Axes and the Swift Swords."

"An alliterative nightmare. What's the difference between the two?"

He shrugged. "Nothing, really. It's a way of creating competition and an esprit de corps. You're trained to trust in circles—the blood family is the highest circle; then the Society; then the world. You eat together, you bunk together and you fight together. You learn to trust the person beside you in battle and you think in black and white terms about the enemies you kill."

"A narrow worldview." Her fingers clutched her bedroll, her knuckles white. "No part of you finds it despicable to treat children in such a way?" Her voice softened. "You don't...perhaps wish for a different childhood?"

Another thought drifted through Cyrus's mind, and though he tried to push it away it lingered; the remembrance of a home, the feeling of his mother's arms around him—maybe more wishful thought than tangible memory. He brought back another thought, a confined room, angry faces surrounding him; like demons at the time, but just children upon reflection. A memory of blood and pain.

"It doesn't matter," he answered, flint infusing his tone. "I didn't have one." He looked at her, glowing blue eyes still visible and shining in the last light of sundown. "What about you? What was your childhood like? You know, before you went to the Brethren."

"It feels as though it were a lifetime ago," Vara said. "I have spent over half my life now away from home—first in the Brethren, then several years with Amarath's Raiders before I joined Sanctuary."

"Isabelle—your sister, I mean—said you don't go home much." Cyrus looked at Vara, who was still. "Why not?" After a pause, he spoke again. "Vara?"

She let out a sharp exhalation of breath. "Let me see if I can answer your question whilst dancing around a delicate subject. As you know, I am the shelas'akur and there are certain...expectations others have of me, expectations I have no desire to live up to. My mother is the foremost among those who feel I should be doing more to fulfill my supposed responsibilities. I prefer not to argue with her, and thus I avoid going home as much as I can get away with."

Cyrus pondered her words until she turned and cast a glance at him. "Tell me what you're thinking, right now."

He froze. "I was wondering how strong-willed your mother would have to be to make you, one of the most stubborn and irascible people I've ever met, want to avoid her."

A light scoffing laugh filled the air in the clearing, almost as if Vara's chuckle were coming from the trees around them. "Yes, well, that attribute did come from somewhere, and I assure you it was not from my father, who is as mild a man as you can imagine. I do miss my father. He was—is—exceptionally kind. What about your parents?"

"Dead," Cyrus replied with leaden words. "Father died in the war with the trolls; Mother...I don't know, sometime after that. I don't remember how, just being dropped off at the Society sometime afterward."

"I'm sorry." Her voice quivered with an empathetic note.

Is that because she's been thinking of her own father or is it because she's letting her guard down? "It was a long time ago."

She cleared her throat. "I should get some sleep since I'll need to relieve you on watch in a few hours."

"Not a bad idea," Cyrus agreed. "I'll be shaking you awake before you know it; get it while you can."

"Yes. Well, goodnight."

"Sweet dreams, Vara."

He turned away from her and began to scan the horizon. Silence fell, broken only by the sounds of owls in the night. Cyrus put his back against a tree, watching the road a few hundred feet away, and looked to his side ever so often, just to be sure that the beautiful, golden-haired elf was, in fact, still there.

Chapter 8

She awoke as the first rays of sunlight broke through the trees. He watched her blink the bleariness from her eyes as she assessed the situation. "It's morning," she said, a look of puzzlement on her fine, chiseled features.

"Yes."

"You were supposed to awaken me in the night." She stood and he joined her, aided by support from the tree he had been leaning against. "Did you fall asleep?"

"No." He wore a tight smile.

"You didn't get any sleep?" Her face fell. "At all?" He shook his head. "You daft bastard. That was as ill-conceived an idea as any you've ever had."

"What?" He jerked from smiling to confused in the space of seconds. She looked at him with an irritation that sent unsettling feelings through him. "I was trying to be nice and give you a full night of sleep."

"You've jeopardized everything with your idiotic gallantry." She rolled her bedroll into a tight wad and wrapped it with leather fastenings. "You'll be tired all day and of less use watching for foes." She threw the bedroll over her shoulder, then snatched up her knapsack and strode toward her horse. "If you fall asleep, I'm leaving you behind."

Cyrus's hand reached under his helm and massaged at his scalp, fingers working through the locks of his hair. "Thank you, for reminding me what married life is like."

She paused, bristling, and rounded on him. "Excuse me?" Her voice contained more chill than the morning air.

"You just caused me to remember why I got divorced," he replied, anger beneath the surface of his words. "Leave it to a woman to take something nice that's done for her and turn it into a life or death situation."

She glared at him, contemptuous. "In case you've quite forgotten, it *is* a life or death situation."

"I haven't forgotten." He shook his head. "I thought I was doing something nice for you, yet somehow you got mad at me for it." He threw the saddlebags back over his horse. "Couldn't you just have been grateful and trust me to figure out a way to stay awake? It's hardly the end of all things."

"Perhaps I overreacted," she said. "But should you ever compare me to a former wife of yours again, you will see quite a different reaction, something akin to the feeling you might have should Fortin step on you." She turned away as she placed a foot in the stirrup and lifted herself onto the back of the horse. "Prehorta is still a few days' ride, but we'll start running into more and more villages as we get closer to human—well, what *was* human territory."

They rode on with few words exchanged. Cyrus spent most of his attention on the roads, keeping an eye on anyone who approached, interposing himself between them and Vara if they got closer than he deemed prudent.

After the third time he had placed himself between her and a group of refugees she favored him with an amused smile. "Are you concerned that a band of broken down old women are plotting my demise?"

"Someone is plotting your demise, and twice they've disguised themselves as refugees. I wouldn't put it past them to have an old woman in their ranks; what better way to sneak up on a person unsuspecting?"

"I suppose you're right, but it feels a bit odd to let you protect me, feeble as those efforts might be."

He let the comment pass as they approached a village. No more than fifteen structures stood clustered on either side of the road. Huts with thatched roofs accounted for all but three of the buildings; two of the last three appeared to be houses of worship; shrines to the gods of Arkaria. The last was a small wooden building that had a signpost out front with the word "Inn" written in large letters across it. Below was another shingle, this one less crafted than the first. It read, "Beggars Begone."

Cyrus started to remark on the sign, but a grunt from Vara turned his attention to the nearest house. On the front door hung a sign with "No beggars!" spelled in bold script. Similar signs hung on every door in the village, even the houses of worship.

"I've never seen the Goddess of Love turn anyone away," Vara said after seeing one of the signs hanging from the door to the shrine to Levembre. "One of her virtues is charity—or so I thought."

"We all have our hypocrisies," Cyrus said.

"Speak for yourself."

After inquiring at the inn, Cyrus learned that there were no spell casters in the village, so they rode on, finding the same in the next town, though it was larger and had even more signs telling refugees to not to bother stopping. They settled later that night, hidden from the road in another copse of trees, and Vara forced him to sleep first this time.

The days went quickly. It was on the fourth day and past the tenth village that it began to rain. It was a cold downpour, the deluge tapping against his helm and his armor, soaking him. For her part, Vara said little, but weathered the damp and cold with little reaction. They continued to pass refugees every hour or so, misbegotten souls with forsaken looks upon their faces. They cried out in hunger, for any help or assistance. The smell of smoke, blood, sweat and terror was heavy on them from the loss of their homes, their family members, their lives.

The rain ceased after a few days and the Plains of Perdamun became more uneven the further north they went, turning from flat lands into rolling hills broken by small forests. Cyrus had traveled this road before; in spring and summer it was a green and verdant land, filled to the horizon with wheat, corn, potatoes and countless other crops. As it was, the grasses had turned brown and the fields were all fallow for the coming winter, which would bring cold but little or no snow.

Vara remained stoic and silent for long periods of the journey. She initiated conversation only out of necessity, but would break her silence if Cyrus asked her an engaging question, which he spent a good portion of his time attempting to craft. It came to his great surprise when Vara broke the silence with a question of her own.

"I have wondered," she began as she pulled back on the reins of her horse, allowing him to come alongside her. The road stretched in a flat line in front of them with no one in sight. "What do you do in your spare time?"

He thought about her question before replying. "What spare time?" He looked at her with a sly grin that he saw returned, even as she rolled her eyes. "We don't have much, what with running the guild and planning expeditions."

"Surely you must find some time to do something other than hack at monsters with your sword."

"Not much, I suppose, but..." He hesitated.

She raised an eyebrow at him, waiting.

"I read."

A giggle escaped her lips, truncated as she covered her mouth with a hand. After composing herself, she pulled it away. "I apologize. Of course, I know you are literate, but I was expecting your answer to be something a bit more..."

"Fitting for a blunt instrument such as myself?" He smiled, trying to disguise the sting he felt inside. "It was brought to my attention after I joined Sanctuary that there was a large gap between what the Society of Arms taught and what I needed to know to be an effective general. So I started reading."

"And what do you read?" She studied him with fierce intelligence; she seemed curious.

"I read about explorations of ancient temples, on the known history of the dragons and the titans. I've read more recent tomes about elven, uh...language and customs..." He paused, wondering what inference she would draw from his admission.

She rode on without reaction. "It is fitting that a general does their best to improve their knowledge. I am not surprised, as you are quite adroit at what you do, and of course competence is not the easiest thing to come by if you aren't working at it."

"What about you?" He drew a curious stare from her. "I've seen you in your spare time; you always park yourself in the same seat in the lounge, always with a different volume."

"You watch me?" She raised an eyebrow but the rest of her expression stayed flat, giving him a moment of unease before the hint of a smile played across her face. "I have noticed. I suspect you know what sort of books I read."

"Always fiction," he said. "Stories of far-off places. I've seen you read one more than most— *The Crusader and the Champion.*"

"Ah, yes. A guilty pleasure, that one," she said with a nod and a smile that was reserved, yet sheepish. "It's about—"

"—A story of love and adventure involving a warrior and a paladin."

Silence filled the air, and Cyrus wondered if the plains had gone quiet or if he had gone deaf. Vara's look was guarded. "Have you read it?"

Fire crept across his face, starting with his cheeks, sending a burning feeling all the way to the tips of his ears. "I have."

She looked to the road, any hint of emotion washed from her next words. "I see. And how did you come by a copy of it?"

"I asked for one from the library in Reikonos." He cleared his throat. "After seeing you read it so many times I assumed it must be good."

"What did you think of it?"

"It's...good. I rarely read fiction, but it was interesting. A very different sort of book than I would have expected you'd enjoy."

"How do you mean?" She cocked her head, a quizzical look on her face.

"Well...uh..." He felt a tightness in his chest. "Let's put it this way—it's not allowed on the shelves of the Reikonos library because elves have a different standard when it comes to what's controversial..."

She laughed. "You're quite the prude, you know that? Dancing around what you mean to say—which is that there are quite a few steamy passages, and you didn't imagine I'd go for that. Let me tell you something, Cyrus Davidon." She leaned toward him even though they were alone on the road, as though whispering a secret she wanted no one else to hear. "I'm quite fond of those parts of the book; I think they're actually my favorite bits. Just because you and your pet rock giant think me a bloodless Ice Princess," she said with a grin, "doesn't mean that I don't carry any fleshly desires."

"I-I-I." He stammered, not sure which of her accusations to respond to first. "I never called you an 'Ice Princess', except to ask clarification from Fortin about what he meant." His cheeks were still flush with the heat as her last statement sank in and he realized what she had said. The words "fleshly desires" rolled around in his head.

"Why not? I am," she said, indifferent. "It's by my own design and efforts that I keep others—including yourself—at arm's length. That doesn't mean that I don't crave the same things you do."

"I don't— I mean—" he stuttered, his mind whirling as he tried to decide what to say next.

"My goodness, I've flustered the great and mighty General of Sanctuary—Hero of the Battle of the Nartanis Mountains, Conqueror of the Goblins of Enterra." A smile threatened to turn into a grin on her lips. "Had I known it was this easy to turn you into a stuttering mess, I'd have started each Council meeting where I expected an argument by whispering a filthy suggestion in your ear."

"You wouldn't have had the market cornered on that. Your

friend Aisling—" he said it with sarcasm but it still drew a look of disdain from Vara—"has done all she can to push the bounds of bad taste in that regard. Nyad also gave me a fascinating glimpse into the sex lives of Terminan elves when I was traveling with her a couple years ago."

"Did she?" Vara's voice cooled. "I suppose this explains the sickness and exhaustion you were suffering from."

"Nothing like that," Cyrus said in alarm. "She just...opened my eyes to the fact that I led a sheltered life." He coughed. "I believe she also called me a prude. Repeatedly."

"Finally an area where the Princess and I—" she put mocking emphasis on Nyad's title—"can agree. Likely the last time, as well as the first." Her face twisted back to the look of mischief. "Now that I know how to torture you—"

"Wait," Cyrus breathed an internal sigh of not-quite-relief. "There's a village ahead with some activity. Maybe we can find a wizard."

Vara's gaze shifted back to the road. "Yes, we'll plumb the depths of your race's secret disdain for biological imperatives later." With a slap of the reins, she urged her horse forward.

Cyrus followed with Windrider a few paces behind her. *I was about to have a discussion about sex with the single most prim and proper elf I've ever met*, he thought. *And one that I have deep feelings for. That could either be incredibly good or insanely torturous, and I doubt I'd know which until it was too late.*

They galloped along the road toward the village. *Maybe I should have waited another minute or so. She might have opened up to me again...or she might have opened up on me, and left me in an even worse mess.* A memory of Nyad's not-so-gentle probing, of her constant badgering until he had admitted that the last woman he'd been with was his wife—now almost four years ago—crossed his mind. *Not sure I want Vara to know that about me.*

Ahead, the village swarmed. It was not much bigger than the others they'd visited, but hundreds of refugees surrounded a series of wagons where food was being handed out. Cyrus caught a whiff as they reached the edge of town and his nose conveyed a message to his stomach, which roared approval after over a week of dry loaves and salted meat.

The scent was lovely; spices and fresh cooked beef, and a smell of fresh bread. The clamor of crowds of refugees, not pleading but squealing in joy and relief from their hunger, filled the air. There was a festive atmosphere and Cyrus cast a look through the crowds of ragged humans and settled on Vara, who wore a smile.

He caught her attention. "Ice Princess indeed. You're smiling at hungry people being given a meal."

She composed herself. "We should be careful. These relief efforts could be a distraction to allow an assassin to close in on us."

Cyrus looked ahead, his eyes fixated on a face in the crowd. Discomfort twisted his insides. "We let them draw us in."

As Vara looked at him in puzzlement, he eased his horse closer to hers and pointed. She saw, but did not react beyond her words. "There's no way we'll be able to outrun them. Not after so many days on the road."

"No." Cyrus cursed under his breath. *This is not going to be pleasant...*

A figure cut through the crowd, taking the utmost care not to knock anyone over, touching weary and downtrodden refugees as he passed, whispering an encouraging word here and there as he went. Upon reaching the edge of the throng he crossed the distance to Cyrus and Vara, the clinking of his aged armor lost beneath the roar of people behind him. His words, however, were not.

Cy turned to Vara, who looked stricken. Before them stood Alaric Garaunt, the Ghost of Sanctuary, his shoulders broad, back straight, and his lone gray eye staring up at his wayward officers. His words came out hard as the armor worn by the man himself, in a phrase that implied suggestion, though his tone carried no hint that it was anything other than a command.

"Let us...have a discussion."

Chapter 9

Alaric led them into the village inn, the door creaking as it swung shut, leaving the noise from the mob outside. Cyrus's eyes took a moment to adjust to the dimness; all the windows had heavy curtains drawn. Wood walls, dark and spotted with age, were illuminated by the light of torches and from a few places where the boards, warped from years of use, didn't quite meet any longer. The air was still but held a faded aroma of old stew.

A long bar stretched in front of the far wall, a row of seats lined up before it. Behind it, leaning on an elbow, was a human woman, her lips curled in a sour expression until Alaric reached into his purse and placed three shining silver coins before her. "I'll take a bottle of your finest mead."

Her expression melted from harshness into something approaching hunger as she snatched them up, nodding. She busied herself with glasses while Cyrus and Vara followed their Guildmaster to a table in the corner. He extended his hand in a gesture for them to be seated, which they did, followed by the Ghost himself.

Alaric studied them, his mouth unmoving, his eye giving away less than usual. He waited, watching them, the silence unbroken until the innkeeper bustled over with three tankards of mead, busying herself with a much more pleasant demeanor than she had exhibited when they first entered. "So nice to have paying customers rather than that rabble outside! Anything else I can get for you? Room for the night? Hot bath?"

"I expect I'm about to be scalded well enough without any aid from your boiling water," Vara muttered under her breath.

"Some privacy, if we could." Alaric looked up at the innkeeper with a smile.

"Don't expect you'll be disturbed by other customers, seeing as we ain't got any," the innkeeper said with a laugh. "If any of that rabble comes through the door, just call me and I'll sort 'em out." She nodded her head again, clutching at the ragged seams of her dress, then backed away and disappeared into a door behind the bar.

"But for this woodpile she calls an inn, she'd be hard pressed to differentiate herself from any of the refugees," Vara said after the innkeeper had left.

"And but for my skill in magic and practice with a sword, I would be nothing but a simple farmer," Alaric said. "Just because this woman has elevated herself above others in her mind is no reason for us to lose perspective." He leveled his gaze on them. "Nor should we become distracted, because a tavernkeeper is not the reason we are here."

Vara cast a quick look at Cyrus before turning back to Alaric. "I won't justify my decision to go—"

With a squeak, the door opened and interrupted her. Curatio swept in, white robes trailing behind him, a serene smile resting upon his face. "Sorry to interrupt, but I am pleased to see you here." He moved toward them, pulling out the remaining chair and seating himself at the table. "By all means, continue."

"I won't—" Vara began.

"I am not here to argue with you," Alaric cut her off.

"I'm not going back." Vara's voice rang through the room. She lowered her head. "I can't go back." Cyrus watched her, looking at the cheeks tinged with red, and knew she was thinking of Niamh.

The Ghost of Sanctuary leveled his eye on her. "I will spare you the requisite speech about how you are not responsible for what happened to Niamh." Cyrus caught a glimpse of Vara's staid expression as it crumbled. "I will cut to the point—since you left, we have had four more...altercations...with members of the Hand of Fear."

Vara's head snapped up but Cyrus spoke before she could. "Was anyone hurt?"

Alaric shook his head. "Three of the attempts were assassins trying to sneak through the gates, unaware that you had left. The fourth..." he sighed, "made it within the walls, disguised as another applicant when Terian managed to ferret him out."

"They will not stop coming." Vara's voice took on a tone of quiet defeat. "Who knows how many of them there could be?"

"Many," Curatio said. "Nyad spoke with her father, the King of the Elves, and he sent us all that they've collected on this cult. They've been operating in the Kingdom for over two thousand years—" He stopped when Cyrus let out a low whistle. "That's nothing for elves, remember—and it would seem they have grown in strength in the last two centuries." His lips drew a grim line across his face, the same as they had any of the times Cyrus had seen the healer deliver bad news.

"Why the last two hundred years?" Cyrus broke his silence as Curatio's eyes darted to Vara. "You're only twenty-nine." Cyrus looked at the blond hair on the top of her head as she fixed her eyes on the tabletop.

Curatio cleared his throat. "Once again..."

"Not up for discussion?" Cyrus turned to Alaric. "I suppose you know."

The Ghost shrugged his shoulders in a way that, to a stranger, would have indicated that he had no idea what was being discussed. Cyrus caught the familiar flick of Alaric's eye as he looked down that told him that the Sanctuary Guildmaster was being less than forthcoming. "It is irrelevant. What matters is —"

The door opened, and a figure was silhouetted in the daylight that flooded into the room. The sun shone off red armor, casting a tinged glow in spots of maroon on the walls.

"Thad," Alaric acknowledged the Sanctuary warrior. "Please, join us."

"Can't; I've come to get you." The big human closed the distance between the door and the table in only a few strides. "Everything is in place. Aisling confirmed it, and we're ready."

Cyrus's ears perked up. "Aisling is here?" Vara turned to him, her gaze so intense he feared a fire spell might have been cast upon him. "I was just curious," he said with a slight stammer.

"Yes, I daresay she is curious as well — about how it would feel to rut in the dark with you like a wild beast." Every word dripped with caustic malice.

"Well, honestly, who isn't curious about that?" Cyrus said, his tone light. The withering glare he received in return forced him to look back to Thad. "What's going on here?"

Thad looked to Alaric before speaking. When the Ghost gave a subtle nod, the warrior answered. "Based on comments made by the captured assassins, we think the Hand of Fear has figured out that Vara is no longer at Sanctuary. We ran into a few of their people coming in from the portal the day before yesterday, but we couldn't be sure, so we've kept a low profile."

Cyrus remembered the mobs surrounding the wagons outside, refugees swarming over them for food and supplies. He pointed toward the door. "You call that a low profile?"

Alaric responded, "That is only a fraction of the force we have in town. Once we realized that the enemy was watching, we knew we couldn't lead them away until you got here. Nor could we confirm that they were assassins until—"

"Vara arrived, and you watched who was watching her." Cyrus nodded at the Ghost with a grudging respect. "Aisling can pick a suspicious figure out of a crowd like nobody else."

"And there you go, wondering what it'd be like to rut in the dark with her." Vara's voice rang off the bare walls. "I don't trust her nor her supposed ability to pick assassins out of a crowd. She's more likely to find the firmest, meatiest, most pigheaded warrior in the land—"

"Are you calling me firm and meaty?" Cyrus looked at Vara, who flushed in embarrassment. "As to pigheaded, I'd say it takes one to know one—"

"Children." Alaric's voice contained a hint of impatience coupled with urgency. "Aisling is quite adept at singling threats out of a crowd, as she has demonstrated on numerous occasions. I trust her judgment."

"So long as you don't trust her with the contents of your purse."

Ignoring Vara's riposte, Alaric continued. "We'll take care of this threat, but before we do, I need to ask you—have you considered where you are fleeing?"

Cyrus looked to Vara. "We have."

Alaric nodded. "May I suggest a brief stop?"

Vara looked at the Sanctuary Guildmaster with a wary edge. "Where?"

"I am not an assassin. But if I were, I would surmise that Sanctuary is the most likely place to catch you unawares." Alaric's hands met in front of him, fingers steepling, as they often did, when he was making a point. "Failing that, next I would try—"

Vara's complexion deadened as she wilted in her chair. Her voice cracked when she spoke. "Home."

The Ghost did not flinch. "I sent J'anda and Vaste along with a detachment of our best to Termina to keep an eye on your parents, but your mother refused our help, and nearly attacked J'anda."

Vara's words came out in a low, almost croaking tone. "My mother would not accept Sanctuary's assistance if she were in flames and we promised to extinguish them."

Alaric nodded to her in deference. "We have maintained a garrison in the house across the street after paying the couple who live there to quarter our forces, which they were only too happy to do when the situation was explained to them. Vaste has checked on them several times since then—"

"If she stabbed at the dark elf, I can only imagine what she'd do to a troll," Cyrus muttered.

"There has been no answer but audible swearing behind the door," Alaric said. "Your family has been warned, but your mother has not taken this threat seriously."

Vara closed her eyes, arms folded on the shining breastplate. "I need to go to them. I need to convince my mother." She blinked. "And perhaps my sister as well..."

"Isabelle has been warned," Alaric said, "and Endeavor has increased their guard. As an officer in Arkaria's foremost guild, I would imagine she is safer than most. Nonetheless, perhaps it would be best if you went to Termina to speak with your mother before going on to whatever destination you have chosen."

A bristling, aggravated feeling rushed through Cyrus at the thought of hiding, quieted by his knowledge that they were up against a foe that did not show its face until it was ready to strike—and that by then it might be too late to save—

"Aisling has picked out three in the crowd outside," Thad said. "They're watching the front door, so I suggest we go out the back."

"Let us not delay." Alaric picked up his flagon and drained the last of his mead before replacing the vessel on the table. "There is, after all, no telling how much time we have before these assassins make a hasty mistake."

Chapter 10

They left through the back door after Thad and Cyrus made certain it was clear, surprising the innkeeper as they passed her. Alaric handed her another few pieces of silver as Cyrus emerged into the sunlit yard behind the tavern, Nothing but fields extended to the horizon.

Cyrus held open the door for Vara, who was still paler than usual. The fading light of day gave her skin a washed-out, almost sickly appearance.

Thad halted them once they were outside. "Someone should wait with Vara while we get rid of these assassins." Cyrus tried to signal the younger warrior to shut up, but to no effect; Thad stared at Cyrus's motions with a look of curiosity that took his eyes off the elf in front of him.

Vara's face turned from pale to an angry red flush. "I'm not some scared, weak little princess, hiding in the shadows of my stronger brethren." She raised an open palm and a blast of force slammed into Thad, causing his arms to pinwheel and the warrior to land on his rump.

She took two steps forward to sneer at him. "Do not make the mistake of believing that because I ran from these cesspools that I did so out of fear for anyone but my comrades; I am a paladin, a holy warrior in the service of Sanctuary and Vidara, the Goddess of Life, and anyone who steps into my path should prepare themselves accordingly."

Cyrus stood back, arms folded, along with Alaric and Curatio. Vara whirled around to face them, her anger yet unspent. "I hope none of you —"

"Lass," Alaric began, interrupting her building tirade, "the three of us have known you long enough to recognize that when you set your mind to a course of action, no matter how ill-advised, it will be unchanged. We have foes to deal with." The Ghost's hand found its way to his sword, and he drew the runed blade, holding it in front of him.

They followed Alaric around the side of the inn, through an alley that led to the main road. The noise of the crowd was still resounding, shouts of jubilation, laughter and glee echoing around them.

Thad leaned in behind Cyrus, Curatio separating the two warriors from Vara in the narrow passage to the street. "You know, it's a wonder she hasn't killed you in the last few days."

Cyrus snorted. "I'm not dumb enough to provoke her wrath unless I'm ready for it."

"There is no preparation for my wrath," Vara said without turning around. "And you're plenty dumb enough."

"How did she hear us?" Thad said, his voice low. "I was whispering and there's a full scale riot of joy going on not a hundred feet away. I could barely hear my own words!"

Curatio shot them a sympathetic look as Vara cast a gaze of annoyance as she pointed to one of her elongated ears. "These? Not just for decoration."

Alaric eased into the crowd, which filled the street to the alley. Cyrus brushed past Curatio, who gave him a reassuring smile as the warrior followed Vara. With a glance back, he confirmed that Curatio stopped at the mouth of the alley, his hands moving to flip up the cowl on his traveling cloak then returning to the folds of his robe where, unlike some healers who preferred to remain unarmed, Cyrus remembered he kept a mace.

"You're not laboring under the delusion I'm some damsel in distress, are you?" Cyrus turned back to see Vara peering at him, question in her eyes.

"Not at all," he said, talking over the raised voices on the street. "I'm just here to help a guildmate in dire need."

"I am not in *dire* need —"

"Well, you're in some need."

Mollified, Vara turned her attention back to the crowd. "Can you spot the assassins from here?"

Cyrus scanned the crowd, trying to take in the small details; happy faces, children darting through the multitude, their voices raised in laughter. The smell of fresh baked loaves of bread wafted through the air coupled with a smell that he knew was Larana's meat pies; a combination of beef, lamb and chicken in a thick crust of delicious dough, one of which could feed several people. His mouth watered; it was his favorite dish long before he joined Sanctuary. He felt the people brushing against him in the crowd, refugees with an air of hope so distant from the ragged desperation of the ones that they had encountered for the last few days that it was almost unrecognizable.

And yet, in the crowd, there were small holes in the

atmosphere of festivity. A man was stock still near one of the wagons, his eyes fixed in their direction. Another, near the door of a house on the other side of the street, was focused not at all on the loaf of bread in his hands but directed to casting furtive glances at Vara.

"I see some of them," he said. "It's the ones that keep looking at you."

"And you don't allow for the possibility that they could be simply admiring my resplendent beauty?" The tension in her voice was the only hint she might be joking.

Cyrus replied in a low undertone, "Their eyes are hardened, sunken; these aren't men who could appreciate beauty in any environment, resplendent or not. They're intent on a purpose and it involves you in an unpleasant way."

She turned away from him so that only her profile was visible, and he watched her look resolve. "I'm certain that their intentions and mine are not matching, so let us dispense with these murderers."

"Yes, let's —" Cyrus was interrupted when out of his peripheral vision came a blur of speed, a brown cloak on a direct line for Vara. A dagger was already extended from the sleeve and Cyrus caught only a glimpse of a man's face as he moved past the warrior. It was contorted with a look of unrepentant viciousness, sadistic glee lighting up the dark-circled eyes as the elven assassin swept toward his unknowing target.

Cyrus's hand was already on Praelior and he felt the familiar sensation of time slowing down. The blade was drawn and moving, flashing through the air in a crosswise cut that opened a gash across the ribs of Vara's assailant, spinning him to his knees. Cyrus brought his sword across the throat of the elf as Vara turned in surprise.

A hush fell over the crowd followed by the first scream, then a hundred others. The calm and docile refugees, so contented only a moment before, saw the peaceful calm shattered and almost as one tried to scatter from the violence in their midst. Cyrus looked to the places where he had seen assassins, but they were all swept up in the movement of the throng, all gone.

One of the wagons flashed and a forked streak of lightning shot from the window. Cyrus could see Larana, her expression one of pure fury, as the bolt struck a figure whose cloak caught fire, forcing him to the ground. Another arced past Cyrus into an elf that was charging at Curatio, a dagger raised above his head. The healer waited with his mace in a defensive posture, but the lightning sent the assassin flying into a wall.

Cyrus turned back as a cry of alarm came from behind him. He was already in motion, his sword up, as he sprang forward, pushing Vara to the side. Distracted by the assailant attacking Curatio, Vara had turned her head as another assassin broke free of the fleeing crowd.

Cyrus brought his sword forward in a blocking motion, batting aside the first dagger of the assassin with his right hand as he interposed his body between Vara and the elven attacker. The assassin was knocked off balance, but brought around his other dagger in a glancing stab that skipped off the metal plating on Cyrus's upper arm and funneled, by pure luck, into the gap beneath his pauldrons.

He cringed as he felt the blade bite into the meat of his left shoulder. Warm blood spurted out of the wound as he slammed his sword into his assailant's face. The assassin's hand slipped free of the dagger's grip, leaving it buried in Cyrus's arm.

The refugees had dispersed, leaving behind a handful of cloaked elves and a near-empty street. Cyrus saw Sanctuary guild members led by Ryin Ayend coming into the village at the north end; the opposite direction from which he and Vara had entered, but they were fighting against the fleeing crowds.

Cyrus maintained a defensive posture, his back against Vara's. Two more elven assassins advanced toward them as he flinched through the pain and felt a burst of lightheadedness.

"Shall we show them the error of their ways?" Vara said.

Cyrus gritted his teeth, the pain in his arm bringing tears to his eyes. "Sure. Why not."

Vara slashed at the assassin closest to her, causing him to take a step back. Cyrus did not wait to see how the next round of her battle went; his foe moved toward him and Praelior came up of its own accord to fend off the assassin's attack. Every clash with the elf's blades jolted him, sending waves of pain radiating from where the dagger was still buried in his shoulder.

Cyrus glanced back; Curatio and Thad were engaged with more assassins that had sprung out at them while Alaric was fighting off two assailants simultaneously. Vara was holding her own against the other, but was in no position to assist him. The pain in his arm was becoming an unstoppable agony, even with the aid of Praelior's mystical strength. He suspected that without it, he would be on his back, helpless.

His assailant struck again and again, each blocked by Cyrus but battering the warrior back toward the inn. Cyrus countered with a clumsy swing, but the blow pushed the assassin back only a few steps, and at the cost of Cy's footing. The warrior fell, the front of his armor a bloody mess, his black plating slick. The smell of it wafted up and his eyes felt heavy. He raised Praelior in front of him, fending off two more attacks by the assassin, whose angular features were cracked by a smile.

"I see you've felt the kiss of black lace," his assailant taunted him. "The mighty Cyrus Davidon, General of Sanctuary, brought low. Not quite so unstoppable without a healing spell, are you?"

"That's not what makes me unstoppable." Cyrus tasted blood in his mouth. His armor felt heavy, and the mild ache in his knees from the position he was in was nothing compared to the screaming pain in his left arm.

"Oh, no?" The assailant grinned as he closed, his boot landing on Praelior, knocking the blade into the dirt.

Cyrus slumped back, looking up and seeing the overhang of the roof of the inn above him. "No...I'm just a so-so warrior..."

"Any other confessions before you die?" The assassin laughed and raised his blade.

"You're about to get perforated with knife blades," Cyrus said, his words slurred. "And I'm going to enjoy it."

The assassin paused, a look of confusion on his face as from above them a shadowed shape detached itself from the roof, flying through the air. The elf looked at the sudden flash of motion. Cyrus reached up and batted the blades aside, knocking them from the assassin's grasp as the shadow slammed into him.

Aisling landed with her weight on her daggers as Cyrus fell over into the dirt, clear of the dark elf's attack on the unsuspecting assassin. He saw her action as if she were moving at half speed; her weapons plunged into the guts and neck of the elf, his grin supplanted by an openmouthed expression of shock, then dissolved by the torrent of blood that spurted from his body at her assault. The dark elf landed with both knees and the force of her impact hid the fact that she stabbed the assassin a half dozen more times in the seconds that followed.

With the lithe grace of a cat, Aisling moved from a crouch to standing, facing away from him. His eyes blurred as she stood silhouetted against the sun, her dark blue skin giving her the appearance that she was a human shrouded in semi-darkness.

Cyrus looked past her to see Alaric, locked in combat with two of the remaining assassins, his sword dancing to either side, keeping them off balance, whirling to avoid his offensive thrusts. A concussive burst of force shot from his hand, clipping one of the combatants and freeing him to focus on the other for a few seconds; all he needed to strike a killing blow on the first before returning to the second and finishing him off as well.

Cyrus glanced back to see Thad and Curatio making quick work of one of the remaining assassins as the remainder of the Sanctuary force arrived. Curatio broke away and came to his side, followed by Vara. The paladin dropped to her knees at his side, Aisling behind her but standing at a distance.

"You silly bastard," Vara said under her breath. "I took mine out without difficulty, but you have to go and get impaled."

"He didn't get wounded by the last one," Aisling said from behind her, every word drowning in accusation. "He got stabbed when trying to keep you from getting knifed in the back." The dark elf kicked at the dust at her feet. "It wouldn't have happened if he hadn't had to save you."

"And where were you while we were fighting them off?" Vara shot to her feet, tense and facing Aisling, who recoiled and dropped her hands to where her daggers rested in her belt.

"I was on top of the inn, waiting for an opportunity to be of use," Aisling shot back, her purple irises seeming to glow in challenge. "And I was, just in time to save his life."

"We have no time for this," Curatio called to the two women as he knelt next to Cyrus. The healer's hands removed Cyrus's pauldrons, then unstrapped one side of his breastplate and backplate while Vara returned to his side and removed the other. Cyrus gritted his teeth again, the pain mounting.

Curatio frowned as he looked at the wound. "Knife went in the shoulder but it skipped off the bone and slid here." The healer's finger traced a line along Cyrus's skin that roared with pain as he did it. "Probably hit an artery." Curatio grimaced and pushed down so hard on Cyrus that motes of light swirled in front of his eyes. The healer's hand re-entered his vision a moment later, a dagger clutched in it. With a sniff, his frown deepened. "Black lace."

"I admit my understanding of human anatomy is very basic —"

Aisling began.

"And limited to the area of the groin," Vara said.

Aisling continued, "But if you can't heal him, won't he bleed to death?"

Curatio's hand dug within his robes, a look of intense concentration on his face that brightened after a moment. His hand emerged, a small pouch gripped within it. "That would be true — if I couldn't heal him."

The words made their way through Cyrus's pain-soaked mind. "Didn't you say the dagger was coated in black lace?"

"I did." Curatio opened the pouch and gathered a pinch of dried leaves between his fingers. "This is going to hurt, and for that, I apologize." He turned to Vara and then to Thad, who showed up at his shoulder. "Hold him down."

Curatio drove his finger into Cyrus's wound, tearing a ragged scream from his throat, followed by a stream of shouted curses, most of which related to the healer's parentage. The wound burned, screaming. Cyrus's eyes were closed, squinted tight, and he forced them open while he tried to control the excruciating pain in his shoulder and arm.

Vara stared down at him, her blue eyes wide with fear, both her hands pushing his left arm to the ground, the veins in her thin neck bulging from the effort. Aisling was lying across one of his legs, which was spasming while Alaric forced the other down. Thad, on the other hand, grimaced but kept Cyrus's right arm contained, unable to do anything useful, such as pummel Curatio to death for whatever he was doing.

In a moment, the healer wiped his bloodied hands together and stood. Cyrus still felt the searing in his shoulder, although it had abated a little. Curatio brought his hands together and closed his eyes, his mouth almost unmoving while a blue glow filled his fists. The light enveloped Cyrus and the pain faded, as though it were a mound of sand blown away by a light wind, a few granules at a time.

Ragged breaths tore from Cyrus's lungs as he sucked in air, his eyes locked on Curatio's. "Not sure I want to know how you did that."

Curatio forced a smile, his expression grim. "I know it hurts."

Thad looked up at the healer. "I thought black lace counteracted all magic?"

Curatio waited before replying. "Alchemists long ago created a cure for black lace as well as the dark magics that carry the same effect; unfortunately, it's from a very rare and expensive plant and I didn't have any on hand after depleting my stock..." His words came out in a low whisper. "...several years ago." He bowed his head. "I should have bought more after we started raising our fortunes in Purgatory, but it wasn't a priority." His head came back up. "Until..."

"Niamh." The name bubbled up on Cyrus's lips, and he tasted bitterness that had nothing to do with the blood from where he had bitten his tongue.

"I had it on a list of things I was going to do. We've been out of it for years. I just hadn't gotten to Pharesia to get it yet." The healer's eyes were haunted, glossed over and staring at the dirt beneath him.

"We've discussed this, Curatio." The voice of Alaric was near silent, stoic. "This is not something we could have predicted."

"We'd seen it before." Curatio's head did not move. "I should have been prepared."

"When did you see black lace before?" Cyrus rasped, fingers kneading into his exposed shoulder, sending spikes of pain down his arm as well as into his chest.

"It wasn't black lace," Curatio said, looking up at Vara. "It was a spell that produces a similar effect. And it had nothing to do with what's happening now."

"Sorry, but we don't have time." Vara stood, a hint of impatience sneaking into her words. "I need to get to Termina to speak with my parents."

"Yeah." Cyrus reached for his breastplate, strapping it on as he attempted to stand, eliciting a murmur of protest from Curatio.

"You're not fully healed—the black lace is still in your system; the rotweed only removed the effects where I was able to touch—"

"You put something called rotweed into my wound?" Cyrus paused, halfway to his feet, leaning against the wall of the inn for support.

Curatio shrugged. "Either that or watch you bleed to death."

"Fair point." Cyrus fastened the last strap and lifted his arms to put his pauldrons back on, but the pain elicited a cringe.

"The rotweed allowed me to heal most of the damage." Curatio's hand reached out to help Cyrus as he stood. "You'll need additional healing over the next hour as the rotweed works its way into the portions of the wound it hasn't affected yet."

"Great," Cyrus said, struggling into his armor. "Either you can come along to Termina or she," he pointed at Vara, "can do it along the way."

"You should go back to Sanctuary." Vara's expression was tender. "I appreciate your concern, but you'll need time to recover."

"I could help," Aisling spoke up, sliding into place at his side. "I'm a very capable nurse. I'd have you up and active in no time. And eventually," she said with an undisguised grin, "you might even leave your bed again."

Vara's nostrils flared as she fired back at the dark elf. "On the other hand, perhaps you should come to Termina simply so you don't die of venereal disease."

Cyrus pushed off the building and drew his arms back from those around him. "I'll be fine. Let's go."

Alaric moved forward, his hand coming to rest on Cyrus's unwounded shoulder. "Larana will teleport you to Santir. Thad and others will accompany you across the river until you reach Vara's home. Do not linger; be quick about your purpose."

"My mother is stubborn," Vara said, her lips drawn in a thin line. "This may not be as quick as we could hope for; she has lived a long time and is set in her ways."

Alaric looked back at her, exuding a calm that only hinted at the deadly threat hanging over her. "Convince them. Do it quickly and get out of the Elven Kingdom. Every moment you wait gives the Hand of Fear more opportunity to target them — and you."

Chapter 11

The winds of the teleportation spell died and Cyrus urged Windrider forward, leading a small Sanctuary force ahead at a slow walk. Every time his horse set a foot down, pain shot through Cyrus's wound. "This way," Vara spoke from beside him, leading them to the west, the sun hanging low in the sky.

"I don't understand," Cyrus said, looking around the square. The portal where they had appeared was a stone ovoid laying with the long side down, runes inscribed around it. It sat in the middle of an open square, mostly wooden buildings surrounding it, in the heart of the human city of Santir. Ahead, Cyrus could see the dirt avenue leading to a massive bridge over the river Perda.

"You'll have to narrow that down," Vara said. "I don't have time to mull over all the things you don't understand in order to try to find a way to explain them to you."

Cyrus gestured around him. "Santir is a human city, with...I think...a couple hundred thousand people. It's not very old."

"About a hundred years old," Vara said. "It was the site of the final battle in the last great war, the one between the humans and elves on one side and the dark elves on the other. What don't you understand?"

"Termina has a population of over a million, and it's across the river," Cyrus continued. "Why didn't we just teleport there?"

"Termina doesn't have a portal," Vara replied. "Rather impossible to teleport somewhere that doesn't have a portal."

Cyrus frowned. "We teleport into the Sanctuary foyer all the time. There's no portal there."

"Actually, there is," Vara said with a smile of self-satisfaction. "It's built into the floor. There's a room in the dungeons—just down the hall from your accommodations last year—you can go in there and if you look up, you'll see it, mounted to the ceiling."

"How did we manage that?"

"I don't know. I would presume Sanctuary was built in the days when the portals were." She paused. "Or somehow Alaric moved a portal into our cellar." She gave it a moment of thought. "Upon reflection, I wouldn't rule that out."

"That brings us back to my original query," Cyrus said. "Why doesn't Termina have a portal of its own?"

Vara's hands gripped the reins of her horse. "No elven city has a portal within its walls, yet all the larger ones have portals nearby. They're all well outside the gates, even in Pharesia."

Cyrus let his tongue run along his teeth, searching for the place where he had bitten it in the battle. "Maybe a defensive measure? To keep someone like the dark elves from teleporting into the heart of your city?"

Vara chewed her lip. "Perhaps, but I doubt it. There is a spell that can be used to render a portal inactive if one fears invasion. Surrounding it with soldiers also allows invasion forces to be routed a few at a time as they appear. Every elven city with a portal is thousands of years old; it is more likely an aesthetic decision." She glanced back to the stone ovoid. "After all, they are rather ugly."

They lapsed into silence as Cyrus took in the scenery of Santir's main avenue. Dirt roads, wet from a recent rain, lay underneath the shoes of his horse, filling the air with a soft sucking noise. People filled the street, shopping from carts and wooden storefronts. Most of the buildings were comprised of wood, as though they were temporary.

Cyrus glanced behind him. Their small Sanctuary army was in tow, spearheaded by Thad and Ryin Ayend. Larana was visible as well, but when he glanced at her she looked away, giving Cyrus a charge of amusement. Her dark hair was tangled around her tanned face, giving her a bedraggled look.

As they approached the bridge, Cyrus noticed a striking change in scenery. The bridge, in addition to being enormous, was composed of beautiful stonework, with statues every few feet along the sides.

Looking down the river Perda, Cyrus saw docks stretching out into the water, with small fishing boats and even a few larger craft at the port to the north. In the distance on either side, Cyrus could see smaller bridges to the north and south.

As they reached the crest of the arching bridge, Cyrus's eyes fell upon the elven metropolis of Termina for the first time. Buildings stretched over the horizon as far as he could see. Tiles dotted the sloped rooftops, red with the aura of sun-baked clay. All the buildings that he could see were built of stone, all made to survive the seasons that occurred in this part of Arkaria.

The avenue in front of him could not have been a more marked contrast to Santir; cobblestones lined the streets and trees were planted every few feet on either side of the road. From where he sat on the bridge, a half dozen squares were visible on the main thoroughfare, each with a fountain. Aquaducts ran across the tops of buildings, greenery hanging from their sides.

In the center of the city, Cyrus could see a structure reaching a dozen stories into the air, capped by a beautiful dome made of shining metal. The stonework glistened in the light, and it was by far the tallest building in Termina.

"The Chancel of Life," Vara said, drawing his gaze back to her. "It's a temple to Vidara, the Goddess of Life. She's the most worshipped deity of the elves. Her temple is largest to reflect her place in our hearts." Her finger traced a line to another building, a mile or so south of the Chancel. It was not so tall but stretched over a space large enough to fit the Chancel of Life within it. "That is the Great Bazaar, the largest market in Arkaria."

Cyrus frowned. "I always thought Reikonos had the largest market."

"Yes, well, being a human you would, wouldn't you?" Vara said in a teasing voice. "This market is the largest, but only because there is more than one market in Reikonos. So, we have the largest market, and you have the most *markets.*"

He looked down the slope of the bridge once more at the Bazaar. He could see the bridge south of him connected with an avenue that ran straight to the enormous market. "I suppose that's an important distinction to make...to someone."

She looked back at him impishly. "Yes, to me. Because it still puts my hometown in front of yours." Before he could respond, she pointed again at the horizon, this time to the north of the Chancel and a square building, devoid of any artistic elements. "See that one?"

"Yes?" The building she was pointing to was boxy, unremarkable—ugly, even.

"It's the center of the elven government in Termina. Did you notice the design?"

He squinted. "It's smaller...and kinda ugly," he said, almost apologetic. He leaned back in his saddle, shifting his attention back to her, waiting for the inevitable eye roll.

It never came. "Indeed it is. You see, all three of those buildings make a statement about Termina. The tallest is the Chancel, placed at the center of the city and the widest or biggest in terms of square footage is the Bazaar. The city designers made it so," she lectured, "to show that the heart of Termina was the love and worship of the Goddess of Life, and that the width and depth of our souls were in worship of her and pursuit of commerce."

"And the government building?"

She laughed. "Ugly, shapeless, and well out of the way of the other two. Termina is the only place in the Elven Kingdom where that attitude about the monarchy would fly."

"Are you...happy to be home?" Cyrus asked with hesitancy.

"I am," she said after a short pause. Drawing a deep breath, she elaborated. "I do miss this city and all its charms." She shifted her gaze from the horizon to him, and he tried to remove the hand he had rested on his own shoulder, as if he could massage the aching pain out of his muscles through the armor. "You need a healing spell."

She raised her hand and under her breath muttered words so low that, like every other spell caster, he couldn't come close to discerning what she said. A tingle ran through his arm and across his chest, as though a warm wind were soothing some of the pain away. "Did that help?" Her voice was an octave lower than usual and filled with concern.

"Yeah." He raised his arm to swing it in a slow arc. "A few more heals, it'll be fine."

"We only have an hour to get it right," she said. "After that, healing spells will have no effect. I need you strong—at your best and ready for what comes our way."

"You're worried about more assassins?" Cyrus raised an eyebrow.

Her jaw tightened. "There are other dangers we'll face that you'll need all your strength for."

"Like what?"

"My mother." She looked away as she said it.

He scoffed. "I've faced the dragonlord, servants and defenders of the gods, and the imperial leaders of the goblins. I doubt I have much to fear from an elven woman."

She turned back to him, eyebrow raised in amusement. "We shall see. Make ready."

They made their way down the wide avenue, taking a left turn several blocks before the Chancel of Life. Their horses cantered along the tree-lined boulevards as the cobblestone roads narrowed. "That wide avenue that led across the bridge? That's called the 'Entaras'iliarad'. It means 'The Way of the Spirit'. It leads to the Chancel of Life; all the main roads in Termina do."

Cyrus pondered that. "So the Goddess of Life is the main deity of the elves? No others?"

"There are pockets where other deities are worshipped, and they have temples." She used the reins to steer her horse around a cart. "Several of the elemental gods are represented — Ashea, the Goddess of Water, for instance, has a loyal following in the Kingdom. Levembre, the Goddess of Love also has a faction. Virixia of Air and Sinaa, Goddess of Peace, have temples in the outskirts."

"Any followers of Bellarum?"

Vara laughed. "Few here, if any, follow the God of War, and they'd all worship in secret. The same with the Gods of Darkness, Death and any of the other 'evil' deities. The Kingdom frowns on the activities and rituals that those gods require in their worship."

"Explains why I've never heard Terian list here as a place he wanted to visit."

She led them down the stone streets, past buildings that were well-maintained and timeless in their design. "This is the old district," she said as they passed a row of homes. "These buildings are several thousand years old, but they've all been refinished." She swelled. "It's the most exclusive area of Termina, with the exception of the mansions on Ilanar Hill, where the greater royals and wealthiest citizenry live."

"So the lesser royals live here?" Cyrus deadpanned.

"Quite a few, yes," she replied, her thoughts elsewhere and missing the sarcasm in his remark. "This is where I grew up."

"Impressive. What did your father do, to be able to afford such nice dwellings?"

"He was...given several businesses to run," she said. "Unfortunately, my father is not skilled at such things, and so he ran each of them into the ground in turn, for varying reasons."

"Ouch. Were his benefactors upset?"

"I suspect at least a little, but there were no shortage of others willing to give him the opportunity." Her eyes had settled in the distance. "He finally conceded he was not disposed to try again and accepted a position with a shipping concern with much less responsibility. It pays well enough, and he's content at his work."

"It's good that he understands his strengths and weaknesses," Cyrus said, shifting once more in the saddle, the pain fading from his wound a little at a time. "Most people don't. But if your father ran several businesses into the ground, how did he afford to live in this — exclusive, as you put it — district."

Vara tugged the reins, bringing her horse to a stop. "We're here."

Cyrus looked up. The building Vara had led them to was three stories tall, sandwiched on either side by residences of similar design, built to share common walls and mirrored on the other side of the street. Tall trees stretched above them to shade everything from the evening sun, giving the avenue a darkened feel. Without exception, every one of the buildings on the street was flawless, the stonework detailed and intricate, unlike anything Cyrus had seen in any of the other cities he had traveled to.

He followed her to the door, five stone steps leading off the street, Thad and the rest of their Sanctuary allies remaining behind as Vara reached the door. Cyrus watched her hand freeze, hovering over the long handle. He stopped a couple steps behind her, watching as a cascade of emotions ran over her profile. He started to reach out to her but stopped. "Are you...?"

"I'm fine." Her head turned and she nodded back at him. "Steel yourself," she warned as her hand closed on the door handle. Before she could finish her thought, the door swung open.

Chapter 12

Framed in the doorway was a woman, her eyes slitted in the same manner as Vara's did when they narrowed. A burgundy blouse and black breeches hung on her, revealing a woman who was still well in shape. Were she human, Cyrus would have guessed her to be in her thirties, but the points of her ears betrayed her elven heritage and made hazarding a guess impossible. Her resemblance to Vara was uncanny.

"Oh, look, our wayward daughter returns," the woman said, her voice crackling with sarcasm. "I heard you were being chased by an order of assassins?"

Vara stood, unsteady, as if she were off balance. "I am."

"How kind of you to come here, bringing danger and death to our very doorstep!" Her mother's face was devoid any mirth, but her tone was mocking and ironic. "I know I told you that I hoped you would visit more often, but I didn't realize I had to include a disclaimer that it would be best to do so when not in mortal peril."

Silence hung in the air. Cyrus felt a sense of awkward embarrassment for Vara, who maintained her stoicism as her mother lashed at her.

With a flick of her eyes, Vara's mother's gaze fell on him, blue diamonds that glittered with all the brilliance of the sun sparkling on a prism, and Cyrus wished that he could make himself small enough to sink between the cobblestones. "And who is this?"

"Cyrus Davidon, this is my mother," Vara said. "She's an overly dramatic, reprehensible old shrew whose mastery of laying on guilt is comparable to a farmer's spreading of manure, and just as prolific."

"But I smell much more pleasant," her mother continued, indifferent to her daughter's insult. With a sniff, her face turned down and her eyes honed in on Cyrus again. "Which is more than I can say of some of us. He's taller than the last man you brought home. But he has the same air about him, the smell of blood and glory and bile so common on a dog of war. It all smells like rot to me."

Cyrus, unsure what to say, caught Vara's eye and mouthed, "Last man?" She shook her head. He took a deep breath through his nose, wondering if she had been speaking about his smell in a literal or metaphorical sense.

"I see you've retained your inimitable charm, Mother," Vara said with an air of impatience. "I need to speak with you and Father if you're quite finished with your initial volley of verbal arrows."

"My dear, my initial volley is plenty to ward off all but you and your sister; why, look, your barbarian friend is cowering." She raised her hand toward Cyrus, who blinked in surprise.

"I'm not cowering...just, uh..."

Vara's mother sent him a look of feigned sympathy. "Poor dear. This one seems a bit slow on the uptake. He must be hung like an ox if you keep him around in spite of his obvious intellectual deficiencies."

"I wouldn't know." The temperature of Vara's voice fell a hundred degrees in her reply. "Can we come in or shall I just move along and come back to bury your corpses?"

Her mother glared at her with great coldness. With reticence and a dramatic exhalation, she stepped aside. "Very well. But you'll need to tie up your ox outside."

"Mother." Vara's tone was warning, bordering on hostile.

"Fine. He can come in." She turned and wandered down the hallway visible through the open door. "Mind the rug, dear. It's new."

Vara wheeled around to him before entering. "Say nothing," she told him. "She is looking for anything with which to skewer you."

"It's like having a conversation with Malpravus, minus the civility." Cyrus closed the door behind him. The interior of the house was beautifully furnished. To his left was a living room. The walls of the house were decorated with tapestries and paintings of all kinds. The one that caught his attention was hanging over the fireplace; a portrait of Vara as a girl.

"Admiring the painting of my daughter?" Cyrus looked back down the hallway to see Vara's mother staring him down.

"Ah, yes," he stammered back. "It's lovely. It really captures the..." His voice trailed off as he stared at the unsmiling visage of a woman he'd known for years. "...the spirit of her." He ignored the irritated eye roll from Vara.

"She wouldn't sit still for the damned thing, even though she was twelve, and she scowled the entire time." An amused smile appeared on her face. "So when you say it captures her spirit, are you saying my Vara is disagreeable?"

Cyrus pondered lying for a split second. *To hell with politeness,* he thought. *She has yet to show me any.* "Yes, she is," he agreed. "Though I'm beginning to think she's not half as uncivil as she would be naturally predisposed to be."

The older elven woman's eyes narrowed and then her expression lightened for the first time since he'd met her. "Yes, she fights her nature, but I've told her a thousand times she should go with her instincts; after all, it takes less energy to let fly the barbs that she produces than it does to suppress them." She looked him over with an appraising eye. "Perhaps you're not as slow as I gave you credit for; but with a face like that, you'd still have to be well endowed for her to keep you around."

"Mother!" Vara's shout crackled through the hallway. "He's not...I'm not *with* him...I'm only..." Frustration rattled through her, causing her to clench her jaw shut. "He's here to protect me; he's not here as my..."

"Paramour?" her mother offered after a few seconds. "Lover? Heart's desire?" She laughed. "Nighttime plaything?"

"There's no need to be vulgar, Mother."

"No need, perhaps, but such desire to be crass is an impulse that I can scarce resist." She led them down the hallway with an imperious wave of her hand. Vara followed, Cyrus a few steps behind, until they emerged in a modest kitchen with a rounded table big enough for a half dozen to eat in comfort. Vara's mother looked to Cyrus. "I would offer you something to drink, but I'm fresh out of the traditional types of poison. I have some old cabbage I've been meaning to throw away — it likely won't kill you, but I doubt you'll see much outside of the privy for the next day or so."

Cyrus decided to let the remark pass. "We should get down to business." He paused, realizing he hadn't yet heard Vara's mother's name. "Uh...what should I call you...? Vara hasn't called you by name; she keeps addressing you as Mother. I could call you Vara's mother...or just Mother, I suppose..." Nerves took over and he could feel himself starting to ramble.

She stared at him. "Do not dare refer to me as 'Mother' unless you wish to insult me, and before you do, I must warn you that I am a formidable wizard and able to strike you down with a single spell." Vara cleared her throat, a look of supreme irritation on her face. Vara's mother sighed, a sound of deepest disappointment.

"Oh, very well. You may call me Chirenya."

Cyrus gritted his teeth. "If you know that there's a threat to Vara's life, then you must realize that these assassins could be after you as well?"

Her mother circled to the table, where she pulled out a chair and levered herself into it with exaggerated effort, as though she were pretending to be old. "I assure you I am still possessed of all my faculties, and I understand that if there is a threat to my daughter that it could well make me a target."

"Listen." Vara seated herself at the table next to her mother. "We need to get you and Father out of Termina."

"And if we don't wish to go?"

Vara blew air out of her lips noiselessly as she looked skyward. "I am appealing to your common sense and, if it exists, your love and trust for me, who has been responsible for quite a few...pleasant contributions to your lifestyle." Chirenya looked around the room. "These assassins are very dangerous, and they have already killed one of our officers in an attempt to get to me. You are not safe. Please." Her voice entered the range of a hushed whisper. "Let us get you out of here."

Chirenya avoided her daughter's gaze. "If I could do as you ask, I would. But I cannot."

A hush fell over the table, broken by Vara. "Where is my father?"

"He's taken ill." Chirenya's eyes pivoted to her daughter. "He's been bedridden for weeks. You'd know this," her finger came up in an accusatory fashion, "if you came home more often."

Her words hung between them. Vara's face was stone, unmoving. Her eyes focused on a point in the distance, beyond her mother's shoulder. Vara's hands fell to her lap, under the table, where her mother could not see, and Cyrus watched as the paladin clasped them together as she continued to stare ahead, one hand squeezing the other.

Standing at the entrance to the hallway leading back to the front door, Cyrus froze, stiffening as he heard a noise behind him. There came the soft click of a lock being plied, then another squeak as the handle turned and the door opened.

Chapter 13

Before it was open, Cyrus was in motion, sword drawn and in hand. He could hear the scrape of Vara's chair and the sound of her blade being jerked from its scabbard as he pounded toward the door. Praelior was extended, ready to strike, but he hesitated as the last rays of sunlight shone off a head of long blond hair that flowed over immaculate white robes, stitched with the runes that marked the woman as a healer.

"Isabelle," Cyrus said in acknowledgment, skidding to a halt and sheathing his sword, embarrassed.

"Cyrus Davidon," said the elven woman who stood before him. "I'd assumed that the General of Sanctuary cut an imposing figure in battle, but to see you charging affirms all my beliefs in that area and then some." She shut the door, casting the hallway in shadow once more.

Once his eyes adjusted, Cyrus saw her lips upturned, fine wrinkles at the corner of her eyes showing themselves. "If I'm that frightening, why are you laughing?"

"It takes more than a hell bent warrior to scare an officer of Endeavor. But if I were, say, a member of the dark elven army? I'd be quaking in fear at your approach."

"Flattery won't help you, dear," Chirenya's voice came from the kitchen. "Your sister is already rutting with him."

"I doubt that very much," Isabelle muttered under her breath.

"Mother! I am not...rutting...with anyone!"

"Well, you should; it would eliminate some of that tension that contributes to the wrinkles on your forehead...you're going to look older than I do soon."

Vara made her way to Cyrus's shoulder. "What brings you home?"

Isabelle unwrapped the delicate shawl from her neck. "Since Alaric sent a messenger warning me about the assassins, I've had a hundred or so of my guildmates encamped in the houses to the sides and back, keeping watch for trouble."

"Wait," Cyrus said. "Endeavor has forces to either side and behind the house?" He turned to Vara and shrugged. "You can't get any safer than that, short of having a detail here."

"Yes, I can only guess how marvelously that would turn out,

based on your reaction to my eldest daughter coming to the door," Chirenya shot at him from the far end of the hallway. "I assume that anyone who knocks on your door at night is lucky to survive the experience. Humans, such primitive creatures, especially the men—"

"Mother," Isabelle said. "Be polite. He's your guest."

"He's your sister's guest," Chirenya returned. "I would have just as soon had her tie him to the hitching post outside." She turned to Cyrus. "You're not going to endear yourself to me..."

"Ever," Vara said.

Chirenya continued as if she had not heard. "...if you go charging about like a bloodthirsty troll at every person that passes through the neighborhood. The High Priestess of Vidara drops by, we have friends—"

"Fancy that," Isabelle said.

Other than a frown directed at her eldest daughter, Chirenya was undeterred. "We are not leaving, not while Amiol is ill, and maybe not even were he well. This is our home and I will not retreat from it. If these assassins show up, I'll be certain to send them in your general direction." She waved her hand at Cyrus.

"I wish to see Father," Vara said.

"He's upstairs," Chirenya said. "I will take you to him, if your sister will consent to watching the barbarian to make certain he doesn't steal any of my fine silverware." She lowered her voice as if she were speaking confidentially. "His kind don't use utensils to eat, so they're quite the novelty—"

"Mother," Vara snapped.

"Oh, yes, very well," Chirenya said with feigned exasperation before looking back to Cyrus. "Do not touch anything. That smell of yours, it gets on everything and you can't get it out, no matter how hard you scrub..."

"Or how hard your maid does, at least," Isabelle said.

Cyrus turned to Isabelle. "How close are your people?"

She smiled. "Seconds away if anyone comes to the door. They only let you two in alive because I allowed it."

"Good." He looked to Vara. "I'm going across the street to talk with our people. I'll send Thad and a few others to loiter in the street while I'm gone."

"Oh, dear, that's certain to depress the property values," Chirenya muttered.

Vara rolled her eyes. "I'll come to you once I've seen Father."

"It would certainly be quieter than me coming back here." Cyrus looked at Chirenya as he spoke.

"But much less witty." Chirenya leaned against the wall. "It's no wonder you girls feel the need to engage in all these foolish invasions and conquests," she told Vara as her daughters followed her around the corner. "There's no one around to challenge your wits..."

Seething, Cyrus walked to the door, pausing in the hallway to take his gauntlet off and rub his sweaty hand along the frame of a painting of a meadow. "Enjoy the smell of that, hag," he muttered so low that it was almost inaudible.

"I heard that," came the shrill voice as he walked out the door. "Keep your hands off my things!"

Cyrus let the door almost close before he replied. "Yes, Mother."

Chapter 14

Cyrus strolled across the street, still steaming. He nodded at Thad and chucked a thumb at the street behind him. The warrior signaled to two other Sanctuary guildmates, who stood up from the steps and followed him into the street as Cy passed them. He walked up the steps as the door swung wide, revealing Vaste, his green skin flushed and an exaggerated grin on his face, displaying his large canines.

"Hihi!" the troll said with over-the-top friendliness. "You must be our new neighbor."

"I am," Cyrus said, "and it looks like I'm going to be in the neighborhood for quite some time."

"Damn. I hate this place."

"Who's at the door?" J'anda's head peeked around the corner of a nearby wall, no illusion hiding his dark elven heritage. "Oh, it's you. I take it you met Vara's mother?"

"I did," Cyrus confirmed.

"And?" The enchanter looked at him with a half-smile, expectant.

"She's a real peach. One laced with arsenic, but still...a peach."

"Apple doesn't fall too far from the tree, eh?" J'anda's half-smile had turned into a smirk.

"Can you assholes stop talking in fruit metaphors?" Vaste's brow was furrowed in annoyance. "You're making me crave pie."

"Seen anything unusual since you've been here?" Cyrus looked past J'anda into the room. A half dozen bedrolls were spread out on the floor, and in front of the window stood two members of Sanctuary, watching the street.

"Other than catching a glimpse of Vara's mother changing her clothes, no," Vaste replied.

"Yeesh," Cyrus replied with a cringe.

"It's okay," the troll said. "She may be a few millenia old, but she's still well put together."

"Don't...ever...tell Vara what you just told me."

"Do I look stupid to you?" Vaste stared down at Cyrus. "I have no desire to stick my head into that barrel of flaming oil." The troll sauntered over to a sofa and lowered himself onto it. "But isn't it reassuring that if ever you break through Vara's icy facade, even when you're old and falling apart, she'll still look as stunning and frightening as she does today? Hells, she'll look like that long after you're dead."

"Thanks for the morbid thought," Cyrus sent a sour look at the healer. "But I'm not interested in—" He halted mid-sentence, catching a look shared between the troll and the dark elf.

"Sure you're not," J'anda said without conviction.

"Tell me," Vaste began with practiced neutrality, "when you lie to yourself like that, does it sound true in your head? I mean...do you often provide escort for hundreds of miles to people in need?"

"If there's a threat of death, I would hope any of us would." Cyrus buried the faint pang of guilt he felt at lying.

"I see," Vaste said with a nod. "And the fact that you've been in mad love with her for two years had no influence on your decision to go?"

"I'm not here to talk about my feelings." Annoyance welled up in Cyrus. "Vara's father is ill and her mother is refusing to leave town." He rubbed his nose. "I have my doubts that she'll want to leave, knowing her mother won't go."

J'anda's eyebrows rose, alarm written on his soft features. "You need to convince her; staying here is suicide."

Cyrus looked across the room at the enchanter. "You've had experience convincing Vara to change her mind?"

"This is not a good place to stand against assassins making a bid to kill her."

"He's right," Vaste said. "We're too exposed."

"I'm not so sure," Cyrus said. "Endeavor has taken over the houses on either side and the one out back; I don't think you could get much safer than that."

"Agreed, but this is not a good spot for a fight," J'anda said with a shrug. "They could come from either direction on the street or through the yards in back—"

"Or they could drop down from a Gryphon," Cyrus added with a disinterest born of fatigue, "smash into the basement with a rock giant..."

J'anda and Vaste exchanged another look. "We, uh," the troll began, "hadn't even thought of most of those."

"Let's hope the Hand of Fear shares your lack of imagination."

"Maybe we've wiped them all out?" Vaste said with a note of hope. "Or done such damage to their numbers that they won't be able to mount an attack?"

Cyrus sighed. "I'm not going to operate from that assumption—I mean, they had a half dozen assassins in a village in the middle of nowhere in the southern plains, on the chance that we were going to pass through on the way to Termina." He shook his head. "No...more likely, they'll come tonight, under cover of darkness, because if they're watching, they know Vara is here now."

J'anda's eyes darted to look out at the street. "How do you think they'll do it?"

"Hard to say." Cyrus put his hands behind his head and leaned back. "You need to be ready to storm the house on a moment's notice."

"My mother will love that," Vara's voice came from the entryway.

Isabelle appeared at her side, glanced around the room and looked to Cyrus with a quizzical expression. "I don't mean to criticize, but don't you have more than two people?"

"We're so good, there's no point in having more," Vaste said.

Cyrus leaned back into the padding of the couch. "How's your father?"

"Sleeping. I'll speak to him when he wakes up." Vara looked around the living room. "We should probably be heading back; Isabelle just wanted to see our operation."

"I have seen it, and I pronounce it very satisfactory," Isabelle said. "If there is an attack, I have faith that you'll all distinguish yourselves brilliantly, just as you have in building Sanctuary's exemplary reputation over the last few years." Warmth oozed out of her every word, Cyrus reflected, amazed at the contrast between her and her sister and their respective abilities to put people at ease or discomfort.

"Wow, you're inspiring," Vaste said. "Can we trade Vara to Endeavor in exchange for you?" Ignoring the paladin's withering glare, he went on. "She hasn't said anything that nice to me in...uh...ever."

"Nor do I plan to," Vara said with a glance toward Cyrus. "Come on then. We're leaving."

Cyrus continued to sit on the couch until her words sunk in. "Wait, me?"

Vara let out a deep sigh. "Yes, you. Mother has consented to letting you stay with us for added protection."

"What heinous sin did I commit to deserve that?" Cyrus looked at her. "Listen, why don't you stay over here at night, away from your parents—and especially your mother. It'll be easier to protect you and you'll be able to go over there during the day with ease."

"Because I refuse to sleep in a common room with a group of men."

"This house has bedrooms," J'anda said. "You could have your own."

"I will not leave my parents unattended," she said, then turned to Cyrus. "Decide quickly if you're going to come with me."

He wrenched himself off the couch, leaving a deep imprint in several places from the edges of his armor. "I'm coming."

She nodded. "Very well. With myself, you and Isabelle, we should be able to hold off any assassins until reinforcements are able to reach us."

"Don't forget Mother," Isabelle said. "I sense that she misses being able to cast a fireball and hurl it at people."

"That explains a lot," Cyrus said, following Vara as she turned to leave. With a wave, Isabelle departed.

"Sleep tight!" Vaste called after Cyrus. "Don't let the vicious she-elves bite! Well, maybe one of them."

As he stepped back outside he almost bumped into Vara, who was waiting for him on the stoop. "You'll be sleeping in my room," she informed him.

He nodded. "All right."

"On the floor. I don't think I need to mention this," she said after a moment's hesitation, "but nothing will be happening between the two of us."

Cyrus felt his cheeks redden as he looked past Vara at Isabelle, who averted her eyes. "We've been on the road together for days, sleeping in close proximity. I think I can handle it without getting inappropriate."

"Yes, well..." Vara said, somewhat stiffly. "There's a vast difference between sharing a camp, sharing a room, and sharing a bed, and I don't want for there to be any misunderstandings between us."

"I get it." Cyrus's cheeks burned and he chanced to look at Isabelle again. Hers were also flushed, and she seemed to be studying the texture of the sidewalk. "I will conduct myself as a perfect gentleman."

"I am certain you will," she replied, turning away from him.

You can tell she was uncomfortable with that, he thought, *because she didn't say, "For once."*

"I doubt I'll do much resting anyway." He fell in line behind Vara. "They'll be coming tonight."

"We've come to the same conclusion," Isabelle said. "If these bastards are as bad as you've said, they'll have someone watching, and they'll have seen Vara by now, which makes it unlikely that they'll hesitate. I have most of my people sleeping now in preparation. We suspect they'll hit around midnight, hoping everyone will have gone to bed."

"I would have guessed after sundown," Cyrus replied. "But it could be any time. It's not like they've been reticent about attacking in the middle of the day."

"Regardless," Vara said, turning to face them as she reached the front steps of the house, "this fight will be different. My parents are to be protected at all costs. I will not have them be killed or used as leverage against me." Her jaw was set. "If these assassins are coming tonight, we face them, we kill them — then we get Father well and get the hell out of here."

Chapter 15

Night fell as if it were the slow drip of dark coffee filtering into a mug, Cyrus thought as he peeked once more out of a second story window onto the street below. Lamps were lit every hundred feet and in the dim light he could see Thad and a handful of others from both Sanctuary and Endeavor lingering on the stones below.

Replacing the curtain, he turned to look around the sitting room. The house was three floors and a cellar; Vara's parents had their bedroom on the top floor, Vara and Isabelle were housed on the second floor, along with a generous living space and bathrooms with running water.

Vara sat behind him, eyes looking toward the stairwell leading up to the third floor. Isabelle sat opposite her, legs crossed, leaning back, eyes closed in deep thought. Cyrus's gaze lingered on her; the healer's traditional white robes were tighter than those worn by Curatio or Vaste and much more flattering. Isabelle was fit, like her younger sister, but her hair was worn loose around the shoulders. In human years, she and Vara looked to be of comparable ages though in fact he knew Isabelle was almost two centuries the elder.

His eyes came to rest on the hem of her robes, then the well-stitched and elegant leather boots she wore that carried not a speck of mud. He brought his gaze back up to find her looking back at him, a sly smile draped across her lips. "We do look quite a bit alike, don't we? I mean, excepting the differing attire."

"What?" Vara's head snapped up.

"Somewhat," Cyrus said, recovering quickly from being caught looking. "But you've got a much more mischievous air about you, more relaxed and less..."

"Tense?" Isabelle looked to her sister. "She'll calm down in a hundred years or so."

"I am not tense," Vara said. "Well, perhaps now I am, seeing as there are people trying to kill me, but on a normal day —"

"You're tense, little sister. I could place my stave in the crack between your butt cheeks and it would snap in two, that's how stiff you are. And it's not a recent problem."

"You do seem a bit tense, dear," Chirenya's voice came from the stairs as she descended from the floor above. "Perhaps your ox isn't doing his job properly; you're supposed to be more tranquil afterward."

"I'm just here to protect her," Cyrus said.

"Oh, yes, and I'm the younger sister of these two, not their mother," Chirenya breezed as she continued down the stairs to the first floor.

Vara returned to her watch of the stairs, lost in thought. Isabelle stared around, languid.

"Did you come here from Reikonos?" Cyrus caught the healer's gaze.

She nodded. "Why?"

"I was wondering how the war was going."

"I suppose you haven't heard all the latest, being on the run as you were."

"Didn't always hear it before that; most of what we heard was about the dark elf movements against the southwest part of the Confederation. I have no idea what's happening around Reikonos, in the north or the Riverlands."

Isabelle stared back at him, cool. "What have you heard?"

Cyrus took a deep breath. "Prehorta got sacked, hard. Survivors said most of the townsfolk fled long before the dark elves got there, but they burned everything and left a garrison force to block trade with the Confederation from the southern Plains of Perdamun. Haven't heard anything since then."

Isabelle took in a deep breath. "It's not been pretty. Since then that particular dark elf army — somewhere in the neighborhood of 100,000 strong — has moved to Idiarna and sacked it."

Cyrus exchanged a look with Vara. "That's the biggest town between Prehorta and Santir."

"Yes. It would seem the dark elves mean to cut off the Confederation from the southern plains."

"They haven't come for Reikonos yet?"

"No." She shook her head. "The Confederation army has held a firm line against any advances north of the Waking Woods and the dark elves haven't bothered to drive east to the Riverlands or sneak past Lake Magnus to hit the Northlands yet. They've focused everything on the southwest; on cutting off the Plains of Perdamun."

"Seems an odd choice," Chirenya's voice came from the stairs again. In her hands was a plate of meats and cheeses, which she carried over and sat on the table between Vara and Isabelle.

"Wouldn't it make more sense to throw everything they have at their enemy capital and knock them flat? Without Reikonos, the Human Confederation becomes a bunch of squabbling little provinces that lack any coordinated ability to fight back."

"I think that is the plan," Isabelle said. "But rather than try to hammer through the defenses around the city—which are considerable—the dark elves have chosen a roundabout way. Perhaps they don't wish to lose all the forces they'd have to commit to a direct assault of the capital, or perhaps they hope to force the humans into a surrender without ever laying siege to Reikonos. Whatever the case, cutting them off from the southern plains is brilliant; at least half the capital's grain supply comes from there with the other half coming from the Riverlands."

"Starve them out, eh?" Chirenya's voice was laced with disdain. "Reminds me all too much of the last war."

Cyrus looked at her face, mottled with a simmering resentment. "How did that go?"

"We won, of course," she said, not bothering to look at him. "But it was a brutal war, and the dark elves never go about anything directly. They didn't come at Pharesia then, either—of course they were more spread out back then; they had cities and towns all throughout the southern plains and the Waking Woods, even in places as far flung as what you humans now claim in the Northlands and Riverlands. They had more to defend than they do now."

Cyrus furrowed his brow. "If they had all these settlements, what happened to them?"

"Abandoned after the last war," Isabelle replied. "In a great wave, the dark elves retreated from everything, claimed their borders encompassed the Waking Woods and retreated into the depths of Saekaj Sovar. It's only been in the last twenty years or so that they've started to emerge again." She chuckled. "For a time, if you saw a dark elf anywhere, it was a rare sight."

"But before the war started—this one, I mean," Cyrus said, "there were enormous numbers of dark elves in Reikonos. We have many in Sanctuary—"

"Indeed, we have some here in Termina and I've heard there are even a few in Pharesia," Chirenya said. "As Isabelle says, all fairly recent. Well, at least on the timescale of an elven life," she said, her final words carrying an edge aimed at him. "I suppose you were just a child when they began to reemerge into the world in numbers."

"So was I, Mother," Vara said.

"Yeah, she's only older than me by a year," Cyrus said.

"And more mature by only a millennium." Vara's impassive face cracked as she looked sidelong at him.

"Regardless, it's an ugly thing, what's happening to the humans," Chirenya said with a sniff. "Though I suppose if your government hadn't been quite so arrogant in sending their forces into the plains, it wouldn't have happened." Cyrus bristled, but bit back his first response—that the elven kingdom had an army present when the war began. "I'm just glad that the King recognizes that it's in no one's interest if the dark elves win the war with your people."

So irritated was Cyrus that it took him a moment to realize what she'd said. "The King recognizes that? How so?"

"Oh, hadn't you heard?" Chirenya spoke with the satisfaction of someone sharing forbidden knowledge. "It's on the lips of everyone in the city. The rumor is, the Kingdom has been selling all sorts of weaponry and food to the humans at very discounted prices that are supposedly financed out of the Kingdom's treasury. They're shipping them up the Perda and along the coast to Reikonos."

Vara was the first to speak. "Let us hope that the dark elves do not consider that an act of war."

"They may consider it whatever they like," Chirenya said. "If they try to begin a war with us they'll be beaten back and taught a lesson for their arrogance."

Vara stood. "That's all the time I have for bravado today. I believe I'll retire to my room." She shot a look at Cyrus. "Coming?"

He nodded to her and followed, prompting Chirenya to let out a self-satisfied guffaw. "Do try to take your time, ox; it will take all you have to relieve the tension she's building now. And don't forget your ventra'maq!"

Vara opened the door to her room, bristling. Cyrus followed and shut the door as the paladin collapsed face first on the bed. She turned her head to look back at him and he could see a tiredness on her fine features. "You may not remember much about your mother, but I daresay you'll never forget mine."

Cyrus did not respond, and after a moment she rolled over, her cheeks flushed. "I apologize. That was...unkind."

He walked to the window, brushing the curtain aside to look onto the darkened street. "You didn't speak any untruths. I don't remember my mother."

"That doesn't mean I was right to say it."

He looked back at her. "What she said...don't forget your 'ventra'maq'? It sounds familiar."

Vara buried her face in the pillow and her reply came back too muffled for him to hear.

He stared at her, in full armor, sunk into the bed as though she were a pouting teenager. "What did you say?"

Pulling her face out of the pillow, she turned back to him, her cheeks red. "Ventra'maq is a potion, mixed by an alchemist." Her face got redder as she spoke. "It's used by women who wish to avoid pregnancy." She propped herself up on an elbow. "You really are a bit of a naif, aren't you?"

He turned away. "I remember where I've heard of it; my wife used to take ventra'maq."

"Ah, yes, your elusive wife." She curled up on the bed. "I have wondered...divorce or..." Her words were soft, and drifted off mid-sentence.

"Divorce. A few years before I joined Sanctuary."

"I see," she said, staring off into space. "I shouldn't be surprised that you were married at some point, commanding physical specimen such as you are."

"What about you? Were you ever married?"

"Close, once," she admitted after a pause. "But it ended...rather badly." Her gaze softened. "How is your arm?"

He grimaced, reminded of the ache in his shoulder. "Better. Still hurts, but not enough to slow me down."

"Take off your armor," she commanded. "Curatio gave me a salve to apply to your wound. There's nothing magical about it, but it should aid the natural healing process." She turned and retrieved a small tin from the saddlebag she had left atop the nearby vanity.

"We're under threat of attack," he said. "Even ignoring the insinuations your mother just made, this is not the best time."

"I always ignore the insinuations my mother makes — and it's the time we have." She strode back to him. "Would you enjoy an infection? Perhaps you prefer to be bedridden for a month? Lose your arm?"

Grumbling, he slid the pauldrons over his head after removing his helmet and gorget. With her aid, he unfastened his breastplate and backplate and slipped the chainmail over his head. He stared at the spot where the assassin's dagger had broken the links.

"You should invest some of your growing fortune in stronger chainmail," she said as she steered him to a chair in the corner of the room. "Sit," she commanded as she walked behind him.

He complied. "There's no chainmail I've ever seen that can perfectly protect you from harm." He felt the cool sensation of the salve running across his skin, spread by her fingers, and let out an inadvertent gasp of surprise.

He looked up at her and she grinned. "Does that hurt you in some way?" Mischief caused her eyes to dance.

"No," he replied. "But your hands are cold." He shuddered from some combination of pain, chill and pleasure as her fingers rubbed the shoulder that had been in agony only a few hours before. She kneaded the tender muscle as she applied a healthy dollop of the salve, massaging the tender lip of skin where the assassin's dagger had pierced his flesh. He groaned as she applied pressure to an area that had not received healing thanks to the black lace. "Now that spot—*that* hurts."

"Tell me something." Her words were calm and soothing, like the ointment she was applying. "You've now trekked hundreds of miles out of your way, putting yourself in the path of countless dangers on my behalf..." She hesitated.

His eyes were closed, and he felt her hands working through painful areas of his shoulder and upper chest. He grunted in discomfort as her fingers moved from relieving tension to stabbing at an unhealed section. "Yes?"

The pressure on his shoulder stopped and he heard the rustle of her armor move beside the chair as she knelt next to him, looking up, her blue eyes wide. "Why?" She continued to stare at him, her eyes fixed on his. "What are you fighting for?"

Cyrus licked his lips. The searing sensation of the salve had worn off and suddenly he felt cold and hot at the same time. He stared back at her, into the eyes of the blond-haired paladin, and saw something beyond the usual intensity there, a hope that he both knew and feared, one that reminded him of the night that J'anda had shown him through magic what he desired in the deepest well of his heart.

"I..."

He started to speak, then stopped. Her hand was on the metal of his greaves, resting on his thigh, sending a thrill through him even though he could feel but a little of the weight. He searched for the words again, and halted, still struck by her eyes. *I need to tell her,* he thought. *I've needed to tell her for years, and this is it...*

He felt a very slight tremor, and wondered if his legs were shaking. "I...what?" Vara had stiffened, her eyes darting around. "What is it?"

She stood and brushed passed the bed, tossing his breastplate to him on her way to the door. She unlocked and opened it as Isabelle appeared on the other side. "Did you hear?" The healer was breathless.

"Yes. The cellar?" Vara tossed another look at Cyrus, who was sitting in the chair, barechested as Isabelle looked around the doorjamb at him. "Come on, get dressed."

"Why?" He fumbled with his chainmail, struggling to slide it on.

"Because," Vara said. "They're here."

Chapter 16

"What?" Cyrus asked. "How did they get in the cellar?" Having looked around earlier in the day, he had found it to be empty, with no windows and no way in or out save for the staircase.

"Did you not hear that explosion?" Isabelle asked. "It shook the building."

Cyrus stood as he began to fasten his breastplate. "I felt...a tremor." He looked at Vara, mortified. "I thought it was me."

She ignored him. "Isabelle, did you get Mother—"

"Upstairs," Isabelle said. "We need to signal your people and mine—"

Cyrus turned and grabbed the chair that he had been sitting in. Raising it above his head, he heaved it at the window, where it ripped the curtain from the wall and broke the glass, flying onto the street, shattering the calm of the evening.

From a few stories below Cyrus heard shouts of "Alarum!" and turned back to Vara, who was looking at him with annoyance.

"You could have just opened the window and shouted for help."

He shrugged as he brushed past her, drawing his sword. "This was faster."

"What was that?" Chirenya's voice rang down the stairwell as Cyrus led Vara and Isabelle into the sitting room. "Ox, did you just destroy my home?"

"Only part of it. More to come."

"Mother, get back in your bedroom and lock the door!" Vara shouted. "They're coming!"

"Oh, all right!" Chirenya's voice was fraught with tension. "But tell your ox that he'll be paying for any of my possessions that he destroys!"

Cyrus stared at the landing below, watching for movement. He waited, focused until a flash running up the steps caught his eye just as a crash of breaking glass came from behind him on the second floor, followed by the sound of the door to the street splintering below.

He turned to see a half dozen black-clad bodies sliding in the windows behind him. Screaming could be heard on the floor above and Cyrus watched Vara rush the stairwell as the first of the assassins reached their floor from below. She lashed out with her sword, a massive, two-handed blade, raking it across the chest of the first assassin, causing him to fall backward and knock down the two that followed him.

Without waiting to see what happened next, Vara ran up the steps, Isabelle at her heels, sword thumping against the railing all the way up. Cyrus shot a quick look at the assassins piling up on the landing, shouts coming from below, and then glanced back to the ones that had broken through the second floor window and were advancing on him. With a muttered curse he turned and sprinted up the stairs, listening as havoc filled the house.

His metal boots clanked on every step. He flew up the stairs and burst through the bedroom door to find a bizarre sight.

The entire third floor was a large bedroom with windows that faced the street. Vara's father lay on the bed, unconscious, blankets tucked around his body. Vara and Isabelle stood in front of him, eyes fixed on the space on the other side of the bed. An orange, flickering light filled the room.

Chirenya was holding five assassins at bay in the open space between the bed and the windows. Her hands clutched a smooth black staff with a red crystal mounted at the top. The elven woman's blond hair was tucked behind her ears. With her back turned, Cyrus could not see her face, but as she gripped the staff it vomited bursts of fire, spheres of blazing flame spewing forth every half second, each flying with unfaltering speed at its target.

Five assassins had broken through the windows, all dressed in black attire with a cowl and mask to hide their features; something similar in spirit but far different in look than the assassins Cyrus had encountered thus far.

And every single one of them was screaming and on fire.

Cyrus stared at the spectacle of a lone elven woman defeating five skilled killers, then remembered that they were far from the only threats. He turned back to the door with a shout to Vara and Isabelle. "Coming up the stairs!" He positioned himself against the wall next to the door.

He led with Praelior, swinging as a blur of black came through the doorframe, his stroke catching the first assassin across the neck. The body dropped to the floor as the next entered, tripping on the corpse. With a step forward, Vara jabbed her sword through the second elf's back, causing him to writhe and then go still.

Cyrus moved to block the door but something exploded in front of him, knocking him aside. Smoke filled his eyes and lungs and he began to cough as he fell to the ground. Tears beaded up at the corners of his eyes and he felt a burning as he tried to blink away the smoky heat. Something whipped through the air above him and he heard a cry of pain, even as he crawled on his hands and knees away from the sounds of battle behind him.

His shoulder bumped something heavy and yet soft. *The bed*, he thought, grasping at the edge and using it to lever himself up, still unable to see through the pain in his eyes. With a tingle, he felt a healing spell run over his face and the tears stopped.

Blinking away the wetness, he rose and saw Isabelle at the edge of a cloud of smoke, her hand extended to him. An assassin appeared from behind her but before Cyrus could shout a warning she turned and a light flashed from her hand, bright enough to blot out the entire room in a blast of white. After it faded, Cyrus blinked and saw Isabelle with a dagger in her hand and the assassin in her grip. The knife came down on his neck again and again, and her white robes were sprinkled with red.

Where's Vara? Out of the cloud of smoke came a whirlwind of activity. Vara stumbled back, appearing at the edge of the billow, an assassin following. She was coughing, her sword extended with one hand while the other covered her mouth. The assassin raised his hands to strike a killing blow and before Cyrus could cross the distance between them, a tinkle of glass came from behind him while something whipped through the air, causing the assassin's head to jerk. An arrow rested in his eye, and the elf tried to speak but nothing came out as his body twitched and succumbed to gravity.

The cloud of smoke had begun to clear and assassins were pouring through the door. Cyrus moved to engage them, positioning himself between them and Vara. He could see Isabelle in the corner of his eye, her dagger extended with one hand while she cast a healing spell on her sister with the other.

Cyrus watched two assassins move to strike him. He blocked the one closest with a careful stroke of his sword, but left himself exposed to the other while he did it. The second came at him with a gurkha; a medium sized blade the length of Cyrus's forearm, the point dripping with a liquid that gleamed in the low light. He raised his right hand to block with the metal of his gauntlet and braced himself for the blow.

Another sound of air rushing heralded the arrival of another arrow, this one coming to rest in the assassin's ear. A strangled screech was cut short and he toppled toward the bed as Cyrus pressed the attack on the remaining assassin, who was joined by another arrival through the door.

Cyrus met the newest assassin with a sideways kick as he slashed at the other, keeping him on the defensive with Praelior's longer reach. The clangor of battle on the floors below was an uncertain quantity; he had no idea who was winning or even who was fighting—whether it was the assassins, Endeavor, Sanctuary or all three.

With another hard kick, Cyrus sent the assassin in the door backward and over the edge of the stairs. A scream was followed by a crashing noise of flesh on wood and then the sound of something breaking. He turned back to the assassin he had engaged with his sword to find him within reach.

Cyrus braced himself for the inevitable pain as the assassin brought his dagger up in a stabbing motion, aimed at the gap at the bottom of his breastplate. Cyrus pulled Praelior back in a motion that would strike little more than a glancing blow against his opponent's unguarded throat. Fortunately, with Praelior, a glancing blow would do all the damage necessary to end the fight. *But will it be in time?* The instinct and concept flashed in Cyrus's mind more than the actual words.

A sword blow struck the elf just inches before he landed the dagger at Cyrus's belly, knocking the assassin's arm aside. Vara's blade punched through the assassin's stomach, turning the leering look of triumph into one of exquisite agony and surprise as her blade ran him through at the same time Cyrus's slipped across his neck. A choked, gurgling sound made its way out of the elf's mouth as he dropped to the ground.

A thundering clamor filled the air as another three assassins entered the room. Their blades were sharp and their steps quiet as they unfolded in a line along the wall toward Vara's father, prompting the paladin to move toward the one closest, her sword rising. As she cut in front of him, Cyrus could see her porcelain face twist with fury.

Her hand came up and a cry of unholy rage left her lips as the assassin closest to her father raised his dagger over the sleeping figure. A concussive blast of force rocked the room as her spell flung the offender into the wall; Cyrus heard the elf's skull crack, and he slid to the floor leaving a smear of blood down the wall.

Cyrus swept forward, bringing Praelior down in a crosswise swipe that knocked the assassin closest to the door's dagger aside as it cut him from his right shoulder to left hip and sent him spinning to the ground.

Cyrus turned his attention to the last of the assassins and watched as a gout of flame engulfed him, wrenching a scream from his lips as another arrow whipped through the window and hit him in the chest, causing him to fall to the floor, still on fire.

"All clear!" came a shouted voice from the stairwell. Heavy footfalls on the steps ended as Thad entered, his sword in hand. "Everyone all right?"

Cyrus looked around the bedroom. Vara was leaning over her father, her hand on his cheek, whispering while Isabelle leaned against the wall behind Cyrus, taking labored breaths.

Chirenya, on the other hand, peered at the body still on fire on the floor before pointing her staff at it. The flames were drawn up in a whirlwind and reabsorbed back into the crystal that crowned her weapon. "I'm quite all right, but tell your friend with the bow across the way to stop putting these killers out of their misery before I'm done with them." She indicated the bodies of the assassins that had come through the windows. Each of them had an arrow through their torsos, their skin charred and blackened where it had been exposed.

"That was my wife," Thad said with a grunt. He raised his hand in a wave across the street. Cyrus turned, and in the third floor of the house where the Sanctuary force had been staying, a familiar elven face stared back at him, barely visible in the moonlight.

Cyrus looked back to the assassins that Chirenya had dealt with and frowned. "I thought there were five of them. I count three bodies."

"Oh, yes," Chirenya said. "Two of them jumped out the window; I presume they were of a mind to end their suffering before I intended it."

J'anda appeared at the door, flanked by several warriors that Cyrus did not recognize. He shot a look at Isabelle, who nodded at him. Her skin, by its nature, was not as pale as Vara's—but she was drawn, her mouth in a grim line, and her complexion was white.

"Isabelle...?" Cyrus said in a hushed voice.

"I'm all right," she said, each word forced. Her robes, normally pure, still bore the stains of blood from her actions during the fight. Except, Cyrus noted, one of the spots at her side seemed to be growing. "I might," she conceded as she began to slip down the wall, "need a little help..."

He rushed to her, catching her before she fell. Cyrus lowered her to the ground as a call went down the stairs from one of the members of Endeavor, a shout for help. She stared up, her eyes fixed on his.

"Vara," he called out. He looked up to see Chirenya swoop down beside him.

"Isabelle," Chirenya said with a lightness he would not have imagined possible. "Dear, why don't you heal yourself?"

The healer's expression was pained, her hand gripping her side. Cyrus pulled up her robes to find the flesh punctured where a kidney would be on a human. "Magic's not working." She tilted her head to look at Cyrus, every word struggling to get out. "Black lace?"

He nodded and looked to Chirenya. "I don't suppose you have any rotweed?"

Chirenya looked back at him with a scowl. "I don't know what that is, but I would never have anything that sounds that foul under my roof." She looked around, surveying the damage. "At least until you and your kind showed up."

"That," Cyrus replied, keeping his voice even for the benefit of Isabelle, who was staring at him with glassy eyes, "is what we need to counteract the effects of what she's been poisoned with."

"Didn't know these...assassins...were using it." Isabelle spoke through gritted teeth. "Endeavor has bloody tons of it." She looked down at her hand, clutching at her wound. "I would have brought some."

"Fear not," came a deep voice from the door, "I have quite a bit." Thad parted the crowd of Endeavor guild members to make way for Vaste, who was wearing a heavy cloak to hide his troll features. As he slipped the cowl back to reveal his green skin and overlarge teeth, Chirenya recoiled, using her body to shield her daughter.

"I will not have some...troll!...work Vidara-knows-what kind of ministrations on my daughter!"

"Then she'll die," Vara said, her voice leaden, standing over Cyrus's shoulder. "Then you'll have only one disappointment to call your own."

"He's one of the best," Cyrus said, before he realized that it might have been more effective to denounce Vaste to Chirenya in order to get her to take his advice. Before he could try and rectify his perceived error, the stately elf removed herself from her position covering her daughter.

"Very well," Chirenya said, pulling herself to her feet. "Fail me not in this, troll, or I shall—"

"Threaten me until I burst into flames, I'm sure," Vaste said, thrusting his cloak into the arms of J'anda as he knelt at Isabelle's side. The troll's long, elegant green fingers reached to his belt, where they fiddled with a small leather pouch. Pulling from them a pinch of ground leaf, he held it above Isabelle so she could see it.

"Yes, yes," the elven healer said, her head bobbing against the floor. "I know how this works. Just do it already."

"As you say." Vaste pressed his hand to her side.

Cringing as he recalled the agony of this particular treatment, Cyrus looked away as Vaste placed his hand against her side. He felt Isabelle beneath him, felt the muscles of her shoulder tauten where he held onto her. A grunt of pain escaped her lips, but no more than that. A few seconds later, it was over.

"I've cast the healing spell," Vaste said. "I suspect she'll be able to heal herself going forward until the hour is up, but I'll stay here just in case." He turned to look at Chirenya, who was standing by the broken windows, staring out into the street.

"Hm?" She turned to look back at Vaste, her expression now haggard. "Yes, that will be fine, thank you."

"Vara?" Cyrus called out to the paladin, who was sitting on the bed next to her father. Her hands were holding his, but her eyes were closed as if she had fallen asleep sitting up. "We need to leave. This place is not safe."

"Not safe?" Thad looked around in wonder. "We just routed at least thirty assassins."

"How did they get in?" Cyrus looked to Thad, who shrugged.

"Most came from the cellar," J'anda spoke up from the door. "There's a hole into the house next door."

Cyrus wheeled around, turning to Isabelle. "I thought your people garrisoned the houses on either side?" She looked back at him, drained, but a look of puzzlement on her face.

"The assassins killed all the members of Endeavor in that house an hour or more ago, before they began the operation,"

J'anda replied. "There's twenty or thirty bodies over there. Most of them died in their sleep. The assassins must have figured trying to approach on the street or the backyard was too problematic, since we were watching this house, but..."

"No one was protecting the protectors," Vaste said with a hint of irony. "So the assassins managed to wipe out a significant force from one of the most powerful guilds in Arkaria without raising an alarm." The troll shook his large head. "That's quite an accomplishment. These are no amateurs we're facing."

"Vara," Cyrus spoke again, approaching the paladin from behind. He laid a mailed fist on her shoulder, as gentle as he could. "We need to leave. It's not safe. We need to get your parents out of here." He looked up to see Chirenya staring at him, expression blank.

"No," came a choked voice that he didn't even recognize. Vara looked up at him, and a righteous anger lit her features and caused him to take a step back. "My father is dying, and I'll be damned if I'm going to take him from his home for whatever time he has left." Her jaw was set, her face steel. "We stay. To the end."

Chapter 17

Cyrus watched her huddle close to her father, who was still unmoving. Whispers from the doorway caught his attention and a quick survey of the room revealed Chirenya now staring out the broken windows while Isabelle was still lying down, Vaste at her side.

"The Termina guard has arrived," Chirenya said, her voice devoid of any emotion. Turning from the shattered glass, she looked to Cyrus. "Someone should speak to them. They don't look kindly on battles in the streets."

"Good thing we kept it in the house then," Vaste said.

"I'll go." Cyrus felt numbness spread through him as he cast a final look at Vara. Her head lay against her father's, her face buried in his cheek. He shot a look at Thad as he moved toward the stairs. "Keep an eye on her. In case anything happens, get her out of here."

The human warrior bowed his head in a show of respect. "Will do."

Cyrus brushed past the Endeavor members who stood guard at the entrance to the room, cramming the staircase with their bulky frames. All were roughly his size or larger; warriors, paladins, and even the occasional dark knight. He pondered the differential between them and the warriors he trained in Sanctuary—on average they were a foot shorter in height and weighed considerably less.

Sanctuary's rangers were miniscule by comparison—few of them were League trained and almost all were smaller by a considerable margin than those he saw from Endeavor. The frame that would pass for a warrior in Sanctuary was small for a ranger in Endeavor.

Every one of them moved aside as Cyrus descended, and upon reaching the first floor he found a half dozen members of Sanctuary lingering in the kitchen and living room. The more formal among them saluted him and he found a familiar face at the front entryway, talking to an elf in full armor.

"Andren," Cyrus said in surprise. "I didn't know you were here."

"I was sleeping when you came over earlier," the healer said with a nod. "Long watch the night before. This is Endrenshan Odellan—Endrenshan is roughly translated to Captain—of the Termina Guard." He gestured to the armored elf, who bowed his head in acknowledgment. The elf, like most Cyrus encountered, was at least a foot shorter than he, with a unique helm that came to a point at the top, with winged ornamentation that extended beyond either side, giving his head a very different shape.

"Cyrus Davidon, of Sanctuary." Cyrus reached out and grasped the extended hand of the guard captain. "Has my comrade apprised you of what happened here?"

"Just basics," Andren replied, his long, dark hair curled below his neck. "About the Hand of Fear and how they're after one of our guildmates."

Cyrus turned his attention to Odellan. "They broke in through the cellar from the house next door, about thirty or so—"

Odellan cocked his head. "Has anyone checked on the people who lived next door, to see if they're alive?"

Cyrus shook his head. "They weren't there. Endeavor had paid the occupants of the house to stay elsewhere—"

The Captain's eyes grew wide. "Endeavor was involved in this skirmish as well?"

"Aye," Andren said with a sidelong smile at Cyrus. "The people who own this house, one of their daughters is with Sanctuary, the other with Endeavor."

"The members of Endeavor that were in the house next door are dead," Cyrus said to Odellan. "They also took over the house on the other side and the one in back, while we have the one across the street." He pointed out the door. "Do you need the local constabulary here to take a statement of some kind from me?"

Odellan's youthful face was lit with a gleam of mirth. "The Termina Guard is the local constabulary." The Endrenshan's short blond hair peeked out from under the lip of his helm, which outlined his face on the sides and forehead. He was possessed of a clean-shaven, ruggedly handsome kind of confidence, the type Cyrus had always associated with the elves.

"I thought you were the army?"

"Army and constabulary are the same in the Kingdom," Odellan said. "We police the cities and defend the Kingdom where necessary."

"One would think you'd never been here before," Andren said.

"I haven't—not to Termina, anyway," Cyrus said.

"I'm familiar with this Hand of Fear group, in passing at least," Odellan said. "We've got a few dead in the last weeks, all attributed to them."

Cyrus's curiosity was awakened. "How did you know it was them?"

"I take it you haven't lost anyone to them yet?" Odellan's eyebrow was raised.

"We have." Cyrus felt a burning in his chest as he thought of Niamh, lively, giggling—and no more. "One of our guildmates, back at Sanctuary."

"My condolences." Odellan's flat face reddened. "But you must have caught them before they had a chance to leave their mark. You said they killed the defenders you had set up in the house over there?" He pointed.

"Somehow they blasted through the cellars. I haven't seen it yet—"

"Walk with me," the guard captain said, already in motion. He led them onto the street, where four columns of elven soldiers stood in formation while a few others milled about outside the houses surrounding them.

The metalwork in Odellan's armor revealed patterns on the chestplate rather than the flat metal appearance that Cyrus was used to. Odellan led them to the front door of the house where the members of Endeavor that had been killed were staying.

Odellan pushed open the door. Inside was a house laid out not much differently than Vara's. The sitting room was filled with dead bodies. A few live members of Endeavor looked up as Cyrus entered with Odellan and Andren, but said nothing.

"The walls." Odellan pointed. Cyrus looked past the corpse of a warrior, a trickle of blood running down the mouth of the burly dwarf, to see spots on the white walls. "For every victim, they do this," Odellan said.

Cyrus looked at the spots. They appeared a deep brown by the light of the lamps. He knelt and realized they weren't spots, but blood, placed on the wall in a hand print. Empty space stood out between the joints and in the center of the palm, stark patches of white interrupted by the dried blood. "A hand print to mark the Hand of Fear," Cyrus said. "Cute."

"Not really." Odellan stared at the carnage. "We've seen a few murders with the hand prints on the wall. Pharesia gave us a warning that this was the Hand of Fear. I guess they caught one in the act, before he made his getaway." Odellan's hand fell to his sword, where it rested as he looked at the bodies surrounding them. "A counselor of the King was killed along with his whole household guard."

Cyrus stood up. "What about in Termina? Who has the Hand of Fear been killing?"

"Mostly wealthy individuals. Usually a lot more well off than your guildmate; the kind that live in the mansions on Ilanar Hill. Half a dozen or so — been quite the rumor mill starting about why they'd be targeting them."

"Seems like the people who own a house like that could spring for a personal guard," Andren said.

"They did," Odellan said. "Some of the best, in fact. We're not just talking about rank and file warriors. These assassins cut through druids, healers, paladins — even one particularly unfortunate dark knight."

Andren perked up. "I don't like the sound of that. Why was the dark knight 'particularly unfortunate'?

Odellan shrugged. "He must have given them a hard time; there wasn't much left of him by the time we found them. They either made an example of him or worked out some frustration on his corpse."

Cyrus squinted, counting the number of hand prints on the walls. "And you're sure it's them?"

"I'm not sure of anything," Odellan said. "Termina doesn't get much in the way of murders; nor does the Kingdom as a whole. Our worship of the Goddess of Life gives our culture more of a respect for it; the idea of taking a life is beyond simple scorn or punishment, it's anathema to our existence. The crime we deal with is larceny, fraud, smuggling, some bar fights and assaults."

Cyrus thought of the alleyways of Reikonos, of the bad ones where no one went unless they were ready for a fight to the death over whatever was in their purse. "Sounds idyllic compared to the Confederation."

"But fairly dull compared to what your guild does on a weekly basis," Odellan said with a hint of enthusiasm animating his face. Cyrus watched the guard captain, who looked to be in his twenties by human standards. "So are you the Cyrus Davidon who led the invasion that dethroned the Imperials of Enterra?"

Cyrus exchanged a look with Andren, watching the elder elf roll his eyes. "I am."

"I heard a rumor," Odellan said, "that it was you and your guild who fought the Dragonlord in the Mountains of Nartanis."

"We did," Cyrus confirmed.

"You'll have to tell me about it sometime," the guard captain said, his detached calmness gone. "I have to ascertain that the person who owns this home is still alive and look around to make sure no one's in distress."

"Sure." Cyrus pointed to the staircase. "Why don't we take a look at the hole they made in the cellar and we'll go up through to the house."

They descended to find a cellar much like the one in Vara's home. Dark, dank walls of stone surrounded an open space that had been used for storage. A few casks and crates were set against the walls and a half dozen bodies lay on the floor, bloody hand prints barely visible on the stone. A tremendous hole was blasted through one of the walls and a few members of Sanctuary and Endeavor were visible on the other side.

"What makes a hole like this?" Cyrus ran his finger along the rough edge. The wall was thick; the blocks used had been quarried to have smooth edges, but the hole was a jagged line all the way around the circle.

"Dragon's breath," Odellan said. Cyrus shot him a quizzical look and the guard captain chuckled. "Not that kind. It's an alchemist's creation, a powder, granules that you place inside a container with a string and you light it on fire and run. It explodes, leaving you with a mess like this."

Cyrus thought back to the fight in Vara's parents' room, of one of the assassins throwing something into the room that exploded. "They used something in the fight; it was small, and it exploded, but it made a big cloud of smoke. Nothing like the damage they did here."

"Sounds like they've got a few different tricks." Odellan stepped through the hole in the wall and looked around from the other side. "So you all heard it upstairs?"

"I didn't," Cyrus said. "I did feel the building shake, but not enough to alarm me."

"So your companions warned you that trouble was coming." Odellan was speaking almost to himself. "Can we go meet them?"

Cyrus gestured to the staircase and Odellan fell into line behind him. They reached the third floor and once again the members of Endeavor that were guarding the door parted so that the three of them could pass.

When Cyrus entered the room, Vara was still sitting on the bed, but she looked much more composed. Her hands were now in her lap, eyes alert. Catching sight of him as he walked in, she let out a small sigh.

"This is Endrenshan Odellan," Cyrus said by way of introduction. Odellan's eyes fell on Vaste, who leaned next to the chair that Isabelle was sitting in, and the captain's eyes widened in slight surprise.

"Pleased to make your acquiantance." J'anda had cast an elven illusion, stepping forward to grasp the hand of the captain.

Odellan's gaze was still fixed on Vaste. "I...can't say I've ever met a troll that wore the mark of a healer before."

"These old things?" Vaste looked down at his robes as if seeing them for the first time. "I took them off a chap I met in a dark alley...after I drained his blood, mutilated his body and danced naked around it for a bit."

"And he jokes," the Endrenshan said. He turned to Cyrus, almost plaintive. "Please tell me he's joking."

"Vaste is a healer, and yes, he has a somewhat warped sense of humor."

From behind Cyrus came a soft cough, just loud enough to be distracting. Turning, he saw Chirenya regarding him with great irritation. "Endrenshan Odellan, this is Chirenya. She's the owner of this home."

The elven woman crossed the distance between them, extending her hand to the guard captain. "Very pleased to make your acquaintance, Endrenshan. I believe I know your commanding officer, Oliaryn Iraid."

"That's like 'General' to humans," Andren whispered to Cyrus. "Probably in charge of the whole city."

Chirenya looked daggers at the healer. "The whole province, in point of fact." She turned her attention back to the captain. "I wish we could have met under more pleasant circumstances, such as the Officer's Ball."

"I am newly arrived from Pharesia, madam," Odellan said with a courteous nod.

"Really?" Chirenya's tone was of pleasant surprise, though Cyrus would have wagered every piece of gold he'd saved in the last few years that she already knew. "You must meet my daughters. This is Isabelle." She gestured toward the chair, where the healer raised a hand in a halfhearted wave. "She was injured in the attack, poor dear."

"So sorry to hear that, madam," Odellan said with a bow to Isabelle, who managed a weak smile in return.

"I wasn't injured at all, fortunately," Vaste said with a straight face. "In case you were worried."

"And my other daughter," Chirenya said, drawing Odellan's discomfited expression back to her, "Vara."

Vara stood from her place on the bed to greet the Endrenshan, drawing a double take from the guard captain. "Pleased to meet you," she said in a low, tired voice. Cyrus saw a slight laceration at her hairline, crimson streaking her normally yellow locks.

"Vara?" The captain's voice tremored with question. "Are you...?"

"Yes," Chirenya answered with a smile. "She is."

Odellan leaned in closer to Chirenya and lowered his voice. "Do you think that...she...might be targeted by this...Hand of Fear...?"

"Because she's the shelas'akur?" Cyrus said, louder than was necessary, startling both Chirenya and Odellan and causing both to look at him as though he had thrown something at them.

Odellan cleared his throat, a loud, uncomfortable noise, as the captain stooped to examine one of the bodies. Chirenya glared at Cyrus with an expression he recognized from Vara's face. The paladin, for her part, seemed to be regarding the whole situation with much more indifference than was normal for her.

Endrenshan Odellan pulled the cowl of the dead assassin's uniform back to look at the ears, running his finger up to the point. "Are all of these assassins elven?"

"All that we've seen thus far," J'anda answered. "I did a cursory look at the bodies downstairs and there don't seem to be any non-elves."

"I wish I could question one of them," Odellan said, his fingers on his chin in contemplation.

Behind the Endrenshan, Cyrus watched Vaste begin to speak under his breath, lips moving as the faint glow of magical energy gathered on his hands. It built to a crescendo, a stunning burst of light that cast the room in brightness. The troll blinked as he finished and nodded when Odellan turned to him in surprise. "Wish granted," he said.

Odellan's brow furrowed, uncertain. "What? AHHHH!" With

a start, the guard captain jumped back as the body he had been inspecting jerked to life and grabbed his leg.

"There you go," Vaste said with a grunt of amusement. "Question away."

"Heal me...please..." The assassin's voice was a whisper, blood spurting from his lips.

"Looks like a lung wound," Vaste said, craning his neck to see from where he was sitting on the floor. "Painful."

Odellan looked in shock at the troll. "Aren't you...going to heal him?"

"After all the trouble we went to putting the holes in him, I don't think I'll patch them up. Besides," Vaste said, "if you interrogate him now, he'll be more apt to answer your questions."

"He's bleeding all over my floor," Chirenya said.

"Please," came the strangled voice of the assassin. "It hurts..."

"You stormed into this house intending to do violence to its occupants," Vaste said from the corner. "Did you not take into account the possibility that they might return the favor?"

Odellan cast a withering glare at Vaste, then knelt next to the assassin. "Who are you?"

The assassin's lips curled into a pained smile, blood dribbling down his chin. "I have no name. I am a Hand of Fear."

"So, more of a title then." Vaste nodded. "And a dumb one at that."

Cyrus held up his hand to Vaste. "Who is your leader?"

The dull eyes of the assassin met his, and from their exchange Cyrus looked away first; the assassin's brown eyes were soulless. "Our leader?" He coughed, bringing up more blood. "His word is death." Cyrus looked back to find the assassin fixated on Vara, who was meeting his gaze unflinching. "Yours. Your family's. And everyone who aids you."

"You're not in a good position to be making threats," Odellan said.

"Kill me; kill all of these." The assassin tried to wave around the room to his fallen brethren, but his hand flopped. "More will come. We will pursue you to the ends of Arkaria." The eyes glowed, still locked on Vara's. "Until the ends of time. We will watch and learn, and our next attack will be more powerful still." He coughed again and a geyser of blood flooded from his lips. "If necessary, we will kill everyone you love, one by one, to get to you. Just like we did with—"

The bloody smile on the assassin's face was frozen as a 'WHUMP!' broke the silence in the room. Odellan jumped back, a two-handed sword sticking out of the taunting elf's chest. Vara had drawn her blade and struck so quickly that no one had seen, let alone been able to stop her. She raised it again, and with a cry of rage brought it down and split the assassin's head from his shoulders.

A cool indifference played across her face, broken by a twitch of emotion, then another. Her perfect mask cracked, and one hand flew to her face, trying to cover it as she stood by herself amidst all of them. Cyrus watched and behind her hands he caught glimpses of her facade breaking.

"Out!" Chirenya's words were frantic, hurried, as she went to her daughter's side, wrapping an arm around her shoulder. "Everyone out!" She looked to Odellan. "My apologies, Endrenshan, but of course we'll continue this some other time."

He nodded. "Yes, madam. I'll come calling tomorrow." Bowing, he backed from the room as the members of Endeavor cleared the path for him, followed by J'anda, Thad and Andren.

Vaste followed after reassurances from Isabelle that she was fine. Still clutching her side, the healer moved to her sister's other shoulder. Vara was deteriorating now, both hands before her face, a choked sob leaving her lips. He was alone in the room with the three of them and Vara's father, still unmoving on the bed.

"You too." Chirenya made a shooing gesture, crossing the distance between them and pushing him toward the door.

"It's not safe," Cyrus said, his protest weaker than he would have thought possible under the circumstances.

"I know you'll stand watch outside the door," she replied as she began to close it in his face. "Isabelle and I will handle this, as we always have. No one comes through that door. I know you'll watch it all night."

"I—" He didn't finish before the door was shut. He stared at it, amazed it was still in place after the battle.

As the sun rose over the wreckage a few hours later, he reflected that Chirenya was right—he did not move until well after sunup.

Chapter 18

Isabelle emerged sometime in the late morning. She looked at Cyrus with surprise as she closed the door behind her; he caught a glimpse of Vara, asleep in a chair in the corner of the room. "I didn't expect you to be out here all night," she said. Warriors from Endeavor lined the stairwells and greeted her with enthusiasm until she gestured for them to quiet. "Aren't you tired?"

"I'm fine," he lied. "How's Vara?"

"She'll be all right." Isabelle flashed him a reassuring smile. "Vara doesn't come apart like that very often so it's all the worse when it happens."

"No, she doesn't show much emotion. Other than irritation."

"Walk with me," she said with a smile.

"Well..." He could feel the internal tension rising. He glanced at the door.

"My warriors will keep watch." She started down the steps and paused, turning to look back at him. "Come on then."

He followed as she strolled to the second floor. Having not seen it in the daylight, he paused, amazed at the damage. All the windows were broken and blood streaked the floors where the bodies were dragged out of the house during the night. There were holes in every wall, glass was scattered on the floor, couches were ripped, paintings knocked from the walls, and chairs overturned and smashed.

Isabelle moved closer to the window, looking into the house across the way. Several of its windows were also shattered. Cyrus caught sight of Martaina in one of them, her bow in her hand, watching. She nodded then returned to watching. The sound of ringing bells filled the streets. The tolling was constant, a melodic noise in the distance.

"You were fortunate to weather the attack with no casualties." Isabelle turned to give him a reassuring smile, then moved closer to the windows to stare down at the street below. Cyrus followed her and was amazed; the columns of Termina guards remained below, still in formation. At its head, standing at attention, was Endrenshan Odellan. On the side of the road was a wagon piled with bodies; the remains of the members of the Hand of Fear, stacked one on top of the other.

"Luck was on the side of Sanctuary." He bowed his head. "I'm sorry about the loss of your people."

He watched her pale cheeks for any sign of rage, but there was none. "These assassins are dangerous when they catch you by surprise, but after facing the Hand of the Gods, the Hand of Fear doesn't seem quite so frightening."

"I suppose it was different for Endeavor when you went through the Trials of Purgatory, but..." Cyrus stared out. "The Hand of Fear has killed more of our people than the Gatekeeper or the Trials ever did."

"We lost very few in conquering Purgatory," she said, "as we had several members of Amarath's Raiders advise us on how best to handle them."

Cyrus racked his memory, trying to remember what Vara had told him about their conquest and the subsequent purge of their ranks. "They came to you after Archenous killed their guildmaster?"

She nodded and looked to him, eyebrow raised in mild surprise. "She told you about that?"

"You sound surprised."

"I suppose I am. She rarely speaks of it to anyone. It's a good sign that after Archenous's betrayal, she's beginning to trust another man enough that she can talk about it."

Cyrus stiffened, sensing there was more to the story than Vara had told him and unsure of how to respond. "Well...when you're...betrayed, as she was...one would tend to take it...personally."

Isabelle laughed, a crackling noise lacking in any mirth. "I think you might be understating it, but yes, being betrayed by your first lover, a man who is to be your husband; being gutted and left alone to die in a place like Purgatory is the sort of thing most people would take personally."

A cold winter wind ran between the buildings and Cyrus felt the temperature drop in his armor, something that had precious little to do with the weather. *So that's what happened.*

Isabelle seemed to catch sight of something on his face that was unexpected. "She...didn't tell you all of that, did she?" Her head dropped as a hand came up to her forehead, hiding her eyes from his sight. "Bollocks."

Silence passed between them before Cyrus spoke. "Before that, was your sister...I mean, has she ever been..." He fought for the words, not sure how to ask the question on his mind.

Isabelle looked back at him, now impish. "Calm? Peaceful? Sweet?" She chuckled. "No, even before Archenous she was just as acerbic and more guarded than most." The amusement left her eyes and she became cold in an instant, as if all her joy had been taken by a single memory. "But he made her untrusting and sapped the vibrancy from her." Isabelle turned to him. "You have to realize that although to humans Vara is a woman, to elves she's still a child; not even lived a half a year if she had the lifespan of your people."

"That's..." He blinked. "Staggering."

"And yet she is a woman, mature—in spite of what our mother thinks—and able to make her own decisions." Isabelle straightened, her chin pointing as she looked at the building across the street. "I daresay that Vara has had to deal with more at her age than most elves ever have to, because of who she is and what it means."

"Because she's the shelas'akur?"

Isabelle turned to look at him, curiosity filling her eyes while her face remained cool. "Do you know what that means?"

"Only in the literal sense," Cyrus said. "'Last hope'."

The hint of a smile blossomed into a wry one. "You could have bluffed me. I might have believed she had told you."

"Twice in a row?" He shook his head. "You knew better this time."

"Probably, but I'm surprised you didn't make the attempt."

"I will find out," he told her. "Someone will let it slip, not knowing I'm around. Probably someday soon, since I'm surrounded by your people here."

Her fingers brushed against the destroyed glass hanging in one of the windows, causing it to fall and break. Without any visible reaction, she said, "When you do, I hope you'll keep the secret, for reasons that will become obvious. But about Vara...she has tremendous pressure on her, of a kind that may be henceforth unseen by anyone, even the Royal family members in the line of succession." Her finger carressed another piece of broken glass.

"What kind of pressure?" Cyrus stared at the blond elf, who seemed fascinated by the shattered glass.

"Three kinds. The first is societal. The shelas'akur is recognized the Kingdom over. They adore her for who she is."

"I've seen that," Cyrus said. "Elves have made mention of her being shelas'akur, even having not met her before."

"There's political pressure as well," Isabelle continued. "The King would love it if Vara were in Pharesia, operating as a member of his court." Her smile thinned, becoming less genuine and more rueful. "I doubt he'd feel the same after a week of her being there. She's never said it, but I know that's part of the reason why she left the Kingdom to study in Reikonos when she did."

"Huh?"

"By all rights, even with her magical abilities she shouldn't have gone to the Holy Brethren until she was nearer to thirty or forty; in fact, given her status, she would have been given instructors from the Leagues and allowed to train at home. Instead, she left for Reikonos at fourteen to become a paladin." She scoffed. "Realize that she took advantage of human standards when doing that—after all, humans may train from the age of six in a League, but that's not normal for an elf. I didn't start with the Healer's Union until I was nearing fifty."

"I didn't realize she had been trained in Reikonos," he said. "I assumed she'd learned in Pharesia or Termina."

"None of the Leagues train here," Isabelle mused, staring at the shard that she had plucked from the window. "Not anymore."

"In Termina?"

"In the Kingdom," she said. "Anyone who needs training would go to Reikonos. Which is why she was able to play off the humans who were in charge of the Holy Brethren in Reikonos, in spite of what I'm sure were screaming protests from the elves in the faculty about her being too young. Of course, that's nothing compared to the last source of pressure on her."

Cyrus waited a beat. "Which is?"

"Mother."

"She wasn't happy when Vara left?" He ran his gauntlet across the sill, brushing shards of glass out the window and onto the street below.

Isabelle's head turned to favor him with a pitying look. "What do you think?"

"She left to study in the human capital?" Cyrus rubbed the stubble on his chin in thought. "Your mother probably went rabid, foaming at the mouth."

"I did not." Chirenya's voice came from behind them, startling both Cyrus and Isabelle, who turned to see her staring at them from midway down the stairs. "But neither was I pleased that my daughter, barely capable of wiping her nose without assistance, took a horse from the stables — "

"One which was given to her as a gift," Isabelle said with muted annoyance.

" — and proceeded to travel hundreds of miles to a savage city with only a note to warn her parents what she was doing." The elven woman's hand was locked on the chipped and damaged guardrail as she descended. "Of course, I didn't see her for almost four years after that — "

"Because you were too stubborn to travel to Reikonos to see either of your daughters — "

" — and after, she showed up only sporadically, usually when she was in trouble." After taking her last step, Chirenya's hand left the banister and her arms folded in front of her, her gaze cold. "Like now, for instance. And of course, she continues to associate with bandits — "

"Excuse me?" Cyrus cut in, outrage edging his voice.

"You're excused; you may leave whenever," Chirenya replied before continuing argument. "Everything that's gone wrong in her life is all attributable to the choices she made from the moment she left."

Isabelle sighed, a deep, disbelieving noise. "I suppose if she'd continued to follow the path you'd laid out for her she'd be much better off."

Chirenya's eyes narrowed at her eldest daughter. "She'd have less scars." Bristling, she changed tacks. "Clean up; we're leaving in a few minutes."

Cyrus caught the eye roll from Isabelle as Chirenya turned to leave. Casting a look back over her shoulder, the elder elf spoke again. "You too, ox. Find a working faucet and clean yourself up; if need be, use the pump in the yard. You'll need to be presentable."

Feeling as if the rug had been jerked from underneath his feet, he stared at Chirenya, almost agape. "Where are we going?"

She frowned. "Are you deaf, ox? Are those tiny ears of yours insufficient to the task of hearing? Men are already such poor listeners; I imagine women with human husbands must be doubly frustrated at their lot. Do you not hear the bells?"

Cyrus listened, hearing the deep intonations ringing down the streets from far in the distance. "I hear them..."

"We go to the Chancel," Chirenya said. "They are calling in the city for morning worship."

Cyrus exchanged a look with Isabelle, who shook her head as if to suggest he not take it any farther. Ignoring her, he said, "I don't know if you noticed, but your house was destroyed last night..."

A surge of heat hit him. Whether from a draft of air or the fire from the elven woman's gaze, he did not know. "Hundreds of years accumulating and collecting possessions in my home, only to watch them destroyed in a single night? It did not escape my notice. But neither has it escaped my attention that my family has endured. So we go to the Chancel of Life to give thanks to Vidara." With that proclamation, she turned and marched back up the stairs.

"My mother is quite serious about worship," Isabelle said, following Chirenya up the stairs. "She'll be ready to leave shortly and you'll get an earful if you're not ready."

"She's serious?" Cyrus asked, alarm rising. "I don't have anything to wear that's not..." He looked down. "...black armor. Nothing that would be appropriate in a temple dedicated to life."

"Armor is fine," Isabelle said in a reassuring tone as she began to ascend. "After all, you did preserve our lives last night with that armor of yours." She paused. "But I would find a working faucet." She pointed to his face. "You have a bit of blood on your face there...and there...and there..." She disappeared up the steps, leaving Cyrus with a growing sense of panic.

Once she was gone, he descended to the first floor and hit the street, mind racing. *She can't expect me to go to the Chancel and worship Vidara, can she? I'm a follower of the God of War!*

So distressed was he that Cyrus didn't notice when Odellan called his name, catching up to him as he reached the front steps of the house across the street. "You look like you're in a hurry," the Endrenshan said.

"I'm in a bit of a bind," Cyrus said. "I just found out I have to go to the Chancel of Life with, uh...them." He pointed at the top floor of Chirenya's house and saw her looking down from one of the broken windows, glaring at him.

"Fifteen minutes," she called down to him. "Wash up or I'll have Vara push you into the horse trough."

"She is...formidable, isn't she?" Odellan said in a muted whisper. "Let's talk inside."

Cyrus shut the door behind them, nodding to Andren, J'anda and Vaste, who sat in the living room, looking across the street.

"Gentlemen." He looked to Vaste. "Troll."

Vaste feigned an offended look. "I, too, am a gentleman." He chucked a thumb at Andren. "Moreso than this drunkard, anyway."

Andren stopped, flask raised almost to his lips. "Who are you calling a drunkard?"

"You."

"Ehh, you're right." The elf shrugged. "Why deny such a beautiful love as exists between me and alcohol?"

Cyrus coughed, embarrassed. "We have company."

Andren looked Odellan up and down. "Yeah, but it's just a young Endrenshan; couldn't be more than a couple hundred years old, if that." The healer sniffed the air for a moment. "To be so young and an Endrenshan—you're not from Termina. I'd bet Pharesia, born and bred, with parents that are mighty high in the court."

Odellan halted and the pleasant expression he had been wearing became a mask. "I can't deny my birth," he said, stiff. "As this is Termina, I hope you'll judge me by my actions and not by my class. I'll accord you the same courtesy."

Andren cackled. "Sounds like a better deal for me than for you, highborn."

Cyrus clapped his hands together, startling Andren into silence. "I only have a few minutes. Vara's mother intends to go to the Chancel of Life this morning, and I don't know whether she intends Vara to go with them."

J'anda, wearing the illusion of an elf, wrinkled his pale nose as he frowned. "What's this Chancel of Life?"

"It's a temple where they worship Vidara, the Goddess of Life," Odellan said. "It's the tallest building in the city. You can't miss it, straight ahead on the main avenue when you arrive. You must be an enchanter with an illusion, because every elf in the Kingdom knows that." He regarded J'anda with suspicion. "Dark elf?"

J'anda looked at the Captain coolly. "Perhaps. Perhaps not."

Odellan nodded. "Excellent idea, using an illusion. Dark elves are not well regarded in Termina at the moment. We do far, far too much business with the humans. I'm afraid we've had a few instances of assaults, mostly by human workers on dark elven merchants. Best not to draw attention to yourself."

"Can we focus on what needs to be done?" Cyrus looked

around the room. "I need a force ready to move in five minutes if Vara's going to the Chancel."

"And if she's not?" Vaste leaned back and the couch he was sitting on moaned under his weight.

"I still need a force ready to move to protect her mother," Cyrus replied.

"Might I suggest," Odellan said, diplomacy and charm layering his suggestion, "my troops and I come along with you, along with any elves or," he nodded at J'anda, "individuals who look elven from your group. It will generate less attention."

"Because a column of Termina guards is discreet," Andren muttered before taking a nip from his flask.

"We'll be able to disperse in the Chancel and blend more easily into the crowd," Odellan said. "Easier at least than offlanders would. Weekly Chancel is a largely elven affair; you won't find many non-elves in the crowd."

"Likely Isabelle will contribute some of Endeavor's forces," Cyrus said, mind racing. "We'll need to leave some people behind, because I doubt Chirenya will leave Vara's father alone and there could be another attack at any time—"

A crack as loud as thunder filled the air and Cyrus froze, looking at Odellan in a moment of gut-punching unease.

"What was that?" The Endrenshan's hand was on his sword, as was Cyrus's. There was a commotion on the floor above them and Cyrus turned toward the door, ready to bolt across the street. Frenzied shouting came from above.

"Hold on!" There was the sound of footfalls on the stairs. "Everything is fine," a feminine voice called down. Cyrus waited in the living room as the footsteps approached, until Martaina appeared in the living room, her hair tousled, her chainmail coif hanging off the back of her head like a cowl.

"What was that?" Cyrus said.

"That old biddy," Martaina snapped back at him. "I was watching to make sure there were no threats and she took umbrage; told me to stop looking in her windows." She ran a dirty hand through her hair. "I told her I wasn't looking in her windows because she didn't have any, and that I wasn't looking but every few minutes, just to keep her and hers safe. She told me to stop it, and I didn't, so she sent a bolt of lightning at me."

She turned to Cyrus. "Then she shouted at me as I was beating a retreat, said to 'tell the ox to get his arse back over there, cleaned up and all', whatever that means."

"Oh gods, that's me," Cyrus said, ducking down the hallway into a washroom. A bronze tub sat in the corner, big enough that Cyrus could sit in it even with his armor on. Polished faucets hung over it, as well as into the sink on the opposite wall. A metal privy filled with water sat next to the sink.

Martaina poked her head through the open door as Cyrus looked at himself in the mirror. Dried blood encrusted his armor, and a few drips had settled on his face. "Facilities are at least as nice as what we have back at Sanctuary, eh?" The elven ranger smiled at him.

"Good thing, too," he agreed. "After all these years, I doubt I could go back to using a chamber pot." Ignoring her chortle, he tossed her his helmet, which she caught.

He leaned down, plugging the stopper in the sink, running the cool water until it filled the basin. While it did, he unstrapped his breastplate and backplate. He slipped the chainmail shirt over his head, sending it clinking to the ground. He reached down, cupping his hands in the frigid liquid, and brought a handful up to his face, scrubbing as hard as he dared, trying to remember where the problem areas had been.

He looked back to the mirror, and the blood was gone. Wetting his hands, he tried to slick back his long, brown hair. Tangles within his locks fought him, and from behind him Martaina let out a soft giggle. He turned to her, ready to snap in annoyance, but she reached over him to let the water out of the basin. Cyrus looked down; the liquid had a deep crimson tinge.

"This is not going to work." Cyrus sighed, then looked down, realizing he had stripped to barechested in front of Martaina without even thinking about it. A flush crept over his cheeks and he felt his back teeth grind in embarrassment.

"You'll make it," she said with a chuckle. "And if you're a few minutes late, it'll be good for that old broad; I doubt she's ever had anyone make her wait." Replugging the sink, she opened a nearby drawer and removed a brush. She ran it through his hair, drawing a wince from Cyrus. "You get stabbed and sliced open in battle, but tangled hair makes you cringe?" She shook her head and laughed. "Human warriors! The Society of Arms teaches you how to keep from flinching from a sword blow but come near you with a brush and you freak out."

"Hair pulling is not part of our combat training," Cyrus

replied. "At least not beyond the hand to hand combat or wrestling practiced within the Blood Families." Martaina slowed the brush strokes with which she was straightening his hair, and he felt the loquacious elf turn into a pit of silence and unease behind him. "Thad told you, didn't he?"

Cyrus could see her reflection; where she had worn a smile only moments before, it was replaced with a drawn look, sorrow behind her eyes. Her nod was slight, but there. "It's not a big deal," he said, trying to make eye contact with her through the mirror.

"It was horrible, what they did to you." She stooped to pick up his chain mail. He took it from her and slid it over his head. "Thad told me it was nothing less than a miracle that you survived, that you were the first—because you were the toughest—"

"If I was the toughest," he interrupted, "it was because of that. I think you're discounting the other warriors the Society has trained."

She fastened his breastplate and backplate together. "I can't tell if you're being falsely modest or if you're really that delusional to downplay—"

"It's done," he said with quiet finality. "That's all that matters."

"As you say," she said, skepticism lacing her statement. She handed him his helm. "Not quite perfect, but as good as you'll get without a full bath and time to clean up."

"Thank you." He turned, taking his helm from her and replacing it on his head. "As for the other thing...if you could keep it to yourself, it'd be appreciated."

Sadness filled her eyes. "You have nothing to be ashamed of. I mean, I'm not a follower of Bellarum, but Thad says you should be proud—"

"It's in the past," Cyrus said. "I'd like it to stay there."

She stepped aside and he moved into the hallway and back to the entry to the house, where he paused in surprise. Vara stood there, her hair around her shoulders. Her expression was prim, her lips taut.

"Hello," Cyrus said, approaching her slow, uncertain.

"Good morning. Mother has asked for our presence on the street in one minute. You have a guard force allocated to stay behind?"

"I do." He swallowed, hard. "You look lovely."

One of her eyebrows inched upward. "I don't see how; I have

had neither the opportunity nor the inclination to do anything more than bathe and let my hair down. It's amazing what fighting for your life in the dead of night will do for one's complexion, I suppose."

Cyrus felt a tightness in his chest. "I've never been to a Chancel before. Am I..." He hesitated. "...presentable?"

She looked him up and down in a cursory manner. "You're no worse off than the unwashed masses that will stand in the back of the Chancel." She tilted her head toward the door. "Come along. Our time is up."

Chapter 19

Cyrus followed Vara, Odellan and Martaina behind them with a few other elves. Chirenya waited in a carriage with Isabelle, its doors thrust open. Vara climbed in, seating herself on the bench next to her mother. Cyrus found himself sitting next to Isabelle, who pushed herself against the wall of the carriage to allow room for his armor. Even so, his left arm pressed against hers, prompting him to smile in contrition.

"You'll have to forgive us," Chirenya said without a hint of apology. "Our family's carriage is designed to be pulled by beasts, not seat them."

"It is also several sizes to small for your rudeness," Vara said.

Odellan appeared at the window. "I have a column ready to follow you. The driver is at your command."

"They always are," Chirenya said under her breath. "Very well, Endrenshan. Proceed."

With a clatter, the wagon lurched into motion. Vara stared out the window, as did Chirenya, while Isabelle playfully nudged Cyrus with her elbow. Chirenya took notice, sending her eldest daughter a scathing look. "Really, perhaps you should have let your sister sit with her ox."

"Mother, please," Isabelle said with a shake of her head. "With their armor, they could not possibly get close enough to keep from bursting out of the carriage."

"It would not be difficult to imagine the two of them in much more intimate positioning than this."

Cyrus choked, prompting all three women to look at him. "Why must you keep accusing your daughter of such... unpleasantness—"

"If it's unpleasant," Chirenya said, "you're doing it wrong."

"I meant," Cyrus's face reddened, "you continue to accuse her of things that she is telling you she is not doing—"

"Things?" Chirenya spoke with cringe of distaste. "Can you not speak plainly? You are a ridiculous man, and thoroughly unworthy of the honor of thrusting yourself between my daughter's legs."

Cyrus clenched his teeth so tight that he thought he heard them crack. "The only thrusting that goes on between your daughter and I is the thrust of her wit, my parry and riposte, and so forth." He looked across to Vara for confirmation, but she had returned to staring out the window, impassive, her hair cascading down her shoulders.

The sound of the wooden wheels clacking against the cobblestones dominated the oppressive atmosphere in the carriage. Cyrus dared not look at Chirenya, for fear of beginning another conflict. Similarly, he averted his gaze from Vara after the paladin sensed him staring and looked at him with a quizzical expression. Isabelle smiled at him, and they exchanged a look every few minutes until Chirenya glared at them both. Finally, Cyrus gave up and looked out the window.

It was obvious they had left the more moneyed district where Vara's parents lived. The houses were constructed in rows, just as in her neighborhood, but the dwellings were smaller, the streets were less kempt and filled with a throng of elves. They moved along in silence, men and women, as one. Cyrus stared out, something odd about the scene tickling the back of his mind, but he dismissed it.

The smell of food sold by street vendors filled the air, filtering into the stuffy carriage where the aroma of the three women was offset by what he had to concede was his less than ideal scent of days of travel and battle. The quiet chatter outside the carriage was a welcome break to the silence within it. The coolness of the outside air was warmed by the bodies close to him in the carriage, particularly Isabelle. Even through his armor, he could feel her breathing against his side. He looked across once more to Vara, who was still watching out the window, and wondered what it would be like to have her breathing against him.

The ride took twenty minutes, by which time Cyrus's legs ached to move. The carriage ground to a stop in front of the Chancel. As he stepped out he reflected that although he'd seen bigger buildings—the Citadel in Reikonos and the Eusian Tower in the Realm of Death sprang to mind—he'd never seen any quite so ornate. The architecture of the Chancel was impressive, with a dome atop the squared building. At each of the four corners of the structure was a smaller tower, and after a moment Cyrus realized that it was from within the towers that the tolling of the bells came.

On every wall were stained glass windows capped by friezes that were carved in such small detail that Cyrus could tell even from hundreds of feet below that craftsmen must have labored on the Chancel for over a hundred years. Columns stretching hundreds of feet in the air lined the entrance and stone steps led up, filled by people answering the call of the bells.

Cyrus reached a hand up to help Vara, who ignored it and stepped down. Isabelle took his extended hand and kept the other on her robes, raising them so that the white hem did not touch the muddy road. Chirenya also accepted his proffered hand, stepping past him so quickly that Cyrus realized she didn't want to acknowledge his assistance.

A phalanx of Termina Guards arrayed themselves around the party, Chirenya exhorting them to "Get moving, knaves." The other parishioners moved aside, and Cyrus caught a glimpse of Odellan walking outside the perimeter of the soldiers.

As they neared the top of the stairs, the entrance doors awaited them behind a small courtyard of columns. A voice cried out in elvish, a gentle and melodic chant of some beauty. Cyrus found he understood some of the words. "It's the traditional call to worship," Isabelle whispered in his ear. Her breath was sweet, filling the air with a wash of mint.

"Chirenya, mother of the shelas'akur." On a pedestal a few feet above the crowd stood an elven woman with dark hair. She wore an expression of utmost serenity, and very little else. Her robe wrapped around her waist, hugging both legs to below her knees but leaving her groin exposed. Her shoulders were covered by a silken cloth that stretched down both arms to cuffs at her wrists, and circled her neck with a simple band. From that band, the cloth ran below her arms, leaving her bosoms visible, along with her belly. "I greet you and your blessed offspring in the name of She who grants life."

"Arydni, High Priestess of Vidara," Chirenya said with a bow. "I offer my humble greetings and present both my daughters to Vidara's grace."

Cyrus felt his stare burning into the Priestess of Vidara's uncovered body. Such a thing would have been unthinkable in Reikonos, where the clothing covered the zones of the body that the Priestess's seemed engineered to display. "She's not wearing much," Cyrus said in a hushed whisper to Isabelle.

"She's a High Priestess of the Goddess of Life," came the healer's amused reply. "Her vestments are designed to accentuate the life-giving and sustaining parts of the female body."

Cyrus watched the High Priestess bow to Chirenya, unable to take his eyes off her. Her skin was supple and free of any blemishing. Her face was pretty and youthful and his eyes lingered a moment too long. He felt a sharp impact on the back of his head, knocking his helm over his eyes. When he readjusted it, he turned to see Vara glaring at him. "Don't leer."

The Priestess turned her attention to Vara and her smile brightened. "The shelas'akur. We are honored to count you among our faithful this week—as we are any week that you deign to grace us with your presence."

"I'm certain," Vara said. "And of course, I am pleased to be here, blah blah blah, you know the rest of the idle pleasantries."

Chirenya's mouth went agape. Cyrus watched Isabelle stifle a laugh and turn away, shaking her head.

If the High Priestess was offended by Vara's response, she did not show it. Cyrus had fixated once more on her exposed bosoms, and this time he moved too slowly; she caught him looking. Instead of scowling, she smiled. "We welcome you, honored guest, with the blessings of She who is the source of all life."

Before he could answer, Vara spoke for him. "He doesn't speak elvish."

"I understood what she said." Cyrus took his eyes off the Priestess to glare at Vara. "I'm learning; I may not be able to speak your language, but I understand most of what's said."

"She who grants life welcomes all races to her sacred Chancel," the priestess said in the human tongue. Her voice was melodic even in the rougher language of the Confederation. "Welcome to our shrine to Vidara. In honor of you, I will conduct the worship in the Human language." She bowed to him, catching his gaze, which he averted to find Vara scowling at him once more, hand raised and eyes narrowed.

They were ushered past the High Priestess's pedestal into the Chancel. When they entered, Cyrus was unready for the scale of the room that greeted him. Big enough for several of Sanctuary's Great Halls to be encased within it, the Chancel stretched forward, benches all lined in concentric circles around a center pedestal. There were four aisles allowing the parishioners to be seated and the benches were already growing full as Chirenya badgered the guards toward the place she wanted to sit.

They seated themselves on a bench that Cyrus would have bet was the place Chirenya regularly sat; she went into the row first and immersed herself in conversation with an elven woman of her same approximate age, who cast curious looks at Cyrus. Vara followed, sitting next to her mother but ignoring the conversation taking place in favor of staring at the pedestal in the middle of the room.

Ensconced on the pedestal was a statue of a womanly figure at least ten feet tall. She was nude, with a baby nursing at each of her breasts. The statue captured her hair swirling around her shoulders with a benign expression on her face. He looked first to Vara at his right, but found her expression curiously blank as she stared at the statue.

Cyrus turned to his left, where Isabelle sat between him and the aisle. She was looking at him and answered before he could ask. "Vidara, of course."

The air was thick with the smell of burning incense, and Cyrus realized that the bells had ceased tolling sometime after their entrance. A gong sounded from behind him, and a rhythmic chant rose as a line of elven women streamed down the aisle, lighting the candles that were placed at the end of each bench. They moved in a procession, almost dancing, each attired in the same revealing garb as the priestess outside and twirling staves that held a lit flame at the end. It reminded him of something he had seen during a carnival in Reikonos, something artful and beautiful, the chanting in perfect time with the lighting of the candles and the movements of the procession.

Down the aisle to his left came the High Priestess, clad as she was before. Cyrus found himself once more transfixed, this time more comfortable in the relative anonymity of the crowd. He watched her as the dancers made way, not interrupting their rhythmic movements. The High Priestess did not dance but instead walked with grace and dignity.

Isabelle leaned over to him. "How does it feel to ogle women that are at least five millenia older than you?"

Cyrus felt his jaw fall before he was able to control himself. "Not all of them?"

Isabelle looked back with a twinkle in her eye. "Yes. All."

"I figured maybe they were less than a millenia old...they look so..." He blushed. "...you know."

She raised an eyebrow. "Comely? Attractive?"

"I meant youthful."

Isabelle chuckled, a light laugh that was only just audible over the chanting. "Elves maintain their graceful looks until the mid 5,000s." She nodded at the High Priestess, who was ascending the pedestal. "How old would you estimate she is?"

Cyrus looked to the center of the room, where the High Priestess stood, arms open in a welcoming gesture as the dancers threaded their way around the pedestal. He looked at her dark, flowing hair, her golden skin, glowing under the light of the candles around her. "You said they were all in the 5,000s, so I would guess early on that scale. 5,100 maybe?"

She shook her head. "5,500 or so. She'll take the turn soon — that's what they call it when we begin to look old. Of course, that will take many decades."

He looked down the bench to Chirenya before turning back. "How old is your mother?"

"It's impolite to ask." Cyrus turned back to see Chirenya hissing at him. "But I'll have you know I'm not a day over 4,500."

The High Priestess clapped her hands together, a sound that resonated throughout the Chancel that was followed by a gong. "In the name of the life-giving All-Mother, I summon you to worship." She spoke for several minutes as the congregation listened. Cyrus watched the crowd as the High Priestess completed a ceremonial call to worship and concluded with a hymn sung by the dancers, who were circled around the base of the pedestal upon which she stood.

Cyrus felt the smooth woodwork of the bench behind his neck as he leaned back and looked up. Over the pedestal, hanging above the statue of Vidara, was another, this one a grotesque figure, with eight arms and the beak like that of a bird but filled with terrible teeth. It was built to hang from the rafters, and looked like an overlarge spider ready to descend on the nursing likeness of Vidara. As Cyrus watched, it began to lower and lanterns projected light directed by mirrors onto the figure, illuminating it.

"While I welcome you in her name, I caution you as ever," the High Priestess said, "to be wary of He that stalks all of the Life-Giver's children. His threat looms large over all we build in our lives, ready to take us at any time should we be careless or grow ill." The High Priestess looked over the crowd and locked onto him. "I speak, of course, of the God of Death — Mortus. He reigns from inside the Eusian Tower in his realm," she continued, "a fearsome place of infinite horror — "

"It's not so bad," Isabelle muttered under her breath as the Priestess continued to sermonize, her eyes off Cyrus now. "Not homey, but I've been worse places."

"Last time I was there," Cyrus said, "one of our less thoughtful wizards set the boiling oil on fire with an explosion."

Isabelle snickered, drawing a reproachful look from her mother. "I bet that made fighting the hydra a challenge."

"Yes, we capped off that expedition with a battle where we fought against the undead skeleton of a dragon I'd killed the day before," Cyrus said. "It was...interesting. I'd rather not go back."

"Agreed," Isabelle said, sotto voce. "I've spent more time in Death's Realm than anyone living has a right to."

"Ever see Mortus himself?" Cyrus nodded toward the hanging statue.

"No," Isabelle said with an emphatic shake of the head. "No mortal has, at least not in living memory. I heard tell about a guild a couple centuries ago that disappeared into Death's Realm; speculation was that he had caught them in the act of pilfering from his treasure room."

"I've only run that expedition with our old alliance," Cyrus said. "How does one know if a god is going to be absent from his realm?"

"Or hers?" Isabelle said, teasing. "There are information brokers that deal in such things."

"I don't know any of them," Cyrus said. "We've been hitting the Trials of Purgatory for the last few months, and of course the Gatekeeper's grown very sick of granting our requests for treasures at the end of the battle; we've flooded the market with the formerly rare pieces of the beasts that live there. We need to look elsewhere for targets to keep our army busy."

"You should join Endeavor in the higher realms," she said with a whisper.

The High Priestess continued to deliver a soliloquy in the background, but he was not catching much of what she said. His mind raced at the thought of taking Sanctuary into the Realms that were being explored by the most elite guilds in Arkaria. "You think we can handle it?" He regretted it the moment after he said it, cursing himself as weak for even asking, fearing he sounded like he was begging for her approval.

"Tearing through the Trials of Purgatory at the rate you are, you won't have much trouble with the upper realms."

Chirenya leaned across Vara, who still sat back, her hands folded in her lap. "This is a time for reflection and holy worship, and the two of you are chattering so loud they can hear you in the backmost rows. Shut up!"

Isabelle made a playful eye roll and obeyed her mother, leaving Cyrus to listen to the words the High Priestess spoke. He felt uncomfortable throughout the service, as if he were there under false pretenses — that they would turn upon him if it were discovered that he was a follower of the God of War. *Other than death, there cannot be any god more opposed to Vidara's principles,* Cyrus thought with a well-honed sense of irony. *I haven't been this uncomfortable since Imina dragged me to a worship for Virixia, Goddess of Wind.*

The Priestess spoke in parables, telling a story about a miraculous blessing that was visited upon the people of Elvendom, and Cyrus tuned her out, thinking once more of the Hand of Fear and the threat they posed. *If I could find a way to track them down...they must have a headquarters somewhere...or a base in the city...how do you find a secret organization?*

"For those who fear, who doubt, who wonder if she exists and if they should tread her path...I say to you that there are miracles that she has performed and blessings placed around us...you need look no farther than this very Chancel to find her works." The High Priestess clapped her hands together once more. "I'd like to call forth the children."

A few of them came forward, down the aisles as the Priestess descended from the pedestal to sit with them at its base. Cyrus surveyed the room again. It was large enough for at least twenty thousand, if not double that. Children gathered around the Priestess, and she launched into another parable. He watched her gentle, matronly manner with the little ones and then looked back to Vara. Her head was bowed, deep in thought. The clean, angular lines of her face gave him pause. At the moment, dark circles hung underneath her eyes, her hair was tangled and she looked tired and careworn.

He resisted the urge to put a hand on her shoulder, to pull her close to him. It was not only inappropriate given the setting, but the fastest way to get slapped on the side of the head regardless of when he did it. He remembered the time a year ago when she had kissed him on the cheek, soft and gentle, a quick peck, and he felt the memory of it bring a tingle to where her lips had brushed him.

My life is tangled beyond belief, he thought. *I'm in a Chancel for a goddess I don't worship, sitting next to the woman who is the biggest enigma I've ever encountered.* He frowned. *Sometimes she seems like she wants me, sometimes I think she'd like to kill me; maybe it's both. I wish I knew how she felt.* He reached up, kneading the bridge of his nose between his fingers. *Hell, I wish I knew how I felt.*

He watched the children returning to their parents at the conclusion of the High Priestess's parable and saw a half dozen walk down the aisle nearest him. Their ears were pointed, but only slightly. *Hybrids,* he thought. *Half human, half elf.* His mind drifted to another thought, of he and Vara...and of children...children just like the ones that were passing him now.

He looked to his right to find her staring back at him, her eyes vacant and with a touch of sadness. "What?" he mouthed, careful to keep from speaking aloud. Chirenya cast him an evil look nonetheless.

Vara shook her head, expression changing not a whit, and returned to staring straight ahead. He sighed, as close to under his breath as he could, drawing another scathing glare from Chirenya, and settled in to listen to the rest of the High Priestess's message.

The worship lasted for a further two hours, during which time Cyrus became more restless. When the High Priestess signaled that the service was at an end, it finished with another procession of dancers leaving the way they came. When the rest of the congregation stood, Cyrus did as well.

The guards that had been seated around them kept them in place while the Chancel cleared; once it was almost deserted, they were escorted to the entrance. Odellan fell into line behind Cyrus just before the door. "I've had some of my people asking questions about the other victims of the Hand of Fear; who their business associates were, what they had in common, that sort of thing. They've discovered a link that I'd like to show you—why don't you stop by my office this afternoon? You know where the government center is?"

Cyrus nodded. "I'll do it as soon as I make sure that..." He looked and found Isabelle talking with her mother in a hushed whisper and Vara, still dazed, following behind them. "...everyone is safe and under guard."

"Very well." Odellan fired off a crisp salute and exited the Chancel, descending the steps while Cyrus stopped with his party in front of the pedestal now occupied once more by the High

Priestess.

"Honored guest," she said after nodding in acknowledgment to Chirenya, "have you learned more about the light of the All-Mother after today's worship?"

"Ah, yes," Cyrus stuttered. "I've learned...much more."

The High Priestess smiled, a knowing smirk that gave the first hint of her age. "And remain unconvinced, it would seem." He started to protest, but she raised a hand to stay him. "Worry not, friend of Chirenya—" Cyrus caught a sour expression on the face of Vara's mother—"we do not badger the unconverted to believe as we do. Your spirit is your own, and those who seek the Life-Giver must do so of their own free will." She bowed to Cyrus. "If you come to us a thousand times more as an unbeliever, you will be as welcome as you are this day."

"I...uh..." He sputtered, looking for something smooth and articulate to say, something which would encapsulate his feelings about long worship services for gods he didn't believe in, spearheaded by millenia-old elven women who looked young enough that they stirred the deepest fires of desire in him. He settled on, "Thank you," and bowed to the High Priestess.

The High Priestess smiled and turned to Vara. "Vidara's grace be with you, shelas'akur."

Vara's head snapped up at the blessing. "It has been, since the beginning." Her voice was dull, dead, but her words courteous enough that they drew a half smile of acknowledgment from the Priestess.

Cyrus followed Isabelle and Vara back to the waiting carriage as Chirenya lingered to speak with the Priestess. The air was cold now, a brisk winter wind whipping through, with the sun shining but bringing little warmth. As Cyrus shivered, he realized he'd become accustomed to the mild winters of the Plains of Perdamun and forgotten how brutal the cold got as one went farther north. He shuddered to think of how bitter Reikonos would be at this time of year.

Once Chirenya joined them, the carriage got underway, and they lapsed into another silence, broken only for a moment when Chirenya looked daggers at Cyrus and Isabelle, saying, "You two couldn't shut up during worship and now you're dead silent?"

Vara continued to stare out the window in a placid calm as they wheeled through the streets. Once more, Cyrus looked out his window, trying to keep from mashing Isabelle under his armor while watching the elves in the streets pass by. The squares and avenues were crowded with people, filled to brimming, all of them clad in cloaks and winter garb. No snow was on the ground nor a cloud visible in the sky; Cyrus wondered if it snowed in Termina like it did in Reikonos.

The clattering of the wooden wheels ground to a stop as they reached the residence. Cyrus once again offered assistance, which was taken by all three women this time; Isabelle with quiet thanks and a smile, Chirenya with scorn and a sudden move to ignore Cyrus, and Vara without comment or emotion.

Something about the street bothered Cyrus. The houses still showed signs of damage from the night before, with windows broken and facades cracked from the combat that took place inside the house, but something was off. There was an eerie quiet on the avenue, with no sound of pedestrians and only the snorts of a dozen horses to break the silence.

He watched Chirenya lead the way up the steps, saw Isabelle follow with reserved silence. From the street he could see the living room through the broken glass, and he stared. A ripple of movement passed before the window as Chirenya opened the door, almost as if the window were the surface of a pond, disturbed by motion within.

He quickened his pace as he followed the women up the steps, and halted as Vara stopped in the doorway, but a moment too late. He ran into her as she stiffened, and he looked around the entryway and realized — the house they were in was not hers.

Chapter 20

"What deception is this?" Chirenya's eyes were aflame, looking around the foyer of the home they had stepped into. "This is nothing like my house!"

"Sorry," came an apologetic voice. Vaste stepped from the corner, where he sat at a table playing a card game with two members of Endeavor that Cyrus had seen but did not know by name. He took a step outside and looked through the window. Although the card game was going on right in front of it, none of the players nor the table was visible from the front step. "J'anda came up with a clever idea — use an illusion spell to switch the facade of your house with this one. Anyone who's passing by won't notice, and assassins might be fooled into attacking the wrong house."

"That'd be a brilliant stratagem, you bloody green idiot," Chirenya said, grinding her teeth, "but for the fact that I'd like to return to my actual house now, and continue to live in it."

"Fortunately, ma'am," Vaste continued, "I have a plan. And it's one in which I will be able to accommodate your request, rather than one that would end with your crabby ass being dumped into the river Perda in a sack at midnight." He smiled so sweetly that it was hard to tell he'd just threatened her. "Follow me," he said, beckoning them toward the stairs.

As they descended into the cellar, Chirenya sniffed her nose. "Are you quite sure that this troll is trustworthy?" she asked Vara. "He's not planning on murdering us in the cellar, is he?"

"I told you that wasn't the plan," Vaste said. "But it is a pleasant thought, isn't it?" He stopped at the base of the stairs and extended his hand, pointing toward the hole in the wall that the Hand of Fear had created the night before. "Your humble abode, madam. And by humble, I mean I've seen mud huts in the troll homeland possessed of more warmth and charm." He smiled again, pointed teeth displayed in a grin of pure antagonism.

"We've increased security in case the Hand of Fear decides to attack again tonight." Vaste patted the banister with one massive green hand as he began to climb the stairs again.

"I want to discuss the security precautions," Cyrus said, nodding at Vaste. "Meet across the street in a half hour?"

The troll nodded and continued his climb. Once he was out of earshot, Chirenya frowned. "I thought his people learned to respect their betters after the last war."

Cyrus bristled, but it was Isabelle who answered first. "I daresay he does, Mother, which is why he doesn't respect you." The healer turned and followed Vaste back up the stairs.

"Well, I never." Chirenya walked through the hole in the wall in a huff, and Cyrus heard her feet echo on the stairs in the next room, on her way up, leaving him alone with Vara, who was still inanimate.

She stood quiet in the dark of the cellar, with only a single lamp to light the room. Her back was to him and she turned, walked through the wall, and made her way to the stairs. Cyrus followed wordlessly.

They passed the first floor and reached the sitting room. Cyrus followed her to the door of her bedroom, which she entered. She made no move to shut it behind her, so he stopped in the frame as she looked out the window, her arms wrapped around her midsection. Her hair lay around her shoulders, still loose, framing her pale face with a golden outline.

After a moment of staring out the window, she turned to him. "Shut the door, please."

He froze, heart thudding in his chest. "Do you want me in the room or outside the door?"

She did not turn back to him. "Either is fine."

He stepped inside, taking care to shut the door behind him as gently as possible. He turned back to find her throwing her pauldrons on the ground as she unstrapped her breast and backplate. He watched as she slid off her plate metal boots, followed by her greaves and vambraces. Next she shed her chainmail, until all that was left was a suit of clothing she wore underneath it all, a white cloth shirt that was stained with years of the sweat and blood of battle, dark pants and worn leather footcovers that she wore inside her metal boots to protect her feet from wear and callousing.

She walked from the missing window to the armoire on the opposite wall before Cyrus's shocked eyes, and opened it after pulling her arms out of her shirt, followed by her head. The worn piece of cloth fell to the floor behind her, leaving her naked to the waist, her back to him. She was careful not to turn lest she expose herself. To the right of her spine, a scar the length of his hand ran up from the small of her back.

He stood in muted shock, unable to think of anything clever to say, nor bring himself to any sort of action. He recalled two years earlier, when Nyad had showed a similar lack of modesty, and after coupling it with what he had seen in the Chancel of Life, he realized for the dozenth time since arriving in Termina that he was, again, no longer in Reikonos. *Far from it.*

He blinked his eyes in rough disbelief. *Years,* he thought, *since I've seen...and now twice in one day...and Vara, of all people...*

"The polite thing to do," she said in, what was for her, almost a normal tone of voice, "would be to turn around while I change my clothing." She chose a dress from the armoire, her back still to him, and slipped it over her head, pulling it down until it covered her to mid-calf. "Failing that, you could at least act as though you've seen those parts of a woman before." She reached down, sliding off her leather footcovers and then shimmied off her pants, using the dress to keep her covered.

"Uhhh...all I saw was your back," Cyrus said, still struck dumb.

Vara paused, cocking her head at him. "I was also referring to your unbridled display of lust at the Chancel."

He shrugged as a flush crept up his cheeks. "It's been...a while." He cleared his throat before speaking again. "I cannot recall ever seeing you in a dress in the years I've known you."

She looked down as if she were seeing herself in it for the first time. "I haven't worn one since the day I left to join the Holy Brethren. I can't recall ever wearing this when I was younger, and it fits marvelously, so I can only assume that either I haven't grown since I was fourteen, or Mother has been stocking dresses in my size in the closet, hoping someday I would come back to the idea of wearing them." She frowned. "It's probably the latter."

Cyrus crossed the floor to where her armor lay and picked up the breastplate. It shone, showing none of the wear and beating that Cyrus's black armor did, even though he knew she had been wearing it for years and through countless battles. He picked up the pieces one at a time from the floor, gathering them together and setting them on the chest at the end of her bed.

She watched him with disinterest, but she watched him nonetheless. "How long ago were you married?"

Cyrus grunted as he scooped up her bracers. "Five years ago we got divorced. We were married for about two years."

"Divorce is not common for humans, is it?" He found her looking back with a curiosity that did not match her languid posture.

"No. It's rare and requires consent of both parties and the court. But she asked for it, I granted it, and the court agreed." He turned away, facing the shattered windows, and looked out to the street. He saw a faint hint of distortion in the air, as though a mirage were outside the window; the magical evidence of J'anda's illusion, visible only from this side.

"And what," Vara continued, "were her grounds for wanting to part ways with such a distinguished warrior as yourself?" She said a moment later, more quietly, "If you don't mind my asking."

"I don't mind." He did not turn to face her. "We got married shortly after I left the Society of Arms, at a time when I was trying to be a guild warrior. I applied to several smaller guilds in Reikonos, and I was traveling constantly." He eased himself onto the bed, still facing away. "She got tired of the lifestyle—of me wandering the world, always seeking battle. She wanted me to give up my aspirations and move to a small town where we could start a family and I could be a guard."

"I have a hard time imagining you as a town guard, standing at a post for hours on end, every day for the rest of your life."

He laughed. "I couldn't see it myself. We argued constantly. She was a flower vendor, and was done every day by sundown. Whenever I got home, on the days I did get home, she didn't know when she'd see me next, or..." He hesitated. "...if she'd see me. Smaller guilds don't have as many healers as the larger ones, so permanent death is more commonplace. She got tired of the worrying, of arguing with me about it—tired of the fight, I guess you'd say."

"Tired of the fight," Vara said. "Yes, I can see that. You, though—you live for the fight, do you not?"

"I like fighting in battles," he said. "But I didn't enjoy arguing with her."

"I meant battle," she said, still draped across the chair. "You worship the God of War, after all. I could tell from the way you acted in the Chancel—outside of the moments when your jawbone was wedded to the floor, drool running freely from your mouth— that you were uncomfortable with the thought of being in a place where another deity was being worshipped."

He shrugged, stung over her mention once more of his

gawking. "It's your idea of worship in general that confounds me. Have you ever heard of a Temple to Bellarum?"

Her face went blank. "I can't recall ever seeing one in my travels."

"That's because worshipping Bellarum is done in battle; with a sword in your hand and the blood of your enemies sanctifying you."

Vara rolled her eyes and let her head loll to stare at the ceiling. "Sometimes you really are quite barbaric."

Cyrus leaned over his shoulder to look at her. "If you don't like to fight, I would suggest you picked the wrong career."

Unmoving, she waited a long moment before she spoke, and when she did, it came out in a small voice. "An excellent point."

He spoke hesitantly, as if afraid to break the quiet. "Do you remember when we staged an invasion of the Realm of Darkness last year?" He cursed under his breath. "You weren't there, never mind."

She did not move when she replied. "As I recall, it came toward the end of summer, right about the time that the convoys began to be destroyed. What of it?"

"There was a moment when we were outmatched. These octopuses were killing us in the dark, and we couldn't see, couldn't fight them. There came a light from the back of our formation, filling the sky, paralyzing our enemies." He chewed his lip, lost in remembrance. "I'd never seen anything quite like it until last night. It was what I saw your sister cast when she stunned that assassin."

Vara lay still on the chair, then nodded her head. "I heard about it at the time—rather a gift horse as I understand it. The spell Isabelle cast is called 'Nessalima's Light' and is every magic user's first spell."

"Named for the Goddess of Light, I presume."

"Aye. But there is no one powerful enough to cast a light of the size you have described. Nessalima's Light can help you find your way in a cave, or allow you to see a few feet in front of you on the blackest night, or blind an enemy for a few precious seconds; but not even the most practiced and experienced spellcasters could bring forth a luminescence powerful enough to brighten the Realm of Darkness. I would suspect something else."

He thought about it for a turn. "So magic users' spells become more powerful as they become more experienced?"

She lifted her head almost lazily. "Yes, but the amount of magical energy it would take to cast and sustain that light would be prohibitive; the spellcaster would be burning life energy to cast that monstrous of a spell."

"How do you...burn life energy?"

She let out a great sigh of impatience. "Magical energy, that which we spellcasters use to craft a spell, is finite; once exhausted, one needs time to replenish that power before casting another spell. However," she said, not raising her head, "if in dire straits and depleted of magical energy, one can continue to cast spells, but it leeches away your life."

"That sounds..." Cyrus caught himself before finishing.

"Ridiculous?" Vara's face was twisted in amusement. "Once, in battle with the Siren of Fire, I watched a young human wizard, fresh from his training in the Commonwealth of Arcanists—the wizard league—cast himself dry trying to extinguish her flames with ice. Once he was out of magical energy, he began drawing on his life. Before the end of the battle, he looked as old as any withered beggar you would run across on the streets of Reikonos." She stopped and her voice turned sober. "He died a month later, still in the care of Amarath's Raiders. He was twenty-five—and looked eighty years older."

She lapsed into a silence again until Cyrus broke it. "The scar on your back," he said. She lifted her head to look up at him. "Is that from Archenous?"

Her head flopped back against the chair. "Yes. A lovely reminder every time I look in the mirror of the value of trust."

He thought about it. "Do you...look at your back in the mirror often?"

"What?" She looked up at him. "No, there's a matching one on my stomach."

"But still," he said after another moment's consideration, "that means you look at yourself in the mirror—"

"Oh, yes," she said, voice cross, "I stare at myself naked all the time. Rather like you at the Chancel, I can't keep my eyes off the female form."

"I thought so," he agreed with a nod. "It's what I'd do if I was a woman."

"Yes, you've proven that well enough already." She lay back again. After a moment, a small laugh escaped her. "You were teasing me just now, weren't you?"

"Yes."

"I absolutely missed it." She stared at the ceiling.

"What's on your mind?" He moved along the side of the bed until he faced her.

"What's on my mind..." She let the words dribble out, slow and soft and completely in line with how she looked. "I'm tired."

"So sleep."

This time she only let out a sound of weakest amusement. "Not that kind of tired. Bone weary. Worried. Worn down by the incessant vicissitudes of my life." She raised her head to look at him. "Vicissitudes means—"

"I know what it means."

She arched her eyebrow. "Define it."

He shrugged, uncaring. "It means bad things that happen to you."

She snorted. "Pithy. But near enough to illustrate the point." She fell back once more. "I'm sick of this—of running, of my father being ill, of my family and guildmates being threatened. I'm well and truly fed up of this whole sordid adventure."

He stared back at her, catching the note of pleading desperation in her voice. "And me?" He said it with a smile, trying to defuse the tension, the raw emotion that was coming off her in waves despite her weary posture. "Are you tired of me yet?"

Her head did not move off the chair, but her eyes found his, and he could see the barest gratitude. "No. I'm not weary of you, Cyrus Davidon, though that may change if you continue to follow me into my bedroom and stare at me when I change clothes." She sighed, the sound of a tired soul. "I am drained and wish for nothing more than an end to these countless troubles. I want peace. Rather like your wife, I suspect, I'm sick of fighting."

When he did not answer, she went on. "When I was young, I fought because I had something to prove. Whether it was in the Holy Brethren or as a recruit for Amarath's Raiders or as an officer for that guild, it mattered not. I had a chip on my shoulder, ambition for greatness, desire and a hunger to conquer and convince everyone of my strength and the rightness of my cause. Archenous's betrayal burned that out of me as I watched my friends and guildmates slaughtered by their own, all because one man's desire for power and riches had grown beyond any level conceivable by those who had trusted him.

"When I joined Sanctuary, I fought to protect instead of increase my riches and power—to defend my friends, my guildmates, and even the people of Arkaria. I channeled my tireless aggression, my irascible, irritable nature into the idea that I was doing some good." She paused to breathe in. "I have fought more battles than I can count, and have even seen guildmates die—but never because of me. Never because of my ideas or decisions or efforts.

"Now I have seen people die because of me. Niamh." Her words came with a mournful certainty. "My sister's guildmates died to protect me and my family. All because someone, somewhere, wants me dead—for what reason I know not." Her expression hardened. "I will root out this Hand of Fear like the vermin they are." She sighed, then her body relaxed, her fury spent, and she lay her head back on the chair. "But after that, I honestly have no idea what I'm fighting for—or why."

She paused, her hands gripping the chair as Cyrus watched her, the most determined, lively, caustic and powerful woman he had ever known, reduced to a moment of supreme weakness. She breathed in and out again, as though gaining strength from the air itself, and then spoke, her words coming as though they were the last proclamation of a soul in utter surrender.

"When this is all over...I believe I am done."

Chapter 21

Cyrus did not speak after her words were delivered; he waited in silence with her for a few more minutes. He started to say something but stopped himself several times, unsure that anything he could offer would assuage her anguish. He listened to her breathing, watched her chest rise and fall with each breath, and thought.

I know how she feels because I've felt that way myself. I don't think she'll believe me...not without telling her about... He sighed softly. *What the hells, why not?* he thought.

He cleared his throat and started to speak, but stopped. At some point, Vara's breathing had changed to something deeper. Her eyes were closed. She had fallen asleep, her arms hanging off the sides of the chair.

Cyrus rose from the bed and shuffled over to her, kneeling at her side. She did not move or acknowledge him in any way. As gently as he could, he placed his arms beneath her and lifted her up, as though he were cradling a child, and carried her to the bed, lying her down. He pulled a blanket from the foot of the bed and covered her, walking as quietly as possible to the door before shutting it with only the hint of a squeak.

Two warriors from Sanctuary stood guard in the living room, greeting him with crisp salutes. *Had they been there before?* he wondered. "Keep an eye out," he cautioned them as he descended back to the cellar and crossed into the other house.

He found Vaste still engaged in a game of cards with the Endeavor warriors as he emerged from the cellar. Friendly banter filled the front room of the house. "He's a cheater," one of the warriors, a dwarf, proclaimed in jest, throwing his cards on the table.

"Never seen anything like it," another said, this one human. "How do you do it?"

Vaste looked up at Cyrus as he entered the room and nodded, scooping a handful of gold coins off the table and placing them in the coinpurse that hung at his side. "It's a game of odds, boys — and you are the oddest I've ever seen."

Jeering laughter filled the room as Vaste followed Cyrus onto the front steps. Cyrus waited until they were halfway across the street before he spoke, and only then in a low whisper. "They don't know you can count cards?"

Vaste laughed, a deep, rumbling sound that came from within his overlarge belly. "No one ever thinks the troll capable of such memory-intensive and mathematical feats." He rattled the coinpurse. "It's made me a lot of money over the years."

They entered the house that Sanctuary had commandeered to find J'anda standing with his hands extended at the front window, eyes closed in concentration. He opened them and looked sidelong at the two of them, but did not speak.

"He says it's taking more and more concentration to maintain the illusion as the day goes on." Andren nodded from a couch in the living room, Thad and Martaina seated opposite him. Just behind J'anda was a human in armor that was bluish in color, covered by a surcoat of purest white. Resting against the wall was a lance that was taller than Vaste, and the human's hand hovered next to it. His eyes looked out the window, searching for any sign of trouble, save for the moment it took him to look to Cyrus and sketch a rough salute.

"Sir Samwen Longwell," Cyrus said in genuine pleasure. "I'm glad to see you here."

"Yes, sir," Longwell replied, his odd accent even more evident to Cyrus after days of listening to the elves speak in their lyrical, singsong language. "Alaric added some more forces to the garrison after the attack last night."

Cyrus nodded. "How are things back at Sanctuary?"

"Tense," the human answered. When they met, Cyrus had asked the man what kind of fighter he was and Longwell had answered with a single word — dragoon. Longwell had proven himself a fierce fighter in numerous battles; a natural leader and a loyal soldier. "We've had more attacks from these Hand of Fear blighters."

A jolt ran through Cyrus. "Any deaths?"

Longwell chewed his lip. "One. A ranger was on guard in the officer quarters and an assassin infiltrated disguised as an applicant — took out our man as the fires and torches were exploding, but not before the ranger let out a shout of alarm." The dragoon lowered his head. "Curatio and Terian captured the assassin — but of course, he wouldn't say a word. However many we've got in the dungeons now, it's a quiet lot. Fortin keeps threatening to eat them, but they won't say a word."

Cyrus shook his head — the safety of Sanctuary members was his responsibility as general. "What was the ranger's name?"

"Doubt you'd know him; he was a new one," Longwell said, "but it was Rin Leviston. Human, from the Riverlands."

"I've seen the name on guard reports," Cyrus said, a flash of the weariness that Vara had described running through him. "Another attack is imminent here and I want to make sure we're ready." He looked to J'anda. "Any idea how long he can maintain that illusion?"

"Indefinitely," J'anda replied, turning to face him, letting his hands drop to his sides. The enchanter strolled to a chair in the corner and flopped down, eyes bright and a smile on his lips.

Cyrus frowned. "I thought you had to sit there and keep casting to maintain the illusions."

J'anda shook his head, a smile creasing his blue face. "No. A lesser enchanter, perhaps. I need only go to the window, cast once every few hours, and stay alive, and my spell will remain in place."

"So why didn't you say anything when we came in?" Cyrus looked back at him, confused.

J'anda held out his hands, palm up, as though he were saying the most obvious thing. "Because I was casting the spell then, of course."

"Oh, of course," Cyrus replied. "Obvious to anyone — except us non-magic users. You know, the overwhelming majority of the population."

"Yes," J'anda said with a hint of wistfulness. "It must be difficult to be so..." His voice trailed off and his hand moved in front of his face, changing his features into those of an elf. "...ordinary."

Cyrus turned back to the rest of the assembled. "I want to bring Fortin here and keep him in the cellar in case the next Hand of Fear attack is worse."

Thad leaned forward and his armor squeaked at the joints. "Uh...boss, you think that this assassin group is going to come at us with more than the forty or so people they hit us with last night?"

"I don't know," said, "but I'd like to be overprepared rather than underprepared if they do."

"I doubt Alaric will have much problem with that," Longwell said, looking back at them from his place by the window. "Fortin spends most of his days stuck in the dungeon since they closed the wall." The dragoon frowned. "He seems tense."

Andren interrupted before Cyrus could respond. "He's a ten foot tall pile of walking rock. How exactly can he 'seem tense'?"

Longwell shrugged and Cyrus went on. "Get him here, if Alaric will part with him. A few more druids, healers and wizards wouldn't go amiss if they can spare them." He halted as the others nodded around him. "I need to go to the government center and meet Endrenshan Odellan—he has a lead on the Hand of Fear."

"Want some company?" Longwell reached out for his lance.

"Yes," Cyrus said. "Andren, Thad, Martaina, Longwell...you're with me." He turned and passed Vaste on his way out.

"That's right," Vaste said. "Leave the troll behind. We wouldn't want any delicate elven sensibilities to be offended by the sight of a mighty green god of healing riding through their city."

Cyrus turned, keeping his expression straitlaced. "I wouldn't want to interfere with the other activities you have planned for this afternoon, such as bilking unsuspecting warriors of Endeavor out of their drinking money."

He turned from the laughter and halted on the front step, less than an inch from colliding with Isabelle, who looked into his eyes with amusement. "Fortunately, our warriors are paid a rather large stipend, enough that they can afford some ill-considered wagering and be none the poorer for it."

The laughter evaporated behind him and Cyrus turned serious. "That was a joke."

"No, it wasn't," Isabelle said, her eyes sparkling with laughter. "Your troll friend is an expert at counting cards. I heard you talking about it in the street."

Vaste looked at her, slight alarm on his face. "I didn't see you anywhere on the street, m'lady, or—"

"Or you'd have curbed your tongue?" She laughed. "I won't tell my warriors. If they're dumb enough to underestimate you, then they deserve to lose their coin. And you didn't see me on the street because I wasn't—I was upstairs, by my father's bedside."

There was a murmur behind Cyrus, then Martaina spoke. "Yes, Thad dear, our hearing is that good—in fact, she heard you whisper that question to me."

"You are going to meet with Odellan, I believe?" Isabelle stared at him, eyes now cool.

"Yes," Cyrus replied, not bothering to lie.

"I'll accompany you." She pivoted and walked back down the steps to a waiting horse.

They made their way along the boulevard in an informal column two wide. Cyrus found himself riding next to Isabelle. "You spoke with my sister," she said, leading them onto a major thoroughfare.

"I did," Cyrus replied, uncertain of how to respond.

"I have never seen her this despondent." Isabelle's cheery disposition had faded; not quite to the depths he had seen with Vara, but she was muted. "Even when we were children, if mother issued an order she did not care for, she would not hesitate to fight back." Her blond hair stirred in the chill breeze. "I hate them for that, this Hand of Fear."

"Not to mention they slaughtered a bunch of your guildmates," Thad said. Cyrus whipped around and the human flinched in consternation. "I'm sorry," Thad said. "It just popped out."

Isabelle remained still on her horse, riding with a serenity Cyrus could not imagine he would have felt in her situation. "You speak the truth," she said, her face hard as flint. "I cannot fault you for that. They died because of my command and I put them in place knowing the risk." She turned to glance at Cyrus. "Still, it does not assuage the guilt."

"You seem to be handling these deaths better than Vara," Cyrus said.

"I've been doing it longer. I'm also older and more in control of my emotions," Isabelle said. "I have been an officer in Endeavor for nearing thirty years. In that time, we climbed from being a guild much like Sanctuary was a few years ago to become the most powerful in Arkaria save two—and perhaps, someday soon, three," she said with a nod to Cyrus. "Within that rank— Amarath's Raiders, Burnt Offerings and Endeavor—is the most brutal competition you could imagine.

"We each push ourselves to outdo the others, mounting harder excursions, more taxing invasions of godly realms, and even participating in the occasional cutthroat guild war; though," she said with a shudder, "thankfully it's been years since the last of those. I have seen hundreds of our own die in my time, perhaps even a thousand or more." She shook her head. "It would be cold to say I don't feel the effects of those deaths last night, but I've seen so much worse, I suppose I'm numb to it."

"Worse?" Thad said again. "What could be worse than your people slaughtered?" Cyrus blanched and shot the warrior another glare, matched by Martaina behind him. "Sorry," Thad said. "Again."

Isabelle seemed not to hear him. "What could be worse than that?" Her voice was far away, dreamlike. "What indeed." She became quiet, and Cyrus thanked Bellarum, hoping that Thad would have no more chances to put his foot in his mouth.

They arrived at the government center a few minutes later. Cyrus had seen it from the bridge and thought it to be ugly; up close his impression was confirmed. Most buildings in Termina had greenery growing from them, vines hanging down the side, even in the chill of winter. The squares had fountains in them that were flowing even now, though Cyrus had seen ice forming on and around them.

The square that held the government center had no charms to speak of. The building itself was a dull grey, with a flat roof and no accoutrements to give it even a semblance of the flair that the rest of the city had. It was as though they designed everything else to reflect the majesty of the city and decided the government center would be solely functional.

Cyrus led Isabelle through the front doors after commanding the others to wait with the horses. As they entered, he found the interior not much different from the outside; an uninspiring entryway where a female elf took their names and handed them to a soldier who led them through a series of hallways.

Odellan sat in an open space, his desk against the far wall, writing on parchment with a quill in his hand. Their escort cleared his throat, then bowed and ducked back the way he came.

"If it isn't the hero of Sanctuary," Odellan said, rising to greet them. With a nod at Isabelle, he amended, "And Endeavor."

"You give me too much credit, Endrenshan, and her —" Cyrus gestured to Isabelle — "not nearly enough."

"The General of Sanctuary is known for his strong swordsmanship," Isabelle replied, "but not nearly so well as he should be for his silver tongue."

"Please, have a seat." Odellan gestured to chairs that were pushed against the wall on the side of the room. When Isabelle refused, both Cyrus and the Endrenshan remained standing. "I suppose you're wondering why I asked you to stop by."

"No, we were in the area and looking for directions to a brothel," Isabelle said with a straight face.

Cyrus blinked and looked at her. "I think you just channeled the spirit of your sister."

"Bah," the healer said. "I taught her everything she knows about acerbic witticisms."

Odellan, seeming a bit lost, reached over to the desk and produced a long piece of parchment. "I hope you'll forgive me for not involving myself in your verbal back and forth—some other time perhaps. I have here a list of the men—and the few women— who were targets of the Hand of Fear." He held it out for them to see.

Cyrus didn't even get a chance to read the first name before Isabelle snatched it out of his hand. "Nonwren, Vadir, Prokhot, Ulonne..." She read a few more names under her breath. "All have homes on Ilanar Hill, all some of the wealthiest citizens of Termina."

Odellan nodded. "There's another commonality, I think, one that's less obvious." He smiled. "If you don't mind me taking a moment to compliment myself, there's not another Guardsman in Termina—and maybe elsewhere—that would have picked up on this."

"Oh, yes," Cyrus agreed, somewhat bored, "very impressive, a list of wealthy elves."

"Not just wealthy." Odellan adjusted his uniform. "All of them are former counselors to the King—every single person on this list has been a member of the royal court."

Chapter 22

"Isabelle," Cyrus said, "you told me if the political elements had their way, Vara would be in the court right now."

"She would," Odellan said. "My father is Prime Minister — which is how I know these people were on the court. Every last one of them has had a close association with King Danay at some point in the last few centuries. Each served a term in their station then moved back to private life here in Termina."

"So," Cyrus began, "why would someone be targeting former members of the court — and someone that would be wanted on the court? You both know more about elven politics than I."

Isabelle exchanged a look with Odellan before she spoke. "No idea."

Cyrus answered with practiced skepticism. "Really. And it doesn't have anything to do with the shelas'akur?"

Odellan shook his head. "She's being truthful. I see no linkage to Vara — at least nothing obvious. But that's not the main reason I asked you to come here." The Endrenshan's eyes glowed with excitement. "I've been waiting for one of our local lowlifes — a gnomish smuggler who I caught with illegal goods — to get back to me with some information."

Cyrus looked to Isabelle, then back to Odellan. "And?"

Odellan smiled. "There's a man that lives on Ilanar Hill, was counsel to the King, and is now missing. I believed him to be in hiding. This gnome bartered his whereabouts in exchange for a reduction in a prison sentence."

"Let's go find him." Cyrus turned toward the exit.

"Absolutely," Odellan said with a nod. "I'll get a few of my men and we'll be on our way."

They left and followed Odellan through another maze of corridors into a barracks, where he issued brisk orders in elvish to a half dozen men standing at the ready. They followed out a side entrance back to the street, where Thad, Andren, Longwell and Martaina waited ahorse. They were moving in minutes with a small column of elvish soldiers following behind them.

Odellan led the way, and the hushed military discipline of the soldiers seemed to carry over to their group; there was no talking as they headed east toward the river, following an avenue that led to the northern bridge that crossed to Santir. They took a right turn at one of the squares and began wending their way through a neighborhood of row homes that looked significantly smaller and much less well taken care of than Vara's parents' neighborhood.

"This is Var'eton," Isabelle said in a whisper. "It's called 'The Lowers' in the human tongue."

Cyrus looked around. The streets were clean and well kept, though the cobblestone was more aged and cracked than in the other areas he'd been, and there was a smell in the air, something like meat. He crinkled his nose and tried to get a fuller sense of it.

"It's the stew that the less privileged eat," Isabelle explained when she caught sight of his wrinkling nose. "It's made with the parts of the animals that no one else wants, and thus is spiced with arinder, a local herb that's quite...pungent."

They cantered along until they reached a house, a two story building made of old, crumbled brick with few windows. Cyrus dismounted and followed Odellan up the steps. "How do you want to handle this?" he asked the Endrenshan as they walked.

Odellan stopped. "He's not a fugitive nor a criminal of any kind. We'll just knock on the door and ask if he'd mind answering some questions. He's in hiding for some reason if he's here instead of at his mansion." With a shrug, the Endrenshan knocked on the door.

Cyrus waited next to Odellan, but there was no response from inside. "Maybe he's not home?"

Odellan chewed on his lip, still serious. "From what I've been told this is a man who has nowhere else to go."

"Perhaps he's not excited to see the law either."

Odellan shook his head. "It's possible he's not excited to see anyone; this Hand of Fear is surprisingly capable. They seem to be everywhere and have incredible amounts of information."

"How do you think they're able to do that?"

"My guess?" Odellan asked before turning to knock on the door once again. "They have spies where I wouldn't have thought it'd be possible to place them — the court in Pharesia, the heights of Termina industry, maybe even in the Chancel. It's hard for me to believe it's so easy to corrupt those institutions."

"That would take a lot of money," Cyrus said. "So where are they getting it?"

"Like so many other things in this investigation, I don't know," Odellan said as they heard a sound behind the door. There was the squeak of a floorboard and the door opened an inch, giving Cyrus a view of blackness from floor to ceiling in the house, with only a slight change of outline in the middle—and a lone eyeball, staring at him from out of the dark.

"I don't accept guests," said the man, keeping the door cracked.

"I am Endrenshan Odellan of the Termina Guard," the captain began. "Are you Arbukant?"

The eyeball darted about, looking at Cyrus and then the Endrenshan. "I might be. What does the Termina Guard want with me?"

"I'd like to ask you some questions about some acquaintances from your days in the court. Perhaps you remember my father—"

"I'm sorry." The door budged not an inch, the darkness within still hiding the elf from sight, and his eye slipped left to right, alternating between the two armored men standing on the doorstep. "I don't want visitors."

"I believe your life is in danger," Odellan went on, "but you already know that. Why not let us protect you?"

"I don't know what you're talking about," Arbukant said, eye wider now. "I don't want to talk to you—not either of you. I have no words for the Termina guard and—" the eye rolled up and down Cyrus, taking him in—"whoever you are."

"What about me?" A soft and familiar voice came from behind Cyrus. Vara stood at the foot of the steps, still wearing the red dress that she'd had on when he left her on the bed. Her eyes were slightly red, and her hair was tangled. "Do you have any words for the shelas'akur?"

"What are you doing here?" Cyrus's words came out in a low hiss.

"Looking for answers," Vara said without a trace of irony as she ascended to the step below Cyrus and Odellan.

The door opened a bit more and Cyrus caught a glimpse of the man inside; at least a portion of him. He looked middle-aged by human standards, and wore dark clothing that looked like a mass of black in the low light of his house. His face had a few wrinkles, and his jowls were exaggerated even though he was not fat at all. He opened the door enough for someone to enter. "I would speak with the shelas'akur," he said. "But no one else. Step inside."

Cyrus interposed himself between the door and Vara as she climbed the steps. "I'm her bodyguard. She doesn't come in without me."

"Are you mad?" Vara said. "He's on edge; don't antagonize the man. Let me see if I can get him to talk."

"Absolutely not," Cyrus returned, not bothering to lower his voice. "You don't have your sword and without the strength granted by your mystical armor you'd have a hard time fighting off a kitten."

Her eyes narrowed. "You'll regret that choice of words later when I unleash a bag of angry cats upon you while you sleep."

"Be that as it may," Cyrus said, turning back to Arbukant, "she's not coming in without me."

As Vara drew a breath to argue, the elf in the doorway stepped back to admit them. "Fine, fine," he said, "but the two of you and no more!"

Vara shot Cyrus a nasty look that he ignored, and he stepped into the open door, pushing her aside to enter first. She made a grunt of impatience, which he also ignored. He rested his hand on Praelior's hilt, feeling the additional strength and speed run through him. Time seemed to slow a degree while he stopped to look around the entryway.

The style of the house was similar to Vara's parents', but the size was much reduced; the hallways were narrower, the flooring was old wood, browned with age and use. There was a smell inside, pungent, and Cyrus thought again of the stew that Isabelle had remarked on.

As Vara passed into the entryway, Arbukant shut the door, casting the room into darkness. "The shelas'akur," he said. "Long have I desired to meet you."

"Yes, well I..." Vara looked around and Cyrus could tell by the way she squinted that her eyes were still adjusting. His had already done so, and his eyes slid over the cracked walls, looking for any sign of danger. "...I'm curious what a man as wealthy as yourself is doing in a place such as this."

"Surely you must know." Arbukant gave her a nod as he locked the door behind them. Vara stood in front of the elven man and Cyrus positioned himself so that he could see anything that happened between the two of them.

"All I know," Vara said, "is that a group of assassins are after me; and they seem to be the same ones that are after you." Cyrus watched her as she spoke, saw the muscles in her neck tense, saw the muscle in her cheek clench with her jaw. "I have no idea who they are or what they want, but they pursue me without relenting."

"Poor dear. You really don't have the slightest idea what this is about." Arbukant stared at her, his hands steepled in front of his mouth. "I have something for you," he said. His eyes flicked to Cyrus and then he reached into the folds of his robe—

And came out with a dagger.

The elf moved faster than Cyrus would have thought he could; but it was the eyes that gave him away. They turned into narrow slits as he pulled the blade free and thrust at Vara, who began to flinch away.

Cyrus's sword accelerated his reflexes so long as it was touching his hand and he had not let go of it since entering the dwelling. As soon as he caught the hint of movement from the old man, the sword was drawn. He had it raised and ready to strike before the elf had extended his arm halfway to Vara, and by the time he drew close to her, the edge of Praelior struck him at the wrist, its blade made of a mystical metal harder than any other. Cutting through flesh was no obstacle; nor was the bone underneath.

The old man's arm was spiraling away before he realized it had been severed. Cyrus followed his strike by stepping into him, shoulder first. His pauldron clipped the elf in the jaw as he forced him into the door, his right hand under the neck and his left still holding Praelior.

"Aiiieeee—" Arbukant began to scream, but Cyrus cut off his airway with the metal of the bracer that wrapped his wrist.

"Why do I doubt your name is Arbukant?" Cyrus looked around the room, listening for sounds of danger. Hearing none, he glanced back to Vara, who stood, shaking, a few feet behind him. "Are you okay?" She nodded and Cyrus turned back to the elf. "Where is Arbukant?" The elf wore a look of pure malice, lips twisted in rage, eyes wide with fury.

"He can't answer with you choking off his airway," Vara said from behind him, her voice brittle.

"He can point. Then I'll think about letting him draw a breath."

The elf pointed to a hallway that led back from the entry. Cyrus released his bracer from the elf's neck and seized his throat with his hand then forced him to the floor. Relying on the strength granted him by his blade, he lashed out with his foot and broke the knob on the front door, causing it to creak and then open slightly.

"Odellan!" Cyrus called. "Get in here!" He looked back to the man they had thought was Arbukant. Odellan flew through the door, his weapon drawn, Thad and Longwell two steps behind him. "He says Arbukant — the real one — is back there." He nodded toward the hallway. "See if he's alive. Be careful — he might have friends."

Cyrus gripped the elf's neck, ready to break it if he heard the slightest sound that indicated battle was coming. *I kill him then get Vara outside and make sure she's safe...* His thoughts ran wild until Odellan called back, "He's dead. Looks like no one else is here."

Cyrus loosened his grip on the elf's neck. "Hand of Fear?"

The faux Arbukant coughed, then nodded, his remaining hand grasping at the bleeding stump of his right wrist.

"How many of you do I have to kill before this is over?" Cyrus said, his anger taking hold. "Let's get to it, because I'm going to win and you're going to lose, and the sooner you realize that, the sooner you and your comrades can get dead. You can't have her, and I will kill every last one of you until you stop coming."

"We will never stop," came the man's low hiss. His eyes were wild, darting from Cyrus to Vara. "When our master commands a death, the death shall be had." He fixated on Vara. "I will say no more," the elf continued. "Do as you will; kill me, imprison me, it matters not."

Cyrus picked him up by the chest and slammed him into the floorboards, yielding a horrifying crack. "I want the name of your master. If he commands fear then I want to meet him so I can teach him a few things." He picked the man's head up and slammed it again. "I can do this all day. I'll just have one of my people heal you between deaths."

"Cyrus," Odellan's voice came from over his shoulder. He turned to the Endrenshan to find him shaking his head. "I can't let you do that. It's not allowable under elven law."

"What?" Cyrus asked. "This?" He slammed the elf's head down again, this time so hard the man emitted a pitiful cry. "Termina doesn't favor the punishment of assassins?"

"We have laws to protect our citizenry," Odellan said. "I can't let you torture the man, regardless of what he's done. He'll face justice through a trial."

"Yes, that seems like a hell of a deterrent," Cyrus grunted. He looked back down at the elf, and was surprised when a choked laugh made its way out of the man's lips. "You think this is funny?" Cy punched him in the mouth and blood welled up from between his teeth, ran down his face, and he laughed again. "You think it's funny to make a woman fear for her life?" Cyrus hit him again, and this time something broke; teeth and maybe more. The elf's nose gushed blood and his eyes fluttered, brushing close to unconsciousness.

"Cyrus!" Odellan's hand landed on his shoulder and the Endrenshan took a knee and whispered in his ear. "I know you wish to hurt this man, but if this continues, duty will compel me to expel you from the Kingdom. Who will protect Vara then?"

Cyrus squeezed his hand tight, his fist cocked and ready to deliver a killing blow to the assassin. "Fine." The elf dropped to the ground, bleeding from the face, the floor already slick with blood, shining from the sunlight creeping across the floor into the entry. "Do whatever you want with him." Cyrus turned to leave and was stopped short by a low, sucking noise. He turned back to the assassin and realized it was laughter; almost drowning in his own blood, the elf was still laughing.

"You...should have killed me..." His eyes fluttered once more and he fixated on Vara, his misshapen mouth contorted in a twisted, now toothless smile. "Your death is coming," he said, spitting blood between every syllable, "because he who is most fearsome has commanded it and so you will die.

"You — and the old one as well."

Chapter 23

Cyrus rode through the streets of Termina, having left the assassin in the hands of Odellan and his troops. Vara was sandwiched between him and Thad, with Longwell and Andren riding in front of them and Martaina behind with Isabelle. The silence was thick and the atmosphere almost as cold as the chill emitted by Vara. "You should not have brutalized him." Vara's words came flat, unemotional, and broke the silence with all the impact of the crack of a whip.

"Perhaps not," Cyrus said. For the past few minutes he had stewed in the memory of what he'd done and felt a hint of remorse — mainly because his efforts had yielded nothing. They were on the Entaras'iliarad, the road that stretched between the Chancel of Life and the center bridge that led back to Santir, and the crowds were enormous, filling the streets with elves wrapped up against the elements. He looked back at Vara again, his cloak draped over the simple cloth dress that was all that stood between her and the icy wind howling through the streets.

"Perhaps not?" Isabelle said. "I think you permanently damaged his face."

Cyrus grunted. "He's not the first. What do you think he meant by saying they would kill Vara and the old one?"

"Maybe he was talking about you," Andren said. "You're looking a bit worn around the edges of late, you know."

Cyrus fired off a rude gesture. "Is your wine-sodden brain capable of grasping that we have a serious threat?"

"Wine-sodden?" Andren said, offended. "I'll have you know I prefer ale."

"Old ones are a legend," Martaina said from the back. "Supposedly immortal, they were the first elves."

"So they're going to kill some immortal elf?" Cyrus pondered, talking almost to himself.

"Yes, except that the old ones," Isabelle said, "if they ever existed, are gone. We elves have a lifespan of six thousand years. That may seem long to a human, but I assure you, it's not infinite."

"Is it possible that they still exist?" Longwell asked. "I mean, would they look different? Or could it be that someone wouldn't know that they're immortal?"

"Yes," Isabelle said with measured skepticism. "I suppose it's possible in the sense that anything is possible; you could get hit by a dead griffon falling out of the sky right now — but it's not likely."

"In other words, you think the legend is bullshit," Cyrus summed up. With a start, he looked back to the Endeavor officer, who wore her customary smile of amusement. "Sorry, I forgot you're not one of my people; I wouldn't have sworn."

"I am familiar with the term, though most of the time I hear it in whispered breaths behind my back rather than to my face." She smiled. "But to your point, most elves would think the legend is 'bullshit' as you so eloquently put it; we live in our communities, and over the millenia we see our friends and neighbors age. Though you might think me still young-looking by human standards, elves can judge my age very close to the mark. It is subtle but noticeable among our own. I would think that someone who lived forever would be discovered after a few decades; perhaps a century."

Thad whistled. "That's a long time to us humans."

"But not to elves," Vara said. "Most elves live in the same communities all of their lives. Termina is unique in that it has attracted enormous population growth by becoming a thriving trade city; most elven cities are dying because people do not leave them except by death, and they do not relocate within them to other neighborhoods because of the rigid caste system. It creates a community wherein you know your neighbors and build a relationship with them from birth until death. Even here, to a lesser extent, it happens."

"So if I was an old one and I wanted to hide out, it wouldn't be practical to do so in the Elven Kingdom anywhere but Termina?" Cyrus chewed his lip as Vara shook her head. He thought for a moment. "Maybe Arbukant was an old one?"

"Yes," Vara said, "and maybe he was a dark elf in disguise. There are no old ones. It's myth and legend."

"Yeah," Cyrus muttered under his breath, "and there's no way goblins could be raiding convoys in the Plains of Perdamun."

"Let us call it unlikely," Isabelle said. "But assume he was — why would the Hand of Fear care if he was a thousand or ten thousand years old?"

"I don't know anything about what they want — other than Vara dead." Cy nodded toward the paladin, who shrugged her shoulders in a worn and noncommital way. "We don't know who they serve, what their agenda is once these assassinations are completed—or why they've been wiping out former members of your King's Court." He nodded at Vara again. "Or a potential one."

They lapsed into silence as they turned from the square onto a thoroughfare. Cyrus steered through the crowds, keeping watch for pedestrians. At one point, a small child darted into the street in front of him and he steered his horse out of the way at the last moment. He looked down at the little one—a boy, no older than five—and watched as his mother darted after him, thanking Cyrus with a stream of effusive words and begging his pardon a thousand times. Cyrus watched them retreat, and noticed the curve of the lad's ear; another half-elf.

"Be on with it, woman," Vara snapped at the mother elf. "If you keep apologizing to this lout, he'll get a swelled ego."

Cyrus looked back at the paladin, her cheeks red from the burn of the wind. "You don't even have an ounce of gratitude to me for saving your life back there, do you?"

She rolled her eyes. "As usual, you look for praise for doing what is expected. I almost wish you hadn't; then I wouldn't have to go through the motions of puffing you up into a bloated and gelatinous mass."

They rode down Vara's street and dismounted. The illusion remained intact, the facades switched for the two houses. The front door flew open as they approached and Vaste stuck his head out. "Hihi."

"Hihi yourself, you grotesque," Vara said. "Get back indoors before someone becomes suspicious."

"I will, after I've stripped naked and done a dance in the middle of the street," Vaste said. "I thought you might like to know—your father is awake and he's been asking for you ladies."

Cyrus turned to Vara. Her face was frozen, eyes squeezed tight from where she had just hurled an insult at the troll. She shivered in the breeze, and after a moment's wait she was in motion, running toward the door. Vaste ducked back inside in time to avoid being shoulder-checked by the much shorter elf.

"So she does have some emotion other than anger," Andren said. "Who knew?"

Isabelle laughed. "She does. Not much, but she does." With a nod to the members of Sanctuary around her, she proceeded toward the door, much slower and with more dignity than Vara had.

Cyrus watched the two of them go and turned around. "Be vigilant. We have no idea what will come next."

"I'm going to go out on a limb and guess...pineapples," Andren said.

"Pineapples?" Longwell's accent was even more obvious in his confusion. "What do pineapples have to do with anything?"

"Oh, they don't," Andren said. "I'm just sick of saying 'assassins'."

Cyrus shook his head and entered the house in time to see Vaste sitting back down at the table in the corner, the same warriors from Endeavor seated around him.

"This time will be different," the dwarf told him as Cyrus headed past them to the cellar stairs.

"Sure it will," Vaste agreed. "After all, you can only lose so many times in a row, right?"

He shut the door, making his way between the houses then up to the second floor of Vara's home and found himself hesitating at the landing. *It's a family reunion,* he thought. *I'll wait for her down here, keep watch in case someone comes upstairs.* He walked toward the sitting area and realized, not for the first time, that he hadn't slept since arriving in the city.

He positioned himself in a chair, his back to the broken windows, and felt his head rest against the padding. *Just need to close my eyes for a few minutes,* he thought. *Or maybe an hour.*

The fatigue from the battles of previous days and the ever-present pain from the wound in his shoulder finally caught up with him, settling over him like a blanket, and soon enough he was in a deep sleep.

Chapter 24

"I think you've ruined my chair."

The words jolted Cyrus awake. He blinked his eyes and realized that he was cold, terribly cold, his cloak missing. He was seated, and his neck had a cramp from the position he'd adopted while sleeping. Bleary, he looked up to see the stern face of Chirenya leaning over him, examining the fabric of the chair next to his shoulder. "Your armor seems to be rubbing off," she said in annoyance. "Are you really so ridiculous that you took the time and effort to paint it black?"

"No," he said, his voice sounding far away as he tried to orient himself to his surroundings. "It was my father's, but it's the metal, not paint, because it's yet to scrape off and it's been hit quite a few times."

"Then what are you rubbing off on my chair?"

"Blood, probably," he said, hand finding his face and trying to rub the cobwebs away. He looked around the room, still wrecked from the battle the night before. He took it all in and looked back to Chirenya. "I kinda think this chair is the least of your decorating problems."

"Cheeky," she said, her eyes narrowing.

"Where's Vara?" he asked, now irritated.

"Still upstairs, with her father," Chirenya said, straightening up. "They haven't seen each other in nearly a year, you know."

"I can't imagine why."

"What is that supposed to mean, ox?"

"What is it with you and oxen? Did you have an affinity for romancing farm animals in your day?" Cyrus countered. "Is there a particular reason you don't like me, or do I just fall under your blanket contempt for humans?"

She glared at him. "You wish to have this conversation now, do you?"

"Why not?" he said. "I doubt I'll get back to sleep anyway."

"I have no problem with your people," she replied. "In my experience, humans are decent enough."

"Then what have I done to offend you? Is it that I guard your daughter? You'd rather her go wandering alone with these assassins after her?"

A sigh of deep disapproval came from the elf. "Don't be ridiculous. While I'm not pleased about the situation she's in, I don't mind that she's got a loyal bodyguard — no matter how ox-like he may be."

"Then what is it?" His words came out suffused with exasperation. "I realize you're a mean old hag to everyone, but you seem to have a particular disdain for me."

"Perhaps it's not for you," Chirenya said. "Perhaps it's more for your type."

"My type? Warriors?"

"That's a start. 'Adventurers' would better encompass it," she said with a haughty sniff. "I know who you are. I've met your kind before; the sort that thinks they're a hotshot, noble and ambitious, with plans to conquer the whole world in order to better your pocketbook. You travel Arkaria and use your considerable martial abilities to steal from unsuspecting dragons, goblins and gods. Oh, yes, you are noble indeed."

"What?" He blinked in outrage. "I've stolen from evil gods, yes, like for example the God of Death, the God of Darkness — you know, bad guys, in that they've been responsible for actual atrocities. I've stolen from the goblins, who, when they were the Goblin Imperium, not only fit the criteria of 'evil' but pretty much defined it, since a great many of their treasures came from convoys they'd destroyed and stolen from over the years. And don't get me started on the dragons I stole from," he said with a shake of his head. "They were plotting to bring about the destruction of the entire mortal world."

"Oh, yes, always a justification for everything. I'm sure in your mind you think you defend the less fortunate."

"I do," he said with annoyance. "I did save the world from the Dragonlord, after all. And I helped overthrow a nasty, oppressive regime that was choking its people and raiding convoys."

"And there was no benefit in it for you?" She looked at him triumphant as his face fell. "I thought so. My daughter and I have gone round and round about her choice of profession, and I doubt you'll say much to sway me. In fact, likely as not, it's her profession that has got her in this trouble."

"You don't know that," Cyrus shot back. "It could be because she's the shelas'akur. And you can't possibly hate me for being a warrior in her guild; I joined Sanctuary long after your daughter and have had no sway over her decision to remain with us or to be an adventurer."

"Fine," she snapped. "My issue with you is as follows—while I'm certain you make a fine plaything, Vara requires a husband. An elven husband."

Cyrus leaned back in the chair and emitted a short, sharp bark of a laugh. "I'm. Not. Having. Sex. With your daughter," he said with exaggerated emphasis. "She's made it quite clear that nothing will happen between us."

"Yes, I'm sure that's what she said," Chirenya replied with a slow nod.

"What is that supposed to mean?" Cyrus shook his head in exhaustion.

"Vara has been a rebel her whole life," came the measured response. "First she fought against the various social customs I expected her to observe; then she bucked the traditions regarding training of magic users by running off to the Holy Brethren at age fourteen; and then she went completely mad and joined a guild rather than use her abilities to serve her king and country." Chirenya's face was lit in the glow of a nearby lamp, serious and stern. "Then she brought home her fiancé—a human, shirking all expectations once more. Worse, an adventurer—an egomaniacal, power-hungry bastard that ended up stabbing her in the back, almost causing us to lose her—" her eyes blazed—"the last hope of our people.

"So you see," Chirenya said, her calm restored, "I have my reasons for being displeased with both adventurers and humans that come home with my daughter." Her smile returned, polite. "I have no desire to see her tread the same path again."

"I'm not Archenous Derregnault," Cyrus said. "To confuse me with him would be a grave mistake in addition to being one of the most insulting things you could say to me. I would...NEVER...hurt Vara. And why do you keep going back to the romance argument? She and I are not together."

"You deny that you have feelings for my daughter?" Chirenya's hands cupped one another. "Because you should understand..." She lowered her voice, so low that Cyrus could barely hear her. "I had a fling with a human once—it lasted about forty years, and while immensely satisfying on a physical level, at least at the start, I got to watch him die in the end." The elven woman's face was grim. "For me it lasted the equivalent of six months to your race, and he had lived a lifetime. Elves have a concept—covekan. Have you heard of it?"

Cyrus felt an unexpected tightening in his chest. "Yes. It's the idea of a long-developed emotional bond between your people."

"Even if I were to ignore Vara's responsibilities as shelas'akur, my desire for her to embrace a less deadly career path and assume that you're a decent—nay, perhaps even wonderful—man, humans cannot become covekan." She drew herself up to her full height so that she could look down at him, a calm resignation upon her. "You would love her all your life and you would be nothing but a passing memory in hers, something that would wreck her heart and spirit for a hundred years or more.

"Suppose you should give her children?" She smiled, but it was a fake one, one that didn't even come close to touching her eyes. "You would wound her doubly; half-elves have less than a quarter of the lifespan of a pure-blood elf. You would bless her with children that she would outlive by several thousand years.

"Perhaps you think me cruel. I assure you, I am not; I am her mother, and I want what is best for her." Chirenya turned to leave, but looked back once more over her shoulder. "Protect her, Cyrus Davidon, protect her from harm. But remember this: the physical harm that will befall her would be nothing compared to the emotional harm of life with you. I don't hate you," she said with conviction as her hand slipped onto the banister and she began to climb the stairs. "But I love my daughter—both of them. And I, too, would do anything to protect them from harm."

Chapter 25

Cyrus staggered out of the house, still exhausted, beckoning to Thad once he reached the street. The warrior trotted up to him, Longwell and a few others lurking nearby. "I'm going to get some sleep. Go up to the second floor of the house and wait there." He walked past them, then stopped as a malicious thought crossed his mind. "Sit on the furniture, relax, and keep an eye on things."

"Sit on the furniture?" Thad looked at Longwell with a guarded skepticism. "That sounds like something Vara's mother won't like."

"If she says anything to you, let her know I told you to do it."

Leaving Thad shaking his head, he opened the door to the Sanctuary safehouse. J'anda greeted him with a nod. "Come to rest? There's a bed in a room on the top floor that's unoccupied."

"How is that?" Cyrus shook his head, trying to clear it from the fog of sleep and the spinning caused by his argument with Chirenya. "We've got a ton of people here."

"Yeah," J'anda said, "but most of them sleep during the day, when we're least likely to be attacked by the order of shadowy assassins, and we moved about half our number over to the house on the other side, taking over for Endeavor. They had to reshuffle people after their losses in the attack."

Cyrus sighed, a long, deep breath of tiredness leaving his body. "You'd think with as many people as Endeavor has, they'd be able to move more in to replace their losses."

The door squeaked behind him, and Isabelle stood framed in it, hands on her hips, causing her robe to cling to her frame, hinting at curves that weren't usually apparent through the white cloth. "Unfortunately, we'll be moving considerably more out." Her voice was laced with irritation. "I've been wondering when it would happen, and it has."

"What?" Cyrus looked at her with curiosity.

"The dark elves have moved two armies into position to hammer the Confederation lines around Reikonos," Isabelle began. "The humans are taking heavy losses south of the city, and the Council of Twelve has invoked Endeavor's Homestead clause." Her pretty face was filled with a putrid expression. "I've got to leave, and take every one of my guildmates. We're to report along with the rest of Endeavor for assignment at the front within forty-eight hours." She held up an envelope. "I'm sorry, but you'll have to take up the defense here yourselves."

Cyrus felt his stomach drop at Isabelle's words. *Reikonos*, he thought. *They've finally started moving on my city.* No matter that it had been years since he had lived there, no matter that there were more terrible memories there than pleasant ones, the human capital was still home to Cyrus. It hung there, in his mind, and always felt as though it were a warm blanket of comfort, waiting for him on the day he should need it.

He looked to J'anda; the dark elf was startled, even through the dwarven illusion he wore, but nodded. "I'll send one of our druids to Alaric and see what he can spare, in addition to that..." He looked at Cyrus. "...other request I already forwarded."

"Sorry to spring this on you." Isabelle's voice fell, along with her eyes. "I'm only one of our council and we have no guildmaster, unlike you. The others have been generous in assisting, and would doubtless have offered more, but this is an order we cannot refuse lest we be ejected from Reikonos."

"How would they eject one of the most powerful guilds from the city?" Cyrus spoke out of pure curiosity. "Your guild could destroy every city guard they have."

"They have a way, I assure you," Isabelle said with a shudder. "It was almost used once before when the Big Three made some defiant decisions and became somewhat intractable in our dealings. Regardless, you need to make preparations to defend Mother, Father and Vara." She raised her head, her chin jutted at Cyrus. "I would like a word with you in private."

"We can step out on the street..." he began after a moment's hesitation.

"No." She shook her head. "In private. I heard him —" she jerked her head toward J'anda —"say that there was a room available on the third floor."

"As good as elvish hearing is," Cyrus said, "I wonder if we might have to travel halfway to Prehorta to have a private conversation."

"And run into the dark elven host that's wrecking the human territories?" Her dark smile of amusement lasted only a moment before returning to seriousness.

He led her up the steps past a sitting room on the second floor filled with members of Sanctuary, and then to a small bedroom on the third floor in the back of the house.

"I heard your conversation with Mother," Isabelle began after shutting the door. "I wanted to caution you not to take anything she says to heart."

Cyrus felt a small laugh leave him before he could stop it. "Which part should I not take to heart? The part where she told me I was a selfish thief or the bit about how I'd stab Vara in the back like Archenous—or all the remarks about sex—because it never gets old, being taunted about the sex I'm not having—"

"With the woman you're in love with?" Isabelle cut him off, staring at his cheeks as they turned scarlet. "Yes, I know. It's obvious to those of us who have been around a few centuries, which is why Mother continues to bring it up even though she knows you've yet to do so much as touch Vara in an 'inappropriate' way."

"As if your sister would allow anyone to touch her inappropriately—"

"She would." Isabelle's eyes bored deep into his. "She would let you; not quite yet, but soon enough. That has Mother worried enough to try and drive you away."

He stood, his mouth agape. "I don't think you know what you're talking about—I mean, your sister—"

"Whom I have known much longer than you," she said. "She is vulnerable right now, but am I wrong in guessing she had grown more...pleasant toward you before this assassin business broke loose?"

He felt a curious stir of hope inside at her words. "Perhaps a little."

Isabelle rolled her eyes, a gesture that made her look more than a little like her sister. "For Vara, that's tantamount to crawling into your bed at night; but I believe she would have become perhaps more aggressive as time went on, less inhibited about her feelings for you."

"I have a hard time believing she has any feelings for me."

"I assure you, she does," Isabelle said. "While she is under considerable pressure and more distressed than ever I have seen her, you have been her stalwart, and she has turned to you more than anyone else besides myself and Mother."

Cyrus took a deep breath, uncertainty swirling, making him feel as if he were spinning. "Why are you telling me this?"

She took a step closer, cutting the distance between them, and raised a hand to his cheek. Her palm was warm, and smooth, and she smelled of flowers as she touched him. "Mother will try and drive a wedge between you. My sister is susceptible to her words, no matter how much she protests that she is not. Yet I see a possibility for her to be happier with you than any time previously." Her hand dropped to her side.

"But your mother was right. I will die long before Vara does." He felt the numbness prick at his heart, displacing the warm flutter of hope with cold reality.

She raised an eyebrow at him. "I would think that this assassin business would have convinced you of the foolishness of that. She could die any day, at any time. You are adventurers and should embrace happiness where you find it."

"I don't know how much longer she'll be an adventurer. She told me she's weary of the battles."

"She's not pleased about having her family thrust into this," Isabelle said. "Vara is a fighter and has been her whole life, even when she shouldn't have been." Isabelle laughed. "There is no one as ornery and combative as my sister, and so long as she draws a breath, she'll fight. She's low now, from the personal battles, just as she was when Archenous betrayed her, but if you see her through this, she'll rise again, stronger than ever." Isabelle's eyes glistened. "And she would make a most excellent consort—and wife—to you."

A ghost of a smile creased his lips. "You say that because you know that I'm the only one that can match her stubbornness."

Isabelle nodded, her hair rolling off her shoulder, her face in a near-smirk. "There are some very good reasons that you two are drawn to one another." She reached out again, this time grasping his hand, gauntleted as it was, and squeezed against the metal. "See her through this crisis, Cyrus Davidon, and hold to your hope; Vara could yet be yours."

Chapter 26

She left him alone after that. He spoke with J'anda about the things that needed to be done and all the while his head spun with alternating thoughts of Reikonos and Vara, Vara and Reikonos. *I should be there*, he thought. But always, another would counterbalance it: *I cannot leave Vara right now. If anything happened to her, I'd never forgive myself.*

But if Reikonos falls to the dark elves, I wonder if I'd be able to forgive myself either.

He awoke the next day after a fitful sleep to find the sitting room full downstairs, packed with both new arrivals and older defenders that Cyrus had seen day after day—Martaina, Thad, Longwell, Andren, Vaste and J'anda were there, as was Nyad and Ryin Ayend, whom Cyrus hadn't seen since the day he arrived, as well as Aisling, who greeted him with a more than friendly smile, and a smaller dark elf who slapped the helm off his head from behind as he entered.

"Nice to see you too, Erith," he said, stooping to retrieve it.

"You disappear in the dead of night after an assassination, not telling anyone, and tromp off to the Elven Kingdom?" The dark elven cleric's irises seemed to glow red in the morning light. "I'm not impressed, General Davidon." Erith Frostmoor glared at him with an icy intensity that fit her surname perfectly.

"That's not true," he said, pushing his helm back onto his head. "I told Thad."

"Like I said, you didn't tell anyone."

"Hey!" Thad interjected. "I am not no one!"

"What's the matter, Erith?" Cy kept his expression neutral. "Did I worry you?"

"Hell no. I was bored. Without you around, there's no one worthy to make fun of."

"Good to see you all," Cyrus said with a nod to each of them. "I take it Alaric sent us the reinforcements we asked for."

"Over protest from some of the Council," Ryin Ayend said with a hint of displeasure.

"What idiot would protest that?" Vaste's green skin turned a degree darker. "Not even Terian is soulless enough to deny Vara assistance in her hour of need."

Ryin Ayend flushed, as did Nyad at his side. "If you must know, it was me."

"You're not on the Council," Vaste said with an air of disbelief. "Sanctuary is not so poorly run."

"In your absence," Erith said, "additional officers were elected—you know, to help run things." She shrugged. "Alaric said you were planning to expand the Council, so he held elections and the members voted."

"They elected you?" Vaste pointed at Ryin Ayend. "Were there no bloodsucking leeches available for candidacy? No man-eating griffons?"

"They also elected Nyad and I," Erith said. "And Longwell."

"I say again, no leeches?" Vaste frowned. "The Realm of Fire is surely frosting over as we speak." He turned to Longwell. "No offense."

The dragoon shrugged, unconcerned. "First I've heard of it. Thanks...I think."

The front door swung open with a click, and Vara entered the room, now clad in a different dress than she had worn previously. This one was a deep green, and left her knees and the bottom of her thighs exposed. The neckline was cut lower than anything Cyrus had ever seen her wear before, revealing a surprising amount of cleavage. It took every ounce of willpower he possessed not to stare openmouthed at the change in the usually reserved paladin.

There was a stunned silence that filled the room at the sight of her clad in such attire, finally broken by Vaste's deadpan. "Somewhere in the distance, I'm certain I hear molten magma freezing and fire being turned to steam."

Vara's eyes narrowed. "I need no sarcasm from you, troll." She looked around the assemblage. "I heard shouting. What's going on?"

"Ryin, Nyad, Longwell and Erith have all been advanced to officer status in our absence," Andren said, a mug of ale in his hand. "Apparently, Ryin was not in favor of sending additional forces to help out here." He took a swig and then positioned his hands as if he were setting two sides against each other. "Now...fight."

"There is no need to fight," Vara said, inclining her head toward Ryin, who was stonefaced, and Nyad, who looked stricken. "It would be inappropriate to ask for guild assistance in this matter; it is a personal problem."

"It's not that," Nyad said, her high voice cracking. "I voted against it too, but not for that reason. We're more than happy to help you in a personal emergency, which this is, or in a matter of defending yourself and your family—which, again—"

"Fine," Vara said, interrupting the elven princess, her disdain for the wizard cutting through the facade of politeness she had displayed only a moment before. "Then what was your rationale?"

"Yes," Erith said, voice dripping with anticipation. "Tell them. I can't wait for the reaction to this."

Vara frowned at the dark elf. "I assure you that I can keep my composure, regardless of what they have to say."

Erith smiled with unrestrained glee. "It's not your reaction I'm referring to." She looked back to Nyad. "Please, do tell. The rest of you," she gestured around her, "sit back and enjoy."

Nyad was frozen in place, but Ryin Ayend spoke up. "In the two weeks since your flight after the assassination attempt, we've suffered a downturn in our activity, and it's adversely affecting the guild and morale."

Andren sat in his seat, his cup of ale extended only a few inches from his lips, expression frozen in befuddlement. "What?"

"What he means," Cyrus said, his voice filling the room with ice, "is that since I've left, there's no general to run our expeditions, so the Army of Sanctuary is sitting idle in the Plains of Perdamun rather than continuing our string of victories that has expanded our power and influence." He glared at Ryin Ayend and Nyad, but the druid didn't flinch away. Nyad did. "What's wrong? Afraid to lead an expedition yourself?"

"I'm not the general," the human said. "Until recently, I wasn't even an officer, so it wasn't my place to do so. You have a higher responsibility to the guild and a duty to fulfill—"

"You're going to have a hell of a time lecturing me about duty with my hands wrapped around your throat—"

Ayend emitted a disgusted noise. "Just like a warrior to move past civil conversation and straight to threats of violence—"

"—wasn't a threat so much as a promise—"

"—perfect representation of your 'all-groin, no-brain' leadership style—"

"—a leadership style it sounds like you're missing, you prissy little tree-loving—" Cyrus rose to his feet, enraged. Days of fatigue had taken their toll, and all the time spent without a target to fight had left him ready to battle anyone. *And this prancing little nebbish just happens to be the first to strut my way.*

"This was worth getting glared at by every elf I passed on the way here," Erith said with obvious glee.

"May I suggest we tone down the discord between officers of Sanctuary?" J'anda had stood and had both hands extended at Cyrus and Ryin, who was still seated.

"I've got no desire to fight him," Ayend said, "but if he takes another step toward me I'll defend myself." His hand was extended as if he were warning Cyrus to stop, but the warrior knew he kept it at the ready to cast a spell.

"A fine way to convince me to come back and lead Sanctuary in battles, pointing at me in a threatening manner," Cyrus snapped at the druid.

"I'm smaller than you and a spell is my only defense should you try and lay hands on me." The man's nose twitched.

Cyrus glared him down. "I'm not going to strike you, but I haven't ruled out grasping you by the neck and shaking you until I get tired of seeing your eyeballs rattle."

Ayend matched his glare. "Try it."

"I'm not leaving," Cyrus said, heated. "I'm not leaving Termina until Vara and her family are safe."

Vara stood silent a few steps behind him, looking around at the new arrivals, keeping her eyes from meeting Cyrus's. "What other news do you bring?"

Nyad spoke, wringing her hands. "Alaric has received a request from Pretnam Urides and the Council of Twelve; the Human Confederation has asked for Sanctuary's aid in defending Reikonos."

A moment's silence was pierced when Vara spoke. "I trust he declined?"

"He did," Nyad said. "He told them that to intervene would violate Sanctuary's neutrality and make us a target for the dark elves."

Cyrus felt his jaw clench. Before joining Sanctuary, the Council of Twelve that ruled the Confederation had been a mythical and wise decision-making body in his mind. *Now that Alaric has shown me their pettiness, I know that at least half are utter fools; reckless, stupid and responsible for the war that is ruining their lands. Our lands.*

"Alaric believed that keeping us out of the war was the wisest course for now. To act precipitously," Ryin said with another superior sniff of his nose, "might bring an unnecessary doom. Of course the Council agreed."

"What's left of it, you mean." Vaste wore a sour look—somewhat intimidating when on the face of a troll.

"The Sovereign of Saekaj Sovar will come knocking on Sanctuary's door at some point if he wins this war," J'anda said. "He still wants me dead, along with the rest of our dark elves." He shuddered. "And he does not forget his grudges."

"It matters not, for now," Vara said. "We have force enough to defend this place, even when Endeavor's troops leave. I..." She stumbled in her words, her voice breaking. "...thank all of you for your assistance."

Ryin Ayend stood, bowing his head. "Though I did not support sending additional forces, know that I volunteered to come here myself to aid you. Nyad as well. We would like to see this order of assassins dealt with. After all, we're edging close to the new year, and shortly thereafter, the winter solstice—it would a good tiding for the season."

Cyrus looked up from studying the lines of his gauntlet. "What's that?"

Ryin Ayend's voice rang out with a stark, derisive amusement. "It shouldn't surprise me; they don't teach you much in the Society of Arms, do they?"

Cyrus felt his soul blacken with rage at the druid's slight. "They spend their time focusing on what's important. Things like fashioning a weapon out of a severed arm and strangling an opponent with their own intestines." His voice became sharp as a blade. "Or your own, if that's what's available."

The shocked silence returned, broken once more by Vaste. "I bet that's come in handy."

The gathering broke shortly after that. The new arrivals greeted Vara with smiles and warm words, and in the case of Nyad, a hug that made the icy paladin stiffen like a cat about to be thrown into a tub of water, her expression a mask of annoyance.

When she broke free, to his surprise she came to him, her eyes brighter than when last he'd seen her. "My father," she began, and halted.

"Is he all right?" Cyrus felt a tremor of worry; not so much for the elven man lying on a bed across the street, but for Vara.

"He's...better," she said. "Still dying, but conscious and

coherent. He has asked to speak with you."

Cyrus stood still until the words sunk in. "Me?"

"Yes," she said with no lack of sarcasm. "Were I on my deathbed, I should seek to avoid you until the last, but he has called for you after Isabelle and Mother told him you have been my 'stalwart protector'." She frowned. "Their words, not mine."

"Of course."

He followed her across the street, into the illusory facade of the house next door, nodding in greeting to the warriors of Endeavor, stern and standing in a line, no longer playing cards in the corner. Something was different, though he could not put his finger on what it was. The warriors seemed...discomfited somehow. The dwarf was edgy, twitching as they passed on their way to the stairs.

The cellar's light seemed even dimmer, reflecting off the walls around him, the stones wet from moisture forming on them. A gleam could be seen in certain places, a yellow reflection of the torchlight on the wetness of the walls. Cyrus looked around and saw two of the spots glowed red. He paused, something waking in the back of his mind, and his hand fell to his sword.

"Too late," a voice rumbled. "If I'd meant to kill you, you'd both already be dead." The ground seemed to shake as a shadow taller than Cyrus separated itself from the wall and moved toward them, eyes glowing crimson. "I thought that sword was supposed to give you faster reflexes, but it appears to have made you slower and less wary."

"Fortin," Cyrus said with a nod. "For about a second there, you startled me."

The light shone upon the rock giant's torso, illuminating his craggy skin. Cyrus knew the truth, that although his flesh was near rock-hard, there was no rock anywhere on him, just a skin that could fend off swords and magic better than any mortal, other than perhaps a dragon. The smell he gave off was of dirt and mildest sulphur; earthy, an aroma that was pleasant but carried fearful memories that reminded Cyrus of facing the Dragonlord for the first time.

"For a second?" The rock giant's words carried annoyance. "I could give you another reason to be startled, this time for longer..." He feinted at Cyrus, who stood still and watched a rocky hand speed at his face, stopping an inch from his nose. "How was that?"

"Unconcerning," Cyrus said. "But be assured, if I didn't know you, I would have run screaming from the room."

The red eyes squinted down at him from the darkness. "No, you wouldn't. You are a warrior through and through, taught from an early age not to flinch from even the most devastating blow, yes?"

Cyrus looked to Vara, who was watching the exchange without interest. "I was."

Fortin began to recede, taking steps back to the wall of the cellar. "You would not have run; I am intimidating, I know. You were not merely trying to impress the Ice Princess, as some men would." A deep, booming laugh rumbled through the room and the rock giant seemed to bow, as best he could. "Ice Princess, your new garb displeases me; where is the metal skin you don for battle?"

"It waits for me, above," Vara answered. "But I am not sure that I want to keep wearing it."

Fortin nodded. "You've doubtless found one stronger. Ice Princesses seem to get many fine gifts; Fortin receives none."

"No, I haven't received a stronger set of armor," Vara answered him with a frown.

"Then what would you wear into battle?" The rumbling voice was baffled. "Surely not this flimsy cloth-skin; it exposes far too much of your soft flesh."

Cyrus caught the flash of danger in Vara's eyes and she wheeled on him, her glare warning him. "Say nothing." He held up his hands in surrender and kept his mouth shut.

"What would you wear into battle, then?" Fortin continued, ignoring her outburst.

"I'm...I'm not certain I'll be going into battle for the forseeable future." Her voice was weak again; the fatigue had set in once more.

"I suppose there will always be a strong warrior such as this one around," Fortin nodded at Cyrus, "easily bent to your commands so long as you continue to display ample flesh." The rock giant shook his head. "I remain uncertain what it is about the chests of women that so fascinate these ones, but they seem to worship those flesh mounds you carry in the front of your clothing; with them I think you could keep a constant guard surrounding you."

Cyrus heard a grinding noise and realized with no surprise

that it was Vara's teeth, her jaw clenched hard enough that he wondered if bits of enamel were splintering in her mouth. "Thank you for that observation," he said, and hurled himself through the opening in the wall before Vara had calmed down enough to respond. His boots clattered upon the stairs, but below he heard the softer footfalls of Vara's leather-clad feet a moment later.

He slowed when he reached the second floor, where a quick glance revealed Isabelle's door was shut and Chirenya sat in the chair that she had awoken him from the day before. She stared out the window, and even the sound of him behind her did not seem to stir her from her reverie.

"Come along," Vara said as she passed him, her long legs carrying her up.

"Right behind you," he said, taking a last look at Chirenya, who still had not moved.

She halted before the door to her parents' chamber and turned back to him, one hand on the doorknob and the other held up, her index finger extended, her eyes aflame. "Do not assume that because I have required help in this matter, or that because I have grown weary of fighting, that I am some weak, defenseless princess, waiting for a strong man to come along and save me." She snapped out every word.

"I have never thought of you as weak nor helpless," Cyrus said, "as demonstrated by the fact that even though you are unarmed and wearing a dress that gives you one tenth of your usual strength in battle—not to mention coverage of your skin— I'm still backpedaling from your ire."

She narrowed her eyes at him, as though she were searching for some sign of sarcasm. "Very well." She moved to turn to the door, but he caught her hand and stopped her. "What are you...?"

He held up his index finger to his own mouth, as if to shush her, and he cut the distance between them to inches, causing her eyes to widen in surprise. "I have never doubted your strength or your courage. I am here to aid you not because you require my help or the help of any others, but because the loyalty and fidelity you have sowed in Sanctuary should be repaid at your hour of greatest need."

Her look of surprise softened, but she still maintained an air of discomfort at his closeness. "I...thank you. But, if you could..." She gestured for him to take a step back.

"No," he said. "I can't." He leaned in close to her and she made to take a step back in alarm, but stopped when her shoulders made soft contact with the door. His hand found her chin and he applied only the gentlest pressure to it, holding it straight. She did not fight him, though her eyes were wide as he brought his mouth closer; they closed when their lips met and he kissed her. He felt her hand against his shoulder, the gentlest pressure, and she leaned into him and kissed him back.

When they parted she looked up at him, breathing deeply, his forehead still pressed to hers, her arms wrapped around him. She swallowed and her hands left his back. She turned, placing her hand on the doorknob, but did not turn it. She paused then spun back to him, her countenance clouded with suspicion and her finger raised once more. "Did you do that because you see me as some sort of 'damsel in distress'? Because, if so—"

He leaned in and cut her off with another kiss, and this time she relaxed more quickly, her arms wrapping around him and her tongue parting his lips, finding his, swirling around in his mouth to his surprise and delight. This time, he broke from her. "I didn't do it because I see you as a damsel in distress. I did it because I finally plucked up the courage to do what I've wanted to do for the last two years." He looked down at her. "And maybe a little because of that dress."

Her hand rested on her breastbone, just below her neck as she tried to catch her breath, her face awash in conflicting emotions. The somewhat serene look turned once more into a frown. "You can face death countless times in the form of dragons, titans, spiders, rock giants, bandits, goblins, instruments of the gods and more without fear, but it took you two years to find the courage to kiss me?"

His mouth hung open. "I...uh...well...to be honest..."

"If the next words out of your mouth are some variation on the idea that I am in some way scarier than all of those things—"

"It's not that you're 'scarier'." He picked his words with care, noting the danger in her eyes. "But if I died facing any of those things, I can be resurrected." He took a deep breath. "If I tried to kiss you and found out that you didn't feel the same way I did..." He let his words trail off.

She looked down. "I see. So you feared that I would leave you rejected? Cast off?"

"Yes. So what say you?"

She looked at him in confusion. "What say I about what?"

"A kiss returned under these circumstances could mean anything — it could be that you're so weary that you don't have the energy to denounce me the way you would if I'd attempted this on a normal day at Sanctuary. That I've caught you when you're vulnerable, or in a rare moment of gratitude and you don't want to say 'no'. But I need — " his hands came to rest on her shoulders and he tried to look in her eyes — "I need you to tell me the truth."

She gave him a subtle nod but did not meet his eyes. "Hm. Well."

He felt as though he had taken a deep breath and was holding it, even though he was doing no such thing. The hopes he felt when she kissed him back were still just embers, waiting to catch fire. "Admit it. You have feelings for me." He pasted a fake grin on his face, and hoped that she would confirm what he had always suspected.

She met his gaze after rolling her eyes. "Fine, I admit it. I do have feelings for you. Or at least *a* feeling — and it is called loathing." She sighed after seeing the look on his face, the disappointment he was unable to contain at her words. "Oh, all right. I do. You...cause a great disquiet in me, upending my simple life and view of things. And it has been so since..." She hesitated. "Well, for quite some time."

He cringed. "I don't know if that's good or bad."

This time her sigh was a sharp exhalation as she leaned forward, pulling him close to her, her lips finding his. He felt her hands on his cheeks, her touch causing him to warm from top to bottom. When she broke off, this time she wore the slightest smile. "My father waits for you within, you know. He told me to bring you to him so that he could thank you for protecting me — and our family."

Cyrus took a breath, his face flushed with excitement, his stomach churning and the steady thrum of his heart in his ears. "I suppose I should go in and speak with him."

Vara smiled at him — a long, slow one that spread to the corners of her mouth and lit her whole face in a way that he had seen few times since he had known her. She was resplendent, radiant, her skin carrying a flush of its own. "Yes, you should. But he can wait while I thank you for myself." She leaned in and kissed him again.

He soon enough forgot about the old man waiting above, the rock giant below, his guildmates across the street, the assassins somewhere outside, and everyone else, as he lost himself in her touch, her kiss, her softness, and the bluest eyes he had ever seen, alive once more after being filled with despair for so long.

Chapter 27

He entered the room a few minutes later, and watching him from the bed was the elven man that he had yet to see conscious. Vara's father wore a light silken shirt that split in a V, revealing his chest, sunken with age and spotted. He had gray hair around the sides of his head but none on top, and his skin was much darker than his daughter's. His face was cracked with a smile as Cyrus entered. The elf waved him over, extending his hand in the customary human (not elven) greeting.

"I have heard much about you," he said in thickly accented human. "My wife and daughters say you..." He struggled with the words. "...have protected them. Although if my ears do not deceive me, I suspect other...reasons?" He thought for a moment. "Motives," he decided. "That is the word."

Cyrus grasped Vara's father's hand and realized he did not know the man's name. "I am Cyrus Davidon, and I have had the honor and privilige of serving with your daughter as an officer in Sanctuary over the last two years. She inspires such loyalty that it was only natural that we would come to her aid when needed."

The old man studied him. "She inspires many things, and I am pleased that loyalty is among them. My name is Amiol—I doubt you would have heard it but through talking with Chirenya, as my daughters would call me—"

"Taedaron," Cyrus finished for him. "In the Human language, we say 'father'."

Amiol nodded. "I am of the old generation. Fifty-seven hundred years old," he said with pride. "I did not learn any of your language until nearly a thousand years ago, so you must..." He paused, searching for a word. "...forgive? Yes. Forgive me, but we did not trade with humans until then, and I have never been good with your words."

"It's all right," Cyrus said. "I speak a little elvish."

"Somehow we will make it through this," Amiol said with a chortle that turned into spasming cough that lasted for nearly a minute. Cyrus started toward the door, but felt the elf's still-strong hand grip his arm, holding him back. "I am fine. You have my thanks, for Vara. For keeping her safe."

He felt the ghostly aftertouch of her lips on his. "It was my duty as her guildmate."

"It was that and more," Amiol said with a glimmer in his eyes. "It was long ago I was a man your age, but don't think that I am so enfeebled that I cannot remember it."

"I would never doubt it."

"I think back on my youth," he said with a sigh. "I am like you; I know no magic. But I was fair with a sword, and fought in my share of battles in the days when we were at the throats of the dark elves, like your people are now." His eyes drifted away, and Cyrus had the sense that he was reliving things from long ago. "I was in the army when it was a shining pinnacle, the spear of Elvendom — before we were united into the Kingdom. I traveled to your human lands, to Reikonos, when it was the Citadel and little else."

"When was that?" The vision of Vara filled Cyrus's head. The remembrance of her touch caused his blood to rush, and he had to work to listen to the elder elf.

"Three thousand? Four thousand years ago?" Amiol shook his head. "It feels like...how do you say? The day before today?"

"Yesterday." *Yesterday I hadn't kissed your daughter yet.* It already felt so long ago.

"Yesterday..." The words came out of the elf's mouth in a slow hiss, thickly accented. "So many of those times seem like yesterday, even though they were millenia ago."

Cyrus pondered that; living thousands of years, watching entire cities grow up. *Reikonos has been the largest city in the world for my entire life,* he thought. *Yet when this man was halfway through his life, it barely existed.*

"You wonder what it would be like to live so long?" Amiol stared at him. Cyrus had not realized he had drifted off, captivated by the question. "It is not so different from your life, I expect, but more of everything — more experiences, more things you have learned, more wounds, more pain, more pleasure, more love." He made a sound of dry amusement. "I have heard humans call elves wise but I suspect we would look foolish compared to someone who has lived so much longer than us. How old are you?"

It took Cyrus a moment to realize the question was pointed at him. "Nearly thirty."

"A child among our people, and yet a man grown among your own." He nodded and stared off into the distance. "Fit to have lands, be married and have children of your own." Refocusing on Cyrus, he asked, "But you have no children of your own? No wives?"

Cyrus cleared his throat. "Humans aren't allowed to have more than one at a time...and no, I don't have a wife. Nor children." *But perhaps...*

Amiol paused. "I was old when I met Chirenya; or I should say she was young. Now I am older still, and she remains as youthful and lovely as the day I met her." He smiled in memory. "And still as stubborn, willful and damnably frustrating."

"I heard that," came a voice from the broken window, wafting up from the floor below.

"Then you heard the 'lovely' part as well, and I'll thank you to take that to heart and stop eavesdropping," he muttered in elvish, still smiling. Amiol folded his withered hands across his chest. "My days come to a close, which is a time of great sorrow among my people, since it comes so rarely. My brothers and sisters, of which there were eighteen, have all preceded me into the beyond." A flicker of sadness lay upon the old man's features. "Because I married so late, and had children even later, I was unable to finish all I needed."

"How do you mean, sir?"

"My eldest daughter is a woman grown," he said. "Tough like her mother, but lighter of disposition. Capable of making her own decisions now, of—" he lowered his voice—"throwing off the yolk of her mother's opinions on how to run her life."

"I heard that too!" Chirenya's voice once more came from below, shattering the calm.

"The illusion on the house doesn't redirect your voice," Cyrus said. He waited for a response, but there was none.

"My youngest daughter is still a child among my people," Amiol said. "She will not be considered an adult until her hundredth year—though she is capable." He smiled. "I still remember the day she was..." He struggled again. "...the day she came from her mother...we would say, 'shelas'."

Cyrus frowned, befuddled. "Hope?"

Amiol looked at him, confused. "No, the day her mother...she came forth from her mother, the day she was...ah...uh..."

Cyrus felt a chill, once more unrelated to the wintery air seeping in through the broken windows. "Born?" His voice was high, his mouth suddenly dry.

"Yes!" Amiol exulted. "I remember the day she was born, so small, but she had a full head of hair, if you can believe..."

The old elf went on, but Cyrus's thoughts buzzed in his head, overwhelming everything that Amiol was saying. Words spun, whirling in his skull, the same two, over and over, and he felt the fool. He thought of the Chancel, of the streets, combing his memory, confirming what he'd seen in his mind's eye, something so odd, and yet undefined; inexplicable at the time.

Shelas'akur, he thought.

Last born.

Chapter 28

He shut the door behind him a few minutes later, leaving the elder elf behind. Chirenya passed him on the stairs, shooting him an accusatory gaze and closing the door behind her. The rest of his conversation with Amiol had passed with leaden speed, as though Cyrus were having it whilst his head was underwater. It dragged, painful in places, as Amiol tried to engage him with questions that he could not find any answers for within the depths of his preoccupation.

Last born, he thought again. *Last born.*

His boots on the stairs made a sound similar to someone knocking on a door. He came off the landing to the second floor and saw her waiting for him at the door to her room, leaning against the frame with her hands behind her, a sly smile resting on her lips that—had this been only minutes before—would have excited him beyond belief at the possibilities.

Now he only wanted to ask questions.

He walked toward her, all thought of her posture gone, the memory of the kisses they'd shared far out of his mind. He brushed past her, eliciting a look of confusion as he strode into the room and stood at the window. "What?" she asked.

He did not look back. "Were you listening?"

"I am not so rude as my mother," she said, creeping up behind him and placing a hand upon his back. "It takes concentration to eavesdrop; I chose not to."

"I see," he said, quiet. "Your father reminisced about the day you were born. Except he didn't say born, because he couldn't remember it; he used the elvish word, trying to bring its human counterpart to mind." Even through his armor, he felt the pressure from her hand increase subtly. "Shelas'akur," he said with a mirthless laugh. "I had it all wrong."

She pulled away. "Not entirely."

"You had to be laughing when I said it the first time," he said, shaking his head. "I was so sure it was 'last hope'."

"It is," she said, "and I did not laugh at you because of it. Not only because we were in no position to be laughing at the time, with Niamh dead just moments before, but because you were close—too close—to the truth of it."

Cyrus felt his hand reach up and grasped at a piece of the window frame, plucking a splinter from it. "How was I close?"

She walked the length of the room, back to the chair she had been in the day before when they had talked. "It's a funny trick of language," she said, hands curled up in her lap. "Thirty or so years ago, the meaning of 'shelas' was 'born'. And then, suddenly, on the day of my birth, it was 'hope' and has been ever after." She let go the trace of a smile. "It's a funny thing."

He turned to her. "There are no more elven children, are there?"

"I am the last," she said in a ghostly voice, hollow. "The last of the pure-blood elves; the shelas'akur. The last born."

"It's what keeps bothering me about this city; there are almost no kids playing in the streets! That's why there are so few children in Termina," Cyrus said. "It's why all the ones I've seen have been half-elves."

"Yes," she said in the same voice. "Humans have become the most popular mating choice for elven women, since elven men can no longer produce children."

"How..." His mouth was filled with the dry dust of the revelation. "How is that?"

She placed her hands on the arm of the chair and used her grip to pull herself to her feet. "No one is sure, but I can say for certain that the Elven Kingdom has not produced a viable generation in over a thousand years. There were fewer and fewer births over the last millennium, until, after my sister's generation—about 1500 children spread out over the course of 300 years—they stopped entirely." She held her chin high. "There was a 250 year gap with no births, not a single one—and then, mysteriously, thirty years ago..."

"You were born." His hand was on his chin, and he was deep in thought. "But why the secret? Why hide this from everyone? Perhaps the humans or someone else could help?"

She laughed at him, but there was no joy in it. "They are the reason we did not tell anyone, the other races. Our lack of ability in breeding puts us at a dreadful disadvantage, wouldn't you say? For every elf killed in a war, we cannot replace them. In a thousand years," she said with doom, "we will have no army— and no Kingdom left because all who remain will be too old to defend it."

"But I've seen children," he said. "Hybrids. Can't they help carry on for your people?"

"Don't say that in front of my mother," she said with a wistful smile. "It may come to that, but let us face it—children of two worlds, humans and elves, for example, do not live as long and they have just as much blood tying them to Reikonos as to Pharesia. That's to say nothing of the complete and utter desperation it has produced in elven men. Even with human women they are infertile; thus it falls to the elven women to propagate what is left of the species—well." She grimaced. "Almost."

"Almost?" He shook his head, staggered at all he had learned in the last half-hour.

"I am the last hope." Her bearing was straight and regal. "There has been a great deal of interest—and pressure—on me."

Cyrus felt a tingle across his scalp as the full weight of what she said hit him. "They want you to...uh..."

She stared at him with grim amusement. "You've got the right of it. My mother would have me, the last born of the elven race, mate with a good pure blood elf as soon as I reach the age of elven maturity, if not sooner." A sneer of disgust drove her beauty away for a flash. "And gods know, there have certainly been enough offers, for when the time comes; high born, low born, royals. 'Just lay back and think of Pharesia,' is my mother's advice." Clouds darkened her face. "I had other intentions for my life, which is why I left."

"Do you still?" His words were quiet, but almost accusatory. "Have other plans?"

"Yes," she replied, just above a whisper. He heard the soft ruffle of her dress as she moved closer to him. "A bit...worse for the wear of late, but I still have...hopes...dreams...things I would like to accomplish. I think..." Her hands found his breastplate and laid there. "...I may find some fight left in me, once I get past this trial." She looked up at him, and though some of the despair had returned, there was hope in her eyes as well. She kissed him again, this time gentle and short. "I am somewhat vulnerable right now, as you pointed out. I hope you find it acceptable to...take things slowly."

Ignoring that his body called out for her, cried for him to sweep her up in his arms and carry to her to the bed, he answered, "That's fine. We can take things as slow as you want."

"Thank you," she said, taking his hands with her own. "I

would not have what I hope to be pleasant thoughts and memories of our time together compromised by all the disasters currently upon us."

Our time together. He froze, thinking of the fact that their time together, however long it lasted, would be limited by his lifespan, not hers. He put it aside. *She has enough on her mind. Let's not bring any more doubts and fears to add to the pile.*

"I'm going to go speak with my father," she said. "Will you wait for me?"

"Of course." He bowed to her, exaggerated, and she laughed.

"Do you mock me, sir?"

He tried to contain his smile, but failed. "Must I stop? Because I doubt you'll keep from making witticisms at my expense."

She laughed again. "Do you like the sound of my voice?"

"I do; it's like a pleasant ringing of bells or the tinkling of a windchime."

"If you like the sound of it that much, I must continue to make fun of you, else I'd seldom speak." She grinned wickedly.

"You were named for Vidara, weren't you?" He stared down at her; even though she was tall, he was mountainous.

"Aye. Because of the 'miracle' of my birth, they gave thanks to the Goddess of Life."

"Perhaps they should have named you after Terrgendan, God of Mischief."

She slapped him on his shoulder. "The Trickster! He's hideous. What are you trying to say?"

He caught her hand as she raised it to smack him again. "That you're mischievous, that's all."

She drew her hand away and turned to walk out the door, halting after opening it. "Wait for me. I'll be back shortly."

"I've been waiting for you for two years; I doubt another hour or two will make much difference."

She smiled, wicked again. "Perhaps, once this is all over with, we can give you a chance to get all that obsessive staring at feminine nakedness out of your system." She walked away, and beneath the folds of her dress, he watched her hips move with a sway that was much more difficult to notice in armor.

When he emerged from the room a few moments later, the sitting room was empty. *I wonder when we'll get these windows fixed,* he thought, shivering from the cold. He heard a squeak and a door opened behind him; Isabelle's door. The healer slid into the room, sly smile on her face. She looked at him and shook her head as if to say, *See?* "You were right," he said.

"Of course," she said, smug.

"I damn you both, your rightness and all else." Chirenya stood at the staircase, fury cloaking her.

Cyrus held his place by the door to Vara's room, unmoving, and unsure which was colder; the anger coming off the woman or the blustery wind coming through the broken windows behind him. "When you thought I was sexually gratifying your daughter you were insulting and demeaning, but not pissed off like this."

"Because then you were but an ignorant ox, unaware of the import of her destiny, of the vital nature of her future." It seemed to Cyrus that a winter storm had swept into the room during the conversation and was swirling around the woman, chilling the air to the coldest he'd felt since he arrived in Termina. "Now you know what's at stake—you know, and you have chosen to act selfishly, all while she's emotionally vulnerable."

"As much as you elves hate to admit it," Cyrus said, grinding out his words with a rough satisfaction, desirous of bursting her arrogance as though it were a full wineskin, "she is a grown woman, capable and mature—"

"By the standards of your child-race," Chirenya snapped back. "You may breed like rabbits in six weeks, but not us. Not elvendom."

"As I understand it, at this point you don't breed at all," Cyrus said. He saw Isabelle cringe at his slight; Chirenya, for her part, simply grew more furious. "Placing the survival of the elven race on her shoulders is hardly fair," he said, pre-empting Vara's mother before she could respond to his jab.

"Too true," Isabelle said. "It's an unfair assumption to think she is immune to the infertility that plagues the rest of our race simply because she's the only elf born in two hundred years."

"It may be unfair, but she could at least try!" Chirenya's words came out as more of screech than a coherent sentence. "You did!"

"With my husband, when I was married, yes. With how many men would you have her try?" Isabelle said, expression laced with irony. "Fifty? One hundred? One thousand?"

"As many as it takes!" Chirenya's eyes were wide with rage, the fury of someone in absolute fear. "As many as it takes to save our race—our way of life—from extinction!"

"Should she bed them all at once, or would it be acceptable to wait a while between attempts?" Isabelle had a tired look, like someone who had had this discussion many times before.

"What do you think, Cyrus?" Vara looked down at them from the stairwell, eyes narrowed. "Being human, your culture has a somewhat different norm, but have you ever before heard of a mother attempt to convince her daughter to become a whore?"

"The situation is grave." Chirenya was quiet now, her eyes lowered. "We stand no chance of survival; you are our — "

"Last hope? Sounds somewhat familiar, as though the words had been repeated so often as to lose all meaning." She trod the stairs, her steps quick, dress whipping behind her. "But being the shelas'akur, perhaps I have a somewhat unique perspective; the men of our race can no longer have children. Not with elven women, not with any race. The women are still fertile, and have babies with humans, dark elves, even a dwarf or gnome, should they be so inclined. Therefore it follows that I am likely fertile, just as the other women of our race are.

"Everyone shouts the name shelas'akur without thinking of the true implications," she went on. "Because if the men are the problem, the only way I'd be a genuine hope to you is if I were a *man* and fertile."

"You are a symbol," Chirenya said, stepping toward her youngest daughter. "You are something that people can believe in when times are dark. You haven't been here in the last years, you don't know; a people without children, without babies, they have no hope. They watch their friends and neighbors grow old and infirm around them and see no youth and vitality springing up to replace it!"

"I have no desire to be a false symbol." Vara took the last steps to the bottom of the stairs. "I have even less interest in doing so whilst giving up my own freedom of choice. If I want to bed a human man," she pointed at Cyrus, "I shall, and to the hells with anyone who dislikes it. If I someday choose to marry and have children with a human, a dark elf or even a troll — "

"Vaste would be pleased to hear you say that," Cyrus said.

" — then I will do so," she finished. "False hope is worse than none at all, and to believe that I am some miracle that will save the pure-blood elves from this calamity is cruel — to them and to me." She looked to Cyrus. "Would you wait for me outside? I'm in the mood for a walk but I'd like to change first." She brushed past him gently and closed the door to her room. He wordlessly walked past Isabelle, who followed him, and Chirenya, who said nothing, lost in her own thoughts.

When they reached the cellar, Isabelle stopped on the stair above him, causing Cyrus to look back when he heard her footsteps halt. "It's time for me to leave. When you come back, I'll be gone. I wanted to wish you good luck, and..." She stopped, as though unsure of what to say.

The dark pervaded the cellar, but he saw the glint of her hair in the daylight coming from the door, open above them. "I'll protect her," he said.

"You'd better." Her eyes blazed in the dark and he saw her clench her fist. "She's worth fighting for."

He took a step up. "So is Reikonos. Keep her safe for me, will you?"

A cocky smile appeared on her lips. "The dark elves haven't faced the 'Big Three' before. I doubt their armies will know what hit them. We'll send them scurrying back to their mysterious Sovereign so brutally that they'll swear Quinneria herself was leading the Confederation armies again."

"I have no doubt."

She turned but paused, as if she wanted to say something else. Her face was a mixture of regret and sadness. "Please...with Vara, just...be careful."

"With the assassins or with...uh..."

"With both," Isabelle said. Her grace was evident, and she looked statuesque staring down at him, the very picture of elvenly grace. "She still bears the scars of Archenous, and to proceed unduly might...inflame them. Be slow and gentle."

"As much as a simple warrior can muster, m'lady." He nodded to her in respect.

"I know you will. Farewell, Cyrus Davidon." She raised her hand. "I suspect we shall meet again 'ere too long."

"I sincerely hope." He found he meant every word of it; the healer was truly one of the most shrewd and yet sweet persons he had met. *I wonder if that comes from being old enough that you're wiser than humans and yet young enough in elven terms to not lose your youthful vitality?*

She left him, closing the door as he continued into the cellar. A rough, rumbling laugh greeted him when he stepped through the hole into the other house. "Ice Princess kisses, huh?" Fortin's rocky face could hardly be described as expressive, yet the giant seemed to be leering at him. "Knew you'd get around to it someday. Or was she controlling you with those fleshy mounds on her chest?"

"Someday you'll learn that those fleshy mounds damn near rule Arkaria," Cyrus said, turning his back on the rock giant. "Those and the gods, and I'm honestly not sure which holds more sway."

He reached the street and thought about walking across the street to the other house, to check preparations. *No*, he told himself. *For once I will back off and trust to let the others handle this duty. I will simply...wait.*

And he did, the minutes passing as sound came from the broken windows above; argument of some kind, muffled enough that it was not obvious what was being said, just that voices were raised. A slamming door could be heard, and then silence.

Cyrus waited on the walk, the wind swirling around him. He had grabbed his traveling cloak from where he'd hung it by the door on the way out of the house, and it helped. The metal of his armor was growing chill, even through the clothes he wore beneath it. The trees on the street maintained some leaf, though he saw some ice forming in the gutters. He stamped his feet, trying to get warm as he watched his breath fog the air in front of him.

I can't believe I kissed her, he thought, feeling like a young warrior again. *I can't believe she kissed me back. I should have done that years ago.* The thought warmed him, and then he shivered as he remembered the first time he kissed his wife. *This time, things will be different. She's an adventurer, after all. Or at least she was.*

The door opened and out Vara stepped, her hair bound once more behind her in a tight knot, the dress gone and replaced with the shining silver breastplate and armor, which sparkled in the light, drawing his attention to her chest. "And still is," he said under his breath.

"Perhaps, eventually, we'll break you of that staring," she said with a smile. "Though hopefully not anytime soon." She held out a mailed hand to him. "Come along then."

He took her hand and fell into step beside her. They walked to the corner of the street, where Thad was positioned, looking toward the Entaras'iliarad with great interest. When Cyrus called out to him, he looked back, then did a double take when he saw Vara's hand conjoined with Cyrus's. "What news, Thad?"

The warrior in the red armor shook his head. "Not sure. Heavy movement down the main thoroughfare to the bridge." He chucked a thumb over his shoulder. "Looks like the citizenry are heading toward the river for some reason."

Cyrus saw, even from blocks away, that there was indeed a massing crowd heading east along the main avenue. Other elves were stepping out of their homes all around and walking in small clusters toward the Entaras'iliarad, talking in hushed voices.

"Any idea what it is?" Cyrus looked around, trying to overhear conversations, but none were audible. He turned to Vara, whose head was cocked in concentration. "What?"

"Shhh." She held a finger up to his lips. He looked to Thad, who nodded approval. A smell of acridness wafted past him, something foul and unpleasant that filled his nostrils, faintly at first, then growing in strength until he could almost taste it, a bitter, burnt flavor in his mouth. Vara continued to listen, her eyes slitted in deep concentration. Chatter of a thousand voices and a far-off tumult to the east were all he could hear, but her finger remained on his lips, pressing softly against them.

After another moment, Vara's head snapped back and she looked stricken as the blood drained from her face. She hesitated then started to say something to him and stopped, her eyes wide.

"What?" He grasped at her arm, holding her as lightly as he could. "What is it?"

When she recovered, she took a deep breath before meeting his gaze. "The dark elves have an army across the river right now." She was nearly breathless from the news, and her eyes conveyed regret for having to tell them. "They're sacking Santir as we speak."

Chapter 29

"Dammit." Cyrus tried to look east down the cross street they stood on, but it ended in a row of houses on the next road. Small pillars of black smoke hung in the sky above. "It must be the same army that burned Prehorta; the one that's been cutting off the Confederation from the Plains of Perdamun."

"Aye," Thad replied. "This'll pretty much finish it if they've left garrisons in place in the towns they've taken. The Confederation won't be able to ship food nor anything else north if they hold Santir; they'll control all the shipping that comes up the river as well." He cocked his head. "You don't think they'd come across into Termina, do you?"

"Doubtful," Vara said. "It would mean dragging the elves into the war; the Sovereign would have to be barking mad to consider fighting on two fronts."

Something about that bothered Cyrus, though he couldn't put his finger on what. "Nothing about this war has made sense, not a thing from the outset until now." He looked east once more and could see the billowing smoke above the skyline. "We should go. Thad...keep watch. If ever there was a moment to strike when we're distracted, this is it."

The warrior nodded. "Wait here a minute and I'll get a few others to go with you."

"No," Vara said. "Let's not wait."

"Sure, it's only your life," Cyrus said. "Nothing so important that we'd bother to take five minutes and gather a few people to protect you from the countless assassins that want you dead."

"Exactly." She began stalking down the street without him. "Come along."

Cyrus shot a pleading look at Thad. "Tell them to hurry." He ran to catch up with her.

When they arrived at the Entaras'iliarad, they blended into the crowd, Cyrus taking care to keep a hand clutched around Vara's arm at all times. She looked back at him, giving him with a smile that cut the cold air. "Feeling particularly protective now, are we? Could it be you're anticipating something at the conclusion of all this?" Her smile was teasing.

"Could be. It has been a while." His reply was curt, and

infused with tension.

She looked away. "You're worried about the Confederation; about the outcome of this battle."

He hesitated. "This does not bode well for Reikonos. They're losing a good portion of their food supply and the dark elves will be well positioned to harrass any shipping that comes up the river bound for Confederation lands."

"You're worried it will come to a siege?" People edged around them on all sides, but the noise of the crowd made it unlikely anyone could hear them. "The dark elves are still at considerable distance from your capital and facing the toughest defenders your people have."

"Aye, but the humans haven't won a battle since the outset of the war." Cyrus felt the uncomfortable ache of his shoulder for the first time in days. "When you lose long enough, the momentum shifts against you and it gets hard to see a path to victory."

"If the Council of Twelve has summoned Endeavor to their defense they'll have brought Amarath's Raiders and Burnt Offerings into the fold as well." She spoke with assurance, and he realized she was attempting to be comforting. "An army of one hundred thousand would fall to defeat against a guild with one-tenth their strength. No nation possesses magic users in the numbers guilds do, and being able to heal wounds and resurrect fighters presents a decisive advantage in combat."

"We don't know that the dark elves don't have guilds of their own to summon to service." The buildings around the avenue had ice frosted on the panes and a thin layer lay over the gutters, causing people to slip, slowing the progress of the crowd. Cyrus could see the bridge rising in the distance. "They could have a hundred guilds fighting for them."

"Doubtful. But I believe they have at least one." He looked at her quizzically and she answered, "Goliath."

He swore, loudly enough that it attracted attention, shocked looks on the faces of nearby elves. "That's where they ended up? I should have known. But I thought the Sovereign of Saekaj didn't forgive his transgressors."

"Apparently he does when you bring an army of several thousand along with you."

They struggled along for a few more minutes, buffeted by the throng of elves around them. Cyrus took care not to use his strength and armor to plow through unimpeded. Vara was not so reluctant.

"Out of the way," she said, shoving aside an elven man.

He stumbled and turned to say something to her, anger writ on his features, when he stopped. "My apologies, shelas'akur. This one did not intend to be in your way." He bowed and spread his arms, using them to push people out of her way as he scooted back. "Make way for the shelas'akur!" The crowd began to part before them.

"Bloody right," she said under her breath. She turned to Cyrus. "I was never much for abusing my status, but occasionally it comes in handy."

"Yes," Cyrus said, voice tight. "A brilliant time to draw attention to yourself, when there are people about who want you dead."

"Please. If I waited to draw attention to myself until no one wanted me dead, I'd never say a word."

The crowd parted. Cyrus looked back constantly, trying to see if the protectors Thad was sending were nearby, but he could not see anything through the crowd. When he looked forward, the span of the bridge blocked his view save for the black smoke filling the eastern sky.

As they drew close to the river, Cyrus felt something small and white land on his cheek. Then another, and another. He ran his gauntlet where it landed and drew his finger to look more closely at it. "Snow?" he murmured aloud.

"No," Vara replied, rubbing her own cheek where some had landed. "Ash." A black smear remained, dampening her usually pale complexion. "From the fires in Santir."

His reaction was visceral and unexpected, a sudden tightening of the muscles in his guts. *I know they're burning the town and plundering everything of value, but the thought of it...* He shook his head in disgust as they followed the road along the river, and the smell of the smoke overwhelmed him. The scent of it was so thick in the air that it filled his nose and mouth, leaving an ashy taste on his tongue.

"Thank Vidara there's not wind today," he heard a passerby say. He had to agree with that; if there had been wind, it would likely have come off the river, delivering so much smoke that breathing would have been well nigh impossible. As it was, more ash streamed down as the fires grew. Although smoke hung over Santir, it hung mostly over the far side of town. The river was still visible, small floes of thin ice on the banks of the dark waters of the river Perda.

The loud voices quieted at the edge of the river and held almost a funereal air. Grim realization set in on those watching their neighboring city burn; the homes, shops and citizens of Santir consumed by the flames and turned loose into the air in the columns of black that blotted out the sky. Cyrus looked across the water from the railing at the raised street that ran parallel to the river. A hundred feet below was a host of docks accomodating the ships that navigated the river. Stairs cut into the side of the riverbank led to the shoreside quay. The wharf was filled with elves observing the destruction.

"I can't see," Vara said. "You, move." Her voice held such command that people moved without even looking at her.

"Not much to see," Cyrus said. Being taller than the crowd had advantages. Across the river, the dark elven army still held in perfect formation near one of the dockside roads in Santir. "Looks like they've got forces massing by the river after marching through the town." He shook his head. "Santir is all wood construction; it's going to burn fast." *And along with it goes the last route for half of Reikonos's supply of grain.*

"The humans never stood a chance," Cyrus overheard someone say. Vara shoved someone out of the way and a few muffled utterances of aggravation were replaced by quiet breathings of "shelas'akur" in utter reverence.

Vara's metal gauntlets clanked as they wrapped around the cold metal railing and she looked across the river, then closed her eyes. "They never did, you know." She opened her eyes and turned to him. "We were through there not long ago and they had barely a garrison of guards. That dark elven host has to be—"

"A hundred thousand," came a voice from behind them. Cyrus turned to see Endrenshan Odellan, a few soldiers with him moving citizens back from Cyrus and Vara. "At least, I'm told." He joined them at the rail. "The King had our riders overfly them a few days ago and they got an estimate before the archers took a few of them out of the air."

"What?" Cyrus blinked at the Termina Captain.

"Flying mounts," Odellan replied, casting his gaze over the water. "Riders on griffons and such, you know." He pointed to the haze of smoke above Santir. Cyrus squinted and saw small figures flying around the clouds of smoke. "We thought they were going north because the march of the army indicated they were heading for the crossing hundreds of miles north of here." The Endrenshan frowned. "Our army rode on that assumption—and they took most of my garrison with them."

Cyrus felt his stomach drop. "You mean your army isn't in Termina?"

Odellan shrugged as though he were trying to be indifferent. "We still have a garrison. And it's not as though the dark elves intend to strike Termina; it'd be an act of war."

Cyrus felt a chill unrelated to the air and leaned toward Odellan. "How many soldiers do you have left in the city?"

Odellan stared out at the water. "Five thousand. Not enough to defend it."

"My gods." A swell of awe and sickness ran through Cyrus and he held tight to the railing as the odd feeling he couldn't quantify came crashing into place. He remembered the words spoken by Andren at Sanctuary only two weeks earlier; it felt like a year had passed.

"Their army came in, all lined up in neat rows, and once they realized there wasn't anyone to defend the village, they just ran wild. Tore up everything in sight, killing the men, dragging away the women, burning everything and stealing what they could carry."

"They're going to cross the bridge." Cyrus's words came as a whisper, but Odellan and Vara both snapped their heads to look at him. He pointed to the massing army on the opposite shore. "Something Andren told me—when they sack a town, they unleash their army, they don't keep it in formation." He sifted through memories of refugees at Sanctuary, remembering similar stories of the dark elven army going wild, burning towns and villages. "Why keep them in disciplined rows unless...?" He let his voice trail off.

"Unless they plan on them going somewhere else." Odellan looked suddenly ill and Cyrus watched the guard captain's hand lash out and his mailed fist hit the railing. "I've heard the same tales," he said, almost in a whisper. "We have no hope of turning them back; not with what we have to fight with."

"Then what do we do?" Vara's eyes were wide. "Termina has a million people and the dark elves are hardly shy about killing civilians; their army tends to seek them out to offer a warning to anyone who would oppose them."

"The body count from their crossing will be astronomical,"

Odellan said, ashen. "We have no time to spare—"

Odellan brought his hand down on the railing once more, creating a noise so loud that everyone in earshot turned to look at him. He turned and stepped onto the railing, boosting himself an extra few feet into the air. Raising his voice, he addressed the crowd, his words loud enough to echo for several blocks. "Good people! The dark elves intend to invade Termina." A moment of silence was followed by mutterings through the crowd. "The city must empty! As Endrenshan and the ranking representative of King Danay the First, I hereby order the evacuation of Termina; abandon your belongings and leave at once! The enemy will be here within the hour!"

An aura of shocked disbelief hung in the air around them for a split second before eighteen different types of hell erupted. Half the citizenry began to speak; the other half began to speak and move, in flight away from the river. Pushing and shoving were rampant, and Cyrus could hear the word spreading in shouts and screams down the waterfront as the crowd began to convulse, pushing back toward the city in a terrible rush.

Odellan moved to the soldiers nearby, issuing orders that Cyrus could not hear. He turned to Vara, who stayed still at the railing and looked stark against the backdrop of the burning city of Santir, ash coming down all around her. "Your parents," Cyrus said.

"My father." She turned to him, panic in her eyes. "He can't travel without help."

"What is going on here?" Nyad and Ryin Ayend appeared, fighting through the crowd. Looking back toward the Entaras'iliarad, Cyrus realized that the news was spreading, the entire waterfront now in motion, the civilians clearing out.

"The dark elven army is about to invade Termina," Cyrus said.

"My gods," Ryin Ayend said, voice a near-whisper. "We have to get out of here!" Nyad paled, her skin a snowy white against the scarlet of her robe.

"Odellan!" Cyrus shouted over the crowd, and the guard captain looked back at him. "What are you going to do?"

Odellan trotted over to him. "We cannot defend the city with the forces we have. All I can do is try to aid the evacuation."

"It is your duty!" Vara's voice rose and her cheeks flushed.

"Duty or no," Odellan said with a shake of his head, "there are three spans to guard—the Northbridge, with the Olenet'yinaii leading to the government center, the Southbridge, with the Ameeras'etas leading to the Bazaar, and the Grand Span that opens onto the Entaras'iliarad. To mount a defense I would need 20,000 soldiers to hold the bridges. Without that number, our position would be flanked and we'd be encircled and destroyed within an hour."

"My father would send aid." Nyad was ghostly pale and Cyrus looked up from deep thought to see her, the Princess of the Elven Kingdom, and he felt a rush of hope.

"There is no way to get reinforcements here in time," Vara said in a ghostly whisper.

"What?" Cyrus looked at her and then Odellan in succession. Nyad bowed her head in resignation. Other members of Sanctuary stood beyond the perimeter of guards surrounding their conversation; Cyrus saw Longwell in particular near the front, watching them with great interest.

"The closest portal is in Santir, remember?" Vara's voice carried a thread of hopelessness. "The next is three days' ride southwest of here."

"Three days' hard ride," Odellan said. "More likely four with an army. Our forces moving north are at least two days away, assuming you could get a message to them." He looked back across the water, where the dark elven army continued to mass, growing larger by the minute, still wrapped in perfect formation. "There will be no reinforcement. The bridges will fall and the dark elven host will march through the city; our pitiful 5,000 will scarcely slow them down." He shook his head sadly. "Tens of thousands will die if they do here what they've done in the Confederation."

"We need to get out of here," Ryin Ayend said. "We need to collect the Sanctuary force and get out of this city before the hammer falls."

"Like hell," Cyrus said before anyone else could speak. "Odellan, could your army hold the Northbridge?"

The Endrenshan looked at him with uncertainty. "For a time, perhaps; it is narrower than the Grand Span. But the dark elven host would simply march around on one of the others and surround us, wiping us out to a man."

"If you can hold the Northbridge," Cyrus said, drawing out every syllable as though each were some precious metal he was loath to surrender, "I'll hold the other two."

A great clamor rose around him as Nyad gasped and Ryin Ayend started to speak. "Are you mad?" The druid stared him down, his brown eyes inflamed with disbelief. "You intend to put Sanctuary in the middle of this war?"

"I intend to defend this city and give its civilian occupants time to escape the murder and death that the dark elf horde would visit upon them," Cyrus replied.

"That will provoke the ire of the dark elves against us!" Ayend's words came out in a shout. "We're to remain neutral!"

"Neutrality be damned," Cyrus said. "Go stand in the middle of the Entaras'iliarad when that host marches through and see how neutral the dark elven army is to you."

"What's to stop them from ending up on our doorstep next?" Ryin Ayend raised his hands above his head as if seeking divine intervention."

"Me," Cyrus replied. He turned to Nyad. "Have you anchored your soul back at the safehouse?" he said, referring to the process by which a spell caster could mark a location and use the return spell to travel back to it later. She nodded. "Go to the others and give them my orders—take Thad and Martaina along with Vara's parents and teleport them out of here—Pharesia, Sanctuary, wherever Chirenya wants to go, there's no time to argue with her. When you're done with that, go to your father and tell him what's happening. Let him know that we're evacuating the city. Tell Andren and Fortin to get their asses to the Southbridge and defend it with their lives."

"Andren will love that," Vara said under her breath.

He finished. "Have everyone else meet us here at the Grand Span, and tell them to make ready for battle."

Odellan spoke. "You're sending two people to defend the Southbridge?" Skepticism ringed his words.

"A rock giant and a healer," Cyrus said.

"A...*what?!*" Odellan was floored. "You brought a *rock giant* into Termina?"

"Does that violate some sort of zoning ordinance? Be upset with me later." Cyrus locked eyes with the Endrenshan. "Will you hold the Northbridge?"

Odellan took a deep breath and his eyes closed. He sat there in the cold air, breathing in and out, the mist from his exhalations the only sign he was still alive. "Yes." His eyes opened. Regret flashed over the Endrenshan's youthful features. "I wish I had fought harder against my superiors when they took my army away. You and your spell casters, few as they are, stand a better chance of success on the Grand Span than my army does." He drew up to attention and saluted Cyrus. "I wish you all the luck, General Davidon. Take command of the defense of Termina, please."

Cyrus snapped to attention and drew his hand to his head in a sharp salute. "They'll not get through us. We'll hold until the morrow; that should be long enough to evacuate the city of all but the most stubborn."

"Aye." With a nod, Odellan broke his salute and barked orders to the soldiers surrounding them. The crowd had dispersed, save for a few gawkers that Odellan shouted commands at in elvish, causing them to scatter.

"Do you realize what you've committed us to?" Ryin Ayend's stunned voice came from behind Cyrus. He turned and found the druid there, looking at him in disbelief. Vara was still next to him, staring across the river, impassive. "You mean to steer Sanctuary into war!"

"I don't." The determination stirred within Cyrus, the anger and rage welling up as though Termina were Reikonos. "But I will fight here, and if it brings us into war then at least it will be for good cause."

"Good cause?" Ayend almost choked. "The dark elves will storm the gates of Sanctuary and kill everyone there if you persist in this course. I fail to see the 'good cause' in that. It's not as though with our two hundred," he said, taking a step closer to Cyrus, "you'll be able to keep them out of the city! You risk your guildmates' lives against an army of a hundred thousand for what? Death and glory? What possible reason could there be to engage in this utterly pointless fight?"

"Pointless?" Cyrus kept his voice calm. "I mean to use the width of the Great Span to funnel the dark elven host into our forces, where their numbers matter little to none. By holding the bridges, I'll keep the dark elven army from descending on an undefended city and leaving a hundred thousand corpses in the streets." He stepped closer and jabbed a finger in Ryin Ayend's face. "If you have a problem with that, take it up with Alaric and see what he says. But if you're not going to help us in the defense, at least make use of yourself by teleporting some elves out of the city while you retreat."

Ryin Ayend stepped away from him, the human's features still shocked. He twitched, as though his brain could not conceive what Cyrus had told him, and his voice was low and gravelly. "You'll die." He looked to the members of Sanctuary that had followed him to the waterfront, Vara's guard. "Anyone who follows you will die."

Cyrus turned to the waiting faces. Within the group of a half dozen he saw the face of Samwen Longwell, who nodded at him and grasped the handle of his lance, which was slung over his shoulder. Aisling's face poked out from under a heavy hooded cowl, looking back at him, eyes glistening in the reflected light. Next to her stood another cloaked and cowled figure, and he realized that the eyes of Erith Frostmoor looked back at him from within.

He took a deep breath. "Right now, I am not your General. I am not talking to you as an officer of Sanctuary. Right now, I speak to you as a man. And in five minutes I'll be standing on the Grand Span, sword in my hand, waiting for the dark elves to cross. I hope I'm wrong, that they'll turn north and go elsewhere. But if they come, I will fight for every inch of that bridge, even if I'm the only one out there." He turned away from them. "If you're willing to do the same, follow me. If you're not, kindly help the elves get out of the way of this bloody swath of destruction bearing down on them. I'll stand alone if need be." He felt a stir of emotion and suppressed it. "It won't be the first time."

He looked to Nyad. "Take that message back to the others— including Andren and Fortin—then tell them to run, not walk to the Southbridge. Go." She nodded once, and disappeared in a flash of magical light that bathed the world in green.

Cyrus did not look over his shoulder; he turned north toward the Entaras'iliarad a few hundred feet away and started walking toward it, not daring to look back.

Chapter 30

He had almost made it to the span when he felt her next to him, armor clanking as she half ran, half walked to catch up. "Stirring speech," Vara said. "I daresay you'll get nearly the whole garrison once Nyad does her bit for King, self and country and delivers your message." She lowered her voice. "Why are you really willing to do it? Risk war and oblivion and all that? This isn't Reikonos, you know."

"No. It's not Reikonos. But there are innocent people here that stand no chance of escaping if someone doesn't buy them time."

"That's it, then? You really are that noble?" She looked at him questioningly. "You're willing to die for faceless masses you've never met?"

He laughed, a deep, rueful sound. "You're the holy warrior. Aren't you supposed to be on board for hopeless causes without question?"

"Yes, but warriors tend to be more mercenary and concerned for survival odds." She drew him up short with a hand on his forearm. "Why are you really doing this? Why here? Why now? Why didn't you go back to Reikonos when you knew the same sort of blow might fall on them?"

"Because you won our bet, remember? This is the service you get from me."

She nearly scowled at him. "Very glib. You picked an odd moment to finally acknowledge my victory in that matter."

They had reached the highest point of the bridge. Cyrus paced a few more feet, shrugging out of her grasp. He looked across the span into Santir, where the skies were black with smoke. He saw the fire was spreading, but the dark elves were massed and moving, the first rank turning onto the street that would lead them to the bridge. He could see the figures in armor, marching, spears over some of their heads. *Mixed infantry*, he thought. *Probably some mounted horsemen behind them. This should be...interesting.*

A line of dark elven soldiers guarded the base of the bridge on the Santir side. *They put a picket on the bridge early on*, he realized. *That's why this span isn't completely flooded with human refugees. They boxed them in and slaughtered them.* A white hot fury took hold of him and he gripped Praelior's hilt tight.

He looked back and saw the half dozen members of Sanctuary that had followed him. *Only Ryin Ayend is missing. Big surprise there*, he thought with a small smile. He looked back to Vara. "You."

She frowned. "What?"

"You. You're the reason I didn't go back to Reikonos to fight." He turned away again. "It's not my home. My life in Reikonos was hell, from the days I was in the Society, to the ones when I was married to the one when we met, when I ran the smallest guild in town and lived in a horsebarn scratching out a living. With Niamh dead, you're the last remaining member of the group that saved my life in Ashan'agar's Den—the day I first encountered Sanctuary." He turned back to Vara. "You're why I'm here. This is your city, this is your home—and mine is with you."

"Gods, that's sappy," she said with a roll of her eyes. "If you didn't want to answer me truthfully, you could have just said so." She started to return to the others who were standing at a respectful distance behind them, but he grabbed her hand.

"I meant it," he said. "You're why I'm here. You're what I'm fighting for. I'll protect these people, because that's what we do, but I wouldn't have been here but for you."

She looked up at him, but didn't pull her wrist away. "You could die." Her words were sedate, drifting like the breath of mist that came out of her mouth when she spoke them.

"Then I die," he said. "But for a reason. I've fought my whole life, dancing it upon the edge of death, and I did it for less purpose than to protect your people."

The words hung between them. She pulled her wrist away, grabbing him forcefully behind his neck and pulling his mouth down to hers. They sat there on the Grand Span, lips locked until the silence was broken by the beating of drums from the dark elven army before them. Cyrus pulled from her and turned to see the enemy formed and streaming toward them, ranks marching up the gentle slope of the bridge, their armor shining in the bare edges of light slipping through the smoke from the horizon behind them as the sun sunk low in the winter sky.

He looked back and saw others approaching from behind at a run, led by a troll that was head and shoulders taller than any of the others. He looked to the north and a mile distant he saw the bridge there filled with armored men to the center of the span.

With a look south, he couldn't see as much, but there was a lone figure in the middle of the bridge, taller than any human or elf, and standing behind him was another figure, smaller, more man-sized. He saw the second figure appear to take a drink from something in his hand and smiled. *My pieces are in place. Almost time for the first move, I think.*

The dark elven column filled the Grand Span from side to side, and at the fore was an officer on a horse, his armor more ornate than the others. He led on horseback, but his men followed close behind, plated boots hitting the ground in time, one row after another. *This should be an interesting challenge, even with Praelior.*

Cyrus felt the press of the others at his back, and looked around to see Vaste arriving at the head of their forces, breathless. "About time," he called to the troll.

"I got here as fast as I could," Vaste said. "You'd think people would be frightened of a howling troll telling them to get out of the way, but apparently they were more scared of the dark elves." He saluted Cyrus in a sloppy snapped off mess that ended with an extended middle finger. "Reporting for ignominious death as a private citizen, sir."

"I don't have time for a headcount," Cyrus said. "How many...?" He looked in question at the group behind Vaste.

"All but Thad and Martaina, who are getting Amiol out of town with Nyad as we speak. She's teleporting them to Pharesia and taking him to the King's Court to put him under the protection of the palace guard. He'll be safe there."

"There's an order of elvish assassins that would love to get their hands on him and you think he'll be safe in the capital?" Vara looked at the troll with incredulity.

"Safer than we're going to be for the near future." Vaste shrugged.

"Safe as anywhere," Cyrus said. "Wait. What about Chirenya?"

"What about me?" The elf shoved her way past Longwell. "I'm here."

"Mother," Vara said, stunned. "What..."

"I'm here to fight," Chirenya replied. "You don't think I'd sit by and let these blue-skinned bastards burn my city down, do you?" J'anda coughed, sliding into place beside her. "Not you." She pointed into the distance. "Those blue-skinned bastards. You're merely a blue-skinned irritation."

"Thanks for the clarification," the enchanter said, miffed.

"It's a great disappointment that more of our kind aren't here to fight," Chirenya said. "Where's their sense of pride?"

"It's tucked away safely behind their sense of reason," Vaste said. "These are not friendly odds, and they'd be suicide for the untrained."

"Lucky we're trained, then." Longwell made his way forward, his lance in hand. "I'm not familiar with the dark elven army," he said to Cyrus. "What will we be facing?"

"I always forget you're not from around here," Cyrus said. "What would you expect an army to bring to a fight like this?"

"Archers." Longwell didn't hesitate. "Mounted cavalry. Footmen...er, infantry, I think you call them. Wielders of magic."

"Likely all the above," Cyrus said. "The foot infantry is easy enough to deal with. The cavalry, less so." He frowned, deep in thought. "I have no idea what to do about the arrows; it's not as though many of us carry shields."

"I can solve your arrow problem," Chirenya said. "Leave it to me."

He raised an eyebrow and shot a quick look at Vara, who nodded. "All right, you handle that." He turned to J'anda. "Anything else?"

The enchanter was still, his hands tucked inside his sleeves, eyes closed. "Sorry," he said, concentrating. "Just a moment."

Cyrus turned, hearing something behind them on the bridge. An army filled the Entara'iliarad; elves, resplendent in the ornate helm that their soldiers wore, marched up the bridge, thousands of them. He felt his heart leap.

"Don't get too excited," J'anda said. "They're an illusion." The dark elf showed his most charming smile. "I thought perhaps a bluff might be in order."

"That is bloody brilliant," Vara said. "If we can hold them here, hurt them bad enough and make them think there's an army waiting behind us, we might be able to force them to cut their losses and run." She shook her head in amazement at the enchanter. "Marvelous, J'anda. Absolutely marvelous."

He bowed, and his smile became dazzling. "I aim to please, madam."

"Form a battle line," Cyrus ordered. "Warriors and rangers in front, and I need someone with a bow..." His eyes came to rest on Aisling, who had slipped to the front of the line, a bow in her hands, peeking out from beneath her cape. He shook his head. "I should have known it'd be you. On my order...you know what to do."

She smiled. "You want to start things off with a bang."

"I do."

They formed in rows as the dark elven army approached, swords drawn. The footsteps of the dark elves were like thunder, marching in time on the cobblestones, the clash of metal on stone sounding the approaching inevitable. Cyrus tried not to concentrate on them, focusing instead on what he would say when the first rank reached him; the dark elves were side by side, a front line thirty wide and at least fifty deep. *Fifteen hundred soldiers,* he thought. *And one officer at the head, the totalitarian figure that rules their entire lives.*

The officer rode a black destrier, a massive warhorse. His helm left his face exposed, but covered the top of his head. At either end of the front row of infantry were the standard bearers; Cyrus recognized the flags they carried as belonging to a dark elven unit whose name he had forgotten since the days when memorizing them was required for him to pass out of the halls of the Society of Arms.

"Hail," the dark elven officer spoke as he closed to within a hundred yards. He held up his hand, and his troops ceased their march behind him. He urged his destrier forward, toward Cyrus, who stood a little in front of the Sanctuary battle line. "I hereby order you to remove yourself from this bridge in the name of the Sovereign of Saekaj Sovar."

Cyrus nodded. "What is his name, by the way?"

"He is the Sovereign." The officer's already stony face darkened. "He requires you to vacate the bridge or die. That is all you need know."

"Among free men, we decide what we need to know," Cyrus said. "But you wouldn't know anything of that, I suppose."

The officer stared down at him, only a few feet in front of Cyrus. "I know a great deal. For example, seeing that you're a warrior in black armor, at the head of a guild force, I know you're Cyrus Davidon of Sanctuary." He sneered. "Interfering with the passage of our army is an act of war."

"Afraid you're wrong," Cyrus said. "My name is not Cyrus Davidon, it is Eloran, and I am but a simple elven pig farmer, here to show you and your army the error of your filthy raping and pillaging ways by slaughtering you to the last man."

The dark elven officer looked back at him in amusement. "If you're an elf and a pig farmer, I'm a gnome and a dressmaker."

"You're tall for your kind," Cyrus said. "By any chance do you have any of your selection of wares handy?" He chucked his thumb toward Vara. "I'd like to buy a dress for my lady. Something slim in the middle that emphasizes her curves, with a short hemline and a deep neckline. Something in black, I think; it'd go well with her complexion."

"You are ridiculous," Vara muttered from behind him.

"Enough." The dark elf made a threatening gesture. "Clear the bridge in the name of the Sovereign, or we will run you down and hang the survivors."

Cyrus cracked his knuckles. "How about I clear the bridge in the name of the King of the Elves, and throw all your corpses unceremoniously into the river?"

The laugh of the dark elven officer filled the air. "You do not have the strength."

Cyrus tossed a look back over his shoulder, where J'anda's illusion of the elven forces marching up the bridge had grown closer and was now only a few hundred feet behind them. He looked to the dark elf on the horse and smiled. "You sure?"

Uncertainty lay fresh on the dark elf's face. "We will crush your forces on the other bridges and flank you."

"Gods bless you young officers; there's no guile in you at all." Cyrus smiled, the most arrogant, infuriating one he could manage. "I have enough men on the north span to hold it and I'm so confident I've only placed two of my fighters on the Southbridge." He looked across the water where he saw Fortin, barely visible, with a line of dark elven forces in front of him, staring him down. Cyrus could not tell how many there were. "What are you, a lieutenant?"

"I'm a colonel." The words came back confident and strong from the mounted officer. "My name is Rorne, and I command the Midnight Slayers division of the Sovereign's army."

"But you're not in charge of the entire host?" Cyrus let a note of disappointment slip into his voice.

"I'm in charge of enough of the army to send you scurrying from the bridge," the colonel replied.

Cyrus rested his hand on the hilt of Praelior, his fingers lightly touching the pommel. "Here's the difference between your thinking and mine." The dark elf leaned forward on his horse, intent on the words Cyrus was speaking. "The thought of sending you scurrying from this bridge never entered my consideration."

A roar of laughter came from the dark elf. "You are wiser than I would have given you credit for; you see already the futility of your actions."

"Naw," Cyrus said, affecting a low drawl. "When I say I never gave a thought to you scurrying from the bridge, it's not because I think my forces are going to lose. It's because every man you send this way will die." He grinned. "Starting with you. Ais—"

Before the last word finished leaving Cyrus's lips, an arrow cut through the air. The aim was true, and the colonel flopped from the saddle, lifeless as a boned fish, the fletchings sticking out from his face.

A shocked silence filled the air for almost three seconds.

Cyrus drew his sword and felt the slow rush of time draw down; every second felt like ten with the power of Praelior flowing through him. He thrust the glowing blade into the air and bellowed his most fearsome warcry; it was so intimidating that the first row of the dark elven infantry took a step back, bumping into the soldiers behind them. He surveyed the foes arrayed against him. *They're fodder. They're weak. Against an army of their own, they'd stand a chance.* His grin became predatorial, nightmarish. *Against me and mine, they're chaff, waiting for the thresher.*

He cried out again, heard the answering call from the Sanctuary force behind him, and felt a rush of satisfaction at the thought of breaking the enemy here, on this bridge. *I may not be able to drive you out of Reikonos, but you won't set a foot in this land.* Cyrus felt the breeze of evening run over him, chilling his cheeks as he took his first step forward into war.

Chapter 31

He charged then and stopped, the air in front of him seeming to catch fire. The heat rolled in a billowing blast, driving him back a step as a wall of flames ten feet tall sparked to life, cutting him off from the enemy and causing his armor to warm.

"Get back, you daft bastard, or you'll catch fire." The words were casual, as though nothing of particular importance were happening. He heeded them, trying to avoid stumbling from the inferno that blazed so hot that he flinched from it. He looked back to see the rest of his force halted, and standing at the fore, hands aglow with the light of magic, was Chirenya. "Might as well start them off with the proper attitude — a healthy dose of fear."

Cyrus looked back to the battle line of the dark elves. Through the fire he could see the front rank of soldiers ablaze. Screams rang over the crackling of the flames, the shouts of agony taking over as the blaze consumed everything within a hundred yards of the starting point. Cyrus watched bodies, wreathed in fire, leaping off the sides of the span into the river below by the dozens.

She just set fire to over half that column, he thought. *A thousand of them, wiped out.* The screams were howling, filling the air with the anguish of the burning. The inferno shifted, moving away from Cyrus and the Sanctuary force, rolling down the bridge as though it were wheeled, leaving flaming corpses behind as it moved forward, hungry to consume more of the dark elven army.

She has to be out of magical energy, he thought. *Even if she's four thousand years old, I've never seen a wizard cast a fire spell that powerful before; she has to be close to drained. Or is she already?* Her eyes were fluttering in concentration, and the glow around her hands had changed from a bright blue to a dark crimson.

"Mother, stop!" Vara's command was sharp, panic rising in her voice. "You'll kill yourself!

Chirenya's eyes opened, drifting, and her knees buckled. "I believe I just cost myself a century of life," she said, falling into the arms of J'anda, who caught her. A thin trickle of blood dribbled out of her nose and onto her blouse. She looked down the bridge and saw hundreds of bodies still on fire, even though the spell had died down, and a smile appeared on her waxy face. "Very much worth it, I would say."

"They'll think twice before sending the next wave," Longwell said, now at Cyrus's side. "No army could stand up to that."

"The next wave will be different," Cyrus said, staring down the bridge. The army massed below, but a ripple was moving through them, their attack halted by the uncertainty brought on by watching their first division slaughtered in fire. "I'd expect archers to start peppering us soon." He stared at the corpses in blackened armor littering the bridge in front of them. "That was a hell of a spell," Cyrus muttered. "Is that how Quinneria beat back the trolls?"

"Not quite." He turned to see Vaste standing calm behind him. "That was impressive, no doubt. But the Sorceress could kill ten thousand with a single spell. Seeing this makes me somewhat glad that Alaric killed her."

"What?" Cyrus looked at the troll. "Alaric killed her? I thought she was a hero—you know, she helped the humans and elves win the war against the trolls—"

"She used unnatural magics," Vaste said with a graveness that sapped all the levity out of the healer's usually sarcastic delivery. "The Leagues declared her a heretic after the last victory." A smug superiority came over the troll. "Of course, the fact that she did so was buried by your people to avoid the inconvenient truth that you only beat the troll armies because of a heretic, not because of how awesome your Confederation is. It gave you humans an inflated sense of self-importance."

"What kind of unnatural magics?" Cyrus looked at the troll, genuinely interested. "Worse than soul rubies and raising the dead?"

Vaste shrugged. "I dunno. Scary stuff, if she killed ten thousand with a single spell. My people speak of it as though one of the gods came down and drove them into the tiny corner of the swamps they still inhabit."

Another question brought itself to Cyrus. "If she was this monumental destroyer, how did Alaric kill her?"

Another shrug. "There's more to the Ghost than meets the eye. I would think his ability to go incorporeal would have taught you that. However he did it, he delivered her body to the Council of Twelve—that's why he's respected enough to get an audience with them anytime he asks for one."

"Can we please focus on the battle?" Vara's sharp voice cut through, shaking Cyrus back to reality. "You know, massive dark elven army against our pitiful little force?"

He looked down the bridge. The dark elven army remained in Santir, shrouded now in the smoke from the fires that were growing closer to the shore of the river, threatening to consume the entire city. *Flame in front of them, flame behind. Shouldn't have burned the city until you were done with your crossing.*

"Speaking of pitiful little..." Cyrus let his voice drift off as he walked to the southern edge of the bridge. Holding onto the railing, he squinted into the distance. The light of day was beginning to fade, and he could see the Southbridge across the water. Chaos reigned on it, as he saw a body flip into the air, followed by another and another. Four more flew over the stone railing and into the icy water below.

A voice rang out, powerful and bellowing: "I WILL EAT YOU ALL AS IF YOU WERE GNOMES!"

He felt Vara brush against him. "I daresay Fortin is holding out against all comers."

"I'm not too worried about him," Cyrus said. "Hopefully Odellan has enough men to hold the Northbridge."

"You lied to that colonel," she said as her mailed hand brushed against his cheek. Ash continued to fall around them, and her shining silver breastplate was tarnished with it, smeared with the remainder of the lives, houses and possessions of the humans who had called Santir home. That thought gave Cyrus another taste of bile in his mouth. "You said you intended to hold the bridge indefinitely, but you told Odellan you would only hold it until morning. Which is it?"

"In the heat of battle, you don't consider retreat," he replied, his words coming slow. "If you think about quitting, you'll likely be doing it when you shouldn't."

"Don't you allow for the possibility you might not win?" She looked at him with clear incredulity.

"Not when I'm fighting." He shook his head. "It's not hard to find an escape route, if it comes to that. But when I'm in the heat of the battle, the words I said to Odellan are not in my mind; holding this ground becomes an all or nothing proposition. To do anything less would allow fear to creep in, and they beat that out of me at the Society."

He looked back to the base of the bridge and his smile tightened. *I thought they'd try this next.* "They're readying the next wave." He pointed to the base of the bridge. "Mounted cavalry."

Longwell thrust his lance into the air. It was over six feet long, with a tri-blade at the tip; the primary three feet in length, with two smaller blades that jutted at a forty-five degree angle to either side of it. The metal was blue, different than steel, and seemingly unbreakable. Cyrus had seen the dragoon ram the weapon into foes at high speed yet it appeared undamaged. *It has to be mystical; no weapon is that resilient, and no man could wield it in a fight against sword and shield the way Longwell does unless it gave aid in the form of speed and dexterity.*

The cry came from down the bridge, among the enemy. Cyrus looked to Aisling, who stood just behind him. "They're calling for a charge," she said.

A row of horses waited at the bottom of the bridge. They began to trot forward, gaining speed as they rode. Another row of horsemen was following twenty feet behind them, and another behind that. *At least six rows,* Cyrus calculated. "Aisling," he started to say, and turned to find her bow already out, arrow notched and looking down the shaft.

"Bet I can take the first row before they get here," she said with a sweet smile. "And I could take you before the second row got here."

"Bloody hell, woman," Vara said. "Leave him be; he's mine — at least for now."

"For now?" Cyrus said.

"I'm willing to join both of you," she said, releasing the first arrow and notching the second, letting it fly as she spoke. A few of the other rangers had loosed their arrows and the front row of horsemen had stumbled, prompting the second row to lose half its number tripping over the fallen first row. Aisling fired off five more arrows in quick succession, downing six more riders. "I'm very flexible, and gentle, if you're into that sort of thing." She loosed another and sent Cyrus a wicked smile. "Or not, if you're into the rough stuff."

"Sweet Vidara, I'm battling the dark elven army to keep them from invading my town while listening to my youngest daughter and her ox being propositioned by a dark elven harlot," came Chirenya's voice from behind them. "How have I wronged you so, Mother of Life, to have you kill me and consign me to the Realm of Death without any chance to atone?"

"You can bring your mother too," Aisling said to Vara, firing off another arrow. "She sounds like she'd be an animal under the covers."

Cyrus cringed. The only sound that could be heard from Chirenya was a deep and uncomfortable, "Oiiiiiiii...."

The fourth row of mounted cavalry had been half downed under the volleys of arrows, and as they came closer into range, a bevy of spells shot forth from the magic users. Bolts of lightning, fireballs and even a blast of concussive force from Vara sent a half dozen more riders to the ground, horses scared and wounded, writhing and snorting, and blocking the next row of cavalry from charging.

"If I don't get to bury my sword in someone soon," Cyrus said, "I may explode." He looked around in time to see Aisling's wide grin. "Don't say it."

"As soon as I get my magical strength back," Chirenya said, "I'll help you with that." She hesitated. "Perhaps I'll wait until we've killed all these dark elves."

"That might be wise, Mother." Vara stood with her hand raised and fired off another spell, unleashing a wave of concussive force that knocked a horseman from his mount, sending him tumbling over the bridge and into the water. "He and his sword are likely to be the most powerful thing standing between you and wasting another hundred years of your life wiping out an infantry formation."

"Not more powerful than you, dear," she said with a mother's assurance.

"They should have sent the cavalry first." Cyrus watched the sixth and seventh rows of horsemen fall to a combination of arrows and spells. "Now there are so many bodies here, the horses aren't that effective." There was a berm of corpses twenty feet in front of them, the result of the most recent charges. Horses and dark elves lay moaning and dying in the pile with the already dead. Cyrus watched one soldier trying to push his fallen horse off of him; an arrow appeared through his eye as the last row faltered and began to retreat. "If they keep this up, they'll blockade the bridge for us and we'll be able to leave their own dead to guard the way."

"How do you think they'll surmount that?" Longwell stood next to him, lance at the ready.

Cyrus sent him a sly smile. "How would you do it?"

"Footmen." Longwell clicked the bottom of his lance against the ground. "But if their infantry saw what happened to the last group, they'll be hesitant."

"Ever seen what happens in a butcher shop?" Cyrus looked back at Longwell, who shook his head. "You're about to; the rank and file that they send up here are going to get slaughtered. Their best chance for success in this position is to send so many at us that our arms get tired from hacking them to pieces."

He waited a few minutes and watched the army below, massing again. The sun had begun to set behind them, and the sound of combat rang out from the bridges to the north and south. Fierce, rumbling laughter came from the Southbridge where Fortin continued to hold against superior numbers but not odds. An obvious battle line was visible in the middle of the Northbridge and it appeared Odellan was holding as promised.

The next round of dark elven infantry marched up the bridge as twilight came, the orange rays of the setting sun blunted by the thickening haze of black smoke that held in the air around them. The ash had begun falling thicker now, reducing visibility.

The infantry came slowly up the bridge, not at a charge but picking their way around the fallen corpses of their fellows, swords drawn and ready for combat. "Looks like we have a cautious lot here," Vara said.

"Wouldn't you take your time getting here if during the whole walk you were stepping over the broken and burned bodies of your countrymen?" Vaste's words contained only a touch of irony.

"I believe I might consider finding another way around," Longwell said. "Say, about five hundred miles north of here."

"They fear the wrath of their generals and the Sovereign more than they fear us." Aisling's face was shadowed, hiding within the cowl whatever she felt.

"Would you like to tell me who this mysterious Sovereign is that commands so much fear?" Cyrus raised an eyebrow at her.

Aisling shrugged, noncommittal. "He's not someone you'd know personally."

He looked back at her shrewdly. "But someone I've heard of."

She cracked a smile. "Maybe. I'll tell you his name if you —"

"No," Vara said, cutting her off before she finished.

"Your loss," the ranger said with another shrug. "I'm a master at..." She leaned in close to Vara's ear and whispered something. The paladin reddened, more embarrassed than Cyrus had ever seen the usually immutable Vara.

"I am eventually going to have to heal someone, right?" Erith's voice came from the middle of their formation and suggested deep boredom. "I'm at my best when I'm challenged, you know."

"Best be careful what you wish for," Vaste said. "You may be challenged more quickly than you know."

"Yeah, well, if wishes were horses —"

"Then they'd mostly be dead, if they're on this bridge," Longwell muttered.

Screeching came from above them; a flight of griffons with riders on their backs soared from out of the smoky haze above Santir and flapped their wings, flying in a straight line a few hundred feet above the bridge, heading toward Termina.

"Were those dark elves?" Cyrus asked, his eyes burning from the smoke hanging in the air. "I need someone to watch our flank. The last thing we need is a flight of those things swooping down on us from behind."

"I'll keep an eye out," J'anda said. "I've been wanting to spend more time at the rear with my faux elven soldiers anyway."

The infantry had closed the last few hundred feet, armor clanking, and began to break into a run. "Here comes the charge," Cyrus said. He clutched Praelior and his fingers dug into the leather grip as he raised the sword, ready to swing at the first foe to come his way.

Another flight of arrows and spells struck down part of the front row. The remainder kept coming, to their credit, and began to howl with cries of battle. Cyrus stepped forward, and Praelior sang, cutting through the cold air, then the neck of the first dark elf to cross his path and the leg of a second. He waded into the battle, brandishing his sword, delivering another cut that felled three more, ripping through their hardened armor chest plating as though it were nonexistent.

He heard a crack of thunder and there was a flash as a druid threw a bolt of lightning into a nearby cluster of armored footmen. The electricity arced between them, leaving spots in Cyrus's eyes as eight dark elves fell in seconds. He blinked the flashes away in time to raise his sword to block the attacks of two more enemies, then countered with a thrust that left one of them dead and the other missing an arm.

The melee was wild as the dark elves pushed against their line. Cyrus delivered a hacking blow that decapitated an enemy and caught a glimpse of Longwell out in front, his spear swinging in wide circles, keeping enemies at bay and leaving behind a swath of dead bodies. His suspicions about the mystical nature of the lance were confirmed when the dragoon used it to pierce one dark elf's breastplate and it came out the back and impaled another soldier behind him. Longwell yanked it sideways, freeing the tip by nearly ripping his foes in half, and promptly slashed down two more enemies with it.

He felt Vara alternate between being at his back and at his side, her blade in constant motion, felling one enemy after another. She caught his eyes once, and he saw the vitality had returned to them; the fire of battle that sent one infantryman scrambling from her assault as she pressed her attack against him, cutting away his light steel blade, then his helm, then his life. She yelled with the fury of a storm and raised her hand, knocking over a line of approaching soldiers with a spell as they closed on her and as an afterthought ran her blade across the throats of two of those she had downed.

Aisling moved through the advancing enemy like a shadow, darting between Cyrus and the rest, losing herself in the melee. She'd pop up and another soldier would fall, clutching at his back, wincing in pain and slumping to the ground, her daggers flashing for a second before she was gone again, after the next target.

Other figures moved through the battle—humans and elves, people he'd never seen before. They appeared behind the lines of the dark elven soldiers, distracting them. Cyrus saw one of them take an axe through the head and keep moving before he realized that they were illusions, cast by J'anda to distract and disorient the attackers. *He has an illusionary army behind us and still has the ability to sow these shades to cause discord among our foes?* He shook his head in amazement as he brought down another enemy soldier.

A ball of metal the size of his fist shot past Cyrus's face, spikes jutting from it in all directions. *A morning star,* he thought. He followed the chain back to its owner and found an infantryman clad far different than the rest. His armor was steel, not the boiled leather of the infantry. His face was like a hatchet, his tall brow sloped up to a receding hairline with black, slicked back hair that hung past his shoulders. His nose was flat and pointed down, and his eyes were illuminated, a cruel smile on his face as he swung the long chain in front of him, his fellow soldiers clearing the way as he approached Cyrus.

Hooting catcalls from the dark elves filled the air as the beast of a fighter attacked again. His morningstar's chain was twice the length of a man. It whizzed through the air and Cyrus barely dodged it again. He brought Praelior down on the chain when it was at full extension, driving down the edge of the blade with intent to cut it so he could close on the warrior unimpeded. His sword came down, hard, the clash of it against the metal chain of the morningstar ringing as Cyrus's full and furious strength, increased by Praelior, was directed onto the dark elf's weapon.

And bounced off.

What the...? Damn, the whole thing must be mystical! Alarm must have registered on Cyrus's face, as his foe grinned in an even more predatorial manner. The dark elf yanked on the chain and Cyrus dodged the rebounding morningstar. The rest of the infantry were pouring in around them, leaving a wide gulf around Cyrus and the dark elven champion with the morningstar. Cyrus could hear Vara's fevered clash with the onrushing forces, and Longwell was using his spear to block and attack the dark elves that were upon him. *This bastard is distracting me, allowing them to slip in and overwhelm us.*

Cyrus used Praelior to deflect the next attack. The dark elf jerked the chain back and swung the morningstar down like a hammer as Cyrus raised his sword. He absorbed the impact across the blade but it rattled his teeth and his arms shook from the strength of the blow, driving him to a knee. *Damn, I need to get closer; if I stay at range he'll tear me to pieces.*

"Watch out!" Aisling's voice rang in his ears and he saw her fighting her way through the melee, trapped behind a wave of enemies. "He's an Unter'adon; one of the Sovereign's sons; he's got mystical armor and weapons!"

In addition to a warrior's killer instinct, Cyrus thought, still at least ten paces from his attacker. The morningstar came around again, impossibly fast, and this time impacted his left arm, one of the spikes finding a joint and breaking through the chainmail beneath. Cyrus felt numbness creep down to his hand and a sharp pain shot up his arm. The weapon winged its way at him again but this time he dodged and it hit the bridge, sending stone fragments in all directions.

A breeze blew past him with a shockwave from Vara's hand, but the Unter'adon flipped out of the path of the spell before it landed, blasting a hole in the rows of soldiers lined up behind him. He glanced over to see Vara return to fending off three opponents, sword moving in flashes in the gathering twilight.

The Unter'adon came at Cyrus again, morningstar gripped by the handle with one hand and the chain with the other, taking half the length out of it as he closed. With one hand he slashed forward with the spiked ball; the other used the chain almost as though it were a short whip. Shifting to his right, Cyrus avoided the business end but the other side, the chain, whipped him across the cheek, drawing blood and knocking his helm asunder.

Cyrus fell to a knee and the chain came at him again, this time striking his breastplate, breaking ribs and cartilage and bringing tears to his eyes from the pain in his chest. *A heal would not be unwelcome right now.* Cyrus saw Aisling fall before him, her white hair untucked from beneath her cowl, her purple eyes having lost their glister in the dark. She hit the cobblestones, blood pouring from beneath the seams of her leather armor, visible where her cloak parted at her front.

Around him was a mass of dark elves, pushing forward. Vara was far behind him now, fifty feet or more. The healers were behind the front line of battle, even farther back than that. *Out of range for a healing spell.* The thought broke into his mind a moment before Cyrus looked up to see the Unter'adon smiling down at him, and he felt the chain wrap around his neck and begin to draw tight.

Chapter 32

Cyrus tried to grasp at the the chain where it coiled around his neck, attempting to unwrap it, but the Unter'adon jerked forward hard and he lost his footing. Both his knees hit the hard metal inside his greaves and he crashed, cheek first, against the ground. *If he kills me here, they'll never be able to recover my body for resurrection – or Aisling's.* His vision blurred from the impact and he felt numerous pains as he tried to stand, fingers grasping hold of the chain in front of him and wrapping it around his gauntlet.

The Unter'adon jerked it again, and the mystical chain closed around his mailed fist, causing enormous pressure. *Let's hope my dad's armor is strong enough to withstand this.* Cyrus yanked back on it and felt the mail squeeze his hand as the chain tightened. He grasped for Praelior, but it was several feet away, its glow barely visible through a stampede of armored legs. *Let's hope someone doesn't pick it up or we're done.*

His hand slipped down and behind him to his backplate. *Thank Bellarum for all those trips to Purgatory.* His fingers grasped as the Unter'adon yanked at him again, but he pulled back with his hand, forcing the dark elf to move closer to try for more leverage. His other hand brushed against the hilt of the curved short blade he hid as a backup. He had acquired it after an expedition through the Trials of Purgatory; after many successes there Cyrus had accumulated a variety of useful objects including a mystical dagger, rings that gave him additional strength, and the blade he used as a secondary weapon.

Composed of an unknown steel, the sword was infused with magical properties, giving it strength beyond its forging. The blade had a metallic sheen with a metal grip wrapped in soft leather. It was plain but effective, and when he pulled it out as he jerked on the chain, the Unter'adon was forced to give him some slack in order to avoid being impaled.

Cyrus took a breath as the chain loosened around his neck. His gorget had protected his throat from being crushed, but the chain had wrapped around his neck hard enough to leave marks. He pursued the Unter'adon ferociously, gripping the chain harder, wrapping it around his wrist and giving himself enough slack around his neck to avoid being choked. The dark elf whipped at him with the excess length, but Cyrus did not flinch as the blows struck his armor.

He spun and wrapped the chain around his chest, slashing at the Unter'adon with his short sword. *Fortunately, I had a lot of experience with this sort of weapon last year*, he thought. He was still at least an arm's length from the dark elf and spun forward again with another slice, wrapping another few feet of the chain around him. They were close enough now that the dark elf couldn't whip him with what remained in the length of the morningstar; he had begun to wrap chain around his own fist instead, preparing to use it to bludgeon Cyrus's head as he drew closer, the spiked ball hanging trapped behind Cyrus.

The dark elven soldiers had moved in around them, and Cyrus became aware that those surrounding them knew that the morningstar was no longer a threat and their champion was in danger. He swiped with his blade at one of the soldiers that got too close, driving him back with a near miss and then cutting the throat of the second to close on him. His reward was for the Unter'adon to attack him while distracted; he heard the impact of the chain-wrapped fist on the side of his head rather than felt it. Scalp tore loose from his skull and he felt blood drip down the back of his neck.

Cyrus turned, head swimming, and brought his sword down on the still-extended arm of the Unter'adon. The mystical blade hit, skipping off the stronger armor, channeled toward the inside of the dark elf's elbow. There, it found a seam and bit into his flesh, ripping a scream from the dark elf's throat. Cyrus jerked his other hand forward, using the chain wrapped around it in the same way the Unter'adon had with him, as a cudgel, and watched the dark elf's forehead above his left eye break as a wash of blood from the impact squirted from the socket.

The Unter'adon staggered and Cyrus dodged attacks from three infantrymen, still tangled up with the dark elf, fending them off with one hand. His vision was spotted and blood was running into his eyes, but he drew upon his Society training to keep them open in spite of the burning. He buried the short sword in the belly of the next dark elf to get too close and lashed out hard with a kick, his rage giving him strength enough to send another flying over the edge of the bridge.

He turned back to the Unter'adon, who was on one knee and rising, the chain fallen from his hands. Without hesitating, Cyrus buried the short sword in his face. *You couldn't even kill me when I was nearly unarmed*, he thought as he pulled the blade out and watched the body fall. The circle of dark elves around him watched with wary disbelief, their fiercest fighter felled. *This will last another second, maybe two. Better take advantage.*

Howling a warcry that startled those surrounding him, he attacked the dark elves between him and the Sanctuary forces. *Praelior was somewhere over...*He saw a dark elf with a glowing blade raised above his head and a sinking feeling entered his stomach. *...there.*

He slayed the enemies immediately in front of him, the chain still wrapped around his fist knocking two of them down with a flurry of punches to the face, his sword finding a weakness in the plate under the other's arm. He knocked the next two in line off their feet and whipped the handle of the morningstar through the air in front of him, knocking the helm off another and breaking the next dark elf's nose. Chaos reigned and he heard foes closing in on him from behind. He swung the handle of the morningstar around again and heard it whistle through the air until it landed with a satisfying *smack!* that told him whoever it hit was no longer a threat.

He unthreaded the chain from his neck as he advanced, loosening it while striking down foes with the short sword, most of them with their backs turned to him. He emerged on the front line of battle and saw the dark elf with Praelior wielding the blade with confidence — against Vara.

He noted the elven paladin, on the defensive, staggering from the assault the dark elf was unleashing on her with the purloined sword. With a shoulder check he knocked a footman to the ground and brought the blade down on the back of his neck, killing him. He pulled the length of the chain and swung the handle of the morningstar up, clearing a space around him, then flipped the handle into his hand. He felt the mystical power of the weapon course through him. *Not as good as Praelior, but it'll do.*

He took two quick steps forward, positioning himself behind the dark elf wielding his sword. Vara was sweating, her strength failing against the repeated blows delivered by the weapon more than the wielder, her face red and the strain obvious. Cyrus knew the dark elf sensed him and watched him begin to turn to counter the threat the warrior posed. *If I had only my short sword, he'd have a chance. Thanks to this* — he clutched the handle of the morningstar tighter—*he doesn't.*

His sword slipped underneath the backplate of the dark elf as he started to turn, but Cyrus threaded the chain around his neck and jerked on it, pulling him onto the blade. It slid through the footman's back then burst through his front, a dent appearing in his breastplate. Cyrus spun the body around, interposing it between him and the dark elven horde at his front, then let go of the chain grip and caught Praelior as it fell, enjoying the feel of it in his hand once more.

A healing wind brushed over him and the pain he'd been ignoring from his scalp lessened. He cast a look back and saw Erith with her hand extended, ghostly look of fright writ on her face. "You wanted a challenge," he said.

"I take it back!"

Cyrus turned back to the dark elves and let out a scream of fury. He waded in amongst them, cutting through them. They fell quickly and he was followed by Vara, Longwell, and a dozen others behind them, driving the dark elven army back. Cyrus was a black blur in the middle of it all. His hands moved without thought, Praelior in one and his short sword in the other. His mind was focused on one thing—forcing his foes back and recovering the body he knew was somewhere ahead.

The dark elves kept coming, but Cyrus was in a blood-fueled rage. He passed the point where Aisling lay and drove on, slaughtering all that came forward to challenge him. He watched Vara and Longwell do the same, and between the three of them they made an unbreakable front line of advance. Other warriors behind them stood ready and rangers fired their bows, weakening the dark elven advance. Wizard and druid spells were loosed as well, but most reserved their magic until needed.

Cyrus halted as the dark elves in front of him began to retreat. He looked around and realized he was three-fourths of the way across the span. The dark elven army was broken; they were fleeing before him.

"Why did we stop?" Longwell sounded almost plaintive.

"Because I'm not of a mind to try and retake Santir," Cyrus said.

Longwell looked around, realizing how far they had come. "Oh. Damn. We ran them off, didn't we?"

"We three," Vara said. The sun had long since set, the light of a thousand torches in the army ahead paling next to the fires still consuming Santir. Her cheeks were red and her breath froze before her as it came out in great gasps.

"Aye, we three," Cyrus said. "But not alone." He looked back at the Sanctuary war party.

"We're still here," came Vaste's dry response. "I did cast a couple of healing spells on you at first, but as you began hitting your stride, I started healing your enemies instead. You know, to give them a sporting chance."

"At odds of roughly 5,000 to one, I would say they still stand a sporting chance," Vara said.

"Did you recover Aisling's body?" Cyrus looked at Vaste.

The troll pointed with his staff, the white crystal in the center sparkling from its own inner light. Aisling sat on the ground beside Erith, her cloak thrown aside, head between her knees as though she were ill. The enemy was fleeing in disordered chaos back toward Santir as he walked over to her. She looked up as he approached. "Did you make it out alive?" Her voice came out as little more than a croak.

"Yes, but only just." He knelt beside her, her white hair streaked with red, remnants of the wounds inflicted when she died.

"I thought I was done," she said. "I saw the Sovereign's bastard about to kill you, and I froze. I knew if you went down we were finished."

"As it happens, there were others of us in the battle," Vara said. Cyrus looked up at her, and after a moment she let out a hiss of impatience. "Oh, all right, it was him that cleared the bridge to recover you, but it was not without help."

"How are you feeling?" Cyrus placed a hand on her shoulder.

"Sick." She moved her head slowly, left to right. "Nauseous."

"Take it easy," he cautioned her. "It'll fade in time."

"I've never died before," she said. "Is it true you lose memories?"

Cyrus swallowed, a lump bulging in his throat. "Yes. But you likely won't know what you've lost until later. If ever."

She stared back at him. "What did you forget?"

He stood, looking down at her. "You'll be back on your feet in no time, but don't push yourself too hard. It's going to be a long night, and we need you at your best."

The dark elf raised herself to a knee and placed a hand on his. "I'm at my best when I'm not on my feet."

"You have blood in your hair," Vara said. "And a little vomit as well."

Cyrus slipped from her grasp, moving back toward the line he had held with Vara and Longwell. The mass of dark elven troops at the end of the bridge was still disorganized.

"Do they have any spellcasters with them?" Cyrus watched the tangled knot of the army with wary concern.

"Likely, but few." Vara sidled closer to him. "Perhaps five, if that, and they will use them sparingly."

"Ridiculous," Longwell said. "Why don't they have more?"

"Because the Leagues that train magic users keep a very strict ratio of how many can work for a government, and what function they'll serve," Vara replied.

Longwell twirled his lance at his side. "And if they violate that number?"

"If the government does it, they're considered to be in violation of the League terms and all their current magic users are recalled," she answered. "If the spellcaster committing the violation is found to be doing so willfully, they're forsaken; unable to be hired by anyone reputable, for any purpose. It's one step above being a heretic; you're shunned everywhere you go." She straightened. "But unlike being a heretic, you aren't hunted to the death."

"Makes sense." Longwell's spear was at rest now. He looked at Cyrus. "You know, you can take that off now." He pointed to the chain of the morningstar, still wrapped around Cyrus.

The warrior looked down and grasped the morningstar's handle, which hung loose off his shoulder. "You know, I don't think I will. It doesn't feel very heavy and it's already come in handy once."

Longwell arched an eyebrow at him. "Planning on losing your sword again? Let me know when so I can pay a visit to a different bridge."

Vara inched closer to Cyrus, and he heard a clink as her armor touched his. "I was...concerned," she said, "when I saw you overwhelmed by that juggernaut."

He smiled down at her. "I was concerned myself." He leaned down and kissed her, their armor making a fearsome clangor as he pulled her closer and their breastplates hit. She broke away first, an uncharacteristic grin on her face. "I've never kissed someone who's wearing armor before," he said with a smile of his own.

"Oh?" She smiled back in amusement as she pulled away and

returned to her spot on their flank. "How was it?"

"Felt great. I'm going to do it again the next time I get a chance." Suddenly self-conscious, he remembered Longwell and turned to find the dragoon staring at him.

"Don't get any ideas; I'm not interested," Longwell said.

"They're rallying," Vara said with an icy calm. She was correct; the torches on the avenue below had reformed into proper lines and were moving forward. "There are archers in their ranks," she said, peering into the darkness.

"Elven eyesight," Cyrus muttered, then turned to shout over his shoulder. "Chirenya! We're about to have an arrow problem. You still think you can solve that for me?"

"I have an 'ox kissing my daughter' problem," came the hostile voice from behind him. "While I burn their arrows from the sky, do you think you could keep your hands, lips and other assorted minutiae to yourself?"

"During that time, yes," Cyrus muttered under his breath. "Afterwards, the things I'm going with do to your daughter would make Aisling blush —"

"Cyrus!" Vara snapped at him.

"I heard that," came Chirenya's weary reply. "I lose a hundred years off my life." She shoved her way to the fore, coming to a halt between Cyrus and Vara. One of her hands rested on his arm and she leaned heavily on him. "And my thanks is you and a request for more pyrotechnics. This would be infinitely easier if you had your own wizards —"

"We do," Cyrus said, lowering his voice. "They're just not as powerful as you."

She looked at him, taken aback. "Aren't you a charmer?"

"Just realizing what your daughter likes about me?"

"My daughter likes the fact that you're an ox, a beast of burden, and likely equipped as such. She is infantile and foolish, and being less than a hundred years old, still very preoccupied with such things."

"Mother," Vara said. Her tone changed in a half a heartbeat. "Arrows incoming!" Her shout drew their attention away and toward the sky.

Cyrus squinted and could barely make out the movement of something in the sky. A light appeared above him as a wall of solid fire, more intense than that which had consumed the first wave of the dark elven army but more compact. The heat brought beads of sweat onto Cyrus's forehead, adding to the already sticky feeling of his skin.

He could see the shadows of arrows pass through the wall of fire that Chirenya had placed above them; after a moment, hot metal began to rain down in drips. He felt a splash of singeing liquid bounce off his shoulder, heard a muttered curse from Longwell and saw his armor streaked with molten steel from the arrowheads.

"I can burn up the shafts and fletchings but metal is another story," Chirenya said, her eyes closed. "At least a burn is easier healed than a projectile which needs to be pulled from your body first."

The infantry was only a hundred yards away now, Cyrus realized, and the rain of arrows must have stopped. Chirenya lowered the barrier of fire, dropping it down on the front rank of the advancing line. Sweat beaded on her forehead, her skin beyond pale and now a shade of gray. Her eyes rolled back in her head and Cyrus felt her knees buckle as she gripped his arm tighter, and he caught her before she fell. Her robes brushed against the chain of the morningstar, which was still wrapped around his chest.

"No more arrows?" Erith asked from behind.

Vaste answered. "Their army is too close; I'm sure they wouldn't want to risk killing their own, since they have no one to heal and resurrect them."

"We don't know that," Cyrus said as Chirenya relinquished her grip on him. "They could have a healer somewhere."

"They pair their magic users in a unit of four or five spell casters," came the faint voice of Aisling. She stood back, her bow in hand, loosing her first arrow as the dark elven army closed. "I would expect to see them soon."

No sooner had the words left her mouth than a fireball twice the size of a man flew from the dark elven lines, aimed at Cyrus. He jumped to the side, pushing Chirenya out of the way as it impacted where he had been standing only a moment before. Another followed, aimed at Vara, who moved forward, ducking under the blast. "At least two wizards!" Cyrus said, moving forward with Longwell, closing the distance to the front line of the approaching army. "Aisling, see if you can—"

"Got one!" the ranger crowed. "The other is hiding in the midst of all those soldiers."

Another burst of flame shot at them, forcing Cyrus to weave to the right while Longwell went left. *It figures she didn't get the more powerful of the two.* The next attack came with two firebolts, each from a different location in the army ranks. "They've either got another wizard or they have a healer!" Out of the corner of his eye he saw Longwell lunge forward with his lance and impale through a footman in the front rank and into the wizard behind him. With a sweep he flung the bodies of both off his lance and over the edge of the bridge. *One down,* Cyrus thought.

He reached the front row of footmen and attacked, slashing through three with his first strike and moving to the next row. He felt a sword land on his right shoulder, stabbing through the chainmail and drawing blood. He turned to see one of the footmen he had just struck down, leering at him, bloody residue across his chest where Cyrus's blow had severed his breastplate. The wound was gone. "They definitely have a healer!" The other two he'd struck down had risen, pressing the attack while they had him surrounded. "No wounding blows or they'll be healed! Kill them all; they won't be able to save their army with resurrection spells!"

He watched the expression of the dark elf in front of him, triumphant a moment earlier, turn sour. His eyes widened as Cyrus brought Praelior across his neck then watched his eyes and head loll backward and roll off his body. *This is going to take way more effort,* he thought, bringing the sword across the next dark elf in line, striking a wounding blow and watching it disappear before his eyes. *Am I going to have to decapitate every single one of them?*

His sword flashed, moving without thought through the enemies before him. He hacked and slashed, watching half the ones he struck down rise again. *I need to find this healer.* He led with his sword, attacking through the crowd, cutting his way deeper into the dark elven army, surrounded once more by the enemy. He heard a shout of protest from Vara behind him, but he ignored it. *At least this time I'm just outnumbered, not overmatched.*

A few rows of soldiers away, he saw a flash of white—a robe, hidden behind armor and near invisible in the darkness that had fallen around them. With a shout he shoved a dark elf out of his way and lopped the head off another. Behind a line of infantry stood a healer, eyes closed, hands raised and glowing. The protective line of soldiers screamed at his approach and charged him, and he felt the bite of a dozen blades hitting his armor. Most bounced off but a few found purchase in the weak points and the sting of the strikes was muted as he fought his way through the warriors that now surrounded him. From beside him he heard Vara shout and glanced to the side in time to see her take the head off another wizard. The man's hands shook as his body fell limp.

It was a deadly ballet; he moved faster than any of them but they weighed him down with numbers and sprung back to their feet after he cut them down; only a few remained unmoving. He concentrated on fatal or crippling attacks—splitting the skull of one in half, removing the head of the next—or ones that would remove them from his path. He aimed an unsteady kick at the last dark elf standing between him and the healer, and felt three piercing attacks land while he did so.

His kick landed, pushing the dark elven warrior out of the way. Using the speed granted him by his weapon, he rushed forward toward the healer, a dark elf so shrouded in the fever of casting healing magics that her cloak appeared to be glowing. "Sorry," he said with sincere apology as he brought his sword against the unarmed woman, striking her down, "I don't like killing unarmed magic users, especially not women, but I can't have you giving my enemies any more chances at life." His slash spattered her robe with red as his stroke nearly cut her in half diagonally from shoulder to waist.

She gasped and looked up at him with stunned surprise, her purple eyes registering shock. Her mouth opened and a horrible sound came out, a desperate, choked moan audible even in the fury of the battle. "I'm sorry," he said again to the eyes that looked back at him. "I'm so sorry."

With that, he turned from her and howled, spending all the internal fury and sorrow he felt, channeling it into the next attack, which brought down eight dark elven footmen with ruthless efficiency. No longer worried about killing in one blow, Cyrus raked them across the chest, severed limbs, destroyed faces with vicious accuracy. *They all have weapons in their hands and they're invading someone else's country,* he told himself, but the image of the dying healer stayed with him.

Cyrus felt a sword strike him in the small of his back and pain lanced through him, causing him to stumble and miss wide with a swipe at a footman that would otherwise have been a killing blow. He looked back at the enemy who had wounded him and brought Praelior around, killing him in one hit. He turned back to the foes in front of him that were barring his passage back to the line where Vara and Longwell held out, but something stopped him. He looked to where he'd cut down the healer and found her, blood pooled at her feet.

But she was standing. Her hands were aglow, her clothing torn asunder by his attack, but she stood. The place where he'd cut her was healed, flawless blue skin with blood beaded up in drops all around the place where his sword had cut a swath through bone, tissue and internal organs only moments before. *Son of a bitch. They must have a second healer; there's no way she was able to mend herself after that.*

Another line had formed between them, and the stabbing pain from the wound in his lower back kept him from rushing them as he had last time. *I need to take her out — merciless this time. They won't be able to reattach her head in the midst of this battle*, he thought grimly. *I should have done it last time — stupid — that's what mercy is when you're outnumbered.*

A shout tore through the night. From far to the south, cutting through the darkness came a voice that rumbled like rocks falling down a cliff. "WHOEVER CONTINUES TO FIRE THESE ANNOYING POINTED WOODEN STICKS AT ME WILL DIE WHEN I VIOLATE YOUR LOWER BODY REAR APERTURE WITH THEM!"

Thank you for the distraction, Fortin. Cyrus charged through the line assembled in front of him, bowling them over and ignoring the pain that made him want to throw himself over the edge of the bridge. He reached the healer in three steps and raised his sword again. "This time I'm not sorry," he said as he brought it around in a horizontal slice. He watched her body drop, the glow fading from her hands as her headless corpse fell to the ground.

A cry of anguish sounded over the fray, a desperate sob that drew his attention even in spite of the fact that he knew there were enemies closing on him. Another row back he locked eyes with a man in a robe who had a rounded face and black hair. When Cyrus saw him, he watched the pudgy blue face turn frightful and knew he'd found the second healer. He ignored the sting of a half dozen more blades as they clashed with his armor and flesh and let Praelior lead him to the man, who turned and tried to escape between the two soldiers behind him. He bumped against their armor, trying to squeeze his fat frame through the gap.

By the time the two of them realized what he was doing, it was too late. *No mistakes this time.* Cyrus brought his sword across, stepping into his stroke and bringing it through the heads of the soldiers on either side of the healer as well. The three of them fell together, and Cyrus felt a grin of triumph as he began to collapse under the weight of all the foes attacking him from behind. He howled and swung his sword in a wide radius, clearing a swath around him, and roared as they closed again, slashing with a circular swing of his weapon that gave him another minute of breathing room. *I'm hurt bad.* With his left hand he felt his back, and it came back bloody. *Thank Bellarum my armor is black or they'd see how bad I'm hurt.* He tried to stand and failed. *Damn. I may be showing them anyway.*

He looked around, and for once there was a gap. Surrounded again, he found himself in the midst of a sea of foes, but none of them close enough to strike. In front of him was the direction that led back to Vara, Longwell and the others, but from his kneeling position he could not see them. The clank of heavy boots awoke him to the danger behind and he rolled forward, feeling an excruciating pain that drew a scream from him as he forced himself back to his feet.

He turned, and before him stood a dark knight. His armor bore terrible angles, with spikes jutting from the vambraces, pauldrons and helm. Slits revealed segments of a humorless face, giving it a somewhat demonic appearance. He carried a two-handed sword that glimmered even in the absence of light, telling Cyrus it was mystical in nature.

The dark knight raised his sword and Cyrus brought Praelior up. He felt the blow land, rattling his teeth. Weak from blood loss, he tried to block the next attack but it was even stronger than the first, driving him back, where the jeer of a footman behind him was followed by a stabbing in his side. He jabbed back with his sword and felt a small satisfaction when he heard a shriek of pain.

The dark knight maintained his distance, circling toward Cyrus slowly. *He's not underestimating me; he knows I'm dangerous even wounded. You'd think I'd have learned by now not to get outside the range of my healers, but no...*

The dark knight attacked again, swinging the heavy blade twice more, and twice more Cyrus blocked, though not without great effort. The strain allowed another dark elf to strike him from behind, and this time when he swung about, the footman danced out of range before he could land an attack, laughing, and Cyrus was forced to turn back to the dark knight.

Every breath was coming with more difficulty, and fatigue was washing over Cyrus. *I just want to go to sleep,* he thought. *But now's not the best time...* The pain ate at him from a dozen places, from two sword wounds where he would have sworn they hacked out most of his lower back, to an ache in his shoulder. The smell of acrid smoke had been in his nose so long he had almost forgotten it, but he noticed it now, along with the growing edge of the cold in the air.

The dark knight brought his sword down again and Cyrus blocked, but this time his balance failed him and he fell to a knee. He raised his sword in time to block the next blow but the strength of it knocked him to his back. *Not now. I have to keep moving or I'm dead.* He began to struggle but the dark knight extended a hand and Cyrus felt a clutching pain in his chest from a spell. A scream tore from the warrior's lips as a sensation like a fiery blade being thrust into his chest impaled him. He started to struggle once more and the searing agony shot through him again.

"Stay down," the dark knight's voice was low, raspy. He closed on Cyrus, his sword held in both hands, blade down. "It will be over in a moment."

It sounded like sweet honey poured into Cyrus's ear. His eyes fought to close and every muscle went slack, no will to move left in them. He felt the blood running down his back and knew that he was bleeding to death. Iron in his mouth told him that he'd bit his tongue and he wondered when it had happened. The clamor of the battle faded, and all he could hear was a great silence. The thousand pains that had plagued him for the last few minutes seemed very far away, and his eyes locked onto the armored figure standing above him. The sword raised, and started to descend, so fast and yet so slow—

Chapter 33

Cyrus watched Vara's blade intercept the dark knight's sword halfway to his chest and she knocked the dark elf back a step. She raised her hand and a blast of force sent the dark elves behind the knight backward, her fury manifested with magical energy. The dark knight held fast, like a man leaning forward in a windstorm, trying to avoid being blown away.

"You were quite right," her lancing voice said as she raised her sword again. "This will be over in a moment." Her hand pointed at Cyrus and he felt a soothing air cross his back, as though the pain in his back had dwindled.

Vara attacked without warning, a leaping offense led with her sword. She clashed with his blade, pushing him back another step and then raining another blow on him. "You would not have had such an easy time with him," she said, voice infused with barely controlled fury, "if he hadn't just finished a suicide mission to kill both your healers."

"Oh, no doubt," came the soothing voice of the dark knight amidst the clash of their blades. "But I would have killed him all the same, just as I'll kill you." His words turned to a bellow. "In the name of the Sovereign!" Echoing cries came from the throats of the dark elves all over the bridge as they rallied for another attack.

Cyrus dragged himself to his feet. He still bled, still hurt, still felt weak, yet Vara's healing spell had given him enough strength to fight on. The nearest footmen were focused on the battle between the dark knight and paladin, and he charged them with a violent attack that sent both of them falling over the edge of the bridge. The Sanctuary force closed, Longwell pressing forward with his lance; for every two enemies he would catch with the blade he would end another with the tip.

Cyrus helped clear the way for the Sanctuary forces, keeping his eye on Vara, who was still locked in combat with the dark knight. He gestured toward Erith and felt strength course through him as his wounds were healed.

The dark knight brought his sword down against Vara, driving her back toward Santir and the still-advancing forces of the dark elven army. They were not speaking, but with every attack from the dark knight, Vara parried or blocked with a grunt. Her cheeks were red from exertion and her counterattacks were coming slower. She raised her hand to cast a spell and he pressed her, interrupting her casting. She fell back, circling to place her back to the edge of the bridge.

Cyrus kept himself toward the middle of the bridge. He fell upon the advancing forces and carved a path through them with Longwell. They had cleared the line between them and the Sanctuary war party, and Cyrus watched as the paladin and dark knight clashed to his right.

He waited, fending off the advancing infantry as Vara wearied. When he sensed she was faltering, he moved forward, exerting his lightning quickness, and struck at the dark knight while his back was turned, stabbing him in the side, his sword punching through the knight's armor and causing him to look at Cyrus, stunned.

"You're a dark knight; don't look so shocked at the treachery of me stabbing you in the back." He slid the dark elf off the tip of his sword, letting the body fall to its knees before he whirled around and delivered a finishing blow. "This is war, after all." He looked to Vara, who was breathing heavy and appeared unsteady on her feet.

"You could have intervened sooner," she said.

"You're a paladin. I thought you'd be mad if I dishonorably intervened in your duel."

"As you pointed out," she said, scowling at him as another row of footmen advanced on them, "this is war and thus the honorable circumstances present in a duel do not apply."

"Didn't your mother ever tell you?" Cyrus looked at Vara, her irritation still obvious. "If you keeping making that face, it'll freeze like that." He turned to see Chirenya, glaring at him. "See? Like that." He made another round of attacks, dispensing with another half dozen infantry, then looked down the bridge toward Santir. "You look tired. Want to take a break? We could bring up some others to hold the front line."

She snorted. "You know that no one could hold it so well as I do."

"I do." He inflicted a crosswise cut to a nearby dark elf. "But I also know we've been at this for quite some time, and it would appear that they've got no intention of retreating anytime soon." He took a deep breath as he pressed the attack again. "In fact, it looks like they'll continue funneling reinforcements down the bridge until either we break or we bleed them dry."

"How long do you suppose you can keep this up?" Vaste's voice broke through after a few minutes of intense battle, during which Cyrus had given very little ground but taken a great many lives in return for it. Arrows whizzed from behind him as the Sanctuary force aided the three of them in holding the line.

"Until they're all dead," Cyrus replied. "Or until the night is over."

"Well, one of those is about to come true," the troll said. "Though I suppose it's difficult to see."

Cyrus pondered the vague reply while dispatching his next four enemies. His hands were cramped from holding his sword, and soreness permeated every muscle. Vara, next to him, was huffing, each breath coming so quickly after the last that he wondered if she might be ready to hyperventilate. The battlefield had begun to lighten, not only aided by the torches carried by their foes, but by another source.

He looked over the bridge and saw the devastation of Santir; the fires had largely burned out, and the smoke had begun to clear. Through the haze, the sun was rising, though it was not visible. It was dawn, Cyrus realized. *We've been fighting for hours*, he thought. *No wonder we're exhausted.*

He dodged the attacks of four more infantrymen and killed them all, taking a moment to assess the situation. He cast his gaze to the Southbridge and saw a figure still standing in the middle of the span, great hands rising and falling with furious power. Bodies were swept over the side in clusters of two and three, and the occasional howls of Fortin that had been audible through the night continued even now.

Cyrus cut another foe down, then another, and turned his attention toward the Northbridge. He blinked as he looked at the span. The night before, it was obvious where the elves held the bridge in the center, even after the battle was joined, as their pointed helmets were a stark contrast to the much more blunted and dull helms worn by the dark elven regulars. The light was still dim and he could not differentiate between them.

"Vara," he called. "Can you see the Termina guards on the Northbridge?"

She disengaged from her next foes, falling back as Cyrus moved to take up her slack in the line. He focused on the combatants moving toward him, keeping light on his feet and battling back, knocking over two more dark elven soldiers.

"I see them," she said at last, slipping back into the fight and taking his place in the center. "You won't like it; they're at the very end of bridge. It would appear they're about to be driven back."

He heard a great hue and cry from the Northbridge, and wondered if that had indeed happened. "How long would it take an army to march from there along the waterfront and flank us here?"

"Twenty minutes," she said as she drove her sword through another foe. "Perhaps fifteen if they hurry."

Cyrus brought his sword down in another slash, sending another dark elf into the beyond. "Then that's how long we have to stage our retreat before we get flanked."

Chapter 34

"I need a druid," Cyrus called over his shoulder. One of them appeared from the battle line behind him, a fresh-faced human. *Gods, I wish Niamh was here.* "I need you to use Falcon's Essence to cross to the Southbridge and warn Fortin and Andren that we're about to be flanked. Teleport them out of the city, back to Sanctuary."

"Are you certain you want to take our most effective fighter out of the battle?" Vara looked at him with incredulity.

"They're going to have to evacuate at some point and Fortin is not so light on his feet," Cyrus said. He turned to the druid. "Teleport them out. We're going to fall back to the Chancel and make sure the streets are clear." With a nod, the druid cast a spell on himself, ran to the edge of the bridge and stepped off, continuing his dash across the air itself.

"Let's start the retreat," Cyrus said, sword dancing to keep the enemy at bay. Four dark elves charged at him. He looked to Vara and Longwell. "You two start backing up, I'll follow."

A burst of flame extended the width of the bridge, burning the dark elves in front of Cyrus. The foes behind the line of fire halted, and he heard a voice over his shoulder. "Enough of your stubbornness." He turned to face Chirenya, her hand extended. "Come along — this won't last forever."

With a last look at the dark elven army trapped behind the barrier of fire, Cyrus exchanged a look with Vara and then Longwell. "Full retreat. Let's go."

They fell back, running across the bridge. The hidden sunrise cast Termina in a pale light, and the Entaras'iliarad was near-deserted, the quietest Cyrus had yet seen it. "J'anda!" he said to the dark elf. "Can you send part of your illusory army marching toward the Northbridge? Maybe we can buy some time."

The dark elf did not answer, but half the illusionary force began a march down the bridge, executing an about-face and starting down the span. Cyrus's eye fell on the harbor. Most of the skiffs and boats had left, but a few remained with the wooden docks and warehouses on the quay. "Chirenya, can you set the wharf on fire? No sense in giving the dark elves a city that's equipped to blockade the whole river Perda."

She halted in her run and raised an eyebrow at him. "Perhaps you have more brains than I gave you credit for." She waved a hand three times and he could see a burst of flame catch on three of the warehouses and one of the larger ships and begin to spread. "That should do it." They resumed their run back toward the city.

Cyrus cast a look back and saw the barrier of fire remained across the bridge. "How long can you maintain that?"

Chirenya was sweating and drawn; whether from the exertion of maintaining the barrier or the running, he could not say. "Another minute or two, perhaps. Enough for us to have a bit more of a headstart." She puffed and then looked at him with a grudging respect. "I know I have belittled you in the past, but I must say, you are quite an effective dog of war."

Cyrus grunted. "But still a dog?"

"With fleas and all, yes." Even through her ragged breathing, he could see she was trying to smile.

They reached the end of the bridge and Cyrus looked ahead to the Chancel of Life. The quiet of the Entaras'iliarad struck him, only a few souls lingering here and there. He watched the Sanctuary force running before him and felt a swell of pride at what they had done. *I hope Odellan's all right; I suspect without a healer he had a hell of a night.*

The smell of the smoke from Santir overwhelmed the city. In the distance, Cyrus could hear the rumble of the army behind them, but the city was quiet, save for Vara's shouts of "The dark elves are coming!" A door slammed somewhere far off, and the sound of the Sanctuary force's footfalls threatened to drown everything else out.

"I need to go home," Chirenya said, and started to change direction.

Cyrus stopped with her. "Why?"

"There are things I should bring," she said. "Things I can't bear to leave behind."

"There's a horde of dark elves descending on us," Cyrus said. "If you have to choose, which is more important to you— whatever you've left in your destroyed house, or your life?"

The older woman glared at him, and he could see the resistance mounting in her eyes, her shoulders tensed as though she were about to lash out at him. Vara was to his right, her hands on her knees, gulping in deep breaths. Finally, Chirenya relaxed. "Fine. You are correct; nothing left behind is worth my life."

"Good," Cyrus said. "Let's sweep toward the Chancel and make sure there aren't any stragglers." An uncomfortable thought presented itself. "Or a glut of people backed up trying to get out of the city."

They moved onward. The fatigue by this point was such that Cyrus felt a great weakness in his arms. The night's exertions had taken a toll, but since he had sheathed his sword his arms had begun to stiffen. *I don't know that I've ever engaged in that much combat in a single night. Evidently my body was not prepared for it.* The cold morning air appeared in little puffs as he exhaled, his cloak long since discarded in the battle. When he had been fighting, it had felt too warm for it; now he could feel the sweat and sticky blood from the wounds he'd suffered cooling on his skin, giving him chills.

A few figures darted in and out of doorways and down alleys as Cyrus approached. *Looters,* he thought. *No time to deal with them now; this city is about to go down in flames anyway, if the dark elves hold to their pattern.*

They ran through the empty squares toward the Chancel, Cyrus's eyes scanning for threats. A griffon screeched overhead, its rider steering it in a slow, arcing circle above them. An arrow shot up, followed by another, and the griffon reeled out of control, spiraling through the third floor window of a nearby building. Glass shattered and bricks fell from the hole left by the beast's crash. Cyrus's eyes flew to where the arrows had originated to see Aisling lowering her bow. She met his gaze as she slung it across her back. "No point in letting them live to harass us later," she said with a shrug.

They ran on, reaching the Chancel square a few minutes later. Cyrus looked back to see the army marching down the Entaras'iliarad behind them, but only a quarter of the way along. *I guess the illusory army slowed them down.* As they followed the road around the Chancel, Vara called out to him. "Here in the square the road bends southwest toward Pharesia, and it is the way most of the evacuees would have gone. It becomes the Olenet'yinaii — the Monarch's Road — here at the edge of the square." She puffed, her breath still coming in gasps. "We should be able to see any stragglers."

They turned the corner and stopped. The road stretched through many blocks and squares until the buildings ended and fields frosted by ice turned into rolling hills. Only a few souls were visible ahead, laden with many burdens.

"It would appear that the evacuation was successful," Chirenya said. "I hate to say we can't do anything for those who remain, but Vidara tends to help those who help themselves."

"No," Cyrus said. "There's one last group to get out."

Vara and Chirenya looked at him, and he pointed back toward the Northbridge. "Whatever is left of the Termina Guard will be shredded if we don't get them out of there."

"And we're likely to be shredded if we attempt a street-by-street defense," Vaste said. "Not that I don't empathize with the plight of the Termina Guard, but neither am I eager to die trying to get to them."

"All we need is a wizard," Cyrus said, "and a few minutes. We can position a frontline—Longwell, Vara and myself, maybe a couple others—to take the heat off of them, and one of our wizards can evacuate us all."

"How many wizards do you have remaining?" Chirenya arched her eyebrow at him.

"I don't know," he replied."But you can do an area-based teleport, can't you?"

"Assuming you're intelligent enough to grasp the blue orb when it appears, yes."

"I think I can figure that out." Cyrus turned. "We go back, around the Chancel and down the Olenet'yinaii. We'll give the survivors of the Termina Guard cover while we extract them, and then we'll return to..." He looked to Chirenya. "Wherever she sees fit to take us."

"Saekaj Sovar, perhaps. I hear it's lovely this time of year."

They moved quickly, and as they passed through the square around the Chancel of Life, Cyrus took a moment to note that the dark elven army moving up the Entaras'iliarad was only about halfway to the Chancel square. He led the way to the next street, and as they came around the corner he saw the Termina Guard.

The street was wide, but not as wide as the bridge they had spent all night defending. The Termina Guard was three blocks away, strung out in a ragged formation that blocked the street, and Cyrus could tell they were in the midst of a brutal fighting retreat. *There are less than five hundred of them left*, Cyrus estimated. *Rough night.*

When they reached the back line of the Guard, Cyrus pushed his way through the rows of bloody and weary elves, Vara at his back and a few others behind them. One of the Sanctuary druids remaining with them hovered overhead using Falcon's Essence and shot a bolt of lightning into the ranks of the dark elves as they continued to surge up the street. From where he stood, Cyrus saw no end to the dark elven forces. They filled the streets all the way to the Northbridge.

"Odellan!" Cyrus called out over the crowd.

One of the elves nearest to him pointed to the front line. "He's at the fore. Has been the whole time."

Cyrus pushed his way to the front line, where there was a slight separation. The dark elves were assaulting the remaining Termina Guards in waves, charge after charge. Two elves died before his eyes while a half dozen dark elves fell in the same space. "Odellan!" Cyrus said again, stepping into the battle and dispatching two dark elven footmen.

"General!" Odellan's voice was weary but relieved. He bore a long, bloody cut across the left side of his forehead, from the peak of his hairline to his temple. His helm was long gone, his long hair red matted with blood. His golden armor was stained crimson as well, and he held his left hand at his side while fighting with his right. "Glad to see you managed a retreat before they flanked you. I was concerned—" he stepped into a charging dark elf and cut him almost in two with a rising slash—"that you wouldn't see us breaking in the dark. I sent a runner to advise you to retreat."

"The city is evacuated," Cyrus said. "There's nothing more your men can do here; we've come to teleport you out."

The clanging of blades filled the air. "Aye," Odellan said, "against these numbers, the city is lost."

Cyrus watched Longwell slide into position at the left side of the street while Vara did the same to the right, as the Termina Guard eased back, swords still at the ready. While Vara and Longwell defended against the next wave of foes, he and Odellan held the center, and the dark elven army seemed to slow its approach, a steady trickle making their way forward rather than a charging line. They waited a few hundred feet ahead, drawing steadily closer.

"Chirenya, now!" Cyrus called. "It's time to leave," he told Odellan. "You and your men go first, and as soon as you've left, the last three of us will grab our orbs and teleport out."

Odellan looked to the left in time to see Longwell kill three dark elves in succession. "All right."

A glowing blue ball of translucent light appeared, hovering in front of Cyrus. Orbs of teleportation appeared in front of Vara, Odellan and Longwell, as well as every member of Sanctuary and the Termina Guard. Cyrus looked back and saw a bevy of flashes, bodies dissolving into the blue fire of wizard teleportation, born off to the destination Chirenya had selected with her spell. Pharesia, Cyrus suspected.

Four dark elves drew his attention back to the fight and he blocked their attacks, knocking over one and impaling another, taking out two more with a slash and then taking two steps backward as he waited for the next attack. He chanced another look at the formation behind him, but it was nearly gone; only a handful remained, including Chirenya and Vaste.

Cyrus looked to Odellan. "Now's the time, Endrenshan."

The Termina Guard Captain hesitated, his hand hovering over the blue orb. "We all go together," he said.

Cyrus looked back; only Chirenya remained behind them, staring at him through slitted eyes. "Come on," she said. "I've had enough of these dark elven beasts. Let us be done with this."

Cyrus looked down the line to Longwell, then back to Vara. "On three. One...two..." He saw the next wave of dark elves beginning to charge, then cast a look back to Chirenya. "Three." He froze, his hand only a second from grasping the orb, and a cold shock ran through him. "NO!"

It was too late; Odellan and Longwell vanished in a blast of blue fire, teleported away. Cyrus watched Chirenya as if she were in slow motion. Her hand grasped for the orb in front of her but came up short, her momentum interrupted by a sudden and vicious attack from behind.

An elf stood behind her in dark robes, a wicked expression on his face and twin daggers in his hands. *Assassin*, Cyrus thought as he watched the first blade buried in the wizard's back. He heard a scream from Vara, a howl of inarticulate fury, and watched as Chirenya grimaced as her hand slipped away from the orb. The elf buried the second dagger in her back, and Cyrus watched as the wizard turned in numb shock, looking at the face of the man who had stabbed her.

Then she went limp and dropped from the assassin's arms, crumpling on the ground, unmoving.

Chapter 35

"NOOOOOOO!!" Vara's anguish echoed down the street and Cyrus watched her charge, all-consuming fury taking hold of her. Her hand glowed white as she moved, casting a healing spell, and he watched the light encompass her mother, then fade, then rise again to no effect. Chirenya was still.

Vara brought her sword forward in an assault that lacked any technique but was born of the fury of a daughter who had lost her mother. Great overhand slashes were thrown at the assassin again and again, but he remained outside the reach of her blade, sashaying and whirling to avoid the paladin's attacks.

Cyrus looked for the orbs of teleportation, but they were gone. *They vanished when she died*, he realized. The next wave of charging dark elves was near now, and Cyrus did not have time to assist Vara. He turned to attack the dark elves and found himself surrounded on three sides. Using an offhand slash he cleared two of the sides, and with a heavy overhand blow he cleared the last.

"We're about to be surrounded!" He looked back as two more soldiers commenced attacks on him. Vara was still hammering at the assassin, her face red with emotion; tears streamed down her cheeks and she leapt forward and caught the assassin with a blade in the shoulder, knocking him off balance. He spun from the wound as she pressed the attack and impaled him on the tip of her blade. A sob of rage flew from her as she thrust the sword deeper into the elven man.

With shocking speed, the assassin forced himself further down her blade, driving it deeper through his chest, all the way to the guard that separated the blade from the hilt. He reached out with his dagger as Vara watched, stunned, and buried his weapon into the gap in her side armor. She cried out and fell to her knees, wrenching her sword from the assassin's body.

"NO!" Cyrus hit the remaining two dark elves attacking him with an assault born of desperation. They flew backward, one missing an arm and the other short a head. He turned and sprinted to where Vara knelt in the street, one hand on her sword and the other at her side. The hand at her wound came forward, pulling the dagger from it. She held it, staring at the bloody blade before dropping it to the ground. She tried to stand, but failed, sinking back to her knees.

Cyrus reached her as she tried to stand again. "Mother," Vara croaked. "I need to see..."

"She's dead," Cyrus said, his voice no more than a whisper. He saw the horror and loss in her eyes as she looked to where Chirenya lay. "We need to get out of here." The next line of dark elves was approaching, no more than a hundred feet away. He sheathed his sword, then hers, and placed her arm around his shoulders, lifting her to her feet.

"I can...walk," she said, trying to shove him away.

"I'm sure you can, but we need to move fast right now," he said as he shuffled them off the Olenet'yinaii into an alley that ran south. "We have to get out of the city before the dark elves catch us, and we're short on magical transportation."

He half-ran, half-walked her down the alley, the morningstar's chain still wrapped around his armor, rattling against it as they went. Far ahead, past dozens of cross-streets, he saw the Entaras'iliarad, still clear. Behind he could see the formation of dark elven soldiers marching down the Olenet'yinaii. Immediately behind him he heard the jeers of a few that had broken off from the column, following them and no more than fifty feet back.

He half-turned and raised Vara's palm in their direction. "Any chance you can knock them backwards?"

"I...what?" Her eyes were unfocused, and she blinked. "Oh." Her hand wobbled in his grasp, and then a blast of energy shot from it, sending their pursuers bouncing off walls from the force of her spell.

"Thanks," he said, "saved me from having to stop and draw a sword."

"Aye," she said, sounding as though she were groggy.

How do we get out of here? His mind was racing. *We'll have to take the Olenet'yinaii out of town, southwest toward Pharesia, and hope that we get a good enough lead on the dark elven army that they don't catch us. We have to get through this alley and onto the Entaras'iliarad before that army reaches this alley, or we're going to be stuck in the city.*

He hobbled along, Vara becoming more dead weight as they went, until finally she went limp and he was forced to lift her up and carry her cradled in his arms. Blood ran down his gauntlets from where the dagger had penetrated her side. *She'll need care. Something to stop the bleeding, and it's doubtful a healing spell will do it. That assassin's blades had to be covered with black lace.*

He cursed himself. *How could we have gotten so involved in the battle that we forgot there were still lunatics out to kill her?* He let out a string of epithets. *They may have succeeded. I'm going to have to carry her to the next town, over uneven roads and with the dark elven army in pursuit, and it's unlikely they'll be very forgiving if I surrender since I did help kill about ten thousand of them last night.* His feet felt heavier with every step, though Vara was relatively light. *Can I carry her to the next town? Yes,* he decided. *I could carry her to Reikonos if I had to. To Fertiss. Anywhere.*

He burst from the alley into the light of the Entaras'iliarad and breathed a sigh of relief when he saw that the dark elven army was still several blocks behind them. He ran the remaining block to the Chancel square, puffing with exertion by the time he reached it. The loud whinny of a horse followed by the sound of hooves beating against the street came from behind, causing him to turn. He nearly dropped Vara, already reaching for his sword to fend off whatever was coming.

Instead, he smiled. The horse whinnied again, hooves clomping to cut the distance between them. Windrider approached from across the square, Vara's mount following behind. "Smartest horse I've ever met," he said as his steed galloped to him. He placed Vara in the saddle and she slumped forward, still unconscious. He climbed up behind her, grabbed the reins to her horse and urged Windrider forward. Vara's horse followed behind, unburdened. *We'll need the second horse; Windrider is bound to get tired of carrying both of us.* He kept an arm protectively around Vara's waist, holding her in place in the saddle, listening to the clink of her armor hitting against his on every step.

They ran at a full gallop for quite some time. They passed out of the Chancel square and headed southwest toward Pharesia, the buildings growing smaller and smaller, from mighty row houses into two story structures, then one story buildings, until finally they became spaced out wooden hovels and then wide open fields. The horse bore them on, still riding at full tilt as the sun rose behind them.

Chapter 36

The land sloped as they headed southwest up to the crest of a hill a few miles away from the city. When they reached the top, Cyrus brought Windrider to a stop. He dismounted and looked back. Termina was laid out before him and he could see the fires still burning in Santir. He could see that Chirenya had done well; the wharf by the river was in flames, thick black smoke covering the Grand Span from the fire. The dark elven horde moved through the streets, their columns dissipated. A full fledged sack was in progress, and he tried not to think about those who had remained behind for whatever reason.

Pillars of smoke were visible above the Chancel of Life. *They're burning the Chancel*, he thought, his mouth dry. Similarly, the government center had smoke coming from it, as well as a few other points throughout the city. A concentrated knot of the dark elven army seemed to be grouped around the Great Bazaar, flowing in and out of it like ants from a hill.

Cyrus reached up to Windrider and lifted Vara from the saddle with utmost care. He carried her to a patch of frosted wheatgrass and set her down, placing his hand under her head and lowering it onto the soft bed of green. Her face was whiter than usual, the flush of battle gone from her cheeks, but her chest rose and fell under her breastplate, now dirty and spattered from the battle. Her hair was still bound and ran to the ground, her ponytail absorbing the frozen dew.

He took her pauldrons off first, removing them over her head with care, and then worked the plate gloves and vambraces from her hands and arms. Next came the breastplate, and finally he rolled up the chainmail at her side. The cloth undershirt she wore was torn above her hip and a small gash spat a thin stream of blood as he raised it. The stab wound was no more than an inch, and the blood around the edges had already begun to crust over.

I'm not a healer, Cyrus thought. *I have no idea how to treat this wound other than to bandage it and hope she doesn't bleed to death.* Vara stirred, murmuring something, but did not awaken. *Dammit. This is so ridiculously unfair. We finally...* He shook his head. *No time for self-pity. We need to ride.*

He gathered up the pieces of her armor and stuffed them in the saddlebags of her horse, where he found a spare cloak and a few articles of clothing. He took a shirt and wrapped it around her waist, covering the wound before setting her back on Windrider. He climbed up behind her and urged the horse forward again.

They rode on, slowing after a few hours because of the increasing congestion on the road. Cyrus tried to bring the horse to a stop to change several times, but the white destrier ignored him. "Don't kill yourself," he whispered, and the horse whinnied. *This is no ordinary horse,* he thought for not the first time. *Something is very peculiar about him.* He held tight to Vara, who grew colder in his grasp. *The nearest portal is three days' hard ride.* The words bounced in his mind, over and over, and he clung to them, hoping he could force time to move faster.

He moved to the side of the road, bypassing the fleeing citizens of Termina and ignoring calls from weary passersby to leave Vara's horse. There was a hunger and desperation among the elves, and their piteous cries asking him for some mercy, for help, but mostly for food fell on deaf ears as he navigated the roads, which grew fuller. It was clear most of them had left as quickly as urged, without consideration for food, drink or shelter of any kind. Many of the refugees even lacked for a decent coat, as though they had run out the door without taking any heed of the weather.

Every hour or so he would pull back the dressing and check Vara's wound. *All this riding can't be good for her. I need to find someone who can actually treat her.*

As sundown approached, the refugees became thicker and thicker. Most of the elves were piteous by now, crying out for food where there was none, and arguments broke out along the road. Cyrus rode on, passing countless quarrels, ignoring pleas to "Just leave me the spare horse!" and hiding Vara's face the entire time, her eyes covered by the cowl of the cloak.

Cyrus was weary as the darkness crept in. Ahead was a crowd thicker than those spread out along the road. As they grew closer he saw a tent set up ahead, the shadowy outline of it visible in the dimming light. Its angular lines jutted up above the nearby trees. It was gargantuan and possessed multiple spires, with small flags at the tip of each.

As they drew closer, Cyrus saw the crowd in front of it. Food was being given freely, served by the bare-chested priestesses of Vidara. Without conscious thought, he steered Windrider toward them. He pulled back the cowl from Vara's head and spoke as the crowd grew thicker. "Shelas'akur," he said, "shelas'akur." Cries filled the air as the elves took up his call, and the crowd parted for them, hands reaching out and brushing her as they passed. He heard women wailing at the sight of Vara's pale face, waxy and still. He stopped and a hue and cry went up from the priestesses as the word was passed to them that the shelas'akur was wounded.

He lowered Vara from the back of Windrider and carried her forward. Priestesses gathered around him and the tent flap opened. A hand emerged and beckoned him forward, the figure silhouetted in the light of a fire burning inside the tent. He lowered his head and carried her through as the shadow moved aside to admit them.

"Over here," came the soft voice of the figure, leading them to a corner where a bedroll was piled with pillows. Cyrus set her gently upon them, brushing her hair out of her face as he did so, reminded of how he had done the same for Niamh when she died. He swallowed his emotions and looked up to see Arydni, the High Priestess of Vidara. "You've done well to get her out of the city in such a state."

"For want of scant seconds, she wouldn't be injured," Cyrus said. "And her mother wouldn't be dead."

"Chirenya?" The High Priestess's face had not looked so lined only days earlier when he had seen her. He could see by the light of the fire and the lamps hung in the corners that she still wore garb similar to what he had seen at the Chancel, her bare bosoms somewhat hidden by the shadows the flame cast.

"She helped us defend the bridges and evacuate the survivors of the Termina Guard," he said as he rolled up the chainmail to Vara's midsection and began to peel away the bloody shirt from her side. "An assassin attacked her after our party teleported away; Vara and I were left behind facing the dark elven army. She managed to kill the assassin, but he struck a final blow." He pulled the cloth from her wound. "A dagger covered in black lace—she couldn't heal herself."

Arydni knelt down on all fours and sniffed the wound, then called for brandy in elvish. "Care for a drink?" she asked with a drawn smile as she dabbed some on a cloth.

"I don't think that will do much for me right now. If my friend Andren was here, he'd be quick to take you up on it."

"You know Andren?" She smiled as she placed the cloth on Vara's wound.

"He's my oldest friend." Cyrus frowned. "You know him?"

Arydni smiled. "I should. He's the father of one of my children, after all."

"Wait...what?"

"It was long ago. He was very young, only a hundred or so, and I was much older, and a priestess. We stayed together long enough to raise our daughter to the age of maturity and parted as friends." She looked wistful as she dabbed at Vara's wound. "How is he? I haven't seen him in so long."

"He's well. He's one of our healers." Cyrus searched his mind for details he could tell her. "He...uh...well, he drinks a lot."

"Really?" She furrowed her brow. "He never touched the stuff in the century we were together, but that was almost two thousand years ago."

Cyrus tried to put aside what she was telling him. "Will Vara be all right?"

"I don't know." Arydni snapped her fingers and spoke words in elvish, and one of the priestesses brought her a small box. It was red, covered with cloth, and when she opened it a needle and thread were within. "I need to close her wound now that I've cleaned it." She muttered more words in elvish and the Priestesses brought lamps and candles closer, casting Vara in the flickering light. Her face was relaxed, and Cyrus could see the small perforation in the skin where the dagger had slipped into her.

He watched as the High Priestess moved her fingers with the delicate precision of a seamstress, slipping the needle in and out of the skin. He held Vara's hand the entire time but the paladin never stirred. When Arydni finished, she handed the needle and thread to one of the other priestesses, then walked to the corner where a basin of water stood. She immersed her hands, taking a few moments to rinse them. She raised them out, and a priestess stepped forward with a cloth and dried them for her; then she walked back and knelt next to Vara, shaking her head.

"I remember when this one was born," Arydni said in a hushed tone. "Her sister, as well. Never was a baby birthed with greater ease than Isabelle. This one, though..." Her hand brushed the blond locks off Vara's head. "Her mother's labor was long and hard." She wore a small smile. "Of course, Chirenya was cursing the whole time."

He swallowed hard, bitterness nearly choking him. He had not enjoyed Chirenya's company, true, and she had been unkind, but... *She was Vara's mother. And she sacrificed more than anyone at the bridge.*

If the Priestess saw his emotion, she ignored it. "She was a miracle from Vidara herself," Arydni murmured. "A true miracle, the lightest spot since this curse began."

Something stirred in Cyrus. "Curse? Are you talking about the infertility of the male elves?"

She looked at him, shrewd, her age and wisdom visible more in her eyes than in her firm and supple body. "She told you, did she?"

"Her father accidentally gave me the words and Vara confirmed it." He squeezed her hand tighter. "She said nothing of a curse."

The Priestess's face bore a flicker of amusement. "How would you expect an entire race of men to go infertile but by a curse?"

Cyrus shook his head. "Is there any spell caster powerful enough to curse an entire race?"

She stared back at him, her eyes looking at his; a knowing look that told him that she knew more than she would tell him. "No. There is no spell caster that could do such a thing."

"Then how...?"

His voice trailed off as Arydni leaned low over Vara, kissing her forehead and caressing her cheeks. "Thank you for saving the shelas'akur, Cyrus Davidon. I know you love her and would fight to your death for her."

"I suppose that to Vidara, to fight is a sin." He lowered his head and his lips brushed Vara's forehead. Still, she did not stir.

When he raised his head back up, Arydni stared at him. "To protect life is the highest calling. To be a white knight dedicated to such cause is to be a paladin, a holy warrior in the All-Mother's service. Some fight for greed, willing to kill another to take what they have; others for love or for lust, and still others for revenge or out of anger. Every day of life is a fight. You can acquiesce in these greater and lesser battles, and find yourself soon enough dead—or dead inside. Or you can fight for what is important to you, struggle for what matters, with word when possible and sword when necessary, and risk death to shape your world such as you would have it."

He took a deep breath and watched the shadows play on the walls of the tent. "How is that any different from...uh..." He hesitated.

"You worship the God of War, do you not?" She stared him down, using her eyes to compel the truth from him.

"I do," he said, though not proudly. Shame burned his cheeks at the thought of the imminent revulsion from the priestess.

"The God of War cares not what your motives are for conflict; he only craves it. You know that to Bellarum, mercy, compassion and tenderness are weaknesses to be purged. Vidara would raise those up as virtues, and commend any who practiced them. It is the same," she went on, "with death. All creatures die and it is a part of life that the All-Mother accepts, for it makes the time of living more valuable and cherished.

"But the God of Death, Mortus, embraces the loss of life, but not life itself. Do you see the differences?" She waited for him to nod. "If so, you are wise beyond many priests and priestesses whose lives have been spent studying the gods and their philosophies." She wore a gentle smile. "Vidara is the Lifebringer, and yet in defense of her own she does command death. Does that seem contradictory to you?"

"Yes. But no more so than the God of Death loathing life, I suppose, for were it not for life, would there be death?"

She laughed. "Another contradiction; I see you have grasped it. To be on a journey of the spirit and follow the path of any god requires either a rigidly inflexible adherence to dogma or a tremendous sense of humor; rarely are both to be found in the same person." Her hand reached over Vara and rested on his shoulder. "You are tired."

He looked across at her, and for the first time since entering the tent realized once more how much of Arydni was exposed. "I am," he said, keeping his eyes on hers, the fatigue settling over him like a warm blanket.

"Rest, for a time," she said. "We will watch over Vara, and tend to her." She extended her hand and a priestess appeared at Cyrus's shoulder. He stood, looking down at the figure of the paladin on the floor below him. He let the priestess lead him away and help him remove his armor, stacking it in the corner where a bedroll waited with another pillow. He lay down and she tucked him in, pulling the blanket up over his body, and he wondered idly when the last time was that that had happened. *Before the Society of Arms,* he thought. *Back when...*

His thought did not finish; he fell into a deep sleep.

Chapter 37

He awoke to a gentle hand on his shoulder, shaking him. When he rolled to his back, he saw it was one of the priestesses, a younger-looking woman with dark hair that hung well past her shoulders, tucked behind her pointed ears on either side. He had a moment of disorientation before the events of the last few days came flooding back to him. Light streamed into the tent from above and Cyrus rubbed his eyes.

"Someone has come for you, sir," the priestess said as Cyrus sat up. He stood and looked to the corner where Vara rested. She remained unmoving, Arydni at her side. Another figure had joined them, huddled next to the High Priestess. She wore red robes, stitched with patterns, and a scarf of black and red silk that lay across her shoulders, hanging to almost below her waist in the style of all spellcasters; the runes stitched into it would have told Cyrus she was a wizard if he hadn't already known.

He didn't bother to put on his armor before walking over to her. "Nyad."

The elven woman stood to greet him, coming at him so quickly that he didn't have a chance to step back. She wrapped her arms around him in a hug and he felt the warmth of her against him without his armor, before she pulled away. "I'm so glad you're safe. I was on my way back to Termina when I heard the crowds on the road saying Vara had been injured and was resting here." Her relief was tangible. "Did everyone else get out? Did Termina..." She let her words trail off, and he could see the pain in her face.

"Yeah." He nodded. "Everyone else made it out except Vara's mother. She cast the area teleport spell, and an assassin struck her down as we were reaching for the orbs. Vara killed him, but not before..." He gestured to her, helpless. "We had to flee on horseback. When last I looked, Termina was overrun." At his words, Nyad's head bowed in sorrow.

"You did well, getting her this far." Arydni stood, joining them. "It's too soon to be certain, but I think she'll be all right; her wound has avoided infection thanks to the black lace."

Cyrus shook his head in confusion. "I thought the black lace was a poison."

"It nullifies magical effects, that's true. But it's hardly a poison. In fact, it has a sterilizing effect, so if you don't die when attacked by a weapon coated in it, you're unlikely to become infected later. We use it sometimes when treating natural wounds or ones that can't be healed by magic."

"Can she be safely teleported?" Cyrus looked down at Vara, who looked as peaceful as she had last night. "We need to get her somewhere defensible."

"Yes," Arydni said. "But she'll need someone to tend to her. I think it best if I accompany you until she's healed. May the Goddess strike me down for my immodesty, but I doubt you'll find a better healer of natural ailments than I."

"You have people to tend to here," Cyrus said. "You've helped us so much, I don't see how we can pull you from your duties any more than we already have."

"There is much care needed here, it's true." The High Priestess folded her arms in front of her, reminding Cyrus once more that she wore nothing to cover her breasts. *It's getting easier to forget that and fail to notice, the more I'm around these priestesses. Or maybe I'm just too tired.* She drew his attention back to her. "But there is no greater duty than tending to the health of the shelas'akur."

"Very well." He nodded. "Can you teleport us back to Sanctuary, Nyad?"

"No," the wizard said. "I have orders to bring you to Pharesia."

"Orders from whom?" *I don't much care for the sound of that...*

"From my father and Alaric, who believes one more assassin remains in Sanctuary, and they're in the midst of rooting them out. He suggested the Royal Palace in Pharesia might be more defensible and my father would be happy to host you."

Cyrus thought about it. *We can't return to Sanctuary. Where else could we go? Fertiss? The gnomish lands? They're not likely to have as much security as the palace of the Elf King. Our list of options grows very thin, and I don't care for that.* "What kind of security do they have? I don't want to avoid Sanctuary for fear of an assassin and end up chancing into one in the Palace."

"My father has guards that he trusts absolutely, that have been with him since the beginning," she said. "He has pledged to employ the tightest security measures. He will guarantee Vara's safety should we go to him; and yours as well, for your part in the defense of Termina."

"All right," Cyrus said. "What now?"

"If there are people hunting you, you cannot go as you are." Arydni placed a hand upon his pauldron, her pale skin standing out against the black metal. "You may be the only warrior in Arkaria that wears black armor, and would be recognizable as the man who travels with the shelas'akur."

Cyrus looked down. "This was my father's armor. I can't leave it behind."

Arydni shook her head, her expression as impish as a woman of twenty. "Nay. When we teleport, we'll need a means to transport Vara; let us take a wagon with us. We'll attire you in the raiment of one of Vidara's Paladins, and I will wear my finest High Priestess robes. We can hide the shelas'akur in the back of the wagon. In this way, it will appear you are escorting me to the Palace to counsel with the King."

"Very wise," Nyad said. "Such things are commonplace. No one will take notice of a Priestess of Vidara riding through the streets of Pharesia."

"Save perhaps any human men with a wandering eye," Arydni said, not looking to Cyrus.

It took them only an hour to make the preparations. The priestesses procured a wagon, which Vara was loaded onto under the careful watch of Arydni. Cyrus placed his armor with Vara's in a heavy canvas bag that was loaded into the wagon and tied down so as not to roll.

Cyrus stared at himself in the simple, freestanding full length mirror that stood before him in the tent. *The priestesses didn't leave much behind in the evacuation,* he thought. Where his armor was normally black as the darkest night, it was now shining steel. *Not quite as bright Vara's,* he thought, *but she'd approve.* He wore a helm that was cylindrical in shape, tapering to a near-flat top with two slits for eyes and a small opening for a mouth. One of the priestesses draped a surcoat over him; it bore the heraldry he had seen on banners within the Chancel of Life; a green field with two trees, a stream running down the middle, and a few flowers of varying colors underneath a blue sky.

"You look very fine, Sir Cyrus," the priestess who was attending to him spoke, her quiet voice carrying a whisper of suggestion.

"I feel ridiculous," he said, tugging on the surcoat. "I'm an instrument of destruction; I'm supposed to be fearsome. I feel like a bunny is going to hop across this coat of arms." He looked down through the holes in his helm. *Even through this...this bucket, I can see I look ridiculous, and I can't see much of anything.*

"Nay," she said. "You look splendid. Were you not the consort of the shelas'akur, I would show you the affection of a priestess for a man who wears the livery of the Goddess."

"You would?" He mused. "Wait...what?" He turned to her, but she curtsied and brushed out the nearest flap of the tent without answering him. "What does that mean?"

"It means that a great many elven women have turned to human men out of a desperation to feel life grow inside them." Arydni's voice washed over him as she appeared at his shoulder. With delicate fingers, she straightened his surcoat. "Human men who come to the Kingdom are courted, and if they are desirous of a bride, they can doubtless find one."

"I've seen a lot of human men with elven women," he said, then nearly laughed. "Some of the men not nearly worthy of the look of the women on their arm."

She stepped before him, making another minute adjustment to his armor. "In a time such as this, hope is harder to come by. Long have our peoples known friendship, but it is never far from an elf's mind that in a thousand years, when we are still in the same positions, have the same King and government, your whole order could be completely different. And yet humans are the most like the elves of all the races. We share little commonality with the dwarves and gnomes, and the dark elves have been our longest and most hated enemy."

She looked at him in the mirror. "I confess it myself, the curious draw toward human men. It is a predisposition that runs through our whole race now. I am a mother one hundred and forty-five times, yet I know I have time in me for a few more, and the desire as well. If I would have one, I have one place where I would need look—to the race of humans." She admired her handiwork in the mirror. "Very good. You look every bit as dashing as a Knight of Vidara."

"How would you know under the helm?" he asked.

"Why, General Davidon," she said with almost a mocking air. "There is more to a Knight of Vidara than rugged good looks, just as there is more to a priestess than ample bosoms displayed openly." She ushered him out of the tent as he blushed and failed to reply. The wagon was a simple vehicle, wood with overlarge wheels, the spokes made of iron. The sides were high and it had padded benches for sitting. *This must be designed so the priestesses can travel in comfort.*

"I will ride in the back with Vara," Arydni said, climbing up. "As a paladin charged with my defense, you need ride up front with Nyad and drive."

He nodded and helped Nyad up to the seat. "Everyone ready?" Nyad looked into the back of the wagon, waiting for a reply from Arydni, who answered in the affirmative. "Next stop —"

"Hush," Cyrus said, grasping her arm. They were in front of the tent, and a crowd of ragged refugees stared at them; elves who only a few days earlier had been warm and well fed, finely clothed in the prosperous garb of Termina, the jewel of the elven empire. Now they were dirty and haggard and homeless, most of them having not so much as a possession to call their own. *They didn't deserve this. The whole Kingdom will be at war now, a war they can scarce afford since they can't make up their losses. It may be wise for them to sue for peace.*

Nyad's hand was raised, and the glow of her spell encompassed them. Different than druid magic, the teleportation spell of a wizard came from a place of power and energy, crackling and coalescing around them with bright colors. There was a flash and the world grew bright then dimmed as Cyrus found himself somewhere completely different.

Chapter 38

Raised swords and spears greeted Cyrus as he appeared back into being. Soldiers of the Elven Army stood before him, a host almost as large as the one that had laid siege to Termina. Though they were clad in the winged helm and steel breastplates he had seen on the Termina Guard, their livery was different with heraldry that showed a city wall covered in green vines, with water flowing down it.

"Lady Nyad." The officer standing at the forefront bowed before her. Thirty or so soldiers were gathered around the portal with their weapons in hand, ready to put down any potential invaders as they appeared. *Easier than defending your city gates when the enemy armies show up, I suppose.* "We are pleased to see you return." With a waved hand, the officer commanded his men to lower their weapons. "Your father awaits your report."

"Thank you," she said as Cyrus took the reins and started the horses forward through a gap that the soldiers made. He watched as they reformed their line the moment the wagon had passed through. The road stretched before them and Nyad pointed him left.

They were in a clearing, and in the distance Cyrus could see the massive trees of the Iliarad'ouran woods. The last time he had passed through, he had marveled; some of their trunks were a hundred feet in diameter and stretched into the sky, blotting out the sun. *They put the Waking Woods near Sanctuary to shame.* It was a green and verdant land, and the air around them was warm, the sun shining down from above. The smell of fresh greenery was all about, the air bearing the scent of nature that had been so absent in Termina and, later, in the perfumed air of the tent of the priestesses.

Trees were all that was visible on the horizon. In front of him was a different sight, something he had not laid eyes on in nearly two years. Pharesia, the seat of Elvendom, was laid out before him, a massive, vine covered wall blocking all but the highest towers and minarets of the city from view. The wall stretched almost two hundred feet into the air, peppered with a window here and there, and complete with parapets, allowing defenders to fire arrows into any invaders while maintaining cover. The stones that made up the wall carried almost a white color, and shone in the sun.

The main gate was big enough that three titans could walk in on each others' shoulders, and wide enough for fifty wagons. *Was it this big when last I was here? Oh, that's right, I met Nyad outside the city.* They entered with a stream of other traffic onto a wide avenue. There were no street merchants but a great many shops on the boulevard. Bakers, armorers, a flower shop that offered a pleasing, familiar aroma were all there — *but fewer than Termina or Reikonos,* he thought.

Trees were in abundance, and every few buildings sat a garden filled with trees and lush grasses, flowers and the occasional water garden. Aquaducts flowed throughout the city, also vine-covered and with occasional offshoots that dumped water sluicing down the sides in waterfalls.

They passed one such garden, with water cascading down onto flattened circular rocks placed around a pool. Next to it was a grassy meadow sandwiched between two three-story buildings. It was a space bigger than two of the row houses Cyrus had seen in Termina, and it backed to the aquaduct's waterfall. Moss grew around the pond made by the falling water, and two gardens grew to either side of it with rich purples and reds, yellows and blues of the flowers blooming in the mid-morning light. A few elves sat around the park, eating, talking and waiting, enjoying the shade.

They stayed on the same road they had entered the gate on, passing through squares with buildings covered in vines, trellises hanging next to every window with blooming flowers and every sill containing plants of some kind. *The residents of Pharesia take their greenery seriously.*

On their right came a large square, fountain at the center, in an odd design that threw off the symmetry of the street. At the far end of the square was a building larger than any other thus far in the city; a squarish structure with towers at all four corners, domed minarets atop each. "It's the Museum of Arms," Nyad whispered. "You remember, where—"

"Where they kept Ventus, the Scimitar of Air, until the Dragonlord decided he needed it more than the elves," Cyrus said. "It's an impressive building." He looked up, where a large domed glass skylight rested.

The horses trudged along in silence. Cyrus suspected Nyad

would have made an excellent tour guide, but the elf seemed preoccupied with her own thoughts. The noise of the wheels clacking against the streets precluded the possibility of conversation with Arydni, so Cyrus contented himself with taking in the varied and beautiful architecture. Though he was certain that most of it had been built thousands of years ago, every building in Pharesia maintained a look of good repair.

The road made a slight turn, and before them Cyrus could see a colossal building. *That has to be the palace.* At each corner of the grounds sat one of the massive trees that made up the Iliarad'ouran forest. They stretched above the walls that encircled the building. Dozens of towers jutted into the sky—some short, some tall, so many he found himself dizzy from the counting. They weaved in and out, asymmetrical, each topped with a minaret of a different color, giving the rooftop a rainbow hue.

As they grew closer, Cyrus saw that the walls surrounding the palace were only half as high as those around the city. The road carried them to the main gate, where they were ushered through with only a nod from the guards. Other wagons were stopped and searched, their occupants staring jealously at Cyrus as they passed.

Once through the gate, the world opened up before them; the palace grounds were even more luxuriant and green than the city. The palace was a mile distant from the wall, Cyrus reckoned, and the space between was all greenery, the only sign of mortal interference being the trimmed hedges, grasses, trees and the tended flowers arranged in beds. Streams flowed through the area and the colors were intoxicating.

"They're beautiful at night as well," Nyad said from beside him. "Father had the gardeners cultivate a night garden where all the flowers within bloom in the evening. As the sun sets above the wall, the colors reflect off the pools and the stone. He has a few plants and flowers from exotic places that glow phosphorescent in the moonlight." She sighed. "I haven't spent more than a week here since I left home; and only then when our exile was rescinded last year. It truly is the most beautiful place I've ever seen."

"I thought the Sanctuary garden was impressive, but this..." He took a deep breath. "This puts it to shame."

Ahead was the palace. Before them, the road divided to run on either side of a reflecting pool and the two roads reunited before a covered entry. "We're going to the north wing," she said, pointing to an offshoot of the main building that sat to the left of the massive central, towered structure. "We'll have it almost all to ourselves." Cyrus steered the horses down the path Nyad indicated, veering away from the main covered entry to a smaller one around the corner. There, a guard greeted them and two more opened the double doors.

A steward waited within, a man who was perfumed and scented, his hair gray all over in spite of the fact that his flesh was still youthful and unwrinkled. He wore silken robes of blue and green, and seemed to walk on the air itself. His eyes were alight with glee at the sight of guests and he bowed and harrumphed while leading them from the entryway into an open foyer four stories tall. A chandelier hung in the middle of the room, twice as big as Cyrus was tall, a circular arrangement filled with a thousand candles, light reflected by the hanging glass on each ring.

He ushered them through labyrinthine corridors. Cyrus carried Vara in his arms, Arydni and Nyad behind him. Beyond the smell of the perfumed man was a scent of a building in disuse. The air was stale and though the hallways were free of cobwebs, Cyrus could sense that they had not been used in quite some time.

"This wing was used to house the immediate members of the royal family," the steward said, his finger running along the wall. "But the immediate family is not so large as it used to be even a thousand years ago, and thus the north wing sits empty." An unmistakeable sorrow filled his words.

The steward led them to a suite, opening the double doors with a flourish to reveal a large living space, the central hub of several rooms. There was an open-air balcony before them, a fountain in the center of the room, and doors on each side. Cyrus set Vara upon the bed in the largest bedroom in the suite. Once he had set her down, he drew a blanket with care and covered her with it, reminding him of when he had done the same in Termina only days earlier.

"When will we see the King?" Nyad asked the steward.

"Mmmm," the steward said, his voice high and equivocal. "He's very busy."

"I'm his youngest daughter," Nyad said with a flush to her cheeks.

"What's he busy with?" Cyrus asked, drawing an amused look from the steward.

"Whatever he wants," Nyad said. "He has advisors that handle most of the affairs of state so he spends his time lurking the palace, prowling through hidden passages, listening to hear what people are saying, playing hiding games with the half-elven children here on the grounds, courting additional wives—"

Cyrus blinked. "Elves can have multiple wives?"

A voice came from the bed behind them; strong, though a bit hoarse. "A product of an archaic bygone age." Cyrus turned to see Vara staring at him, eyes half-lidded. "The only elven men with multiple wives nowadays are royalty—and only because they marry highborn women so singularly useless that they can serve no other function but to adorn a man's arm—and bed."

Nyad flinched at Vara's assessment, her ears reddening under her long hair.

Cy crossed to the bed, kneeling at the side. Arydni sat next to Vara on the other. "How do you feel?" he asked, his gauntlet finding her uncovered hand.

"Not half as poorly as you are dressed," she answered, staring at his helm. "You look absolutely ridiculous, by far more than usual." She cleared her throat and looked around. "What happened? Where are we?"

"The Royal Palace," Nyad said, stepping up behind Cyrus, the steward a step behind her.

"Do you remember what happened?" He removed the helm from his head and felt his long hair cascade around his shoulders.

"My head feels a bit foggy," she said. "But I remember..." Her voice trailed off and when it returned, it was hollow. "Everything." She looked first to Arydni, who nodded, and then to the steward and blinked. "Who the blazes are you?"

He bowed again. "My most pleasurable greetings, shelas'akur, I am but a humble steward of the Palace—"

"You are no more a steward than I am a dancing gnome," she said, her eyes narrow. "I remember your face from the days when I was in the Holy Brethren. You spoke with me the first week that I was there and I never saw you again afterward."

He bowed again. "You have an excellent memory, since that was sixteen years ago and I looked much different than now."

"I thought it curious at the time, as you seemed to be known to the elven members of the staff and yet I never saw you again after we spoke." Cyrus listened to Vara but watched the steward, his hand already on Praelior, every hair on the back of his neck standing on end. "You asked questions no one else had the gall to ask — if I was happy with my parents, or if I was dissatisfied in some way with living in the Kingdom."

The steward guffawed. "I suppose it would be curious; I came that day to discern your reasons for entering the Brethren so far in advance of what was expected. But it was not the first time we had met."

Vara sat up in bed, grimacing as she did so. "Oh? Pray tell, I cannot recall any others."

"We have a long association, you and I. I was present on the day of your birth, and have seen you many times throughout your childhood. In any of those times, I was not garbed in such a way as you would have paid any mind to my face," he said. "In fact, I suspect that even those among you who would normally recognize me cannot do so outside of my customary outrageous attire."

He nodded at Nyad, who was staring at him, curious. "Your mother, after all, taught you never to look the palace help in the face when you spoke with them; it's unbefitting a highborn to look in the eyes of their lessers. I would never have taught you that, but this particular game of royals has helped me play my own game unnoticed for nearly three thousand years, so I dare not discourage it."

Nyad still stared, puzzling at him. Cyrus looked to Vara, who frowned in confusion, while Arydni wore a serene expression, the look of a woman who had figured it out. "What?" Cyrus asked her.

"He's the King," she said.

"No," Nyad said under her breath, "I would recognize..." A slight gasp of disbelief worked its way free from her, and she sat down on the edge of the bed in astonishment.

Cyrus looked to the wizard. "I take it you weren't...close...during your childhood?"

"As close as any father who has fifty children and a country to run," he said with a sad smile. "Even when I'm with them, I'm trapped in the absurd attire of the King, so ostentatious and yet beautiful and intricate I would swear the craftsman spent their entire lives designing them. It tends to draw the eye away from trifling details like my face, which is plain enough."

Cyrus looked to him and saw the truth of it; the King was plain. His cheekbones were average, but his eyebrows were more pronounced. He was not fat, but neither was he thin. The robes of the steward were bright enough to draw attention away from his average features; Cyrus could not imagine what the robes, crown and staff of a King could do.

The King's posture had been the somewhat stooped bearing of a steward. That was gone now, and something more majestic had taken its place. His shoulders were squared, back straightened, and he looked like a soldier at attention – or a King, about to make a pronouncement.

"Why come to us now, your grace?" Vara said. "Why like this?"

He nodded, a slow, careful nod. "Because this is the only way I can come to you, where we can speak without prying ears. The problem with putting yourself at the center of a monarchy is that all your subjects in court put you at the center of their lives. They all crave a minute of my time, then another, and another – and when they don't, you can be sure one of my wives does. There is no privacy for a King, no words or message that can be delivered that aren't listened for and heard by as many ears as can catch them."

He slumped once more, a subtle transformation, as the weight and gravity of the King disappeared and was replaced by the flighty, carefree spirit of the steward. "But no one cares about the pronouncements of the caretaker of the abandoned north wing. The members of the court and the viziers are too busy fawning over the King, trying to curry favor and hoard power to pay attention to me."

"What do you have to tell us?" Cyrus asked him. Nyad and Arydni shot him a prompting look that took him a moment to decipher. "...Your...uh...majesty," he amended.

"It would be 'your grace', as a general rule," the monarch said with a smile. "But since I am not here as the King, let us speak as though I were not one. You may call me Danay."

Cyrus felt a curious lightheadedness. *Danay. As in King Danay the First*, he thought. "What brings you to us?"

"Things that cannot be said in a public setting." He cast his eyes to the windows, saw they were shut, then looked to the door, which was closed, then back to Vara. "Your father is safe, only a few doors down the hall. He is not able to walk, but you may visit him at your convenience." He took a deep breath. "I must caution you, however; his age overtakes him. My physicians assure me that he does not have long to live; a few days at most."

Vara, already drawn and pale from her injury, seemed to grow even whiter at the King's words. *She has to tell her father that Chirenya is dead*, he realized.

If the King noticed Vara's discomfiture, he did not address it. "In a few days, when you have recovered," he indicated her and Cyrus in turn, "the two of you will come before the court and be presented with our highest honors for your defense of Termina. Our spies have told us that between all three spans, the dark elves lost nearly half their invading army and cannot fortify their positions as they originally planned."

His eyes glittered. "The Sovereign of Saekaj played us truly false on that, and his army and council are nearly as filled with spies as ours. His sealed orders for the attack on Termina went out with only two griffon riders, direct to his general, cutting out every member of his council and even the lower ranks of his military until the attack was in motion. We won't be able to easily remove them from this side of the river, but if not for your efforts, we might not have been able to remove them at all; they would have had a hundred thousand yet with which to defend Termina."

"But you will remove them, won't you?" The question came from Arydni.

"We will try," the King said. "We can scarce afford to suffer the losses it will take. My generals inform me that city fighting will be a much more difficult battle than meeting their armies on the open plains; our cavalry and experience counts for less in the narrow streets." He shook his head. "The sole advantage of an army as mature as ours is experience. Close-in melee does not benefit us. With wider spaces our mounted soldiers can perform charges that would cause their infantry to wither."

Cyrus swallowed heavily. "Can the Kingdom survive without Termina?"

King Danay looked at him with a grim amusement. "Not easily, no. Termina was the beating heart of the Kingdom's economy, producing most of the weapons, armor and other equipment that we've been sending to the Human Confederation. All our shipping ran through the city, a large part of our fishing came through the port, along with most of our exports and imports." He shook his head, deathly slow. "Without the taxes from all that, we'll have a shortage in the treasury in the next year. Fighting a war on this footing will be difficult. We'll be on the defensive, forced to focus on expelling the dark elves from Termina then protecting our borders, which is far from the kind of war I'd like to give them for their brazenness."

Nyad spoke up, her voice straining. "Who will take the blame for losing Termina?"

"Now there's an inconvenient truth of ruling," Danay said with a nod. "Nobody predicted this. No one thought that the dark elves would be foolish enough to attack us in the middle of a war with the humans, and yet who looks the fool now? Well, if the dark elves do it's solely because of your efforts, not ours. Also, those of that young Endrenshan, I suppose—Yemer's son, I forget his name..."

"Odellan," Cyrus said. "His name is Odellan."

"I'm afraid that it's irrelevant," the King said with a sigh. "His name means less than nothing now. He lost 4,500 soldiers in the defense of the Northbridge. My generals view that—as would the public of the Kingdom- as an unsustainable loss. Never mind that he saved the lives of hundreds of thousands more, the fact that he lost such great numbers looks...well, it looks bad. Especially when coupled with the fall of the city." The King threw up his arms in a gesture of resignation. "The chattering classes have already gone wild with anger. Odellan is to be expelled from the Termina Guard, stripped of his rank and exiled from the Kingdom."

"That's ridiculous." Cyrus felt the heat of outrage rise within him. "Odellan is a hero. He led from the front and fought through the night the same as we did to protect the lives of the citizens of Termina. He was prepared to sacrifice his life to save the people and you ought to know it."

"I do know it. But do you assume I am all powerful in some way?" The King said it with a laugh, but there was no humor in it. "My generals and the people have spoken. All I could manage was to spare his life, which was quite a bit under the circumstances. It's not as if those lost can be easily replaced by recruiting the next generation of youthful soldiers."

"The grim political realities of running an empire," Vara said with unrestrained sarcasm. "Let no act of great courage go unpunished."

Danay shrugged. "I can do little enough about it. He'll be given transport out of the Kingdom to a place of his choosing, and some money. I suspect, as industrious as he is, he'll end up all right. But that's such a gloomy subject, and so far out of my control. We have more pleasant matters to discuss — such as the honors you're about to be given."

"I'll pass," Cyrus said. "The man you should be honoring is about to be exiled; he fought with a high risk of permanent death, and the gratitude you've shown him galls me. I care not for your honors." His voice was hot with contempt, raising the eyebrow of the King. "...Your grace."

King Danay straightened back into his royal posture, and his mouth became a tight line. Nyad cringed as he moved, and his voice was as unyielding as stone. "While you remain under my protection, you will at least do me the courtesy —"

"You mean give you the political hay —" Cyrus interrupted.

" — of accepting the honors I bestow. You will do so because I have a long and far-reaching relationship with your guild —"

" — every member of which was declared persona non grata in your country just a few months ago for a series of crimes we did not commit —" Cyrus went on.

" — and because it's good manners for a houseguest to humor his host."

" — And that's why we're leaving," Cyrus finished, a cold fury having overtaken him. "You can stick your hospitality straight up your —"

"Cyrus!" He jerked his head away from the rising tempo of his disagreement with the King at Vara's shouted command. Though she used only his name, he heard the implied message. *Shut up. You're arguing with a King in his own palace.*

He's a hell of a King, Cyrus raged internally. *Odellan was the best leader he could have hoped for in Termina; any of his stodgy generals with more experience might have hesitated to evacuate the city, waiting to see if the dark elves made an aggressive move. For his part he gets exiled, cast out of his own homeland and spit on for doing the only reasonable thing he could have in the circumstances...*

"I don't expect you to understand our politics," the King said, gathering up in his robes. "Odellan is not the first good man to be destroyed through no fault of his own, nor will he be the last. But while you are under my roof, you will accept my honors as well." His eyes narrowed. "It is possible you may even enjoy a few of them — titles and whatnot. We will make arrangements in the next few days. Until then, enjoy your stay." He bowed his head, not nearly so low as he had when playing the steward, and withdrew with a flourish, the door closing behind him.

Vara waited a few seconds after he left before rounding on Cyrus, her head whipsawing around as if it had been blown by a hard wind. "He's the King, you daft bastard. You don't address the monarch like that."

"Why?" Cyrus's teeth grated. "Because he has a royal title to excuse the fact that he just helped run an innocent man out of town?"

"No," she replied with heated words, "because he's the King and it's unseemly to do so. You're fortunate he was so forgiving else you might have found yourself hanging from the outer wall."

"Yeah, it would have been a real shame if I'd needed to kill a thousand members of the palace guard today," Cyrus said under his breath.

"The palace guard contains more than just warriors," Nyad said, her voice oddly hollow. "Because governments can only hire so many members of the Leagues, they hold back a disproportionate number to protect their most valuable holdings. Anyone who attacks the palace would be set upon by wizards, druids, enchanters and an army protected by healers." She stared off into space as though she were still shell-shocked. "I had no idea...he looked..."

"Yes, well, leaving aside the obvious questions about her sad and pitiful childhood —" Vara stared down Cyrus, ignoring the mortified look Nyad shot her — "it remains that you would do well to tone down your ego; even if you could kill the entire palace guard it would be for naught because you'd then be the enemy of the elves and be hunted throughout the lands, unwelcome wherever you go."

"Your King can't even defend his own lands, let alone hunt anybody in someone else's," Cyrus scoffed. He looked to Arydni, still at Vara's bedside, "What do you think?"

She shrugged. "The priestesses are always at odds with the monarchy. You haven't lived until you've told off the King."

"I meant about our next move."

"Vara will heal in a few days. You'll be better protected here than anywhere else and if you must accept some ribbons, lands and titles from the King in order to assure her safety until you can return to your guildhall, then bury your pride and dignity in a dark place for Vara's good health." She kept her expression neutral, but Cyrus detected the faintest hint of reproach in her words.

They'll throw an innocent man out of their Kingdom and I'm supposed to smile and accept accolades from a government like that? He looked around to find everyone staring at him. Vara's face was still drawn and her lips were pursed as though she were in great pain but trying to suppress it. *She lost her mother, got wounded in a battle that cost us her hometown, her people are at war and she's still being hunted by the most secretive order I've ever run across.* Shame burned his cheeks. *I don't care for what they did to Odellan, but if I'm going to fight to the death over a matter of principle I'd have it be my death, not hers.* "All right. We'll stay."

The days that followed dragged as slow as any Cyrus had ever lived. He carried Vara in his arms to Amiol and listened to her tell him that his wife was dead. The elder elf took it well, comforting his daughter, who was largely stoic herself. Even her face maintained a stony countenance while she broke the news to him; two silent tears were the only outward expression of her grief. Later that night, he swore he had heard a choked sob, though it might have been a noise outside. The soft, steady breathing of Arydni by the window and the gentle snores of Nyad on a nearby chair held him in place, kept him from going to her. In the morning, the news came from a palace messenger that her father had died in the night.

She took it without reaction, remaining in bed, staring, her knees pulled to her chest but with little more than a blank expression. As much as he wanted to talk to her, Arydni and Nyad were ever-present in her room. The Priestess maintained a constant watch on the paladin, taking no meals, very little liquid refreshment and less sleep than Cyrus, who had taken to resting for brief periods on the fainting couch in the corner of the room.

Nyad remained in close attendance as well. After recovering from the shock of her father's secret, she had prattled on about the palace, its history and the life of growing up in it until Vara had broken her silence and told the wizard in no uncertain terms to either shut up or leave. She had managed almost ten minutes of silence, after which she had begun to talk about Pharesia and the history of the city.

Days passed, then a week, then two. Servants brought meals of the finest elven delicacies; fresh vegetables from every corner of the Kingdom, citrus fruits garnishing and braising the meats that they supped upon. Everything was delicate, exquisite, and portioned so small that Cyrus had taken to asking for multiple servings to be brought with every cart lest he starve to death.

"The elven people are more about well crafted foods than abundances of it," Nyad sniffed when he mentioned it.

"Well I'm about eating what it takes to maintain my frame," he said. "Although that does explain why you lot are so small."

"And you've overfed both the fat in your belly and betwixt your ears," Vara had replied. Two weeks after they had arrived, her color had returned and Arydni was satisfied with the healing she was experiencing. "Though I suppose that dates back to your days in the Society of Arms, where they breed the next generation of war boars by dividing you neatly down the middle and telling you to kill everyone on the opposing side."

"That's not quite how it works," he said, calm. "But the training program does encourage healthy amounts of eating."

She rolled her eyes and then rolled off the bed. She had begun walking without his assistance only a couple days earlier. The King's Physician and the Chief Healer for the realm had both visited her at various junctures and conferred with Arydni in conversations that had involved dense elvish words that Cyrus did not know. After they had left, his companions had summed up what was said—that Vara was recovering nicely. Notice had been given that a ceremony would be held in the throne room in which Cyrus and Vara would be rewarded for their efforts, along with the other defenders of Termina.

"Brilliant," Cyrus breathed. "Won't a public ceremony draw the attention of the dark elves to the fact that we breached our neutrality and declared ourselves their enemies?"

"I think that the tens of thousands of dead bodies we left might have done it for us," Nyad said. "It's not as though we could keep secret what was done there; the surviving members of the Termina Guard that we saved told their family members and friends, some of the Termina survivors saw us taking up defensive positions—"

Vara interrupted her, frowning at him. "It's not as though there are countless warriors that dress entirely in black armor walking the paths of Arkaria. That dark elven colonel identified you the moment he set foot on the bridge. There is no hiding our involvement."

"I had hoped," Cyrus said, "that we might be able to defend the survivors and retreat without word getting out. At least not anything that could be conclusively proven."

"Conclusively proven?" Vara's laugh drew his attention to where she stood by the balcony, staring out onto an empty courtyard filled with swaying trees. "The Sovereign declared a death mark on our entire guild with much less evidence and for much less of a crime. Still, I suspect he's rather occupied at the moment, making war on the two largest powers in Arkaria. Perhaps we'll go unnoticed for a time."

"Perhaps," came a voice from behind them. "And perhaps not."

Standing in the doorway was Alaric Garaunt.

Chapter 39

"Alaric," Cyrus said, jumping to his feet. "You're here," he said. The words sounded lame in his ears. The old knight stood before him with arms crossed, like a disapproving father, and a twinge of shame interspersed with more than a little fear washed through Cyrus's innards at the sight of his Guildmaster.

"I am," the Ghost said. "I've come along with our guildmates for the ceremony—and to speak with the two of you." He nodded at Cyrus and Vara. "It has been some time and much has transpired...since last we spoke. Cyrus...I would have words with you, alone." He turned from them and walked out the door, with nary a look back to see if he followed.

With an uneasy feeling, Cyrus trailed after him, through the main living space and into a bedroom on the other side of the suite. "I'm sorry," Cyrus said as he shut the door. "There were a million people in Termina and I couldn't allow them to be slaughtered by the dark elves; you know they wouldn't have had much remorse about making a pyre of the city with all the residents in it."

The cool eye of the Ghost looked through his helmet at Cyrus, sending a chill through the warrior. Alaric reached up and removed his helm, revealing his gray-streaked hair and eyepatch. Of late, the Guildmaster had grown a beard, short but full, matching his hair in color but perfectly uniform in length. If nothing else, it helped to further cloak the already impassive paladin's emotions.

The smell of the room swept over Cyrus; the rich aroma of citrus wafted in on the breeze, so much warmer than the one he felt in Termina, a hard chinook that could cut through him. This one was pleasant, carried a trace of warmth even in the thin chill of the midday. Light made its way in, stretching across the floor in small, angular shafts, conforming to the open arrangement of the balcony doors and windows. The room was decorated in rich reds and dark wood paneling, different from the lighter colors of the room they had stayed in. *Maybe I should send Arydni and Nyad over here,* he thought, then mentally slapped himself for it.

Outside, the noise of crickets and distant voices far below the balcony could be heard, a faint murmur that underlay the silence within the room. Cyrus tasted an almost coppery flavor in his mouth, the anticipation of bloodletting upon him, as if the Ghost was going to strike him for what he had done.

Alaric's eye did not betray his emotional state, leaving Cyrus in turmoil until the Ghost spoke. "I am aware. I find no fault with your actions in Termina; had I been there, I would have done the same. If not for the fact that you were so very far from a portal, I would have attempted to move our army into place to reinforce you. If not for you, things would be going much worse for the elves than they are."

"Oh?" Cyrus felt a stir of hope. "They haven't told us anything in weeks; do you have news?"

"I do. The battle rages around Reikonos, though the line is holding. The elves have managed to keep the Sovereign's forces contained in Termina and have made excellent progress in pushing them back. Fully a third of the city is back in elven hands, though the price has been high." The Guildmaster made a fist. "I doubt the dark elves will easily surrender such a choice foothold; we've been told that more dark elven forces are marching to assist their brethren in holding the city, which bodes well for the Confederation, as it removes forces that might otherwise have been moved against their capital."

Cyrus felt lightheaded but oddly relieved. "This war is spinning out of control."

Alaric stared down at his clenched fist and when he answered, his tone was flat. "Wars are not known for being exercises in control, brother."

"I know that; I only meant—"

"I know what you meant." The Ghost unclenched his fist. "The Sovereign, on the surface, seems to be overreaching. Starting a war on two fronts seems foolhardy, yet the dark elves have won every battle that matters thus far. The best thing that could happen for Arkaria is for the Sovereign to have overextended; however, I fear that he may not have. One would think that when the Human Confederation aimed to begin this conflict, they would have been better prepared for it."

"I had never known, in all my years living in Reikonos, how petty, vain and power-mad the Council of Twelve was until you brought me before them," Cyrus said with no small amount of consternation.

Alaric wore the hint of a smile when he answered the warrior's statement. "Why should they—and Pretnam Urides in specific—be different than any other mortal? Are we not all petty, vain, and power hungry in our own ways? When you came to our doors looking to gain better weapons and equipment from our expeditions, were you not seeking to expand your influence for your own gain?"

A flush of embarrassment caught Cyrus by surprise. *He always does this.* "I suppose, but—"

Alaric interrupted. "The difference is means and motive. If you fight only for yourself, if you are willing to kill innocent parties to get what you want—only disaster can follow. There's nothing wrong with wanting, so long as you work for it and don't put your desires before everything else—including other people."

"That seems like a pretty big difference."

"Whether you kill one or a million innocents with this intent, you are still a murderer. The only difference is scale." Alaric scratched at his beard. "But we have other things to discuss. I was told you were reluctant to attend the ceremony?"

"I was," Cyrus said, feeling the muscles in his jaw tense. "The Elven military has caused the ouster of a genuine war hero and I don't care for it. But I'm willing to go along with the King's wishes since we've taken shelter here."

"Very good." Alaric gave a perfunctory nod. "I realize that it might be difficult for you to understand that kings and councils make grave decisions that are sometimes unrelated to their own personal desires, but it frequently happens. And it rarely has anything to do with honor."

Cyrus felt the unease once more, thinking of Odellan, left to scratch out a life for himself wherever he may, never to return to his homeland. *I felt that, last year. I would not care to see anyone else have to suffer it, especially someone so undeserving of that fate.*

"I sense your unease," Alaric said. "But the King has accepted the judgment of his generals, and his generals have made your Endrenshan the scapegoat. Much as you might wish to change that, you cannot."

"I realize that," Cyrus said, shaking his head.

"Your uncompromising loyalty toward your comrades is admirable," Alaric said, turning away from Cyrus to face the balcony. "This Odellan is a hero, obviously." He turned back to Cyrus. "Yet, with the dark elves sure to number us among their enemies, we need ties to the nations that fight against our foes. Do not judge the King too harshly for what he must do to protect his country. Accept his accolades with grace."

"I will," Cyrus said, still reluctant. "But I don't have to do it with a song in my heart."

"If you did, you would not be Cyrus Davidon," Alaric said. "All that aside, you have missed quite a bit in your absence. We have purged what I believe to be the last of the assassins from our ranks. However, it would be difficult to be certain as we've had a massive influx of new recruits in the last month or so. We've taken pains to tighten security, and I think Vara will be well-protected in our midst now."

"We need to track down this Hand of Fear." Cyrus tightened his hand inside his gauntlet.

"The assassins we have captured have said nothing that would betray even a hint of who their master or masters are." Alaric leaned against the railing of the balcony. "They appear to be fanatics, true believers in their cause, whatever it might be."

"We need a plan," Cyrus said, stroking his chin. "They seem to have limitless numbers. We can't hold back these maniacs forever. Not at Sanctuary, not here. They will eventually get a lucky shot, and Vara will die."

"Aye," Alaric said. "Nor would we want to adopt the policies that the King has put in place to protect her here."

"What policies?"

The Ghost winced. "Let us call them...severe. Should anyone unapproved approach your suite, they are killed if they cross beyond a certain threshold."

Cyrus felt his stomach turn in disgust. "That is...barbaric."

"Too true," the Ghost said. "But it has resulted in the killing of two confirmed assassins. And one very confused gardener in search of a privy."

Cyrus nearly choked. "They killed...an innocent man?"

"It would seem. The palace guard is not to be trifled with."

"That...horrible!" Cyrus recoiled in disbelief. "We can never tell Vara."

"Agreed. This is all the more reason we should return to Sanctuary as quickly as possible," Alaric said. "We will continue to try and find this Hand of Fear organization when we return. All appearances to the contrary, they are surely not a bottomless pit of recruits and they must be hiding somewhere—they are not an ethereal menace, after all."

"And you would know, being something of an ethereal menace yourself."

With a smile of slight amusement, Alaric started to speak again, but stopped at a sound from the other room. Cyrus turned and opened the door to find a herald who bowed to him. "The King of Elvendom awaits your most gracious presence in the throne room." His message delivered, the man withdrew.

"We will speak again later," Alaric said, passing him as Arydni, Nyad and Vara joined them from the other chamber. "Now is the time for you to accept your rewards with all the decorum I've come to expect from you."

"Or at least the decency not to start a blood feud with the entire Elven Kingdom." Vara's words were sharp, and she did not blink away when he looked at her with mock offense.

"Am I correct that after the ceremony, you'll be returning to Sanctuary?" Arydni looked at them with her usual serenity, the sunlight from the balcony windows giving her a kind of tired luminescence.

"Yes," Vara said, her voice quiet.

"Then this is where we part," Arydni said. "I am pleased that you have mended, shelas'akur, but you have no more need of my ministrations."

"I cannot thank you enough for what you have done," Vara told the priestess.

"It is the duty of the All-Mother's servants to take scrupulous care of her greatest blessing," the priestess said. She turned to Cyrus. "It was my very great pleasure to make your acquaintance, Cyrus Davidon. I hope that Vidara will bless you in all your endeavors."

"My thanks to you," Cyrus said with a bow. "I cannot bring myself to think of what might have happened without your assistance."

"You are too kind," she said. "I wish the best for all of you; I would not presume to say that we have seen the last of each other, but rather to say farewell for now." With a bow, she exited the room. Cyrus realized after she left that she had been clad in the same priestess garb for the last two weeks that she had worn when first they met—and he had scarcely noticed.

The walk to the throne room was long. Cyrus marveled at the complement of eighteen guards that surrounded them. Nyad walked with them and Alaric trailed slightly behind Cyrus and

Vara, who were side by side. Vara stared into the distance, clinking together her gauntlets, but the sound was lost in the noise of plate boots clattering on marble floors.

The air carried a sweet smell and Cyrus couldn't help but notice vases filled with flowers throughout the palace. Trees filled earthen planters as they entered a hall larger than Sanctuary's Great Hall, the floors marble with circular patterns, seals and crests everywhere. He could scarcely see the far edge of the hall, and the roof was hundreds of feet in the air, supported by pillars that were as large in diameter as two horses lined up front to back. Vines and plants grew out of shelves that ringed each pillar and the walls were covered by three tiers of planters filled with trees, flowers and the odd pond and waterfall.

A hundred gigantic chandeliers hung from the ceiling, each with candles flickering, casting light over the hall. Above, massive skylights were open, allowing light into the room. The edges of the hall were lush and green, the center impressive with mosaics on the floor and carefully shaded marble that was patterned into royal seals.

"This is the main hall," Alaric said from behind him. "It is the entrance to the palace and where anyone who desires an audience with the King would wait. It was designed to be so large and intimidating that no foe could look upon it and think that the Elven Kingdom was anything other than a dominant force."

"The 'look at me! I have money so I must have power!' approach," Cyrus said. "How novel and free of insecurity."

Alaric let out a low guffaw. Several of the palace guard shot him scandalized looks but Cyrus ignored them. Near the middle of the hall was a crowd — over a hundred people waiting. Cyrus might have ignored them if not for the fact that within their ranks were a tall, green-skinned healer and a figure made out of rock. He smiled as they were led near the entrance to what he assumed was the throne room, and the Sanctuary army that had helped him defend the bridges of Termina made their way forward, forming into lines that would allow them to fit through the double doors.

One figure in particular stood out, his surcoat much cleaner than when last Cyrus had seen it. "Longwell," he said, breaking free of the guardsmen, who moved to allow him to pass and then drew tighter around Vara once he had done so.

The dragoon detached himself from the Sanctuary army. "Good to see you, General," Longwell said with a curt nod, his accent lilting. "I was not surprised to hear that you escaped from Termina. I apologize for not remaining until after you, Vara and Lady Chirenya had removed yourselves from the field of battle. It shan't happen again."

"You could not have predicted what would happen," Cyrus said to the dragoon, whose head was bowed, his helm carried in the crook of his arm. His brown eyes burned with the fires of contrition. "The fault was mine for not urging Chirenya to leave first."

"Knowing her even the little I did," Longwell said, "I doubt she would have heeded you. I saw in the moment I grasped the orb what was happening; knew as I reappeared at the portal north of Sanctuary that you'd not be returning with us."

"There was nothing you could have done," Cyrus said. "Your courage was exemplary in the bridge defense and I hope the King recognizes you for your efforts. Without your lance, I don't know how we would have done it."

The dragoon's swarthy skin showed only the barest redness, but Cyrus could tell he was blushing. "The honor is in serving. All other awards are ancillary."

Cyrus turned from the dragoon to see J'anda standing in the front row, his elven illusion looking particularly radiant. Vaste nodded and smiled, a gesture that seemed to be a compliment of sorts. Thad and Martaina stood side by side, the warrior's red armor contrasting with the green hues of Martaina's boiled leather, her hair done up in an elaborate braid, a radical departure from its usual muss. Lurking under a hood, Cyrus could see Aisling, and when he caught her eyes he couldn't shake the feeling that she looked ready to dart away at the first hint of trouble.

The ground shook as Fortin made his way to Cyrus, who looked up at the rock giant in mild surprise. "Fortin. You were exceptional in holding the Southbridge; I've come to expect nothing less than excellence from you in every endeavor."

The rock giant leaned forward with sudden speed and Cyrus took a step back, afraid Fortin might be falling on him. To his surprise, the stony warrior knelt and bowed his head in a solemn silence. Even kneeling, the rock giant was as tall as Cyrus. "Thank you, General Davidon," his words came out in a rush. "Never before have I killed fifteen thousand of you fleshbags in a day." His head raised and the red eyes glowed, his rocky mouth creasing a curved line upward on his face. "That. Was. Fun." He stood as suddenly as he had knelt and turned, returning to stand at the back of the Sanctuary army. As he walked away, Cyrus could have sworn he heard Fortin whistling a tune.

"He's bloodthirsty, even by your standards." Andren's voice cut through Cyrus's haze and he turned to see the healer at his side, shaking his head at the back of the retreating rock giant.

"How did it go for you in the bridge defense?" Cyrus looked to his oldest friend. The circles under the healer's eyes were darker than usual, likely the result of being awakened long before noon.

"Oh, that." Andren wore a look of mild embarrassment. "Wasn't much to it. I spent most of my time hiding behind an upturned wagon. I think I might have cast one heal, and it was because I was bored, not because he needed it."

A strong odor of alcohol wafted from Andren as he spoke, and Cyrus felt a flash of rage. "Are you drunk?"

The healer's brow creased at the accusation and his eyes turned stormy. "Well, I wasn't going to go into this royal nest of vipers sober now, was I?"

Cyrus looked back in astonishment. "Unbelievable."

"You don't know what it's like being back here," Andren said, lowering his voice. As Cyrus listened to him, it almost reminded him of pleading. "I hate this city and these high and mighty bastards that think they're better than everyone. They lord it over you because their mom and dad were sixteenth generation members of some house that got land and a title ten thousand years ago when they handed them out and mine were from peasant farmer stock and grew the foods they ate while they didn't work a day in their lives."

"All right, fine," Cyrus said in a hiss. "Do you want to leave?"

"Hell no." Andren looked back at him in befuddlement. "I'm about to get an award from the King!"

"I thought you said you hated royals and highborns!"

"Well, yeah, but he might give me something—like land, or a title."

Cyrus looked at him through half slitted eyes. "You just said you hated the people that got those things handed to them."

"Well, that's because *I* don't have them, isn't it?" The elf shook his head as though it were the most obvious point.

Cy felt a sudden urge to strangle the healer, but resisted it. "I'm constantly impressed by your ability to have lived two thousand years and still be utterly blind to your own contradictions."

"Thanks," Andren said. "I think."

Voices behind him turned Cyrus back to the bevy of guards clustered around Vara and Alaric. The paladins spoke to each other in hushed tones along with a third figure, a member of the court. He rejoined them to find that the elf they were talking to was a minister of protocol, there to assist them through the ceremony.

Cyrus listened to the man, a gray-haired, foppish fellow named Erdnim, as he described the formalities of the ceremony. Each of the members of Sanctuary that participated in the battle were to be given honors, a medal and ribbon, with a small award of gold. Larger awards were to be made to J'anda for his illusory army, Erith, Andren and Vaste for healing the front line of battle, and Aisling for slipping behind the enemy lines and fighting amongst the dark elves. They would receive a title along with their medal and gold. The largest awards were to come to Cyrus, Vara, Fortin and Longwell, for being the front line on the bridges.

"Along with each of these awards comes a granting of land and the title of Lord," the protocol officer said, his perfumed smell forcing Cyrus to take a step back.

After a moment, the minister's words sank in, and Cyrus blinked. "I'm sorry, did you say a land grant and a title?"

"Yes," Erdnim replied, his pointed nose inhaling deeply as he raised it into the air. "The men will be Lords, the shelas'akur will be invested with the title of Lady, and each of you will be granted a parcel of land that the King feels would be appropriate given your stature."

"So for me, it's likely to be in the swamp outside Gren," Cyrus said under his breath, referring to the troll homelands.

"Hardly," Erdnim said. "That is not within the boundaries of the Elven Kingdom."

The doors opened and they were ushered into the throne room in a procession. Vara's guard melted away once they entered. *Probably because the entire room is filled with guards.* The throne room was long and rectangular, with members of the court seated on either side and the King's throne against the far wall, by itself. Upon it was a figure covered almost entirely in robes.

The robes were multicolorored, with subtle hues of red, yellow, blue, purple and green. *If I hadn't seen it, I wouldn't believe those colors could ever go together*, Cyrus thought. Yet somehow they did, with the cloth achieving a shimmering sheen, glossier than even the finest silk. From this distance, Cyrus could see woven patterns in the cloth. The cloak covered the King's head and hair to just above the forehead and the sides of his face from the temples down to his chin. Upon his head rested a crown of glistening gold, silver and other metals, shining more brightly than his robes, studded with precious stones that reflected the same colors as his attire. The points of the crown jutted almost a foot above the King's head. *That crown must be worth more than half of Reikonos.*

As he approached the throne, Cyrus realized that attired as he was, there was no way to notice the King's face. The monarch's hands rested on a stave that bore enough gemstones to put the crown almost to shame, and every finger was adorned in rings. Cyrus led the procession of Sanctuary's heroes with Vara, Fortin and Longwell and the rest forming ranks behind them. He had watched Alaric break away at the back of the room, finding a place to stand near the doors.

Cyrus brought the formation to a rest at the base of the steps that led up to the monarch, where the Minister of Protocol gestured. Banners matching the King's robes hung from above, bearing heraldry of different units of the Elven army. He looked until he saw that the one hanging directly above the King was of the Termina Guard—a city by a river against a light blue background. It seemed to be hanging lower than the others around it—in a place of honor.

The ceremony was long, but touching. Each member of the force had their name called across the assemblage. Cyrus saw more than a few decorated members of the Termina Guard in the crowd at the back of the throne room, watching and cheering when appropriate.

When the time came for the highest honors, J'anda was called before the King first, knelt and had a medal placed around his shoulders. The King whispered something in the dark elf's ear that caused the enchanter to chuckle, then spoke in his loudest voice, "Arise, Sir J'anda the Cunning."

Erith was next, and dubbed Madam Erith the Pure-Hearted, which caused Cy to snicker and her to shoot a dirty look over her shoulder at him. Aisling was dubbed "the Crafty," and Cyrus watched as the King whispered something to her and she whispered something back to him that caused the monarch to laugh out loud. "Gods, I hope she didn't do to him what she does to me," he said under his breath. Vara turned her head to glare at him.

"Do you think the King feels a bit odd giving so many awards to dark elves when his Kingdom is at war with them?" Longwell's voice was just below a whisper.

Cyrus ignored Vara's attempt to shush them. "He strikes me as the sort to be grateful for whatever help he can get."

Andren was called next before the King and pronounced "Sir Andren the Vigilant." *Except when he's drinking*, Cyrus thought. Vaste was the last of his group, and towered over the monarch by almost two feet. "You will be the first troll ever given this award," King Danay pronounced.

"I'm not surprised," Vaste said. "It's difficult to honor someone when you've been so busy killing them."

He knelt for the King to place the medal over his head and arose "Sir Vaste the Wry." With an exaggerated smile and a long wave fit for a beauty queen, the troll made his way back to his place in the formation.

"Now we award those who tended the front line of the bridges, who fought until Termina was empty of our people. They led this struggle with courage and skill, and are deserving of a great reward and even greater renown. Each shall receive land and the title of Lord—or Lady, in the case of the shelas'akur." A rumble of applause made its way through the crowd and Danay stopped to acknowledge it. Cyrus looked to Vara, but she stared straight ahead, a little flush on her cheeks.

"The first of these heroes is a warrior like no other. In the heart of battle, he held against all the forces that came against the Southbridge, and threw them back with no weapon but his own two hands. Come forward, Fortin of Sanctuary." The rock giant moved toward the King, who flinched as Fortin dropped to a knee, causing a reverberation through the floor that forced the monarch back a step.

"For his bravery, Lord Fortin shall be awarded a landhold of ten thousand acres in the foothills of the Heia Mountains," the King said. "It is a territory filled with caves, rocks and scarcely a mile of arable land—per his request." The King wore a subtle smile. "For this, you shall be known as Lord Fortin of Rockridge. Arise a Lord."

Fortin stood, dwarfing the King with his stature, and bowed

once more before stepping back to the line. Longwell was called and stepped forward as the rock giant returned to their line. "Why not pick a spot of land that you could sell?" Cyrus asked in a low voice, once more disregarding the shushing noises coming from both Vara and Erdnim.

"Because I wanted something to remind me of home—that could be my home, someday," he replied in a gravelly rumble that sounded nothing like his usual timbre. It took Cyrus a moment to realize that the normally stoic rock giant might be crying—or at least his version of it.

"Sir Samwen Longwell," King Danay began, "a dragoon from a land we know not, defended the center span with tremendous effort, holding a third of the bridge from harm at his own peril. He did not flag, he did not fail, and he did it all without a word of complaint. Those who can wield a weapon as he did are few and valuable; those who do it with unquestioned honor and loyalty are worth more than a field of emeralds." The King said the last with a smile, and a ripple of amazement ran through the assemblage. Vara gasped next to Cyrus, but when he made to ask her about it, she silenced him with a look.

"To you, sir, I give ten thousand acres in the plains and meadows south of Pharesia, stretching from the sea inland. They lay in the sight of the Heia mountains, but are a green and fertile land, ripe for cultivation if you so desire." He gave the dragoon a benevolent smile. "Rise, Lord Longwell of the Emerald Fields." He rose and bowed once more to the King, who nodded his head in acknowledgment.

Cyrus had a thought and turned to Vara. "If he awards this land, are we obligated to defend it?"

She shot him an acidic look and finally broke her silence, her voice low. "No, and I doubt you'd need to, based on where he's assigned it thus far—south of Pharesia is far from the war."

But not from the titans. Cyrus thought of the enormous, beastly inhabitants of the southern lands beyond the Heia mountains. *Or the dragons, south of them.* He shook away the thought. *Neither has come in force over the mountains for millenia.*

"Vara..." the King called her forward. Her hair was down again and her armor was in perfect order once more, shining in the light of the throne room. "Lady Vara defended her homeland, rather than remaining neutral as her guild would have allowed her to do, and defended the Grand Span against all attackers from dusk until dawn. When the shelas'akur was born, it was expected that she would be our hope in a dark time and lead our people back to greatness, warding us from the dangers that assailed the spirit of our great Kingdom.

"What was not foreseen was that she would choose to take up arms and protect the Kingdom from invaders as well. When one is born to great duty and honor, as she has been, it would be easy to shirk the concerns of the physical, to put aside the burden of sword and shield and consign oneself to an easier life. Instead, she took up the blade of honor as one of Vidara's holy warriors, and fought to protect her homeland in a way that none of us could have expected from one so...exalted." He gestured to her and she knelt.

"There is a village to the north that sits on a crossroads of great importance. The Lord of that place was known to you, I believe, for a gift he gave in your youth. He died in the close of the year last, and left no heir behind. In times of peace, the crossing is a land of quiet fields and solemn woods, cool streams and pleasant weather. I pronounce you Lady Vara of Nalikh'akur. Rise."

Cyrus felt a slight, sharp exhalation as Vara rose and bowed her head to the King. She made her way back to them with stilted steps, dazed, a jumble of thoughts written upon her face. He waited until she was closer and then leaned toward her to whisper, "Isn't that where...?"

"Yes," she said. "It is."

"Finally," the King continued, "General Cyrus Davidon. Most guilds, headquartered far from the territories that are defended by elves and men, would not have dared to involve themselves in the defense of Termina. Guilds that make their home within the walls of our cities are understood to have a vested interest in protecting the homeland. Not so with a guild that finds themselves in disputed territory; for them, it might be more expedient to remain uninvolved in the war and let it pass them by rather than expose their home and fellows to the harm that might befall them from hostilities.

"But not this man. When all manner of ill swept into Termina, he did not use his wizards to flee from the fires of war. He took up arms and defended the Grand Span, holding it against impossible numbers until daybreak to provide our people a chance to flee for their lives and safety. Then he ordered a careful retreat so as to be certain that our civilians had made it safely from the city streets.

That would have been far more than was called for by an army and a general that had already gone so far out of their way to assist us.

"Not so for this warrior. He led his troops to cover and assist the evacuation of our own Termina Guard, allowing the remaining survivors to escape the city when otherwise they would have been killed. He stayed behind, planning to be the last man out of the city, when events beyond his control trapped him with a wounded companion. Yet he still managed to fight his way out, saving our beloved shelas'akur from certain death."

"Before I conclude our final award, let this be known. For the nine heroes I have recognized individually, each will receive one further reward. When the day comes that our armies retake Termina, each will be given a mansion on Ilanar Hill, to be maintained by the Kingdom in grateful thanks for their service, and so they may ever dwell among the citizens they saved and own a piece of what they fought so hard for.

"Come forward, General Davidon." The King's eyes were fixed on him, and even through the robes, they made an impression, piercing him the way that Alaric's did. Cyrus made his way in front of the King and hesitated before going to one knee. "For bravery and action above any that would be expected, I name you a Lord. The courage you have shown is worthy of more than any title I could give you. If I awarded you a holdfast in the Kingdom, I think it would be wasted on a man such as yourself."

He leaned in to Cyrus and spoke in a whisper. "Instead, I award you that which I think you will have more use for; but be aware it is not mine to freely give. It comes with strings that must eventually be severed for you to truly possess it."

Cy looked at him, confused, as the King went on. "Cyrus Davidon of Sanctuary. Your actions are beyond my ability to repay with a simple Lordship—though I award you that title. I cede and commit to your care a swath of land that has long been claimed by the Elven Kingdom, but today I renounce that claim. I give to you the Southern Plains of Perdamun, from the Waking Woods and the Bay of Lost Souls to the south fork and western bank of the river Perda north to Prehorta. I give them to you, in their entirety, and make them yours to defend."

He looked at Cyrus with compelling eyes, light but alive, searching through him. "Stand, Lord Davidon of Perdamun. Arise as the Warden of the Southern Plains."

Chapter 40

The applause was deafening as Cyrus walked, stunned, back to his place in the line. *What does that mean? It's not as though the humans or the dark elves are going to just give up their claims to the southern Plains of Perdamun.* He blinked. *But if they did...that would be a hell of a gift. I'd damned near have my own kingdom. An empty title,* he decided as he rejoined the line. *Probably did it as a means to keep me from holding land in his Kingdom,* he thought with a grim smile as the King concluded the ceremonies and the crowd began to disperse. But the words "Warden of the Southern Plains" continued to rattle around in his head as he followed the procession to the exit.

"What a marvelous ceremony!" Erdnim's voice was a high squeak. "Have you ever seen anything so magnificent?"

"Not since I looked at my naked body in the full length mirror this morning," Vaste said, drawing a look of horror from the Protocol Minister, who edged away from the troll's smiling visage.

"Lord Davidon," a familiar voice came from behind him. He turned to find Endrenshan Odellan, clad in his finest, and still bearing the helm of the Termina Guard.

"Odellan!" Cyrus moved to meet him, thrusting his hand out and seizing the guard captain's. "I had heard you were to be exiled."

"Aye," Odellan's face was stern, not lively as it had been before. "I'll be teleported out of the Kingdom at sundown; but they let me stay for the ceremony honoring my men—as well as for yours. I owe you my thanks—and my life."

"It should have been you up there," Cyrus said, his voice louder than it had been a moment before, drawing offended looks from members of the Royal Court around them. "You should have gotten the biggest land award of all of us."

Odellan shrugged, his face gray. "It was not to be; my only regret is that I wasn't able to fall in battle for my country and thus save one more of my soldiers to return home."

Cyrus leaned in closer to the Endrenshan. "If you had, it wouldn't have saved a single one and likely would have cost you more."

Odellan's mouth upturned. "It is kind of you to say so."

"What do you plan to do when you leave?" Cyrus studied the elf with rapt attention.

"I don't know." Odellan's face went slack. "I have considered going to Reikonos to pledge my sword to their defense; I've heard they are seeking volunteers," he said with a shrug. "Or I could go to Fertiss to join the dwarven army. It's more peaceful there, but I'm not sure I'd enjoy the quiet."

"Or you could apply to join Sanctuary," Cyrus said, "and have all the adventure you could stand and get wealthy in the bargain."

The elf's eyebrow rose. "I've wondered about that; if I'd be able to make it. If I had what it would take."

Cyrus brushed him off. "Doubtless. You're a veteran officer that commanded the defense in one of the largest battles in the last twenty years. That's more experience than our applicants usually have."

"Yes, but I commanded the forces that *lost* that battle."

"So did I," Cyrus said, scoffing. "We were outnumbered twenty to one with no reinforcements; we weren't expecting to win, just to fight long enough for your people to escape. That takes more than martial prowess, it requires tenacity and honor, and you have it—and that's what we're looking for in Sanctuary. Say the word, and you're in. You can come with us when we leave."

Odellan froze in place. "Yes," he rasped after a moment of quiet. "I'd be honored beyond belief."

"We're fortunate to have a war hero such as yourself." Cyrus clapped him on the back. "Get your things and return here; we'll wait for you."

"If it's all the same," Odellan said, "I'd rather go out and see the city for the rest of the afternoon, and have the wizard the Kingdom assigned to transport me drop me off at the portal near your guildhall this evening." His voice broke a little as he spoke. "I appreciate the kindness you've shown and your offer, but if I'm to leave my homeland forever, I'd like a little longer to say my farewells."

Who would I even say goodbye to back in Reikonos? Cyrus wondered. "I wouldn't begrudge you that."

With a nod, Odellan left, striding through the crowds as another elf approached Cyrus, handed him a small scrap of parchment, bowed and left. Cy opened the paper and looked at the words scrawled within.

Meet me in the eastern gardens under the northwest tree. We need to talk one last time before you leave. Bring Vara. — The Steward

Cyrus frowned and crumpled the paper in his fist, making his way back to his allies. He eased up behind Vara, who was standing on the outside of a small circle of conversation that included Andren, Vaste and J'anda. She appeared disinterested, her eyes unfocused, staring into the distance. He rested a hand on her shoulder and she started, turning to him in surprise until he handed her the parchment. He watched her furrow her brow in concentration and then turn to Alaric, who was talking with of several members of the Royal Court.

Cyrus turned to leave, but found Aisling barring his path. "I was worried after you didn't show up at the Pharesia portal when we left Termina. I should have known you'd make it through somehow. Still—" her hand found his cheek and he felt the warmth of her as she pulled close—"you made me worry." He tried to turn to look at Vara, but when he caught sight of her there was no emotion on her face; her expression was flat and she stared at him with dead eyes.

"I have something for you when we get back to Sanctuary," Aisling whispered. "Something just for you."

He pulled away from her, trying to hide his discomfort. "I'll give you points for being less suggestive, but I don't think I want it."

She laughed. "Oh, you will. It's not what you think. Although...you'd want that too, if you knew what you were missing." She gave him a wry grin, and without waiting for a response she bounded away, slipping into a group between Longwell and Erith, casting a mischievous look over her shoulder at him. He returned his gaze to Vara, who was unresponsive and followed him as he led the way out.

"You don't think this is some sort of trap?" She broke the uncomfortable silence as they exited through the steps on the north wing of the palace, crossing the road below, the one they had entered the palace by days before.

"I don't think so, but you never know." He felt his hand drift to the hilt of Praelior, keeping it from swinging as much as it normally did when he walked. "I'm a little surprised the King felt a need to talk to us again after..." He let his words drift off.

"After you insulted him?"

"Among other things." They followed the paths into the

garden, heading toward the massive tree that stood above the palace on the northwest side of the grounds. The wending road was deceptively long, carrying them past walls that had flowers growing out of terraces, others where the vines had blooms as bright as any rose Cyrus had seen. So captivated was he that he didn't realize that they hadn't spoken since entering the gardens. He started to say something, but thought the better of it. *She's lost in her own thoughts; best I let her have this moment. It may be the last she has outside, under the sky, before we return to Sanctuary and she's caged until we rid ourselves of these damned Hand of Fear creatures.*

Fountains burbled and after nearly an hour's walk they arrived at the trunk of the tree. It grew out of a large fountain, its trunk forked into a hundred pieces as it neared the ground. The bark-covered base twisted and expanded at the bottom of the trunk, like a cypress tree Cyrus had seen in Nalikh'akur on the edge of the swamp. But unlike that, this tree trunk was a hundred feet wide in the middle and rose up in the air a thousand feet, stretching above all the buildings in the city.

The fountain that it was planted in showed no sign of cracking, which Cyrus thought curious until he saw the bottom was dirt. The whole area carried a more earthy aroma than the flowered part of the garden. This deep in the gardens no one appeared to be about; they had not seen a living person in almost half an hour.

"I was worried you wouldn't come." Cyrus turned at the sound of a voice from behind them. The King strolled up, his pace leisurely as he passed a pot of green plants and stopped to pick at them. "After all, the request of a steward hardly carries the same weight as the command of a King."

"I was more worried that it wasn't you that sent it." Cyrus kept his hand on his sword and the King noticed it and nodded, a very slight smile curling his lips.

"It's wise to remain prepared in such times. Did I hear correctly—you offered Odellan a place in your guild?"

Cyrus looked back at him. "I did."

The King pursed his lips before he replied. "Good. I have a message, and it comes to you because of your friend Odellan."

Because of him? Cyrus waited, the tension returned, and he gripped the hilt a little tighter.

"The bequest I gave your people—the mansions in Termina," the King began, his hand resting on his chin. "I could only give them because of the deaths of their original occupants, almost all of them without a clear heir."

"Ah," Cyrus said. "The ones that died by the Hand of Fear."

"Yes," the King said with a subtle hiss. "Odellan's father gave me a list of their names, and this is a place where once more I owe your new guildmate a debt."

"You could try pardoning him," Cyrus said.

The King winced, and Cyrus could see the monarch's regret. "If only I could. But these dead, I knew every one of them."

"Because they were part of your court, yes?" Vara spoke up. She sat on the edge of the fountain and a clank of armor on stone distracted Cyrus. *I'd like to see her with her armor off again*, he thought, mind drifting.

"They were," he agreed, his words hushed. "At various points throughout the last few thousand years, I counseled with each of them — in the early days of establishing the Kingdom, every one of them was vital; my most fervent supporters. They were the wealthiest and wisest among us, the last remnants of a group that cast support behind my grandfather 10,000 years ago, allowing him to establish the foundations upon which my father built and which I used to unite our people into the modern Elven Kingdom. With their deaths, this group has been nearly wiped out."

Cyrus frowned. "Do you mean to say that this group had forerunners that supported your grandfather? Or —"

"No," King Danay said. "These elves — these men, mostly — they supported my grandfather during his days, then my father during his, and finally me."

Vara looked at the King with great concentration. "If you mean to say these men lived 10,000 years ago...that is impossible. Elves do not live that long."

Cyrus felt a sense of awe as a piece fell into place. "Except the old ones."

"Quite so," the King breathed.

"I don't believe it." Vara leaned to her side, resting her hand on the fountain's edge.

"But that Hand of Fear assassin said he'd kill you and the old one." Cyrus looked from Vara to the King, his eyes wide. "You said 'nearly' wiped out. How many are left?"

"Only one now," the King replied, his face reserved as he seated himself next to Vara and ran a hand through the water, admiring the ripples that came from it.

Cyrus leaned toward him. "The last old one — their life is in danger. Who is it?"

The King did not look up from where he held his hand under the water. "I cannot say; I remain bound to a promise I made three thousand years ago to keep their secrets, one that they extracted from me before they helped me gain the throne. I cannot give away the identity of the last of them, not so long as they yet live."

Cyrus felt as though his lips were cracking as he spoke. "What do you expect us to do with this information if we can't speak with the last of the old ones? They may know why the Hand of Fear is after her!" He pointed to Vara, who sat silent.

The King removed his hand from the water and shook it off, causing droplets to fall. "I expect you to return to your guild and inform your Council of all you have learned. I will get word to this last one and see if they wish to be revealed to you. Absent that, perhaps this information can give you some insight into these assassins and their intentions." He wore a look of tiredness and regret. "I thank you again for your service to the Kingdom..." He turned to Vara, and nodded, his face suffused with pain. "...and I pray that you will come through these dark times unscathed, my Lady."

"I'm afraid it's too late for that," Vara said with a sadness of her own. "But I thank you for what you've done—sheltering, protecting and honoring us. And now, giving us what you were able to tell." She blinked, and Cyrus saw the light catch on a few droplets of water in her eyelashes. "I thank you."

"As with all of our meetings," the King began, back in the hunched posture of the steward, "the pleasure is all mine." He reached for her hand and kissed it, then turned and walked a long, meandering circle around the tree to disappear behind the trunk.

Cyrus waited with Vara, who stood staring down at the water. He moved forward to embrace her, but she held up a hand to halt him and turned away. He watched a few drops fall from her eyes and cause tiny ripples of their own in the fountain. "I'm fine," she said at last. "We should get back to the others; they'll be leaving soon."

"Not without us," he said. She still had a hand out to keep him at arm's length, but he grasped at it with both his own, the plate mail around his fingers clinking against hers. She did not stop him, but finally pulled away and began walking toward the path they had arrived on. They walked back in silence. She led from a few paces in front of him and after he had tried three times to walk beside her, he gave up because every time she increased her pace to keep him from drawing even.

They arrived back at the palace to find Alaric and Longwell standing at the edge of the gardens, waiting for them with Nyad. "Ah, good," the Ghost said upon catching sight of them, "now we can leave."

"How did you know where we were?" Cyrus asked in puzzlement. The Ghost held up the small slip of parchment with the King's note. "Didn't realize I dropped it."

"You didn't," Alaric replied. "Aisling pulled it off of you and gave it to me once you departed."

Cyrus thought about it. "I didn't even notice."

"Hard to believe, engaged as you were with her thrusting her pelvis into you at the time," Vara said in a voice of quiet accusation.

"I didn't..." Cyrus started to say. He stopped when he realized that her voice had been as dead as her look. "Never mind. We need to meet with the Council."

"I am afraid that will have to wait until the morrow, when Ryin Ayend returns to us. Let us go home, my friends," Alaric said with a soothing demeanor, and turned to nod at Nyad, who seemed to awaken at his words and nodded back before casting a spell.

The light of the magic swirled around them and Cyrus felt the tingle as it consumed him, and he closed his eyes. When the bright flashes stopped, he opened them to find himself in a familiar setting that he hadn't seen in over a month. The fire roared in the hearth of the foyer and a pleasant buzz of activity filled the room.

In the lounge he saw Andren, a horn of mead in his hand raised in salute to Cyrus. He turned round to look into the Great Hall. No refugees were visible but he caught a glimpse of Larana within, who froze at the sight of him, staring unabashed, her face awash with relief. He turned from her, embarrassed, after nodding in greeting, and felt Alaric's hand come to rest on his shoulder. The Ghost had a hand on Vara in a similar manner. "Go to your quarters if you'd like; I'll send for you once I've assembled the Council for our meeting on the morrow." He gestured toward a couple of familiar warriors who were standing nearby at attention, and they both fell in line behind Vara as she made her way to the staircase.

"Vara," Cyrus called out, and watched her stiffen and turn to him.

Her face was wrought of all emotion, even the hostility that she wore in the early days he had known her. She had fallen once more to the exhausted, weighted state he had seen her adopt in Termina. "Perhaps later," she said, and turned away without further explanation. Her guards followed her up the stairs, Nyad a few paces behind them.

"Are you not glad to be home, brother?" Alaric stood at Cyrus's shoulder.

"I am," he said without enthusiasm. "But I can't help but recall the night I left, and the events of that day." He looked into the Great Hall, remembering the steps he had trodden with the burden in his arms, the red hair bouncing from his every step as he carried Niamh to her resting place.

"Yes," Alaric said, a pall hanging over him. "I was sorry that you missed Niamh's burial."

"I was sorry about that too, but it seemed more urgent to get Vara out of here before it could happen again."

"Agreed. That this threat has persisted as long as it has is disturbing." Alaric shook his head. "I cannot fathom the depths of this group's desire to kill Vara. They have continued to attempt strikes here, even after it is obvious that she is no longer with us."

"What do you mean?" Cyrus felt a sudden and intense burst of curiosity. "How many assassins have you rooted out in the last month?"

"A dozen," Alaric said. "Aisling tipped us to all of them, one by one, and we observed them carefully, starting the day you left. When cornered they attacked, causing grievous woundings. I doubt Curatio has left the Halls of Healing in weeks, so busy has he been tending to the injured. The last, however, was the worst," the Ghost said, "a female who posed as an applicant. She nearly killed Scuddar In'shara and hurt a half dozen others trying to gain access to the Halls of Healing."

"She did?"

"Yes," Alaric said. "We speculate that she thought that Vara had returned here after the fall of Termina and was trying to 'finish the job' as they say."

Cyrus felt his thoughts churning, in a jumble. "Makes sense. It wasn't obvious where we were, I guess."

"Aye," Alaric said with a small smile before clapping a hand on Cyrus's shoulder. "You look weary, Lord of Perdamun. You should get some rest."

Cyrus frowned. He caught a glimpse of Larana, staring once more at him through the open door of the Great Hall, and he looked away, back to his Guildmaster. "Didn't the Human Confederation give you a similar title to 'Ward of the Southern Plains' or somesuch last year? I'm sure I heard Pretnam Urides call you Lord Garaunt."

"Lord is an honorific in the Confederation, not a true title. They merely made me a steward," Alaric replied, his smile enigmatic, "without ceding any claims they have on the lands. I'm afraid it's not nearly as impressive as a Lordship and convincing a power that has claimed this land for some 10,000 years to cede their claim."

Cyrus waved him away, thoughts still swirling. "It's hardly impressive. Other than the pissing-for-distance competition that the elves, dark elves and humans held here last year, a major power hasn't held a serious claim to these lands for over a century."

"Still," Alaric said, "ceding an ages-old claim is not something that the Elven Kingdom would do in normal times. I'm afraid things have become dark indeed for them, that King Danay is acknowledging that the elves are not equal to the task of holding anything beyond the bounds of the river Perda." He shook his head. "A stunning admission. But a topic for another time."

Once more, he clapped Cyrus on the shoulder and the warrior felt the warmth of his Guildmaster's touch; not physically, through the plate glove and mail that separated them, but the affection of the Ghost for his "brother," in the way that Alaric Garaunt had always had for the charges under his command. "You are tired. Rest. I will send for you when I have assembled the Council."

"That's...not a bad idea," Cyrus admitted, letting his feet carry him toward the stairs. Every step was familiar yet foreign to him after his absence. *How long was I gone?* he wondered, his body still weary. *I didn't sleep well in the palace, that's plain.* Something tickled the back of his mind, some words spoken that he couldn't remember. *There's something I'm missing, something I've forgotten. Gods, I wish I wasn't so tired.*

His feet moved without his mind's assistance, up the stone stairs, past the floors that held the applicant quarters, the members' rooms, and the double doors behind which the Council met. The glorious stone that made up the walls and floors of Sanctuary blurred. The familiar smell of the wood fires burning in the hearths should have put him at ease, but all they did was remind him of Niamh, of the flash of red when she would whirl around, eyes aflame...

That was damnable, he thought. *To lose her to some vile assassin...* He felt a pang at the thought of the assassin hitting his true target. He remembered the night in Termina when they'd poured into the house of Vara's parents, had killed so many members of Endeavor, and of the dawn on the streets, after the battle for the city, when a lone assassin had struck down the most forceful person Cyrus had ever met...

And still they struck here in the aftermath of that. Attacked the Halls of Healing trying to get to Vara, because they didn't know where she was. He shivered as he turned the knob and opened the door to his room.

He stepped into the privy off his chambers. A small room, large enough for a tub, a metal plumbed shower in the corner, and a sink and full-length mirror. He stepped to the basin and turned the faucet, feeling the water run out as cold as a Termina morning. He splashed some over his face, which was still unshaven, and watched the droplets catch on his beard. He stared at his blue eyes in the mirror, eyes with dark lines beneath them. *They didn't know where she was...*

The buzz in his head was disrupted by a shock, and he straightened back to bolt upright. *But they did know, didn't they? They sent assassins to Vara's chamber in the Palace; the guards killed two of them. How could they have sent assassins to her chambers, in an abandoned wing, if they didn't at least have an idea of where she was?* He felt himself grow cold as words echoed in his head; the last piece fell into place, and he sprinted to the door.

Chapter 41

Within a few minutes the Council had been summoned, absent the presence of Ryin Ayend, who was explained to be visiting family overnight in Reikonos. Cyrus looked at the small circle around the chambers—Alaric, his eye clear and bright, more visible with his helm removed; Curatio, staid but wan and with less sparkle in his eyes than he used to have.

J'anda and Vaste sat in close attendance with Nyad nearby, all three looking slightly rumpled. Longwell, on the other hand, was stiff and looked somehow to be standing at attention even though he was sitting in his chair. Erith looked bored and tired, and had taken the seat to Cyrus's left that had been occupied by Niamh until so recently. The addition of the officers gave the room a crowded feel, and Cyrus found himself bumping elbows with Longwell, who apologized for each occurrence.

Terian Lepos stared at Cyrus with a smug, self-satisfied grin, after nodding at the warrior when he entered. "Good to see you, man in black. I'm guessing after fighting off a constant rush of assassins and the entire dark elven army, a couple weeks in a palace must have been quite the vacation."

"I didn't find it all that restful, sleeping as I was on a fainting couch."

"They have beds the size of a commoner's house and you opted to sleep on the couch?" The dark elf shot him a look of revulsion and swung around to Vara. "I heard you finally caved in and locked lips with this lummox, but you couldn't find it in yourself to let him into your bed?"

Vara had remained silent thus far, her head down and preoccupied, but at the dark knight's jest her blank expression was replaced by a scowl. "I'm sorry, I was rather more occupied with healing a wound I suffered in battle, mourning the death of my mother and father, and thinking of the other two people who shared the room."

"Nothing wrong with having an audience," Erith said as she studied her nails. "It makes you perform better."

Alaric cleared his throat, drawing the attention of everyone at the table. "You summoned us with some urgency," he said, looking to Cyrus. "Is this about what the King told you and

Vara?"

"No," Cyrus replied, his fingers folded in front of him, mailed gloves laying on the table. "And yes. I mean, what he told us was incredible, but —"

"It was nonsensical," Vara said.

" —I was just thinking," Cy continued, "about all that's happened in the time since we left, both here and to us in Termina, all the assassin attacks —"

"Perhaps you might fill us in on what the King told you that was so damned important," Terian said, his amusement gone.

"In a minute," Cyrus said. "But first, I have a question."

The dark knight threw his hands up in the air in exasperation. "Always with the dramatics. Can't you just cut to the point when you have one of your 'revelations' instead of dragging us unsophisticates through your mental hoops?"

"No," Cyrus replied, "because otherwise you might begin to slip into the accepted wisdom that all warriors are unthinking idiots and you'd stop appreciating me."

"If I appreciated you any less, it'd be quantified as hatred. Get to the damned point."

"Soon." Cyrus took a deep breath, looked once around the table, and stopped on the healer who sat at Alaric's right hand. "Curatio, how old are you?"

"You'll reinforce that assumption of 'unthinking idiot' yet," Vaste said.

Curatio sat forward, his tiredness tempered by a slight sparkle of amusement. "I am however old you think I am."

Cyrus leaned forward, not breaking eye contact with the elf. "I think you're at least ten thousand years old. How far off am I?"

J'anda let a loud, scoffing laugh while Terian snorted. Chuckles filled the air as Cyrus continued to stare down the healer, who did not blink, but whose smile had frozen on his face. "Damned far off," the enchanter said. "Elves only live six thousand years, after all. You know that." J'anda looked around the table, but his expression halted at Alaric, whose fingers were steepled in front of him, his eyes watchful and serious.

"You are off by quite a bit," Curatio said. He adjusted in his seat, not looking away from Cyrus, not breaking eye contact. "I don't remember the exact day I was born, and the calendar has shifted somewhat since then, but it was something on the order of 23,000 years ago — give or take a few."

Vara was staring at Curatio with open eyes. "'We will kill you...and the old one'."

"What?" Alaric straightened, turning his attention to Cyrus.

"Something one of the assassins said when we were in Termina," Cyrus replied. "I didn't report it to you, likely because the next day Santir was sacked and we were fighting for our lives. The assassin was posing as a man named Arbukant—" he turned to look pointedly at Curatio and watched a flicker of recognition fall over the elf's face, and for the first time he caught a hint of age behind the healer's eyes—"who was the second to last survivor of a group that the King claimed supported him and his father and grandfather before him as they put together the Kingdom; he said they were the 'old ones' of Elvish legend—the first elves, immortal."

J'anda was the first to speak after several seconds pause. "I can't believe..." He turned to Curatio. "You are one of these...an 'old one'?"

Curatio looked aged, solemn, for the first time since Cyrus had known him, and the voice he answered in was brittle. "The last of them, apparently."

"You were the one who saved us in the Realm of Darkness last year," Cyrus said. Curatio cocked his head at the warrior. "You used Nessalima's Light, but you have more experience using magic so it's brighter than that of others, and you drew on your immortal life to feed it once you ran out of magical energy."

"Aye," Curatio said with a nod. Every movement seemed to be ponderous, slow. "The expedition was in danger of being overrun...I couldn't chance that happening because, unlike Enterra, there was no possibility of rescue if we had fallen."

"You've been there," J'anda said, leaning forward, resting his elbows on the Council table, his eyes wide and hungry. "You've seen history, the rise of the Elven Kingdom, of the Sovereignty, the wars between them—"

"Many have, that still live in the Kingdom," Curatio replied.

"But you were around for the War of the Gods!" J'anda's exclamation hung in the air, but caused the healer to sigh.

"I was," Curatio said after a moment. "10,000 years ago." He turned his head to look at Alaric, and almost seemed to be drawing strength from the Ghost, who sat silent, the lower part of his face hidden by the hands he had folded in front of him. "I have seen..." He hesitated. "Many changes, many wars...many things...I wish I had not."

"My gods," J'anda said. "You were around when the Dark Elves came forth from the caves of Saekaj for the first time."

"I always heard that the dark elves were made from the torture of the first elves by Yartraak, the God of Darkness," Nyad said with a look of innocence.

Terian answered, his eyes narrowed in irritation. "That's a myth, one so insulting that I'm not going to respond to the notion that my entire race is nothing but a beleaguered offshoot of yours." He looked with sudden uncertainty to Curatio. "It is a myth, right?"

"Yes," the healer said. "But the dark elves interbred with several of the first elves and as a result gained longer life than your race originally enjoyed."

"So here's the question," Cyrus cut off any further digression. "Why does someone want to kill you and Vara, the oldest and youngest of the elves?"

Terian's ears perked up. "Wait, Vara is the youngest of the elves?"

"Oh," said Vaste with mild surprise. "That explains a lot, actually."

"That's supposed to be a secret," Nyad said, her voice strained.

"I expect we can keep that amongst ourselves," Alaric said. "And it does seem more than coincidence that the assassins are targeting the youngest elf and the oldest. The question becomes why? What do they have in common other than being at chronologically opposite ends of the elven populace?"

It was Curatio that answered. "It is hoped that Vara is immune to the curse of infertility that plagues our people; I and my fellow 'old ones' *were* immune, without doubt."

"You can have children?" Nyad stared at him, incredulous. "How do you...I mean...who...?"

The elder healer leaned forward on the table, neutral in his expression. "Seventy years ago, I fathered two children with a human woman. Since elven men are currently incapable of fathering children with anyone, it showed me that I was immune to the curse."

"Who was it?" Vaste stared at the Healer with a sly grin.

"No one you'd know," Curatio said, brushing him off. "The children, both girls, are in the Riverlands of the Confederation and will live close to a thousand years because they're my daughters—

and are, in essence, as pure-blood as any elf that walks in the Kingdom these days."

"Then...you could save us!" Nyad's voice was almost a cry, a jubilant noise of broken despair.

Curatio was unmoved, indifferent. "No, I can't. Not like that."

"What?" The wizard's face registered shock as her jaw fell open. "Why not?"

Curatio took a deep breath and drew his hand to his face. "Because we made a pact, the other old ones and I. We vowed not intervene and become, as the only men capable of doing so, the saviors of the elven race. It was a calculated decision, to let human blood continue to intermingle with ours." He didn't look up from where his eyes were fixated on the table. "We had good reasons; it was a decision made by very wise men. And we were wrong, but it's too late to do anything about it now."

There was a long silence. Nyad looked almost collapsed at the other end of the table, Vara maintained her indifference, and Curatio had slumped in his seat, the most defeated Cyrus had seen him.

"So let's say you're immune to this...curse," Terian said, breaking the silence. "Which you say makes elven men infertile? Why would anyone curse the elves that way? Who would want to kill you?"

"When in doubt," Vaste said, "I blame Goliath."

"The infertility of the elves stretches back nearly a thousand years," Vara said. "I doubt even Malpravus would orchestrate a scheme that would not bear fruit for several millenia."

"Perhaps the Sovereign of Saekaj Sovar?" J'anda said, trading a look with Erith and Terian. The dark knight, for his part, looked murderous at the enchanter. Erith shook her head.

"Perhaps," Alaric said. "He does take a notoriously long view of the game."

"This is not a game," Nyad snapped. "This is our people—our lives."

"Not to him," Alaric said, calm.

"Who is this Sovereign everyone keeps being so damned mysterious about?" Cyrus looked around the table, irritation overwhelming him. *Of all the mysteries I've run across since joining Sanctuary, this one annoys me the most.*

"Sorry," Alaric replied. "Not yet. While it could be him, this is another secret that requires protecting for reasons that would become obvious if you knew the full details. And it may," he held up a hand to ward off Cyrus's response, "come to that, but not yet. Should we find the answer to who holds the chain of this Hand of Fear organization, I suspect all our questions will be answered."

"They have a master," Cyrus said, his hand curled into a mailed fist. "They've said he ordered the deaths of their victims."

"And we have no idea who it is?" Terian looked around.

"It could be anyone," Vara said. "For all their attacks, we still know next to nothing about the Hand of Fear."

Silence reigned for a moment as Terian scratched his chin. "I know something."

Alaric's words cut through the quiet. "You tortured one of them, didn't you?"

"Maybe." The dark knight's normally cool expression was even more reserved.

The fire crackled behind Alaric's eye. "I specifically told you—"

"You keep me around to do the things you're not willing to do yourself," Terian said, blazing defiance. "Protecting this guild from outside harm is my only priority, and if it's between bleeding some gutless assassin who had a hand in killing Niamh and waiting for the hammer to fall on another of my guildmates, it's an easy choice. Besides, it didn't even require that much effort. The last one we caught was human, a young one. Folded easy, because he wasn't a true believer like the others."

"Who's the master?" Cyrus leaned forward, intent on the dark knight.

"Not sure," Terian said, some of his smugness disappearing. "This human was seemed to be more of an initiate. Whoever they are, the Hand of Fear is running low on experienced assassins. This one was unsure of who they serve, only that 'the master is great and powerful and mighty' and all that crap. But he did know where the lair was, after some..." He looked away from Alaric's piercing gaze. "...coercion."

"I will not accept this sort of behavior, Terian," Alaric said in warning.

"If anyone ever kills another one of our guildmates this way, I suspect you'll accept it again," Terian replied. "Unless you'd like to see us keep losing people to these murderers."

"What you have done is beyond our code of honor." Alaric's voice carried a warning. "It is not how we comport ourselves in this guild."

"No? When it's them or us, I pick them to suffer and die every time. Sorry if that makes me cold, but that's how it is."

"We will discuss this further in private." Alaric's eye was narrow. "For now, we must eliminate this threat once and for all."

"Their base is in Traegon, in the Elven Kingdom," the dark knight said. "They used to have an army of master assassins. My sense is that they've gone through a lot of them lately, but we should still expect a tough fight. The initiate told me that there's a closed door in their headquarters, that only the initiated are allowed inside, and that they come back from behind it with orders from the master." He smiled. "So if we're lucky..."

"There's a portal just outside Traegon," Nyad said. "We can get my father's permission to strike; he might even add some of the army to assist—"

"No," Cyrus cut her off. "Get his permission, but don't let him tell a soul. Hand of Fear has shown a remarkable talent for learning things that they shouldn't know; they must have spies in his court. We can take a small army and hit them and maybe we'll catch this mysterious master at home."

Alaric turned to Nyad. "Go now. Every moment we wait gives the enemy further opportunity to place assassins within our walls again."

"Aisling is keeping an eye on everyone that walks through the door," Curatio said. "She seems pretty good at singling out the ones that are here for nefarious purposes."

"Which she should be," Vara muttered, "since she herself is here for nefarious purposes."

Alaric ignored her and turned his gaze to Cyrus. "Put together a small strike force—thirty or so of our most elite, in preparation to strike. Be ready to move as soon as Nyad returns." Cyrus nodded and Alaric turned back to face the occupants of the circular table. "If we are fortunate, this may be the last day that we need concern ourselves with the Hand of Fear."

Chapter 42

"I'm going, right?" Andren asked as Cyrus sat at a table in the Great Hall, nibbling on a turkey leg that Larana had wordlessly set in front of him. He had smiled and nodded at her in thanks, and she retreated, casting the occasional look back at him. Even now he saw her through the open passthrough in the wall where she was hard at work in the kitchen preparing dinner and sending him furtive glances, looking away every time he caught her.

"Yes," Cyrus said, turning his attention to his oldest friend. "I need a few healers, so I think it'll be you, Erith and Vaste."

"Yes!" The healer pumped his fist. "Revenge for Niamh at last."

"This isn't for revenge," Cyrus said, setting his quill down in the jar of ink. "This is to protect our guildmates from further harm. This Hand of Fear, they intend to kill Curatio and Vara."

"Well, yeah," Andren said, looking insulted. "But I find no wrong in taking a bit of vengeance for our favorite druid."

Cyrus did not respond; Curatio had entered the Great Hall and was making his way toward them. Cy nodded at his approach and the elder elf slid a chair out and sat down. "I'm going with you," he said with an odd determination.

"I'm making a list right now," Cyrus replied, feeling the need for a sudden caution. "I...believe it would be safest if you remained behind, along with Vara."

The Healer shook his head. "I'm afraid not. I need to come with you."

Cyrus exchanged a look with Andren. "I have several healers," he began, "we can make it without your help."

"It doesn't matter how many healers you have. I'm coming along—exercising my prerogative as the Elder of Sanctuary." Curatio stood; his words had come out the same way one might deliver a simple statement. With that said, he turned and began to make his way back toward the foyer.

"I doubt we'll need your skills—" Cyrus said to his retreating back.

"Doesn't matter," Curatio called over his shoulder. "You'll have them." He disappeared through the doorway.

"I believe the Elder of Sanctuary just told the General how it is," Andren said with barely contained glee. "I can't remember you ever taking orders from anyone and liking it."

"I don't like it now, either," Cyrus said. "But he's more experienced than any of us and I'm sure he has his reasons."

"So is it true?" Andren's hand was wrapped around a horn of ale, and his light beard already dripped with the brew. "He's an 'old one'?"

"The last." Cyrus dipped his quill back into the ink and added Curatio's name to his list in small script at the bottom. "How would that feel, outliving everyone you've ever known?"

"Not fun. Not that all the elves I know are dead, but I've been shunning my own kind and hanging around you more-mortal races for a few hundred years now. While you certainly know how to have more fun than the elves, it tends to come to a damned abrupt stop far earlier than I'm ready for it to."

"Which reminds me," Cyrus said, a smile coming to his face. "We have a mutual friend; she helped me care for Vara and bring her back to health."

"Oh?" Andren took a deep slug from his horn.

"Yeah, her name is Arydni—"

The mouthful of drink that the healer had taken erupted from his lips at the mention of the Priestess's name, covering the table, the parchment and Cyrus's breastplate. Andren made a strange, deep choking sound, as though he had inhaled some of his beverage. "I guess you remember her," Cyrus said.

Andren coughed, pounding himself on the chest before taking his hand away and clutching the table. "It'd be tough to forget that one. I haven't seen her in about two millenia. Has she taken the turn yet?"

Cyrus raised an eyebrow at him. "You mean has she started to age to fit her years?"

"Yeah."

A flash of Arydni in her priestess attire, with her supple flesh and ample bosoms, came to Cyrus's mind. "She has not."

"Really?" The healer's voice carried a note of hope. "Maybe I should track her down after this. You know, reacquaint myself."

Cyrus looked back to the blank spot under Curatio's name on his parchment, dipped his quill and began to write another name. "I thought you had women enough to keep you occupied here in Sanctuary."

"I do," Andren said. "But Arydni was a whole different kind of woman. Not like these naïve human girls I've been playing around with; she was almost three thousand when I met her, and the things she knew how to do..." He shuddered, a smile cracking his face as he stared off into space.

"Keep it to yourself." Cyrus shook his head. "I've already seen almost all of her; I don't need to imagine what she's capable of, it'll give me..." He let his words drift off.

"Nightmares?"

"Quite the opposite, more like." Cyrus shook his head. "Bellarum himself couldn't help me if I got caught muttering her name in my sleep."

"Yeah." Andren scooted his chair closer to Cyrus. "What's going on with you and the shelas'akur?"

"I don't know," he said. "She's been distant since her mother and father died. I won't crowd her now that she's been through all this; I'll just wait and give her time to figure things out." He shook his head. "It's not as though she's going anywhere, and if I were in her position I think I'd be wrecked, losing my hometown and both my parents in the course of a week."

"Yeah. Lucky for you that you don't have any parents to worry about." He shook his head. "Or a hometown, really."

Cyrus stiffened. "Reikonos is still my hometown."

"Really?" Andren's voice was measured incredulity. "If I'd have gone through what you went through at the Society, I'd have said good riddance and left the place behind the minute after graduation."

"Yeah." Cyrus felt a pang of bitterness. "It's done though. It doesn't matter. In the past. All that matters now..." He paused as he caught sight of a flash of blond hair, and a tight smile appeared on his face. "...is the future."

Andren and Cyrus remained silent and watched Vara storm her way through the Great Hall. Her hand toyed with the sword in her scabbard and she stopped at the edge of the table and looked to Andren first. "Drunk," she said to him with a nod of acknowledgment, then turned, focusing on Cyrus.

"Shrew," Andren said, drawing a withering glare from Vara and an eye roll from Cyrus. "What? She insulted me, I fired back."

"I stated a true fact about you." She cocked her head and glared at him.

"As did I," he returned and took another swig of his ale. "Would you rather I lied and called you 'sweetheart'?"

Vara let out a breath of exasperation and turned back to Cyrus. "I am coming with you to Traegon. There will be no argument."

"You sure about that?" Andren said, then buried his mouth back in his cup when she glared at him again. "Just asking."

Cyrus stared back at her, impassive, as she began to speak. "These monsters have killed one of our comrades while trying to get to me, drove me from my home and killed my mother." Her anger was white hot and visible on her face and in her mannerisms, the way she swung her finger around to point at Cyrus. "I don't care what oafish, protectionary nonsense you might have in your head about keeping me safe; I will be attending this attack, regardless of what you say—"

He didn't blink away from her assault, but reached down and grasped the list between his thumb and forefinger and lifted it with care to avoid the wet ink, angling the written words so she could read them, then pointed with his available hand to the line below Curatio's name.

She halted her tirade, confused, then followed his finger and stared at the parchment in concentration. "That says my name. Is that—that's the list for the raid?" He nodded, and a flicker of uncertainty was visible as she froze in place, finger still pointed at him. "That's...well, good."

He nodded. "I won't bother to try to talk you out of it, but I will ask you to remember that our priority is to capture or kill all the members of Hand of Fear in their base. No pursuing vendettas that may result in allowing any of them to slip the net, all right?"

She drew herself to rough attention, hands at her sides, her head held high and chin pointed at him. "I assure you that I am well in control of myself and will remember my duty."

"I'm sure you will." Cyrus lowered his voice. "Can we talk?"

Hesitation marked the paladin's body language, as she rocked back on her heels and half-turned. "I...think we should wait to speak until this is over. I..." She turned away from him and lowered her head. "...I have quite a bit on my mind at present, and I don't feel up to the challenge of a deep and thoughtful conversation."

Cyrus watched her and felt a ripple of concern roll through his belly. "All right," he said, even as a voice in his head screamed that it was not. "We'll talk after. Be ready to leave; as soon as Nyad returns we'll be teleporting to Traegon." He half-smiled. "Do you remember when we were in Traegon last?"

"We were only in Traegon once together," she replied, and began walking toward the exit. "And I can't recall anything of substance happening there." She did not say anything else as she left, wandering out into the foyer toward the lounge.

"Well, that sounded promising," Andren said the moment she was out of earshot.

"Shut up," Cyrus said, but the words lacked any conviction.

"It's almost as though the two of you got married or something," Andren said, drawing Cyrus's gaze. "About thirty years ago," he clarified, causing Cy to shake his head. "Seriously, even when she hated you she wasn't that cold and dismissive."

"She lost her parents and her home," Cyrus said without emotion, turning back to the parchment and staring at the names, trying to keep his mind away from anything else. "You'd be lucky to handle it half as well." He shook his head and tore the parchment in half. "Find these people. Tell them I want them to come with us."

"I'm drinking," Andren said, his voice approaching a whine.

"Take your mug with you and find them while I track down the other half. This is important. If you're in that much of a hurry to get back to drinking, hand off half of your list to the first person at the top of it and get them to do that for you."

Muttering all the way, the healer made his way out of the Great Hall as Cyrus gathered the other half of the parchment. He tried not to think about Vara, but failed. *She's been through a lot. After Narstron died, I wasn't even half as functional as she is right now, and I'd just lost a close friend. She got to watch a guildmate die for her benefit, then saw her hometown overrun by enemies and watched both parents die.* He shuddered and shook his head. *If Reikonos had been taken by the dark elves, it'd be enough for me to be edgy and isolated. She had a lot more happen than just that.*

By the time he'd rounded up his half of the list and made his way back to the foyer, Andren was already sitting in the lounge. "See?" Cyrus asked him upon entering the room. "Was that so hard?"

"Nah," the healer said. "Easy as pie."

"I finished finding everyone on the list," Cyrus heard Longwell's voice from behind him and turned to see the dragoon carrying the parchment he had given Andren. "I told them all to assemble here, that we could get the call to go out at any time."

Cyrus stared down Andren, who looked back, unflinching.

"See? It's done."

Cyrus sighed and looked around the lounge and foyer to see most of the people from his list already scattered throughout the area. Vaste and J'anda were lingering near the main doors with Erith and a few others, and Curatio stood in front of the huge hearth in the foyer, his back to the room, absorbed in watching the fire. Vara was seated in her usual place in the lounge, looking out a window, on the edge of her seat, rocking back and forth from nervous tension.

He heard the scuff of a boot on the stone behind him and turned to see Aisling seat herself on the arm of his chair, leaning in, her teeth flashing a wide grin. "Hi there," she said in a voice so low it sounded almost like purring.

"Aisling," he said. "Thank you for continuing to keep an eye on the front doors for us—"

"That's nothing," she said, dismissing him. "You haven't come to get the gift I have for you."

"Yeah...I don't want to be rude, but I'm not interested in—"

"I told you it wasn't that," she breathed in his ear. "It's this." Something slipped from her long cloak, a sword, glinting in the light of the dimming sun coming in through the windows on the far end of the lounge. "But you really should take me up on the other at some point, because it's not fair to knock it if you haven't tried—"

Cyrus's eyes alighted on the sword she held before him. Runed, the blade was massive, bigger than Praelior by a few inches, and glowed a faint red in the steel. It looked familiar and he studied it with curious intensity before looking up to Aisling, whose purple eyes blazed with excitement. "It's from the dark knight you killed on the bridge." She sighed as she looked at it. "The devilish part of me wanted to sell it, but I just couldn't." She thrust the hilt toward him. "It's yours; you did kill him, after all."

"But you brought it out of the city." He gazed at the glow from the blade. The light reflecting off it gave it an evil look, and he felt discomfort staring at it, even though he knew it was a finely crafted weapon.

"Even still." She rested it in his hand and forced the hilt into his other. "It's yours. I kept it for you; I know it's not as good as what you've got, but maybe you can give it to someone who will use it. Seems a shame to waste a weapon like this by selling it to someone outside the guild. It's near priceless."

"Aye," Cyrus said, lost in the red glow. "I carried out the morningstar that the Unter'adon tried to kill me with as well." He shook his head and closed his eyes, feeling his fingers close around the hilt. "I'm sure I can find someone who can use them." He nodded at the dark elf, who looked at him with expectant eyes. "Thank you."

"Cyrus." The calling of his name brought his attention to Alaric, who stood behind him. Cyrus got to his feet, nodding at the Ghost, whose eyes settled on the sword he held. "A fine weapon; tinged with the strength of Yartraak, if I'm not mistaken."

"The God of Darkness?" Cyrus stared at the blade in surprise. "It's not a godly weapon, is it?"

"I think not," the Ghost said, a slight smile peeking out from the bottom of his helm. "While mystical weapons are enchanted and bear powers a normal blade can't hope to match, a godly weapon is of a whole different caliber. A mystical weapon can help a man hold off an army; a godly weapon can help him carve through said army, leaving nothing behind but a bloody swath." Alaric stared at the sword and reached out for it, taking it when Cyrus proffered it to him. "This is a fine mystical blade, and it bears the touch of the Lord of the Dark, but it's no godly weapon; his weapon is—"

"*Noctus*, the Battle Axe of Darkness," Cyrus whispered in memory. Alaric raised an eyebrow and nodded. "I saw it last year when we were in Yartraak's Realm."

Alaric handed the weapon back to him. "I will accompany you to Traegon," the Ghost said without preamble.

Cyrus kept his composure but inside he felt a curiosity; the Ghost rarely left Sanctuary. "You and everyone else, it seems."

A hint of amusement drifted across the visible portion of Alaric's features. "Curatio and Vara are going as well, I take it?"

"I assumed Curatio would have told you."

"He didn't need to," the Ghost said. "Now that he is aware of the Hand of Fear's interest in him, you would be hard pressed to keep him away from them. Knowing that they sought him as well as Vara, he feels responsible for Niamh's death, and he'll pursue this until the truth comes out about their leader." The Guildmaster of Sanctuary's lips faded from a smile into a hard line. "And I would not care to be this 'master' when Curatio finds out who he is."

"Curatio is a healer," Cyrus said. "They're not renowned for their offensive abilities."

Alaric's eyebrow cocked at Cyrus. "Healer or not, he is a fearsome foe, and you would do well not to underestimate him. I assure you he did not survive to the age he has by being unskilled in the arts of war." A memory made its way forward, a vision of a long ago incursion into the halls of the goblins under the mountain of Enterra—of Curatio with a mace in hand, killing goblins as the Sanctuary force was overwhelmed and destroyed. Alaric stared at Cyrus, apparently aware of his being lost in thought. "What?"

"The first time we went to Enterra." Cyrus licked his lips, which felt suddenly dry. "Do you remember it? When you had to come and rescue us?"

"I do." The Ghost was quiet. "You speak of the night we lost your friend, Narstron."

"Yes." Cyrus felt the sting of the memory, but pushed it away. "Did Curatio die that night as well?"

"Yes; there were no survivors among you save for Niamh, who teleported out. Make no mistake, he may be immortal, but only in the natural sense. He can still be killed by weapons and spells." The Ghost smiled. "He's just more difficult to kill for being so damnably canny."

"I can hear you," came Curatio's voice from across the foyer.

"There was never any doubt," Alaric said. "I meant every word of it."

"Did you know he was an old one?" Cyrus honed in on Alaric's eye, which did not dodge away from him.

"Of course. Curatio and I have known each other for a long time; there are no secrets between us."

"But plenty between you and the rest of the Council," Cyrus said with a great sigh.

The Ghost's eye glittered. "Perhaps. Know me for as long as Curatio has and that will change."

"How long would that be, exactly?"

A chuckle came forth from Alaric. "I am human, brother. Whatever skills and abilities I may possess, I am still a man. Be assured of that."

"I believe you," Cyrus said. "But that doesn't really answer the question, does it?"

Alaric chuckled again. "I suppose not."

Any further inquiries that Cyrus might have put forth to press the issue were put aside when the blast of a teleportation spell brought a red robed wizard into view. Nyad's blond hair tumbled down as she shook off the effects of the travel and looked around, her eyes alighting on Cyrus and Alaric. With a single nod, she told them all.

"Time to leave," Alaric said, voice almost a whisper. "Time to end this hunt." Without a word said by Cyrus, the men and women he had placed on his list were already moving toward the center of the foyer, ready.

"Gods, I hope so," Cyrus replied, following his Guildmaster to the heart of the raiding party.

Chapter 43

They appeared outside the city after dark. Snow was falling and the roads were already covered. The crisp air flooded Cyrus's nose and lungs, helping him stave off the desire to sleep. When challenged by the guards at the gate, Vara rode forward to speak with them, her stallion seeming to have more spring in its step than when last he had seen it. He patted Windrider and turned to Alaric. "Who do I owe thanks to for retrieving my horse from elven territory?"

"I believe it was Ryin Ayend. After you had gone to the palace, he teleported into the Kingdom and retrieved them from the Priestesses of Vidara." Alaric coaxed his horse along with minimal effort.

"I have a hard time getting a read on him," Cyrus said. "He takes positions that I find indefensible—like not wanting to help Vara or get involved in the war—and yet he still assists in the oddest and most useful ways."

"He's quite the contrarian," Alaric said. "You may not like or agree with him, but you can't argue with his loyalty."

"Aye," Cyrus said, grudging. "I find it easier to see the world in absolutes—either someone is on my side or they're not."

Alaric laughed. "I can't say I haven't seen the world from the same perspective myself, in my youth. But Arkaria is a complex place. To try and label people good or evil is futile and a simplistic way to look at the world."

Cyrus looked down at Windrider, who trudged along the snowy road without any urging from him. "I wish it was that simple. Good guys and bad guys, and obvious which is which."

They passed through the gates, opened by the guards at Vara's behest. The Traegon guards watched them warily. "Did you explain why we're here?" Cyrus asked Vara, who nodded. "Did they say anything?"

"They asked to see the King's letter, then requested that we try not to burn down the city in our efforts to apprehend the assassins."

"Burn down the city?" Cyrus frowned. "Why would they think we would do that?"

She ran a hand along the side of her horse's neck. "The King's letter was explicit in that it required them to stand aside and allow us to do anything to capture our quarry, even if it involved burning the city to the ground."

"You can see how high in regard the monarchy holds the cities of the common people," Andren said from off to the side. "Whole damned Kingdom tilts to corruption on the side of the royals."

"Now you're part of the status quo, Sir Andren, in case you've forgotten." Vaste graced the healer with a smile. "Do be vigilant, watching from your mansion as the royals continue to do all the things you've bitterly railed about for years."

"Never should have taken that title," Andren mumbled.

"What about the gold?" Vaste smiled, a wicked one that exposed his teeth.

"Well I wasn't going to pass that up, was I?"

The town was much smaller than Pharesia or Termina, but almost every building possessed a tower capped by a minaret. Following Terian's instruction, they made their way to a warehouse on the far edge of town. The building was made of bleached sandstone, and even in the dark Cyrus could see it would appear near-white in the light of day.

Cyrus dismounted and studied the sides of the building. "No windows to speak of," he said, thinking out loud. "They won't see us coming." He pointed to a nearby door. "Since we have no idea what's inside, one door is as good as another. We might as well come crashing through that one."

"You have a strategy in mind for this, I assume?" Vara climbed down from her horse with athletic ease as Cyrus crossed the ground to the warehouse at a trot. He did not slow as he approached the door but sped up, crashing through shoulder-first, filling the air with a horrible cracking noise as he plunged into the darkness. "I should have bloody well known it would be something as stupid as that," he heard her mutter.

She climbed through the wreckage of the door behind him, sword drawn. They were in a lamplit room with no one in sight. He moved forward to allow the others to join them, and the room began to fill as he moved around. There were paintings on the wall, furniture of a typical elven style with red silk cushions, and a smell of incense filled the air.

"I'd tell you to be on your guard," Cyrus said in a whisper, "but if you weren't already, you wouldn't be here. Split into two groups. One with me, going this way, and the other goes with—"

he glanced back and saw Alaric, sword in the paladin's hand — "with Lord Garaunt, going that way. Take them alive if you can, kill them if there's any possibility they might escape."

He led the way through a door to his left, keeping his sword in hand in front of him, ready to block. The glow of the blade allowed him to see slightly better in the dimness. He heard Vara's soft breathing a step behind him, and heavier breathing following her at a distance, punctuated by an occasional snort that told him that Vaste was in his procession. He walked down a long hallway, weaving around tables placed on the sides of the hall, filled with candles and statuary.

A noise ahead caught his attention. He swept forward, careful to muffle the sound of his boots by staying on the plush carpeting that ran down the middle of the hall. Another noise came and he crept forward with a single finger pressed to his lips in warning for quiet. The noise came from a door on the left.

He reached it and found it closed, and heard another sound from within, a creaking noise that caused a chill to run through him as he leaned against the wall and started to move his hand toward the knob. Vara took up position on the other side of the door, a line of others behind her starting with Terian and J'anda and followed by Vaste. Cyrus held up his hand with three fingers extended. *Two...one...*He opened the door with his shoulder, sword in hand as he charged into the room.

Cyrus came to a halt as he determined the source of the noise. Behind him Vara stopped before running into his back, but Terian did not, causing her to bump forward into him. The source of the creaking was obvious now. A rope hung from the rafters, looped around the neck of the only assassin in the room, and his body swung in a slow, lazy circle hanging before an altar with a massive statue on it that looked familiar.

"Cut him down," Cyrus said, still focused on the dead man. The body was clothed in red robes, a more ornate version of the garb the other assassins had worn. A twang was followed by an arrow streaking through the air and cutting the rope in its flight. With a snap it broke and the body tumbled to the floor.

"Why would he kill himself?" Terian said.

Cyrus leaned over the corpse. It was an old elven man under the hood, eyes clouded with near-blindness even before he had died, the warrior realized. His hands were gnarled and the stiffness of death had begun to set in. "He was infirm. Blind, crippled hands, who knows what other kinds of ailments." Cyrus reached down and closed the old man's eyes, then felt down to the belt, where he removed a blade from a scabbard. It was a familiar dagger, one with the blade of black and the eight-sided pommel that held the circular snake emblem he had seen from every assassin of the Hand of Fear thus far.

"You think maybe he was the master?" Andren's voice punctuated the silence.

"No," Cyrus said. "I think he was the last of their order, and that he killed himself to atone for their failure."

"Really?" Terian's voice carried skepticism. "After all these attempts, one relentless assault after another, you think they finally reached the end of their numbers and this guy just gave up?"

"I'd ask him, but he's already cold." Cyrus pushed back to his feet. "I think if you've got a secret order and you're sending initiates to fulfill your mission, you're running low on people."

The dark knight looked around the room. "Yeah. Maybe. But if this guy's not the master, how do we find out who ordered Curatio and Vara's deaths? It's not like Alaric is gonna let me torture anyone else to get the answer."

"You won't need to." Curatio's voice came from the doorway behind them. "Alaric sent me to tell you that we've swept the rest of the building; there's no one else here."

"So they're all dead?" Vaste wondered aloud.

"We should be on our guard for a while," Cyrus said. "They may have a few more making their way toward Sanctuary, or in hiding, but other than that I think...they're done." He looked back to the body of the old man lying on the floor, and he caught sight of an overturned stool that the assassin must have stood on while preparing for his demise. "Without knowing who the master is, I don't see how we can't truly put an end to this."

"Simple enough," Curatio said. "The answer resides here — in this room."

Terian's head whirled around. Cyrus kept his turn more reserved, scanning for signs before coming to rest on the statuary of the altar. Vara stepped in front of him, fixated on the same thing he was, and he followed her up the small steps.

The altar was wooden, with two wide, sturdy legs parallel to each other. It was big enough to support the statue, which looked to weigh a few hundred pounds. *From where he hung, and the way he was facing, it was almost as though he was sacrificing himself to...*

"I don't get it." Longwell's voice came from behind Cyrus. "What? The statue was the master?"

"A representation of him, at least." Vara's words came out in breaths, low and hushed.

The figure carved in stone had eight arms, radiating around him and jutting from his shoulders, back and torso. At the torso his legs split into four muscular supports for an oversized thorax. The head perching at the top of the long neck was beaked, like a bird, but open-mouthed to show fangs, and the statue was detailed enough that there were a hundred or more of them visible. The eyes were dead and lifeless in the stone, but large. It was an alien thing, and the expression was of pure malice.

"This is ridiculous," Longwell said, stepping up to the altar. "This? They serve this...this thing?" He shook his head. "I mean...what is it?"

"Mortus," Cyrus said. "It's Mortus."

"Mort-what?" Longwell placed a mailed fist on the statue and slid it across derisively. "Is it a creature? A beast? A monster? A ruler? A greengrocer in Reikonos? What?"

"No," Curatio said, still quiet. "Not a creature, nor beast, nor ruler, not of these lands, at least not of late. It's Mortus. And of all the masters they could possibly serve, this is...by far, the worst I can imagine."

Longwell threw his arms up in despair, still looking at the healer. For answer, Curatio looked back at the dragoon, stared into his eyes, and spoke in a voice that cracked with terror and dread, so frightening in a normal voice, but one that drove sheer terror into Cyrus's soul knowing that it came from a being 23,000 years old. "Mortus is a God.

"The God of Death."

Chapter 44

"I'm afraid," Longwell's voice rang across the Council Chamber after they had returned to Sanctuary, "all this talk of gods runs right over me like so much water in a stream. I don't believe it, I don't understand it, and I'm surprised any of you, who seem so reasonable in all else, could buy into it." The dragoon shook his head, his hair wisping as it fell on either cheek. "They're not real."

"Oh, they're real enough," Curatio said. The healer wore a traveling cloak still fastened around his neck. They had returned from Traegon and immediately gone to Council. "The gods are real enough to touch you if you should get in their way, real enough to kill you if you should cross them."

Longwell snorted. "I'm not trying to be disrespectful, but from an outsider's perspective, the idea of gods sounds... ridiculous. Forces, beyond our sight, manipulating people? Ludicrous. They tell similar fairytales in my own lands, but only the peasants believe them."

"It's no myth," Terian said, causing Longwell to roll his eyes. "The Gods of Arkaria are quite real, not some imaginary figment. Many of them have been seen in the last few hundred years, and interfere in the affairs of mortals to this day."

Cyrus leaned forward and looked to Longwell, who was still shaking his head. "Weren't you with us in the Realm of Darkness last year?"

"Aye, I was. But I didn't see a god in that place; just a hell of a lot of darkness, and some creatures that—while extraordinary—don't require a god to exist any more than any of us do."

"Putting aside the question of whether deities exist," Erith broke in, "why would Mortus want Vara and Curatio dead?"

"He has good cause to want me dead," Curatio said, his voice ragged. "I have no idea why he would want Vara to die."

"What did you do to piss off the God of Death?" Terian looked at the healer with barely concealed awe.

Curatio smiled, a wan, sad curve of his lips. "You are aware that the vast majority of the Elven Kingdom worships Vidara?"

Terian nodded. "I've heard that, yes."

"I brought her word into the Kingdom." He paused. "I evangelized for her thoughout Elvendom until she was the widest accepted deity."

"Mortus hates Vidara," Cyrus said. "I haven't heard you speak out for Vidara since I've been here. Do you not believe in her any longer?"

Curatio shrugged, and it gave the effect of making him seem even more resigned. "I still believe in her in the same way I believe in anything I can see with my own eyes and feel with my own hands. I just don't worship her as I once did. All my evangelism was after the War of the Gods, 10,000 years ago, when the beliefs were still spreading..." He hesitated. "...among the disbelievers and those who followed the...old ways."

"Supporting the opposing god would be reason enough to make you an enemy, I suppose," Vaste said. "But again, we come back to the other questions — why Vara and why the other old ones?"

"Vara is a symbol in the Kingdom, yes?" J'anda looked around the table. "Perhaps it was an attempt to destabilize the elves?"

"Arydni, the High Priestess of Vidara, told me that Vara was a gift from the Goddess of Life; the only hope since the curse began," Cyrus said. "If Mortus and Vidara are bitter enemies, locked in perpetual struggle over mortals, then would that make one of the battlegrounds the Elven Kingdom?"

Alaric cleared his throat. "The biggest, actually. The original elves were near-immortal. Can you imagine any greater affront to the God of Death?"

"Six thousand years? I imagine he might be offended by a lifespan of such length," J'anda said.

"Indeed," Alaric continued, "the God of Death has long hungered for more souls from the elves than he receives. In addition, his tools are not limited to death, but also the means of fear."

"Hand of Fear," Cyrus murmured. "What greater is there to fear than death?"

"Quite a bit." The Ghost placed a hand on the top of his helm, which was resting on the table. "That said, there is something that might cast this entire situation in a different light."

"And that is?" Terian spoke after Alaric had paused for a moment.

"Since none of you but the elves among us have had cause to know of this curse that afflicts their people, you would not have had cause to ask yourself from whence this curse came." Alaric's face had resumed its harder resolve; his eye was a gleaming gray.

"I thought of it for a while last night," Vaste said, clicking his staff against the ground. "But I assumed that if anyone knew for certain who had done it, we'd have been told."

"No one knows." Vara's voice was scratchy, a choked whisper, as though she were straining to speak. "It has been the greatest mystery of the last millenium, and the secret in general precluded too much idle searching for the answer outside the Kingdom."

"Cursing every male in the Kingdom with infertility?" Erith broke her silence. "What sort of spellcaster could even muster such a spell? Even if there was such a thing, who could cast it?"

"No one person," Nyad said. "My father's counselors suspected an army of dark elven wizards, traveling throughout the Kingdom, over the course of a hundred years—"

"No," Alaric said. "Not the dark elves. It was Mortus."

"You sound certain." Vaste eyed the Ghost.

Alaric's demeanor left no room for doubt. "I am."

"Told you himself, did he?" Terian quipped.

"No," Alaric said. "He did not. Yet I know that he did it."

"What kind of spell could even do that?" Longwell looked at Alaric. "I don't buy into this idea of gods—he'd have to be using the same magic as everyone else, so what kind of spell does such a thing?"

Alaric laughed, but it was hollow and mirthless. "He does not use the same magic as anyone else. The gods have powers of their own, things beyond the knowledge of mortals, and this is one of them."

Cyrus stared straight ahead. "Beyond the knowledge of mortals...but are they beyond the use of mortals?" His eyes flicked up to catch Alaric's gaze, and the Ghost did not look away quickly enough. "Could a mortal use a spell that the gods use, like we would use one of their weapons?"

Alaric hesitated and looked to Curatio, who for once remained cooler in his disposition than Alaric. The healer looked to the Guildmaster, and in a resigned voice, almost devoid of any emotion but a hint of accusation, said, "You didn't tell me it was him."

Alaric looked to Curatio and something passed between them, something so subtle Cyrus could not quite interpret it. "I was sworn."

Curatio nodded, his jaw jutted out, as though he were chewing on the inside of his lip, and turned back to Cyrus. "Yes, but with some qualifications. *Some* mortals could use *some* magics that that gods wield, but only the most powerful spellcasters, and the spells would drain them, being somewhat more energy intensive than a simple healing spell, for example."

"Heresy," Ryin Ayend said in a low, hissing voice.

"If a cure to the curse existed and we found it in the Realm of Death, could you use it?" Cyrus stared down Curatio. "You, who have the ability to burn through more magical energy than any mortal."

Curatio did not speak for a long moment, nor did he break from Cyrus's gaze. "Yes. I likely could."

"Assuming such a thing existed," Ryin Ayend said, his eyes aflame with shock, "what you speak of is heresy, and reason enough for the Leagues to hunt you across Arkaria to the end of your days."

"Which would be quite the merry chase," Curatio said. "I daresay I'd just outrun them until they died, then go on living my life."

"Even if you did such a thing, how would this help you and Vara?" Ayend looked from the healer to the shelas'akur. "Mortus sent assassins after you; stealing a spell to heal your people after he cursed them is hardly going to endear you further."

"Since he already means to kill us," Vara said, her response icy, "I don't see how things could get worse if we further offend him."

"Perhaps they wouldn't for you," Ryin said with a hint of exasperation, "but they would for us—as in Sanctuary. We have enemies enough without adding the God of Death to our list."

"Speak for yourself," Terian said. "I'm always willing to take on new candidates if they're worthy, and I think the God of Death would be a pleasant enough challenge." Terian looked down the table, his long nose seeming to point at Cyrus. "What are you proposing?"

"Nothing that radical." Cyrus balled his fists inside their metal shells. "We've been on expeditions to Mortus's domain in the past, while he's absent. I say we do so again, only this time with the specific purpose of finding something that would help us break the curse inflicted on the elves." He looked at Vara with a sidelong glance and saw her watching him. "If we save the elven people from this calamity, perhaps it will give the God of Death something else to focus on."

"I still have no idea why this so-called God of Death would cast a curse on the elves like this," Longwell said, shaking his head as if he could make the whole situation disappear. "And I've yet to hear any genuine, empirical evidence that convinces me that he is real, so if you want to raid his realm looking for something that doesn't exist, why not? What's the worst that can happen?"

"We could be caught by Mortus and smashed to a juicy pulp," Vaste said.

"If we find and use some forbidden magic of the gods, we can be declared heretics and become the enemies of everyone in Arkaria from now to the end of our days." Ryin Ayend had his hand over his eyes as though massaging a headache away, but his words were clear.

"I'll take the dishonor of heresy upon myself," Curatio said. "None of you need fear it, since none of you could use the spell anyway. But I doubt we'd find a cure; what we need is the curse itself, because with it I have a starting point for deriving a cure."

"Branching off from accepted, League-taught magics," Ryin Ayend said. "That's more heresy. Will it ever cease?"

"Your Leagues have a great many rules," Longwell said with a shake of the head. "I say we have nothing to fear in this Realm of Death and if the rewards are anything like what we found in Darkness's Realm, it will be worth it."

"Other than being mashed by a god," Vaste said, "I'm inclined to agree. We've fought through the Realm of Death before. If we can do what every guild before us that's assaulted a god's realm has done and find a time that Mortus won't be home, I vote we do it."

Nyad spoke with a gasp. "Yes." The wizard looked haunted.

Curatio smiled. "I see no reason why not; the God of Death has never before troubled himself when these things have happened to him in the past."

One by one, around the table was a slow series of nods of assent. "This is madness," Ryin Ayend said with a heavy sigh, "but as I see no more direct harm coming to us than we are already in line for, I vote 'aye'."

Vara was in a daze, but blinked out of it when her turn came to speak. "I do not know if this will help Curatio and I or not, but should we find the spell, and should he be able to cure the curse, it will help my people." She bowed her head and closed her eyes. "And that is all I have left to care about."

Alaric tore his gaze from her. "I would echo the sentiments of others in my words of caution. Gods are not to be trifled with. Were we to achieve this, it might distract the God of Death from our friends; but that is mere hope. He is not known for being a forgiving sort, nor of a mind to relinquish a goal once set. While the Hand of Fear may be destroyed, he has other servants who will take up the fight and follow his commands." With sorrow he looked to Vara. "I do not know that this will end your torment, but I will give everything in me to attempt to make it so."

Vara was sickly white when she answered, but it was with a mechanical voice. "I thank you. All of you."

"I leave it to our general to work out the details," Alaric said, nodding to Cyrus. "With that, let us adjourn."

Cyrus remained in his chair while almost everyone else beat a hasty path to the exit. Vara looked back at him as though she were about to say something, then turned away, disappearing through the door behind Nyad. Cyrus turned to find Curatio staring down Alaric.

"You should have told me," the healer said.

"I should have." The Ghost looked back at him. "But I was sworn to secrecy."

"And you violate it now?" Curatio's words came out low and accusatory, harsher than anything Cyrus had heard from him.

"Lives are at stake, and you know this may be part of a larger plan by Mortus." Alaric stood facing Curatio. "I am sorry I did not reveal..." His eyes flitted around the room to find Cyrus watching, as well as Terian. "...what I know...sooner. I did not wish to —"

"I know what you didn't wish to do," Curatio said, voice rising. "I know damned well what you didn't want to admit to. To hell with it, Alaric. It was always you anyway. I thought I made my peace with..." An agonized grunt came from Curatio, and he shook his head, face awash in unexpressed emotions. "Damn it all. I'm 23,000 years old, I shouldn't..."

"You are a man," Alaric said, soothing. "Regardless of age, you share the same flaws as the rest of us, tempered only by greater wisdom than any other."

Curatio stared back at him for a moment before reaching out in a fit of pique and knocking the Ghost's helm from the table to the floor. "To hell with wisdom. To hell with tempering. And to hell with you." With a snarl, the healer swept from the room, his cloak trailing behind him.

Alaric stooped to retrieve his helm and placed it upon his head. "I am sorry you had to witness that."

"It's kind of like watching Mommy and Daddy fight," Terian said with a sadistic chuckle. "I've never seen even a hint of discord between the two of you before."

"Yes," Alaric said with a sigh. "I'm afraid there's much more to it than my witholding information. But that is a story —"

"For another time," Cyrus and Terian chorused.

A flicker of amusement made its way across the Ghost's face, but did not reach his eye. "What can I do for the two of you?"

"Nothing for me," Terian said. "I need to talk to Cyrus."

Cyrus stared at the Ghost, who, after the argument with Curatio, seemed somehow smaller than he had ever looked before. "I...I have nothing that can't wait."

Alaric nodded. "If you'll excuse me, gentlemen, I feel the ether calling." He took a deep breath, and Cyrus watched his armor rise with the inhalation. As it began to sink with his exhalation, the lines of the Ghost's armor began to fade, and the streaks that ran down the plate of his mail blurred and became insubstantial, a thin mist filling the room around his feet, as Alaric became the Ghost in deed as well as name, and the fog disappeared from the room.

"Of all the weird things he does, that's the weirdest," Terian said with a shake of the head.

"What do you need?" Cyrus leaned against the table, watching the dark knight.

"Ah," Terian said with a smile, "I need nothing. In fact, I come to you with assistance." He straightened. "I can help you with invading the Realm of Death."

Chapter 45

The light was dim in the Brutal Hole, a bar in the slums of Reikonos. Though he had seen it when living there, Cyrus had never trod in the establishment, which was for dark elven laborers that worked on the waterfront. The patrons were surly, protective and quarrelsome when standing outside, thus he had never been motivated to find out if the interior was as shabby as the broken down wooden facade.

Until now, he thought. *It matches.* Terian had dragged him here with the assistance of Nyad, who was waiting for them at the old Kings of Reikonos Guildhall only a few blocks away. The bar had a dim mirror stretched behind it, the edges scarred and blackened from age and poor use. The whole place had a smell he associated with unwashed garments mixed with saltwater. *I'm used to smelling the death and horror of battles, and this place has a scent that makes me ill. What does that say about it?*

Terian took a deep sniff. "Smells like home," he said with a serene smile.

"Remind me never to visit Saekaj," Cyrus said, taking a sip of the green ale in front of him. He kept his head hidden under his cloak, less worried that the patrons might start a fight with him than he'd end up killing all of them and have to answer to the Reikonos authorities. He looked around the motley crowd shouting crass comments at the woman behind the bar; she matched every one of the dock workers profanity for profanity, causing them to laugh even more.

"It's no worse than here," the dark knight assured him. With a slug of his ale, Terian looked back at him. "Aren't you pleased to see that your city is still standing?"

Cyrus was reminded of the discomfort in his belly as they teleported into the main square. As it appeared before him, he let out a slight yet obvious sigh of relief. They were stopped by Reikonos guards that were stationed around the square and detained because of Terian's presence. Once Cyrus's identity had been established, the guards had let them pass with a glare at the dark knight, who shrugged the whole thing off. "If my city was under siege by humans, they'd kill any of you trying to teleport in." He grinned. "Your people are far too merciful."

"Let's hope it doesn't cost us the war," Cyrus had said without amusement.

In spite of the frigid Reikonos winter, the hearth was empty of a fire, with only the faintest embers still burning within it. "Wood is worth more than gold right now," the woman behind the bar had said when she brought their drinks. She looked with suspicion on Cyrus's downed hood, but didn't press the issue. Terian had thrown extra coins her way to expedite her retreat, which she took without question and returned to the bar and the rowdy longshoremen gathered around it.

"How much longer?" Cyrus kept his voice low, in spite of the fact that it would be near impossible to be heard over the din the drunks were causing, another peal of raucous laughter filling the air.

"Now, I think," Terian said as the door opened, allowing a sliver of sunlight to cross the floor. The obnoxious laughter of the crowd at the bar stopped as a figure entered, also hooded, and swooped past them with a shuffle, drawing the attention of the dock workers as it passed. After a moment, the laughter returned; a choice comment in dark elvish reached Cyrus's ears, which he didn't fully understand but grasped enough of to shake his head at the crudity.

The figure approached them with caution, shuffling on a leg that appeared unsteady. When it reached them, Cyrus was struck by the trailing stench that came in its wake, overwhelming any of the horrible fragrances of the bar. It smelled of the decay Cy had pondered earlier, overwhelming and gutwrenching. With a nod, it sat, and the lamplight caught features that were gray as a stormy sky.

With a sudden sense of revulsion, Cyrus pushed back against the chair. Terian's hand gripped his, holding him down as he reached for his sword. "Don't," the dark knight said.

"It's...it's a..." Cyrus reached again for his sword but Terian blocked him with a gauntlet, clanking metal against metal.

"A wendigo?" The creature slid forward into the light, revealing a wreck of face. His eyes were sunken in the skull and a skeletal hand that reminded Cyrus of Malpravus slid across the table and picked up a gold coin from a stack in front of Terian. Its mouth was mangled, twisted with jagged teeth, and when it breathed on him Cyrus felt a need to vomit. "I am, a creature of Mortus that has long since fled the master's realm."

Cyrus yanked his hand away from Terian and held it in front of his nose. "What brings a foul servant of a foul god to Reikonos?"

"A foul place." The wendigo's mouth twisted into a smile, giving it a more grotesque look than before. "I come here to meet you, to treat with you, to offer you information for coin—are insults all I am to receive?"

"Don't act so offended," Terian said, sliding the stack of coins off the table and into his hand. "You're a wendigo; your skin is rotted and you smell like a troll brothel on Sunday morning. Hrent, this is Cyrus Davidon. He's faced your kind before."

"You've fought the footsoldiers of death?" Hrent reached across the table, emaciated gray hand facing up, pointed toward Terian. "Then you know most of what you'll be up against if you're planning on going to the Realm of Mortus."

"Aye," Cyrus said, holding his breath. "Is there still a hydra and demon knights?"

The rotted face of the wendigo twisted again. Milky white eyes stared back at him from beneath the hood. "Perhaps. Perhaps there's more. I find gold helps me recall."

Terian shared a look with Cyrus, then dropped a half dozen coins on the table. "Start talking. If what you say sounds good, more may follow."

Hrent reached out and grasped at each of the coins, bringing them up to his teeth and biting them one by one. "All right," he said when finished. "Yes, there's a hydra and a host of demon knights; nothing different about them. But there's more now."

"Such as?" Cyrus said from behind his gauntlet.

The gray finger beckoned, and two more gold pieces were tossed upon the table. "Might be skeletons. I can't recall." Another gold piece clinked in front of the wendigo. "Yeah, skeletons. A whole army of them. Not particularly strong, but a nuisance when coupled with the demon knights and my brothers." The thin fingers came up to Hrent's face and scratched the skin, long claw digging into dead flesh, leaving a mark but no blood welled up within. "Something else, too." He nodded at the small but growing pile of gold in front of him and two more pieces landed upon it. He nodded again and Terian threw two more. "They've changed their strategy. They don't hide anymore; everything waits in the fields of Paxis by the portal. Except the hydra. You won't have to face him unless you go looking for him."

Cyrus exchanged a glance with Terian. "Anything else? A dragon skeleton or anything like that?"

The sunken eyes watched him. "No. Nothing like that. All that's left is the time."

"When?"

The long claws clicked on the gold, and Terian poured five more pieces out of his coinpurse and slid them across the table one at a time as Hrent bit them, his long teeth leaving little flaws in the face of the metal. "Tomorrow," he said, scooping them all off the table. "He'll be gone for three days; has a meeting with Bellarum in the Realm of War. Those two...they do go on and on," Hrent said with a smile that made Cyrus's stomach turn.

"Anything else you'd like to tell us?" Terian watched him expectantly.

The wendigo licked his split and cracked lips with a dry tongue. "Might be I'll have some information on Yartraak soon; I'm making inroads with some of his former servants, but he's a secretive bastard, that one."

"We'll see," Terian said. "I doubt that will do you much good."

Hrent slid the last coins into a leather pouch and Cyrus watched them drain into it through his rotted fingers. "Nice to know I've got a new customer to sell to," he said with a pointed grin. "Tired of dealing with Goliath all the time. I do miss Endeavor and Amarath's Raiders; they always had class—"

"You sold information to Goliath?" Cyrus left his seat and leaned across the table, grabbing hold of Hrent's cloak and yanking him back.

The sunken eyes were wide with sudden fear. "Yeah, they bought off me a few times. What of it?"

"Cyrus..." Terian's tone was warning and the warrior looked across the bar. The rowdy longshoremen were all looking at him, his hood now behind his head, face exposed for all to see.

"Never mind," Cyrus said to Hrent. "Come to us again when next you have information. Go on." Without hesitation the wendigo grabbed his pouch of gold and limped from the bar. At the counter, the dock workers watched Cyrus with sullen faces. He parted his cloak at the front so his armor was obvious, and rested a hand on Praelior. "Reckon I'll be leaving now, too." He led the way, keeping watch on the resentful eyes of the dark elves as they passed, flipped a silver coin to the bartender as he left, and she flashed a grateful look.

"So now we know when," Terian said, walking beside him through the slums. "Can we put together an assault by tomorrow morning? Because it'll take us at least a day to get to the portal to Death's Realm."

"We're a little out of practice," Cyrus said, steering around a vegetable cart that had only a few meager pickings left on it. "But the numbers are in our favor with an army of over three thousand, so a little sloppiness won't harm us as it would have when we were a hundred or two hundred strong and reliant on larger allies." He let out a breath and watched it fog the air in front of him. "The larger question is, can we trust him?"

"Who?" Terian cocked his head back in the direction of the bar. "Hrent? Not remotely. But he's sold to others and he wants more people to sell to, so I think his information is accurate."

"Listen to what you just said." Cyrus shook his head in amazement. "We're about to invade the Realm of a God, searching for the cure to a mystical curse, and on the say-so of one of his former servants."

"When you put it that way, it sounds like fun."

Cyrus laughed. "When I put it that way, it sounds like madness." The mirth vanished from his face. "That's a sobering thought."

"No, it's not," Terian said. "It makes me want to drink." They turned down an alley and Cyrus caught a sidelong glance from the dark elf. "This really is crazy. Why are you doing it?"

"I'm just spearheading it," Cyrus said after a moment's pause.

Terian stopped him with a hand on his arm. "We're talking about crossing into the Realm of the God of Death and upending one of his schemes that is so nefarious, it ends in the death of a whole race. Do you have some kind of hero complex or just a death wish?"

Cyrus looked to the next building, the old horse barn where Nyad was waiting for them. "We've done it for lesser reasons. For gold, armor and weapons."

"Yeah," Terian said. "But what's the reason this time? To find some miracle cure that probably isn't even there? I mean, do you think that just because we show up and steal some of his stuff, Mortus will forget that he wants Vara and Curatio dead?"

"No."

A hard look found Cyrus from the dark knight. "Then why?"

There was a long pause. "Because we have the power now.

Because this is their last hope and there aren't any others. Because we could save an entire race from dying out." He took a deep breath and struggled with it, feeling the chill deep in his lungs, awakening an ache there.

"That it?" Terian stared him down.

"Yeah. That not enough reason for you?"

The dark knight looked away. "That'll do, I guess." He turned, going the last few paces to the old guildhall, where he opened the door and stepped inside.

Cyrus waited, hesitating just a moment before following him. *And...because...I can't bring back her mother and father.*

Chapter 46

The quiet of night overwhelmed him. His window was open, and far below, the occasional whinny could be heard from the stables as well as voices from the guards walking patrols along the high walls that protected Sanctuary. A low, rhythmic snoring was audible from across the hall in Vaste's room. It was not so loud it disturbed him on a normal night. *But this is not a normal night,* Cyrus thought.

Surrendering thoughts of sleep, he wandered to the window. The sill was stone, square, and high enough for him to rest his elbows as he leaned forward and out. He looked to his left and saw, two windows down, that Vara's was open. *She's been through hell since Termina. Her city lost, her mother dead, then her father. Still, after years of dancing around it, I kissed her and she kissed me back. I feel selfish thinking it, but I hope she gets through this rough patch soon.* A welling of guilt came up from deep inside him. *I just wish she'd let me help her in some way.*

A sob echoed through the night air, jarring him out of his thoughts. It was followed by another. He snatched a cloth shirt and pants and struggled to get them on, then walked down the hallway, his bare feet padding along on the cool stone. "At ease," he said to the six guards stationed in the hallway. Quietly, he knocked on Vara's door.

"Who is it?" came the muffled voice from the other side.

"Cyrus. I heard you through the open window. Can I come in?"

After a moment, a small reply made its way to him. "Yes."

He opened the door, and she sat on the bed in full armor. The only visible light was from the moon outside. Her back was facing him, her head angled toward the window, but bowed instead of looking out. He shut the door behind him.

The silence filled the space between them, with only the ambient sounds to disturb the peace. She sniffed, enough to catch his attention, but still she did not turn. "Why did you come here?" she asked him at last.

"Why did you let me in?" He said it as gently as he could manage.

"If I hadn't you'd likely take the same approach as putting a castle under siege; stand outside the door and hammer it, break it down and storm inside." She sniffed again and turned to him. Her face was dry, though her eyes were red and swollen, the traces of tears still visible even in the moonlight.

He breathed in, then out. "You're right. I likely would."

"Yes. Since there's nothing you can do to help me chase away these annoying emotions I'm grappling with, you might as well just leave me be."

"I see," he whispered. "When we were in Termina, I tried to show you how I felt about you, and regardless of whether you feel the same or not, what I was trying tell you was that—whatever you're going through, you don't have to be alone unless you choose to be."

She laughed, a short, sharp, bitter sound. "But I am alone. My mother and father are now dead. The bedrocks of my life, perfectly fine only a week ago, when I was taking them for granted, are now gone, permanently. The home where I was raised, the place of all my childhood memories, is destroyed. Perhaps the Elves will reclaim Termina, perhaps not, but either way, it's shattered. My sister remains at a distance—you are closer to her than I am—and I feel responsible for the deaths of at least two people in my guild."

She laughed again, and it was a hollow and frightening sound. "I didn't even know one of their names, and the other I've been less than kind to for years." She turned, pulling one of her legs onto the bed, and a tearing noise resulted as the cloth sheet caught in the joint of her knee armor. She looked at it dully for a moment and then grabbed at it with both hands, standing up and pulling the sheets from the bed, heaving them across the room toward the privy, where they came to rest in a tumble. "I didn't even know the name of that warrior, or ranger, or whoever it was, who died at the hands of an assassin, right out in that hallway! And it was my fault!"

Her words came out as a shout, and she lanced out with a foot, kicking her bed, which buckled under the force of her attack. The mattress flew into the wall and he heard shards of wood from the frame hit the stone. The door behind him opened and the guards rushed in, weapons drawn. "It's all right," he said them.

He turned back to Vara, who was attacking the headboard with her fists, punching holes in the wood with each strike, over and over until it snapped in half. She threw both pieces across the room, where one of them splintered and the other broke a bookshelf, sending a shower of books to the floor. "Leave us," he told the guards.

He could read the eyes of the guards, both humans, both skeptical, but they closed the door and he could hear their voices in the hall along with the officers of Sanctuary who had been awakened by the din.

Vara slid to her knees, her breathing heavy, face racked with emotion, but still she retained her composure, and he watched her. He knelt at her side and without conscious thought his arms slipped around her. "I'm sorry," he whispered. "I'm sorry about...everything. I'm here if you need me." He reached around and touched her face, his skin against her cheek and felt wetness there. He leaned in and kissed her, felt the pressure of her lips against his, felt her return it for a moment, and then he saw her eyes open and she pulled from his grasp, standing up and walking toward the window.

"I'm sorry," she said, leaning on the sill, refusing to look at him. "I can't. Not right now. Please...leave. We can talk about this afterward. I just...I'm sorry." She turned and he caught a glimpse of the anguish behind her eyes. "I'm truly sorry."

"It's all right," he whispered, climbing to his feet. "It can wait. If there's anything I can do —"

"There isn't. Please. I just need to be alone."

He nodded and left, shutting the door behind him. He passed Curatio, Terian, Longwell and Vaste in the hall, ignored their questioning looks and said, "She's fine. Just...going through all the turmoil you'd expect her to be going through."

He shut the door to his quarters and leaned against the wall. *I hope I didn't make it worse. I hope she...at least asks for help soon. I...* He clutched at his hands, entwining them to keep from shaking. *I need her. I don't know when that happened, but I do.* He returned to the window and looked to his left, but hers was shut, and the quiet was overwhelming, as if everything that had been making noise just a few minutes earlier had died. He lay down upon the bed, certain he wouldn't be able to sleep, but only a few minutes later, he slipped into unconsciousness.

Chapter 47

Cyrus's sleep was restless and dream-filled. Shadowy figures with glowing red eyes harangued him, demanding the answers to question after question. When he finally awoke, he considered it something of a blessing that he had been able to sleep at all given how troubled his mind had been.

The journey to the portal to the Realm of Death took all day to reach. It involved a long hike overland out of Sanctuary's gates. While Cyrus and many of the others rode horses, there were not nearly enough for the entire army, as there had been when last he had been there. They reached the edge of the Bay of Lost Souls at sundown, where a group of wizards led by Nyad had been hard at work conjuring boats out of the sand.

By the time they reached the edge of the sea, the army was tired, and they built fires and supped on stew that Larana fixed out of stores she had brought on a wagon train. They bedded down by the water, and Cyrus fell asleep listening to the roar of the bay after a short meeting with the Council to discuss strategy.

The dawn broke over the eastern horizon and lit up the water with a thousand sparkles of light. The conjured ships were ready to carry them across the choppy seas, and after a breakfast of cold beef and hard bread they set out. The skies were blue, but the rocking of the boat made Cyrus feel ill, and he was thankful when the Island of Mortus appeared.

After they landed and offloaded their personnel (the horses and wagons had been returned to Sanctuary by the least experienced wizard and a handful of helpers), Cyrus found himself staring into the portal. It was like any of the countless others he had seen but for one critical difference: whereas the ones in Reikonos had a center that was empty save for when someone teleported into it, this one crackled with dark energy, a blackness that seemed to suck all the light toward it. He shuddered and remembered that the portal to the Realm of Darkness carried a similar, ominous feel.

The army assembled in marching order behind him as Cyrus stared into the darkness. *Will this work? Will we accomplish anything here or just kill another god's army and take his pointless treasures?* His eyes found Vara, still distracted, staring into the distance, beyond the horizon and the sea. *Will she ever have room for happiness in her heart again? Or will it remain as black and gloomy as...*His eyes flitted back to the portal and watched as it leached the light from the air around it.

"General," came Thad's quiet baritone. He turned to see the warrior in red, who tossed him a quick salute. "Your army stands ready."

Cyrus looked over the host gathered before him, filling the island to the edge of the sea in a formation best suited to squeezing through the portal a rank at a time. He raised his voice, ready to give the last commands before they moved forward. "The last time we were here, there was no battle to be had on the other side of this." He pointed to the portal. "We marched to Eusian Tower in order to find and defeat Mortus's minions. I'm told that today, things will be different, that we'll be opposed from the moment we enter Death's Realm. And that's fine.

"The last time I was here," he said, his words cold but clear, as though remembering an unpleasant memory, "it was for the purpose of depriving the God of Death of his treasures, to raise our fortunes by lowering his. Hardly a noble purpose. Today we come for a different reason. Two of our own have been marked for death by Mortus, and countless others stand at risk of a curse he has placed on them." Cyrus kept his words vague, trying to keep the secret of the elves. "We come here today not to enrich ourselves, though surely that will happen as we storm Mortus's Realm. We come here to try and find a way to protect those whom we hold dear, to save others who have been marked without knowledge, without reason — without sin."

He squeezed his fist tighter in his gauntlet. "There is no more noble goal than fighting for others. Remember that, as the servants of Mortus come at you. Their visages are horrifying, their strength is great, their numbers are countless, but we are not here for ourselves. You do not wield sword, or cast spell, or sling arrows for yourself alone. We fight for others, for life, for our comrades. Remember that, when things grow grim. Remember that, when you become weary. No god can make you stand in a place of harm if you choose not to; but the bonds of fellowship have kept many a fighter from running when his heart was filled with fear.

"For the last months, our comrades have been under attack from the servants of Mortus. Wounded. Chased." He hesitated, overcome by memory and emotion. "Some have even died. All in his name. We can't strike at a god, but today we can make the servants of Mortus feel fear. Feel death. We fight for others. And we won't be afraid."

He drew his sword, raised it above his head, and howled a cry of battle. It was answered by thousands of voices, and weapons were upthrust with his. Cyrus turned, pointed to the portal, and charged through it, the feet of his army thundering behind him.

Chapter 48

When he appeared on the other side of the portal, the red sky drew his attention first, followed by the endless fields of faded grass that stretched off into the distance. The faint smell of decay was present under the scent of the earth wafting up from the fields. He could hear the wind rustling through the grass, watched it sway almost hypnotically, and felt the weight of his armor as the breeze slipped through all the nooks and crannies in the plate.

The first howl started like a gust of wind, but persisted even as the breeze died. It was loud, high-pitched, and followed by a rattling noise that sounded like teeth clacking together. A skeleton sprang from the grass, its bones held together by nothing more than magical power. A light was awake in its eyes, and it sprang for him, teeth wide and a rusted sword in its grasp.

The skeleton hacked at Cyrus, forcing him back more out of surprise than from the strength of its attack, which was formidable considering it had no musculature. Five more skeletons sprung out of the grass behind it, and another eight behind them, popping up in rows, an army springing from the ground. They clutched swords and maces, flails and hammers.

After dodging the first blow, Cyrus attacked, hacking the skeleton in half with a swipe that avoided the ribcage and severed the spinal column. He started to fend off the next attacker when he felt a shooting pain in his foot; looking down, he saw the skeleton he'd cut in half had used its upper body to crawl to his leg and ram a sword into the gap in his boot armor.

Cyrus swept his sword around, severing the head of the skeleton, and brought Praelior up to block the attack of the next three skeletons that fell upon him. More were rising in the distance and he heard the strains of combat beginning in earnest behind him as the Army of Sanctuary continued to flood into the the Realm.

Hobbling, Cyrus stepped forward, sword swinging, bones flying as he tried to make every attack count. He felt the bite and sting of a hundred swords, finding the gaps between the plate at his sides, poking holes in the chain mail. *At some point maybe I should get something like what Orion used to wear,* he thought as another prodded into his flesh above his left hip. *On second thought, I don't recall it doing him all that much good last time we met.*

There was a roar behind him and Fortin broke forward, wading into the bony defenders of Death's Realm. His arms flew one after another and a rain of bones filled the air. Arrows whizzed by Cyrus's ears, knocking skulls from necks, driving the light out of the eyes of the undead. A healing wind ran over him, chasing away the thousand stings and leaving only mild pangs in their place as he bolted ahead. Fortin had a half-dozen skeletons hanging from him as he turned, and a hand came around, swatting at them like so many flies, breaking them to pieces.

A shriek in the distance caught Cyrus's attention, and he smashed two more skeletons as he saw the next threat; wendigos, their gray flesh visible through the army of bone. He could smell them approaching, the same stink of rotting flesh that he'd caught from Hrent in the bar, and he remembered the teeth that could rip out a throat with little effort.

They hit his vanguard with a fury, pushing the Sanctuary force back into their fellows still coming out of the portal. Wendigos leapt into their midst and screams filled the air, from friend or foe he could not tell. Three skeletons and two wendigos made their attack on him. He hit two of the skeletons so hard that their bones were smashed to powder and the wendigo that caught the sword blade was hacked almost in half. It staggered and made to attack him again, but fell, bloodless, to the ground, where it struggled to return to its feet.

The fiends fought with more strength than their small bodies showed. Cyrus spun out of the way of a wendigo's claws and struck two skeletons, knocking the head off one with a solid punch and caving in the skull of the other with the pommel of his sword. He saw another wendigo driving an unnamed warrior to the ground, teeth sunk into the man's neck, blood squirting as the undead creature pressed his attack with feral savagery. A lance speared through the middle of the beast, allowing the Sanctuary warrior to drop to the ground, clutching his neck. Longwell appeared wielding the weapon and threw the wendigo through the air to the far side of the battle as though he were tossing a piece of fruit from his blade.

A fire sprung up before him, washing in a wave over the undead; large enough to surprise him, but not nearly as big as the inferno Chirenya had summoned in Termina. It rolled forward, pushing a ten-foot gap in the middle of the battle, giving Cyrus room to maneuver forward and allowing the other Sanctuary fighters space to wield their weapons. Cyrus pressed ahead, following the flames until they dissipated a few hundred feet away. He struck at the wendigos that flooded from behind it when it vanished, bringing Praelior to bear as quickly as he could wield it, cutting and ripping through his foes.

He felt Terian bump into him a few times and even looked back once, exchanging a nod and a smile with the dark knight in the heat of the battle. Longwell was nearby, the area around him cleared by his massive lance, and Vara carved a path of her own, along with Alaric, whose magical blasts sounded occasionally and were followed by a rain of bones as the force of his spell punched through the skeleton army, destroying all in its path.

He caught sight of a few others as the chaos prevailed; Scuddar In'shara of the desert, his blade sweeping wendigos before him like a reaper cutting through stalks of grain; Menlos Irontooth the northman felling skeletons by the dozen as his wolves swept through their ranks, depriving them of legs and arms and spines, crushing them in their jaws and howling as they brought them down. Odellan attacked with particular fury, battering skeletons to pieces with sword and shield, alternating between slashing with his blade and bashing with a large shield that bore the heraldry of the Termina Guard.

When Cyrus had thought the battle nearly over, a horn sounded at the far edge of the fight and he remembered the last of Death's defenders. The demon knights stood nine feet tall, with muscles bulging in grotesque ways. Cyrus had never seen anything akin to them, even in the Society of Arms, where warriors turned pride in their muscles into a fierce competition. Their skin was tinged red, stretched over faces that were more teeth than anything, and their ears stood straight up, pointed in the air. Each of them carried a weapon of their own and rather than the rusty blades and cudgels of the skeletons, they were steel or better, shined to rival Vara's armor, wielded by an enemy who was familiar with them.

The howls of the demon knights broke over Cyrus and his front rank as they faced the last wave of skeletons. Others had broken through their line into the Sanctuary army and a melee was being fought as the last of the bony undead were falling upon them. Wendigos were still in ample supply, leaping back and forth from target to target, striking with quickness and disappearing to find their next victim.

Cyrus was bleeding from a dozen wounds, and a wedge of skeletons had cropped up between their lines. No healer was near him, as no spells were forthcoming. He fought off the next attack by a slew of skeletons, hacked the head off three wendigos, and then the demon knights were upon him. As they strode into the fray, they swept aside their allies that got in the way; Cyrus watched one swing a sword to clear its path, cleaving a wendigo in half and sending it through the air.

He dodged the first strike of the demon knight and brought Praelior down upon its leg, hacking into the muscle and bouncing off the bone. He spun and withdrew his weapon, watching as the demon knight fell to a knee, where it was impaled through the face by Longwell. *I hate to assume this is going to be easy,* he thought, allowing himself a smile, *but* —

The blow from the next demon knight was not telegraphed, and he didn't see it as he spun to face the creature, but somehow when he had completed his turn, there it was upon him, too close, and the cudgel landed under his side. His armor slammed into his ribs and he felt bones break along his flank as his side seemed to catch fire. The demon knight followed up as Cyrus dropped to a knee, causing the warrior to catch a punch that broke his nose and clouded his vision.

He saw the creature reach back and swing the cudgel again. It hit him flush on the chest and the agony in his side spread, becoming a screaming pain in his sternum. It took all that was in him not to fall to the ground; instead he remained on one knee with his sword in hand.

Another punch found him, sending his helm spiraling away, and Cyrus saw a flash as the red sky turned bloody, a crimson he had seen times beyond number on the battlefield. The stalks of wheat swayed above him and the demon knight filled his vision. There were other faces, too, demonic visages, not like the skeletons he had faced before, but distorted — shades of living bodies, mouths wide and features misshapen, screaming in torment. He could hear them, their cries of agony, and they were everywhere; laying on the ground, suspended in the air, the shouting, screaming creatures of damnation.

The sky snapped into focus and the red faded, along with the shades, and it took a moment for him to realize he had been healed. He rolled, avoiding the cudgel that was coming down at him, and it struck a glancing blow on his shoulder that made it go numb to the elbow. He pulled up, sword in hand, and surged to his feet as the cudgel came down for another stroke. He fended it off by striking it at an angle with Praelior, causing the demon knight to smash a cluster of skeletons.

The demon knights were among them now; most were fighting off two or three Sanctuary combatants. *Lucky me. I get you all to myself,* he thought as he watched Menlos and Scuddar taking turns distracting and then attacking theirs. Vara and Alaric outmatched another, driving it to its knees and pounding it with successive spells that battered it from two directions. Longwell had speared one with his lance and was spinning it in circles while Aisling attacked it from behind. She would sting it, burying her daggers and then darting away while Longwell pushed his lance into the wound and withdrew it, causing a spatter of blood.

Team tactics. Glad I taught them not to fight fair. But I got left without a partner. He gripped Praelior and glared at the cudgel-wielding demon knight. "You snuck up on me when I wasn't looking." The beast swung the cudgel overhand and Cyrus dodged, avoiding the blow. The cudgel hit the ground with a teeth-rattling impact, and Cyrus swung his sword at the beast's arm as the knight began to retract its weapon for another attack. Cy misjudged his aim and only grazed the forearm of the knight, opening a gash a few inches deep. Black blood pooled in the wound and began to drip onto the ground.

"Bet that hurt," Cyrus taunted as the cudgel came at him again and he whirled out of the way, this time striking at the fingers of the demon knight when its arm was fully extended. Cyrus felt the blade hit and watched three of the demon knights digit's spin off to the ground. The next swing of the cudgel was wild to one side and Cyrus managed an attack that severed the demon knight's unwounded appendage, sending it spinning to the ground as the creature let out a howl and began to attack with his stump, battering Cyrus to the side.

Didn't see that coming, Cyrus thought, shaking off the motes of light from the hit. The demon knight's forearm had whacked him across the skull, and without his helm, he felt it. The demon stormed up to him and raised a fist with two fingers, bringing it down with alarming speed. Cyrus held up his sword and heard the impact as well as felt it. The screech of pain from the demon knight was near-unbearable, and the black blood splattered all over his armor, covering his face.

The demon knight struggled, clutching at its stumps. While it was distracted, Cyrus darted in, blade flashing, and struck it in the gut, dragging the weapon across. A spurt of blood and the beast fell to its knees, gurgling. The wicked teeth were still visible, frightening and a threat when Cyrus stepped in behind the creature. "I guess you weren't here last time I visited. I cut off the head of one of your brethren, stabbed another through the heart and rolled a dragon skeleton downhill into a whole passel of your kind."

He raised Praelior and brought it down, severing the head of the demon knight before it could utter a response. "I find the old ways are best, wouldn't you agree?" He spat, removing a thick coating of blood that filled his mouth. "Of course you would. You're dead. The dead don't argue."

"Malpravus might disagree with you." Vaste's voice came from behind him, and Cyrus turned, having forgotten the battle. A few skeletons still moved on the ground and one demon knight was being toyed with by Fortin, but otherwise the fight was over. Members of the Sanctuary army loitered around the field, corpses of wendigos and demon knights scattered on the trampled ground along with an assortment of unattached bones.

"Thanks for the heal," Cyrus said, surveying the scene before him. "Looks like we won."

"Was there ever any doubt?" The troll's smile carried a hint of mischief. "Still, I won't be comfortable until we've left this forsaken place behind, hopefully with a cure in hand. Or something that can lead to a cure. Or possibly just some pie."

Fortin picked up the last demon knight and brought him down over his knee, filling the air with a cracking noise. The rock giant roared and pulled the head from the creature's body, holding it aloft amidst ragged cheers from some of the Sanctuary combatants. "I suppose that's a sign that the battle is over," Cyrus said.

"And a sign that the party has begun," Vaste said.

"We can move when you're ready." Curatio wandered up to them, making his way over the debris that littered the battlefield. "Few deaths, few injuries, and a large and motivated army make for an easy conquest of this realm."

"The God of Death should put more effort into his personal guard." Cyrus shook his head. "We'll head for the Eusian Tower in five."

They assembled in formation, with the weakest and those newly resurrected pushed to the back of the army. In the far distance stood the Eusian tower, a structure larger than any Cyrus had seen, a staggering black spike that stretched into the sky. "I've only been in the first level," he said, staring up at the heights. "What do you suppose is at the top?"

"Damned, more damned, and still more damned," Vaste replied. "It's their stock-in-trade here in the Realm of Death. Remember the boiling oil? Remember the cavern of ice?"

Cyrus shuddered. "Couldn't forget those. Glad we don't have to jump through those hoops this time."

"Yes, hopefully someone's left the master's chambers open for us to plunder."

They trudged on and every once in a while Cyrus would step to the side of the column, looking for the back of his army as it snaked off into the distance. The Eusian tower grew closer and closer, stretching beyond where the clouds would have been—if the Realm of Death had any.

"The Fields of Paxis go on forever," Cyrus said under his breath.

"Not forever," Curatio said, "but near enough that you can see forever from them."

Cyrus smiled. "I suppose the few more minutes it will take us to get there must seem like such small and inconsequential things to someone who's lived as long as you."

Curatio waited before answering, seeming to take in the red skies and peaceful grasses that blew around them. "Aye, small things perhaps, but the stuff life is made of. If you seek to have the minutes pass faster, then what you seek is death, unintending as you may be. Minutes are all we have."

They were at the tower moments later, climbing the great steps to file through the enormous doors. They crossed a bridge onto the grand, circular platform at the heart of the tower that branched off in four directions. On the wall opposite where they entered, two gargantuan doors stood open, large enough for five dragons to climb on each others' shoulders and enter.

"Based on the scale of the chambers of the gods I've seen," Vaste said, "I can't imagine fighting something of the size they must be."

"I've always told you size matters," Erith said from behind, drawing a dirty look from the troll.

Cyrus looked back; his army stretched across the bridge and out the doors. "There's no way a wizard will be able to cast an area teleport with us strung out like this."

"Kinda reminds me of Enterra," Erith muttered.

"That's the problem with having an army so large, it's like a snake, how it stretches," Terian said, looking up into the darkness above them. "Where are we going?"

"This way." Cyrus led them through the doors. The tower was silent save for the noises of the Sanctuary force marching through. The smells of cold air and hot oil had mixed to form something unsavory that settled in Cyrus's nostrils when he was on the platform and failed to leave as he entered Mortus's chambers.

The doors gave way to a balcony that overlooked a treasure room. Staircases curved down either side and there were pedestals lining the walls as well as shelves crammed with items that stretched to the far end of the room. Underneath a banner that held a picture of a hand reaching down to pluck a human being was a portal that crackled with light energy, as though it were the opposite of the one that had brought them into the Realm.

"Where d'you reckon that goes?" Erith asked the question Cyrus had already been wondering.

"Nowhere we'll be exploring today," Alaric said, surprising Cyrus by appearing at the front of the army. He hadn't seen the Ghost since the column had begun its march. "Shall we officers begin our exploration?"

"Company halt," Cyrus called out. "Officers, let's take a look around. Everyone else, hold position here."

Cyrus descended to the floor, Alaric, Curatio and Vara immediately behind him with the other officers trailing.

"What went there?" Longwell pointed, indicating a large pedestal in the middle of the room, empty of whatever it once held.

"I'm going to guess Letum, the Staff of Death," Cyrus said, moving past it without looking back.

"You sure?" Longwell peered at the empty space.

"Pretty sure."

Cyrus passed minerals, vases and other assorted treasures, pointing them out. Vaste followed behind, scooping up the less fragile items and stowing them in a burlap sack. When the troll picked up a glowing orb, he squinted at it. "Is this...?"

Alaric gazed at it. "It keeps anyone from teleporting out of the realm while Mortus is not here—preventing anyone from leaving save through one of the portals."

"Let's smash it," Terian said. "I don't like feeling trapped."

"Here," Curatio held his hand out, and Vaste gave it to him. Without words, Curatio cast a spell and the light left the orb. "Now it's intact, and we can sell or keep it as we choose."

"Breaking it would be more fun," the dark knight said.

The treasures were minor in many cases; most not worth taking, pieces of old weapons or other junk. They passed several bookshelves filled with old volumes. "You think a cure is in here?" Cyrus pulled one of the tomes, its pages cracked with age and wear, the writing all in runes that although familiar were unreadable to him. "I don't even know what this says."

"It's called literacy," Erith said with a snicker. "It involves reading books, not eating them."

"Fine." He walked over to her and held the page in front of her face. "Use your amazing gift of literacy and read this to me."

She squinted at the page. "It says...uh...um..." She looked at him and blinked. "It says you're stupid."

"Really? I thought it said you're incredibly mature. By which I mean old."

"It's written in the language of the ancients," Curatio said, looking over Cyrus's shoulder. "There are few who can read it."

"Can you?" Cyrus looked back at Curatio, questioning.

The elf smiled. "Of course. I am rather ancient, after all."

"Why haven't I ever heard of these ancients?" Erith pulled a book off the shelf then discarded it after one look.

"Because you're uneducated," Cyrus replied. "Listen to lessons, don't run your mouth through them."

"You're about to learn a lesson—"

"The ancients were wiped out during the War of the Gods," Curatio said, taking the book from Cyrus. "They left behind quite a few remnants of their civilization—for those who bother to look."

"The portals," Cyrus said with a sudden realization.

"Very good." Curatio's finger ran up and down the page of the book and he smiled. "And the Citadel and Colosseum in Reikonos. Some other scattered artifacts, great and small, exist."

"How were they wiped out?" Vaste asked the question, the troll standing at a distance, leaning against a shelf.

"It all comes back to the War of the Gods," Curatio said, still splitting his attention between the book and the words he spoke. "When the gods were challenged over meddling in mortal affairs, they lashed out, striking down those who offended them greatest. After the upheaval in the pantheon that came from some of their own — Bellarum, in particular — instigating attacks against them, they needed an example of what happens when you challenge their might.

"So, they chose the largest, most prominent civilization, the greatest threat to their power, and destroyed them." He turned a page. "Very little was left standing when they were done."

"That's not how I've heard the story told," Nyad sniffed. "I always heard Bellarum, the God of War, in his wickedness, showed mortals how to breach the realms of the gods. He sent his armies to wreak havoc with them and when Eruditia, Goddess of Knowledge, was slain with Bellarum's Warblade, the other gods and goddesses banded together in outrage over the atrocity and destroyed his army, punishing him for a hundred years before allowing him to return to the Pantheon."

"Yes, well, I would certainly trust the word of your nannies over the testimony of someone who was actually present at the time," Vara said, voice laden with sarcasm.

"As always, there was more to the story than is widely known," Alaric spoke up. "History records considerable fighting on Arkaria at the time, between an alliance of dwarves, elves and gnomes standing against the titans, the trolls and goblins on the other side. The dragons had risen up from their isolation. The gods were picking sides and at the heart of it all was the ancients."

"Also," Curatio said, looking up from his book, "a guild called Requiem, composed of some of the first humans to arrive on these shores from across the Sea of Carmas, was in the middle of the fight."

Cyrus looked around, and his eyes rested on Longwell, who blushed. "That's the land I'm from, yeah."

"Oh?" Cyrus raised an eyebrow at the dragoon. "I...actually didn't look at you on purpose, but...interesting."

"So how did it all happen?" Erith looked at Curatio. "I mean, I'd always heard Nyad's version, more or less, and about the alliances fighting each other."

"A story for another time," Alaric interrupted, drawing an acidic look from Curatio as he closed the book the elf was holding.

"We are in the Realm of Death, after all, and our armies are waiting for us."

Cyrus had stopped at a pedestal that held a single piece of parchment, covered in runes. "What about this?"

"Because the perfect place to display the curse you're using to kill off an enemy race is in plain sight," Vaste said, deadpan.

"It is when there's a barrier put around it by the God of Death himself," Alaric said.

"So it's unbreachable?" J'anda walked to the edge of the pedestal. "Because you'd need one of the godly weapons to break down a barrier put in place by the gods, correct? Or be a god yourself, I suppose..." His fingers hovered over the outer edge of the barrier, a faint glow obvious only by close examination.

"Which means it's...out of reach," Cyrus said, numb, staring at the parchment.

"Not exactly," Alaric said, voice taut. "If you would all stand back?" Exchanging a curious look with J'anda, Cyrus moved away from the scroll, followed by the other officers. Alaric looked at the pedestal then drew his sword, *Aterum,* and a blast of force shot from the tip with a power greater than his usual spells.

The energy hit the barrier and coruscated, crackling against it, filling the air with blinding flashes as the barrier dissolved under the force of the Ghost's spell. The energy faded, leaving the piece of parchment in the center of the pedestal. Shocked silence prevailed among the Sanctuary officers as Alaric returned his sword to its sheath with precision.

"Wow," came Vaste's voice, laced with irony. "It would appear someone's got a godly weapon and didn't bother to tell the rest of us. I'm sure this will be a hotly debated topic in the lounge tonight, but probably not in the Council Chambers, at least not now. Maybe in—"

"—the fullness of time," Cyrus chorused along with a few of the other officers. If Alaric was amused, he gave no sign. Curatio appeared to be suppressing a chuckle.

"No, we can discuss it when we return to Sanctuary, if you wish," Alaric said, somewhat prim. "But I cannot guarantee I will answer all your questions."

Vaste shrugged. "Well, it's progress."

Curatio approached the pedestal and picked up the parchment, holding it in front of his eyes, reading it. He murmured under his breath in intense concentration.

"So?" Erith looked at him. "Is it...?" Her voice trailed off.

Curatio did not answer at first, still staring at the page. "It is," he said. "The curse comes from a branch of dark magic long forgotten."

"What kind of spell caster would have used it?" Erith said with mild curiosity.

Curatio looked to Alaric, then back to Erith. "I...I'm not sure. It...it needs more study."

"Anything else worth taking as long as we're here?" Vaste pointed to the bag he carried. "I have room for more plunder."

They scoured the room, taking a few more choice objects before returning to the staircase and the guild members waiting. Cyrus looked over the heads of his army and saw that the formation stretched beyond the bridge and platform and out of the tower. "As spread out as we are, a wizard spell will not get all of us home in one casting," he said to the officers waiting. "We need to evacuate in phases."

"At least we did away with the barrier to teleportation," Terian said. "Otherwise we'd be heading back to the portal we came in by, right?"

"We didn't clear the dungeons underneath us," Cyrus said. "There could be enemies waiting in ambush."

"Still thinking of Termina?" Longwell's voice was quiet, so low that Cyrus knew it was meant for his ears only. Still, Vara turned her head and caught his eye before flicking her gaze away.

"I need the strongest fighters to stay until everyone else is out," Cyrus announced. "If you came with us to the Hand of Fear raid, I want you to remain behind until I give you the order to accept teleport. We'll start here and begin walking our way up the line, teleporting out as much of the army per time as we can." He looked to Nyad. "Care to begin?"

The elf nodded, and her hands lit up with spell energy. A blue orb appeared in front of Cyrus, the surface flaring with the magics contained within. Flashes lit the walls around him as he watched about three hundred people disappear into the teleportation spell, leaving behind forty or so.

"Move up," he ordered, striding back across the bridge, where the platform was filled. Fortin rose above the rest, and when Cyrus saw the rock giant, he called out to him. "We're doing an area teleportation spell to send the army back to Sanctuary, Fortin. I need you to stay behind and help cover the retreat in case any of

Mortus's creations are lurking."

"Sounds like good clean fun," the rock giant replied. "Unless of course they are lurking, in which case it'll be good messy fun." Fortin laughed, a deep rumbling sound that reminded Cyrus of the noise he heard while visiting a quarry. The rock giant stopped and peered at Cyrus. "Messy...because of the blood of our enemies covering our hands, you know?"

"I caught that, yes."

The next teleportation spell cleared the platform and bridges of the Eusian tower, sending another five hundred or so members of the Sanctuary army back home. Cyrus followed the bridge to the exit, stepping out under the red sky to see the remainder of his force crowding the stairs. Another few hundred more were sent on, followed by another wave as the path widened into the Fields of Paxis. Less than three hundred remained, Cyrus estimated as the wind rushed past, stirring the tall grass.

"This is it," Cyrus said. "Veterans, hold off until the last of our people are away." A teleportation orb from the last spell cast still lingered in front of him, hovering like a glass ball filled with light, waiting for him to seize it. "I don't think there's anything that's going to try and attack us now, but there's no use tempting fate."

Nyad raised her hands to cast the final teleport spell, and Cyrus looked away. The winds were stirring the grass again and he remembered the horrific things he had seen when the demon knight nearly killed him. *What the hell were those?* he wondered. A murmur ran through the army behind him and he snapped to attention as the lights of the teleportation orbs guttered out, like a fire being snuffed.

He turned to Nyad, his heart racing. She stood before him, a perplexed look on her face. "Let me try again," she said. Her hands moved, the light filled them and she released it, but no orbs appeared. "I...don't know what's happening! I can't seem to summon—"

"I know what this is," Alaric said, voice filled with menace.

An icy hand grabbed Cyrus by the heart. "No. You don't mean..."

The breeze turned into a howling wind and the air crackled with power. Red forks of lightning sprang from the space behind them on the tower steps, lancing out, a maelstrom of pure magical fury splitting open the sky. From it emerged a behemoth; a creature with four legs anchored on a rounded pelvis, a thorax that sprouted eight arms, each twitching. The head appeared from the rift last of all, and it bore the beak of a bird, but was open so that jagged teeth were visible even in the flickering light cast by the portal it had opened.

It descended as though it were being lowered on a wire, gently, from the rift, which began to seal shut behind it. Within seconds, the tongues of red lightning had receded, revealing the sky above, now an even darker maroon than before. The maelstrom had been replaced by an eerie, still calm that settled over the entirety of the Realm, and a silence hung heavy over the last remnants of the Sanctuary army, punctuated by the realization that their escape, which seemed inevitable only a moment before, was now impossible.

Mortus — the God of Death — had returned home.

Chapter 49

"If Bellarum thinks he can talk to me that way he is mistaken, I am the God of Death..." Mortus spoke, a loud, grinding sound that sent waves of horror through Cyrus. The God of Death's face was angled away and he seemed not to have noticed the Sanctuary army at his back. *If he just goes back into his tower, we can run for the portal...*

A scream tore from the throat of one of the newer recruits and Mortus swung around to see them standing at his feet, an army of ants when compared to him. Cyrus knew that he barely reached halfway to the God of Death's knee, so large was the deity. *He's going to kill us. He'll splatter us all over his realm and there's nothing I can do...*

"Interlopers! Intruders!" Mortus shouted in a deafening cacophony. "To me, defenders of death! To your master!" Cyrus pushed his way forward, trying to interpose himself between the God of Death and the Sanctuary remnants. "My servants, I summon you! Heed my call and destroy these thieves, these—" Mortus looked left and right, as though waiting for something. "You...have killed my servants." *Need to attack him now, give the others time to flee...*

"We have," came a voice from Cyrus's side. A hand came to rest on Cy's gauntlet, already on the sword. "Strike at him and we all die," the Ghost hissed. "Wait." Alaric raised his voice and spoke to the God of Death in even tones. "But they are such a little thing for one so great as you to resurrect."

"Alaric Garaunt..." The God of Death's voice carried a rasp and rattle that shook the Fields of Paxis. "The Army of Sanctuary."

"None other," Alaric said with a short bow. "Plainly, you have caught us in the act of doing something we should not be doing. I call upon you, the mighty Master of the Hereafter, to forgive us, and realize that while you may allow us to walk away today, all of us will be subject to your domain—death—eventually."

"Sanctuary..." Mortus rumbled once more, and the birdlike head looked over them, eyes searching. "The shelas'akur..." He fixated on Vara, then his head swiveled to Curatio. "And the last of the old ones. With the two of you in my realm, I hold the final demise of the Elvendom in my hands."

"Yet you have already masterfully set the fall in motion," Alaric said, soothing. "No one can undo what you have done. Why hasten a painful demise? You could show mercy, knowing that none will escape you in the end. Let us go. Show Arkaria and the other gods that you do not fear mortals. Allow us to leave your Realm in peace."

A low, hacking laugh came from the God of Death. "As a god, what need have I to fear mortals?"

"You need not," Alaric said. "Yet with our deaths you buy nothing you will not eventually have anyway. But with mercy, you might convince others of your righteousness."

"My righteousness..." Mortus's arms hovered around him as he peered down at Alaric. "You are still deft, Alaric Garaunt. You barter for the lives of your people with all your cunning." He stared down at the Ghost. "Your bargain is accepted...if..."

Cyrus felt a scant thrill of hope. *My gods, Alaric talked him out of it. He's going to let us...*

"...you leave behind either the old one or the young one."

Alaric was still as statuary. "I take your meaning as...Vara or Curatio?"

"Call them what you will." The beak clicked. "I will let the rest of your number leave if one of them remains as a sacrifice."

Alaric did not move, did not speak, as though paralyzed. Cyrus had never seen the Ghost halted into inaction.

Curatio stepped forward, his head held high. "I have had a long and storied life. I will remain behind."

"No!" Vara shoved Longwell aside, stepping to the front of the line. "You can give our people hope with what you know," she whispered, at Curatio's side. "You're the only one who can read...it." She looked up to Mortus, towering above. "I will remain with you, God of Death, as your sacrifice."

Cyrus saw Curatio thrust the parchment into her hand as he pulled her close to him, but she refused it. "You are young, and have much to live for."

She shoved him away roughly, sending the healer back a few steps. "I do not. I am weary of this life, of living in a world that would take everything from you a piece at a time, until you have naught left." She looked back to Mortus. "If you would have me be your sacrifice, strike swift and true. End it—and be quick about it."

"Done." The ragged voice of the God of Death crackled over

the assemblage and he raised a hand above his head. Cyrus could see it, aimed at Vara, far enough away from all the others that the blow would strike flush, and she would be ended. Her eyes were closed, her head was bowed. She was ready.

"NOOOO!" The voice was loud in his head, an agonized scream of such force that it even delayed the God of Death in his attack for a split second. Cyrus was already in motion by the time he realized that the voice was his, and Praelior was in his hand by instinct alone, raised above his head as he checked Vara with his elbow, sending her rolling away from where she had been standing. He held Praelior aloft as though it were a shield that could protect him from harm; the foolishness of the gesture dawned on him only at the last.

The fist of Mortus descended upon Cyrus, slow, as if he were moving in half-time. A scream filled reached his ears and pain wrenched through him. He felt himself come apart, and he knew it was done.

Chapter 50

The screaming reached Cyrus's ears first, followed by the realization that he was not dead. He blinked, his head heavy, his vision blurred. Without knowing, he pushed himself to his feet, felt the balance catch him enough to stand, and he looked down. His armor was covered in blood; his own. His nose was dripping, and the seams of his armor dribbled crimson onto the sands and grass that surrounded him.

"You're healed," came a voice from behind him. He whirled to see Curatio. "I healed you before his attack took you apart. Now go!"

Cyrus turned back, the scene returning to clarity in front of him. Mortus was screaming in agony. The hand he had attacked Cyrus with was gushing ichor, black fluid that sprayed from the stump as the God of Death swayed from side to side. "Interlopers! Thieves! Oathbreakers!"

Cyrus felt his head clear and thought suddenly that Mortus was...smaller, somehow...than he had been when he'd first appeared. "I made him bleed," he said in shock. The God of Death's head swiveled and focused on him, and three more arms rose to an apogy, ready to strike him down. "I made you bleed!" he called out to the face.

"Let us continue that trend," Alaric said, "lest we die." The Ghost leapt through the air, his sword drawn and raised above his head. The jump carried him high and he swung the sword as he began his descent. Alaric's aim was perfect—the blade cut through two of the raised arms of Mortus and sent them flopping to the ground as the God of Death screamed and raised his head into the air in agony.

He can be hurt. He's not invincible. Cyrus heard the words in his mind. *The God of Death is not invincible. Does that mean...?* He rushed to the front right leg of Mortus and brought his sword around. Another scream tore from the deity's mouth, and Cy retracted his blade to find a gash several inches deep in the calf. He pulled back and sliced again, opening the wound further, causing Mortus to stagger.

"Bring him down!" Terian's voice washed over Cyrus, and he saw the dark knight attacking the opposite front leg, his sword a frenzy of attacks, none of which seemed to be having near the effect of Cyrus's. Praelior struck again, carving deeper, to the bone, and causing the God of Death to stumble and fall to a knee.

Longwell jabbed his lance, burying it a couple of inches into the god's pelvis and wrenching another agonized cry from the beak. Vara was present in the fray, along with the others; Odellan hacked at the god's foot until Fortin pushed him out of the way and sunk his hands into the gash, ripping it wider. Alaric soared through the air in another jump and Cyrus watched two more arms flop to the ground.

Fire crackled and bolts of lightning hit Mortus, drawing more screams from him as Cyrus pressed the assault. Two arms were still flailing along with one stump, and the deity was trying to force himself back to his feet, but the Sanctuary force was swarming, striking, like ants attempting to devour wounded prey. Cyrus climbed to the last arm moving on the deity's left side and struck it, taking three hard attacks to hack it from the body.

The last arm swiped at Cyrus, forcing him to jump out of the way, and he swung, grazing it. A squeal came from Mortus, and Cyrus ran his blade along the abdomen as he dodged across and cut into the last arm, which seemed to move more like a tentacle with a hand at the end than a human appendage. It flopped to the ground and Cyrus turned, burying his blade in the God of Death's chest, wrenching another cry.

This time, there was no doubt; Mortus shrank before Cyrus's eyes. *He's getting smaller as the battle goes on*, Cyrus thought, plunging the blade through the deity's chest again and again. The beak swung down to bite him and he ran his sword across the side of the God of Death's face, drawing a shriek. The deity's whole body bucked and threw Cyrus off. He fell ten feet and landed on his back, looking up into the face of Larana, who was whispering under her breath, before he rolled back to his feet, sword in hand, ready to strike again.

Mortus was smaller yet, now just twice the size of Cyrus. His legs had collapsed under the attacks of the Sanctuary army, and his head was drooping. "I...am...the God of...DEATH!" An explosion of magical force sent all the combatants that had been crawling over him flying, and Cyrus skidded back a few feet on one knee, sword in hand. *I'll finish him*, Cyrus thought, dragging himself to his feet, intent on nothing else.

Without his arms, Mortus's upper body was oddly cylindrical, oozing ichor from the wounds he'd sustained. Three of his legs were removed, and the last was kicking, trying to right himself. His head and neck sagged under the weight of keeping his body upright without arms to balance, and every movement threatened to put him sideways on the ground. He now stood no taller than a man. His attempts at movement reminded Cyrus of an insect, plucked of all its legs, as the God of Death struggled toward the stairs, retreating from the Sanctuary forces.

A lone figure stepped in front of him, cutting off his escape. "I tried to get you to see reason," Alaric said. "I begged you not to doom us to this course of action. I gave you every opportunity to escape with your pride intact, with the illusion of infallibility that you and yours have worked so hard to create."

"You can leave," Mortus wheezed. "You can leave without sacrifice!" His leg thrust out, trying to gain traction on the steps and pull him past Alaric. "Let me be!"

"The God of Death is not forgiving," Alaric said. "Did you think I forgot?"

"Please...Alaric! Please!" Mortus halted in his attempts to escape, his beak flapping in desperation.

"I said the same to you not ten minutes ago. You were deaf to my request."

The God of Death coughed, and black ichor spilled down his long torso. His voice changed, from desperation to something else, and a loud, sucking noise came when he spoke. "You...know...what this...means..."

The Ghost reached under his helm and grasped it with one hand, removing it in one smooth motion, letting it drop to the ground. He looked down at the broken Mortus, his eye coldly impassive as he raised his sword, Aterum, above his head, grasping it with both hands. "I do." He brought the blade down in one swift motion, and the head of the deity rolled from the body, which toppled over.

A loud hissing filled the air, and Curatio cried out as if in pain. He clutched the parchment bearing the curse, the one they had liberated from Mortus's chambers. Fire raced across it like a flame consuming a bit of chaff, and it disappeared from his hand with nothing but a wisp of smoke left behind to show it had ever been there.

A low, deep rumble filled the air, and the sky turned black. Red lightning flashed and ran down the sides of the Eusian tower.

The smell of ozone descended as the air crackled and exploded around them. The figures he had seen before, the screeching phantoms with black eyes and mouths open in horror, were appearing in physical form, their lord and captor now dead. Their screeches resounded, horrifying, shrill, and they began to drift toward the Sanctuary raiders.

"NYAD!" Alaric's call echoed over the booming of the thunder as the Eusian Tower released another wave of souls. "TELEPORT!"

Cyrus did not see the wizard work her magic, nor hear her in the fury of the storm as the winds whipped around him, but he saw the flashes of blue as people started to disappear. He watched Nyad go, then Curatio, and Ryin Ayend, Erith and Vaste, and countless others. Larana was silent, her orb in front of her, her eyes hollow and watching Cyrus when he saw J'anda reach out for her, grasping her in his arms and vanishing in the magic of teleport.

The tormented souls were swirling in a vortex above them now, the tempest of control broken loose with the master of the realm dead. They swept closer, and Cyrus exchanged a look with Longwell and Odellan, who remained, and Alaric, as the last few of the raiders disappeared, leaving the four of them alone with one other.

Vara was on her knees, her sword at her side, eyes dull. He cried out to her, but couldn't hear the voice in his own head over the howling of the unnatural event taking place around them. She looked over her shoulder, meeting his gaze, and he felt a shudder through him.

She has no hope left.

The orb of teleportation glittered before her, waiting to be seized. She hung her head, a silent figure in the midst of the most destructive force Cyrus had ever seen. The tower was cracking; he could hear the structure buckling even over the wind, and it was a terrifying sound. The souls of Mortus's damned were edging closer.

He ran forward, crossing the ground to her, watching the phantoms eddying across the ground like a stream unblocked, rushing toward her with soulless eyes, gaping mouths open and screaming. He hit his knees, wrapped his arms around her, gripped her close and reached out for the orb.

He watched Longwell, Odellan and Alaric seize their orbs, felt

Vara fight back, trying to writhe out of his grasp as the magics consumed them, pulled them out of the Realm of Death, and carried them home.

Chapter 51

When the teleportation magic receded, Cyrus was left holding Vara in his arms. She was limp, motionless, but he felt her breath against his neck, and her hair was tangled across his face. He stood and lifted her to her feet. She did not fight him.

The foyer was loud with conversation; explanations flew from those who had remained for the battle with Mortus to those who had left. Exclamations, curses and disbelief all flowed freely in the hall. Cyrus walked Vara to the stairs, ignoring the inquiries that came his way, steering past Alaric, who stood stonefaced, watching everything that was transpiring, and past Longwell, who had sunk to the floor, shaking his head in disbelief.

He climbed the stairs and she leaned on him for every step. He opened the door to her quarters and helped her to the bed. He unstrapped her armor and set it to the side, and still she did not resist, did not fight back, did not say anything. As soon as her armor was off, she curled up on her bed, facing away from him. He started to leave, but she spoke.

"Will you...stay with me?"

He turned to find her looking at him, her eyes filled with fatigue and sadness, and something else, something undefined that recalled the day they first met. "Yes. I will."

He sat in the chair by her bed until she slipped off to sleep; it wasn't more than a few minutes and she was breathing softly, unconscious. He crept from the room, taking care when shutting the door and admonishing the guards who had taken up posts outside to not allow anyone to disturb her for any reason.

He went to the Council Chambers and found them already full, no conversation taking place within. It was a grim and quiet group of officers inside, and Alaric seemed to be the grimmest of all, staring down at the table, not acknowledging that anyone else was even present.

"So," Terian broke the silence as Cyrus took his seat, "I'm just gonna say it. We killed a god." He leaned back in his chair and frowned. "When you say it out loud, it sounds kind of bad."

"We killed a god," Vaste repeated. "Yeah, I think that's bad."

"We're heretics for certain," Ryin Ayend said.

"Doubtful." Curatio held his hands cupped in front of his

mouth. "No one gives a damn about the God of Death except some truly dark souls on the fringe of society. No one from the Leagues is going to care enough to declare us heretics; hell, most of them will congratulate us on a job well done."

"Won't..." Nyad twitched. "...won't the other gods be upset with us? You know, for being mortals who killed a god?"

"That is what the legends say." Erith cast an uneasy glance around the table.

"I'm starting to believe your legends after tonight," Longwell spoke up. "But should it really be that easy to kill a god? I mean, I had some trouble piercing him, but it seemed like Cyrus and Alaric were cutting through him like he was a fresh softbread."

"Yes," J'anda said, his eyes narrowed in suspicion, "if I didn't know better, I would swear both of you were wielding godly weapons."

Alaric looked up slowly. Then, without warning, his hand went to his hip and removed his belt, scabbard and all, and threw it on the table. "This is Aterum, the blade forged by Marei, the Goddess of Night, daughter of Yartraak, 10,000 years ago."

Terian looked down the table at Cyrus, who shrugged. "Mine's Praelior. Not sure what its story is."

"Oh, but you do," Alaric said, eyes filled with sudden intensity. "Praelior was assembled by you, it's true, but the quest was given to you by the God of War himself."

"I—" Cyrus started to protest, but stopped himself. "How did you know that?"

Alaric ignored his question. "Praelior was forged by Drettanden, the Demigod of Courage, who poured his very essence into the blade to give it the power it now holds. After his death, it was disassembled and scattered by the gods, so as not to be a threat to them in the future."

Vaste let out a low whistle. "Should have hid it better."

J'anda looked back at Alaric. "I have never heard of this Drettanden nor Marei."

Alaric sighed. "That is because they are both dead. The legend, which isn't widely circulated because of how weak it makes the gods look, holds that Drettanden was killed by the Guildmaster of Requiem—the same man that killed Eruditia with Ferocis—and beginning much of the destruction that took place during the War of the Gods. Marei was killed around the same time period, one of countless others." He looked around the table. "Their names are buried in obscure tomes; gods and goddesses who died in that war and whose names lay forgotten in the dust of time."

"Wait," Nyad said, a confused look on her face. "Is that why we don't know the names of the God of Good and God of Evil? Were they killed during the war as well?"

"Doubtful," Curatio answered. "Alaric and I have done considerable research—some of which is aided by my memories, some of it hampered," he said with a smile. "The good news is, I doubt we need to worry about any immediate reprisals from the gods. Mortals have killed gods before, and the division in the pantheon works to our advantage."

"But what about the legend?" Nyad pressed. "If the gods didn't unite in fury over Eruditia's death, what was it?"

"There's no evidence that they united against anyone but Bellarum." Alaric stood and walked to the balcony window.

"In other words," Terian said, "you don't think we have anything to worry about. Other than the threat of the dark elves sending an army our way, someone else declaring war on us, or the gods themselves coming down and smiting our little haven off the face of Arkaria."

A knock at the door sounded, startling them all. "I wonder which of those it is?" Vaste asked, sending a smile Terian's way.

Thad peeked his head through the door. "Sir Longwell, you have a messenger—a man named Teodir—here to see you."

Longwell blanched. "He's one of my father's men," the dragoon said in surprise. "But he'd have to have traveled months to get here."

Thad nodded. "He's waiting for you in the foyer."

Longwell looked to Alaric, the question in his eyes, but the Ghost did not turn from his place at the window, staring out across the plains. "We are adjourned," he said. "We will assemble again tomorrow at some point."

Cyrus waited as the others filed out. Curatio was the last, sending a final look at Alaric that was as mysterious as it was brief. When the door closed, he spoke. "How did you know that Bellarum guided me to my sword?"

"Not now," came the knight's quiet reply. His words came out even more weary than usual.

"But I—"

"I SAID NOT NOW!" Alaric's fury blazed, and Cyrus flinched back from the heat in his words. He hesitated, unused to fleeing from anything, but took slow steps to the door and shut it behind him, placing it between them like a shield, to protect him from the anger of the man who was the closest thing he could remember to having a father.

Chapter 52

Vara stirred when he shut the door, even though he closed it as quietly as he could. *Damned elven hearing.* She rolled over to look at him, and he could see by her eyes that she had been crying again. *In her sleep?* She sat up, the fire in the hearth still crackling, spitting its warmth across the room. "Hello," he said.

She nodded at him. "How fares the Council?"

"Awash, athwart and abuzz."

She scrunched up her face, perplexed. "What?"

"Never mind. They're confused. Alaric is as upset as I've ever seen him. He yelled at me when I asked him a question. I can't recall him doing anything like that before."

She pulled her knees close to her chest, wrapping her arms around them. "We did just kill a god. It's a rather heady feeling."

"Apparently I'm the only one excited about that," Cyrus said. "I mean, if you can kill one—"

"Don't. That road leads to madness; to a quest that has no good end and no real purpose."

"I suppose not." A moment passed, and he found the courage to speak the words on his mind. "In Death's Realm, you were ready to—"

"I was." She cut him off. "Perhaps I still am; I don't know my own heart at the moment. Things seem very dark indeed, as though all my hopes were drained along with my spirit."

"There's always hope."

She lowered her head. "No. There's nothing left now. My people are doomed. My parents are dead." Her hand reached up to her face, brushing a strand of hair away from her eyes. "My hope is gone."

"I know it seems that way right now," he said, a hand stroking her shoulder, feeling the cloth of her undershirt against his fingers, "but your life is long, and the black despair that covers you now will lift, given time and fortune. Trust me. I know."

"You didn't know your parents." Her words came out free of accusation, but they stung all the same.

"True," he recovered from the pain of her last statement. "But my wife left me, and I lost Narstron—"

"Let us not compare agonies. My last lover stabbed me through the back and then killed all my friends."

"I am not minimizing your pain," he said, trying to keep his voice soothing, "but you eventually recovered and continued living your life—"

"And that's worked out marvelously for me."

"It gets better," Cyrus said in a whisper.

"Does it?" Her words were bitter, tinted with the emotion within her. "Tell me, warrior of Bellarum, how it gets better? I realize that you got over your parents quickly and easily by burying your sorrows in the bosom of your 'blood family' when you joined the Society—" he rankled at her words, feeling the swell deep inside, wanting to correct the wrong of what she said, but he held it in—"but some of us don't open up that easily, don't have anyone to go to."

"You can come to me," he said, eyes burning. "I have been here for you."

"Can I?" She stared at him, dull, dead in the eyes. "Can I truly?"

"Yes!" He felt the words flowing over him, the feeling, and he let it take him. "I have loved you since the day I first saw you. I have dreamed about you, about what it would be like to be with you, and all I've wanted—all I've ever wanted—is to be with you, to love you...to have you love me."

She stared back at him, unflinching at his admission. "And in a hundred years, when you are dead and I yet live, who am I to go to then?"

He heard her speak the words, but they hit him with almost physical force, stunning him. "What?"

"In a thousand years, will you be there for me? In two thousand, will I have forgotten your name? The touch of you against my skin? Will my memories of you be vivid, painful and bright? Or will they dry up like water in the desert, and leave me without remembrance of the blue of your eyes, the lines of your face, the callouses on your hands?"

He felt dry in the mouth, and stilled himself lest a tremble make its way through his body. "What...are you saying?"

"It will not work, Cyrus. It can never be, you and I. For I am elf, and my life is long and my duties are as great as my sorrow. We will not, cannot be. Not ever."

He staggered off the bed, barely in control of himself, feeling drunk though he hadn't had a drop. "You don't mean that."

She looked at him coolly. "I mean every word of it. I thank you for trying to comfort me in my hour of need, but I'll have you take your leave now." She turned over in the bed and lay down, facing the window.

He staggered away and through the door, not bothering to shut it behind him, letting the guard do it instead. The world seemed to carry a strange hum, loud enough in his ears that he couldn't hear anything around him as his feet carried him down the stairs to the foyer. There was still a gathered crowd, and a great many hands slapped him on the back as he passed. He felt them dimly, as though they touched him in a dream.

He found himself sitting in a chair in the lounge, staring out the front window into the darkness. *Did she ever feel the same as I did? Was she just confused after having so many emotions running through her for so long? Is this because of that bastard Archenous Derregnault? If I killed him, maybe...*

He looked up in surprise when he realized Longwell had spoken his name several times. "I'm sorry, what?"

"Didn't mean to disturb you," Longwell said. "I wanted to say farewell."

"Farewell?" Cyrus tried to shake off the veil of confusion that hung around his head. "Where are you going?"

"Home," the dragoon said. "I leave on the morrow. My father's kingdom is invaded and the situation is grim. My father finds himself at war against long odds against our neighbors. He sent one of his knights to bring me home."

"Where is home?" Cyrus asked the question almost ruefully, as much to Longwell as himself.

"Over the Endless Bridge, across the Strait of Carmas, in the Land of Luukessia. It's a large place, but only humans live there; three kingdoms forever jousting back and forth over territory." He looked down at his boots. "I hoped to escape that life of constant, pointless combat, but my father calls, saying things are dire. Luukessia has been deadlocked for a thousand years, and it seems the northern kingdom of the mountains has grown strong enough to upset the balance. My father needs every hand he can find."

"Does he?" Cyrus said. "Could he make use of me?" He looked up at the dragoon, finding Longwell's eyes startled.

"I daresay," Longwell replied. "My father could use any able sword he could get, to say nothing of the fiercest warrior in all Arkaria."

"Keep talking like that and you'll swell his head." Terian spoke, crossing to join them from where he had been seated by one of the hearths. In his hands was something familiar, a scabbard, the one that held the sword that Aisling had brought Cyrus from Termina.

"That's mine," the warrior said, pointing at the weapon in Terian's hands.

"Oh?" The dark knight's voice was suddenly cold. "How so?"

"Aisling brought it back from Termina for me," Cyrus said. "I was set upon by a dark knight, and we battled. I killed him."

"Ah," Terian said with a bow. "In that case, here is your prize, good sir." He knelt with exaggerated pomp and proffered the hilt as a squire would, holding the scabbard for Cyrus to draw the sword.

"It's all right," Cyrus said with a shake of the head. "I kept it because I thought one of our brethren could use it; it's a finer sword than most any and it seemed a shame for it to fall into disuse or be sold."

Terian looked back at him, emotionless. "Aye. I've been looking to put aside my axe for a while. If you'd be amenable, I'd take it off your hands until a day comes when you have need of it."

"I doubt that day will come," Cyrus said. "Use it freely. I gift it to you."

"A princely gift. I hope the day comes when I can repay you for what you've done." Terian took the scabbard and fastened it into his belt, then turned to Longwell. "Would your father have need of a dark knight in this Land of Luukessia?"

"My father would find use for any who came with me," the dragoon said. "His letter asked me to bring along any assistance I can provide. As I said, we know no magic in those lands, so anyone who fights with the aid of it, as you do, would be worth a hundred or more ordinary soldiers."

"Then I will go with you into the east," Cyrus said.

"We leave on the morrow," Longwell told him. "We have a long ride ahead of us; I hope to have a wizard teleport us—"

"To the portal on the beach on the Sea of Carmas?" Cyrus asked.

"You know of it?"

"I've seen the Endless Bridge, once," Cyrus said. "I wondered where it went at the time."

"To another land," Longwell said. "A green and beautiful place, but a long journey. It's two days' hike south on the beach, then five long days across the bridge. We must be provisioned amply before crossing, for there is no fresh water nor food to be found on it. At the other side lies the first kingdom of the three. They would let one man pass — perhaps two or three. Any more and we will be challenged. All told, it will take us near two months to make it to my father's lands from here."

"I'll pack my things," Cyrus told him, "and see you on the morrow."

After nodding farewell to Terian, he climbed the stairs and hesitated at the landing where the doors to the Council Chamber were. After a moment of doubt tugged at him, he stopped. *I owe him at least an explanation.*

The door creaked as Cyrus entered. The hearth burned with a fire that warmed the room, and the smell of wood burning gave him a last sense of home. Alaric remained standing where Cyrus had left him earlier, and did not turn when the door opened. "Samwen Longwell is going back to his homeland, Luukessia, to help defend his father's Kingdom, which is under attack. I wanted to let you know that I'll be going with him, as is Terian."

The Ghost turned, and Cyrus saw neutrality on his face. "The land of Luukessia is torn by war?"

"Aye," Cyrus replied. "Longwell's father has a kingdom there. They are in need of able hands to wield swords."

"Enrant Monge." Alaric's words were quiet. "Very well. We have a problem to attend to before you leave."

"Oh?" Cyrus rested a hand on the back of his chair.

"Because of our rising fortunes and the notoriety you garnered in your defense of Termina, we have accumulated over a thousand applicants who have little to no combat experience. Without a general to lead them, they will languish. Indeed, the attack on the Realm of Death was the first taste of battle for some of them, yet most were not even through the portal by the time the fight was over." He walked to the table and leaned over it. "If you are to be absent for...as long as you are likely to be gone...we will need these new recruits trained."

Cyrus stiffened. "If you have to appoint a new general, I understand —"

"I will put out a call for volunteers to join you; you will take as many of them with you as will come," Alaric interrupted him.

"They are of no use to us until they have known combat, and we are unlikely to be engaging in any invasions in your absence. A land without magic is a good place for them to learn what battle is about. You will assemble forty to fifty experienced veterans and magic users, and I will send word to the newest recruits, whose experience is lacking, and see who is willing to accompany you."

"I'm...certain Longwell's father will be pleased at any additional assistance we can offer."

"His son has earned our loyalty." Alaric gripped the back of the chair. "We will repay that fidelity in kind; we will help stave off the ruin of their kingdom and it will assist us in preparing our forces."

"We'll likely be gone for several months," Cyrus said, looking away from the Ghost's piercing gaze. "You're certain you're all right with that?"

"Whatever calamity comes our way will not be dissuaded by whatever inexperienced warriors go with you. We can defend Sanctuary against most any danger with even a few hundred defenders." He looked at Cyrus, unblinking. "But I suspect your absence will be...noticed."

"I'm not so sure of that," Cyrus said under his breath.

"Before you go..." Alaric held out a hand, as if to stop Cyrus. "I know the revelation that the gods are not invincible intrigues you. I do not want you to use the Army of Sanctuary against the gods in the future, do you understand? I want your word."

"My word?" Cyrus blinked in disbelief. "Do you really think my mind is on that right now?"

"I think I am about to send you across the world at the head of an assemblage of our forces, and I want your word that no matter what happens, you won't go after the gods." Alaric's eye burned with a fire and he closed the distance to Cyrus. "We were lucky that Mortus is so ill-favored among his own kind, lucky to kill him without any casualties. That luck may not extend to another god, and I don't want you getting the idea that hunting deities is anything other than utter foolishness."

"He died so quickly Alaric—"

"*We...were...lucky!*" The Ghost reached over and seized Cyrus by both shoulders, shaking him. "If you lead your guildmates into battle with another god, there will be death. Put aside your pride and listen to what I am telling you!"

"All right," Cyrus said. "I...won't go after them."

"I want your word." Alaric's hands still rested on Cyrus's pauldrons and he held firm.

"I promise," Cyrus said, his words coming out soft and low.

"Very good." Alaric looked away and strode back to the window. "Assemble your veterans. I will give the orders for the recruits to meet you in the yard on the morrow. Take at least five wizards or druids with you to send messages back with your progress."

"Thank you," Cyrus said. He paused, uncertain what else to say. "I'll...see you in a few months." He turned to leave but Alaric's voice halted him at the door.

"Farewell," the Ghost called out.

"Goodbye," Cyrus returned. "We'll see you then."

As the door closed behind him, Alaric's reply was nearly lost, but Cyrus could have sworn, underneath the sound of the fire crackling in the hearth, he heard a whisper.

"No...you won't."

Chapter 53

The day dawned bright, sunny and glorious, with just the hint of bitterness that accompanied late winter. The warmth of the sun was offset by the chill of the morning air. As Cyrus made his way down the steps, he found the foyer in a state of odd quiet. *I'm late,* he thought, *but the rest of the guild must be sleeping it off; undoubtedly they had a celebration.*

He passed the doors to the Great Hall and saw a lone figure inside. Larana sat at a table and turned when he passed, her face smudged. She stared at him for a long moment without saying anything, then rose and made her way to him. He waited for her, stunned and curious in equal measure as she stopped, grabbed hold of him and hugged him close, finishing by giving him a simple kiss on the cheek. Her eyes were wet, and he felt a droplet splash as she pulled from him and ran back into the Great Hall, disappearing into the kitchen where he could not see her.

He turned mechanically and walked out the front door of Sanctuary, ready to go to the stables. He halted at the top of the steps, blinded by the harsh light of day and stunned by what he saw once his eyes adjusted.

"Company...present arms!" Thad's shout jarred him back to awareness. The grounds were filled with members and recruits, with a company of at least a thousand assembled in formation, ready to march. The officers waited in two rows on the steps, presiding. To either side of the formation stood well-wishers, members cheering for their brethren, laughing and waving.

Alaric approached Cyrus, clasping a hand on his shoulder. "Your army awaits, General."

"There must be over a thousand here," Cyrus said in awe.

"Eleven hundred and fifty, but who's counting?" Vaste, as always, weighed in with no small amount of irony.

"You, apparently," Terian said.

"I don't..." Cyrus stuttered as he looked over the assemblage. "I mean...I didn't think..."

"You never do," Erith sighed, "but we love you anyway."

"Did you think that these new warriors would not want to follow their general into honorable battle in a new land?" Alaric squinted at him in the daylight. "They fell over themselves volunteering; in fact we had to refuse numerous veterans in order to keep the numbers within reason, else you'd have taken nearly everyone with you."

Cy looked again over the crowd, overwhelmed. "I see." He turned his eyes to the bottom of the steps, where horses awaited. He saw Aisling, shifting back and forth on a stallion next to Terian's destrier, which waited for its master. Odellan waited, his winged helm standing out in the crowd. Martaina Proelius waited ahorse, whispering something in her mount's ear while Mendicant the goblin looked bizarre on a pony.

"Anything to say to your army before you depart?" Alaric indicated the assembled crowd.

"Uh..." Cyrus coughed, then cleared his throat. "Today, we take the Army of Sanctuary into a new land, in support of a very dear friend. This is the heart and the essence of what we do. We hear of someone in need, and do all we can to assist them. There is no more faithful friend than Sanctuary — and no more faithful enemy, either, if it comes to that. Mortus learned that last night." He saw Alaric blanch out of the corner of his eye.

"When I joined Sanctuary, it was for a far different purpose," Cyrus said, voice straining as he shouted to be heard. "I came here to get better weapons and equipment, so I could pursue my ambitions of being a more powerful warrior. I was willing to invade any land, take from any god, goblin or dragon that had what I wanted, and do whatever it took to achieve my aims. But what I learned in lessons about honor, brotherhood and fidelity here changed my mind.

"We march now to a far off kingdom, without hope for reward, because a friend has asked for help. This is our true mission. What we've done in the past, be it striking down the Dragonlord or invading Enterra, has been for noble reasons. No other guild would do these things, and yet they are what define us. We fight for honor, for our brethren, and for those who can't fight for themselves.

"Thank you, all who have come to wish us well. We will go and do our duty, and return before you know we're gone."

At the last word, he walked down the steps toward Windrider, who waited next to Aisling. It felt like the longest and loneliest walk he had ever taken. He took the reins from her and threw his saddlebags across the haunches before stepping up. Terian joined him, as did Longwell and Curatio. Cyrus looked at the healer in confusion. "You're coming?"

"Aye," the elder elf replied as he mounted his horse with ease. He looked away, toward the horizon. "I think it would be for the best if Alaric and I parted ways for a bit."

Cyrus raised his hand in salute, and was matched by those lined up on either side of his army. He looked back to the assembled officers, all of whom were present save one, either on the steps or ahorse with him. He urged Windrider forward, leading the riders around. The army, neatly broken up into six blocks of soldiers, executed a turn toward the gate and began to march as he took the lead, the others behind him at a canter.

"We'll teleport once we're beyond the wall," he said to Nyad, who rode next to Ryin Ayend. "You know the portal we're going to?" The elf nodded. "Good."

He stopped just beyond the gate, moving Windrider to the side of the road, and looked back, beyond the wall, above the crowd, to the tower in the center of Sanctuary. Far, far up the side, he looked for the windows almost at the top, where the officers were quartered. One was open, and a dot of blond hair was visible, even so many stories up.

Does she know that I've been fighting for her all this time? Does she care? Does it matter? The cold cynicism blanketed him, chilling him far more than any winter could. *Time to go back to doing my duty,* he thought, *and fighting for Sanctuary.*

He turned and rode back to the front of the line, leading his army away, out of the gates — and off to war.

NOW

Epilogue

Cyrus blotted another tear from his eyes and cursed himself for his weakness, then shook his head. The rain continued outside, and the dreariness caused him to curse again, before he turned his attention back to the words in the book.

Niamh is dead. I can scarcely believe it. She was such a force of personality, such a mischievous dreamer, such a happy spirit that I could not believe her age when first I heard it. I was certain she had to be of the youngest generation, like my sister, but no, she was over six hundred — and still young at heart, wild and free, happier and more full of life than anyone I have ever met, even the humans.

Until now.

And because of me.

I don't know if these assassins have come to Sanctuary because I am shelas'akur or for some other reason, but I know that more than I can express, I mourn Niamh. Any brightness that may be manifest in my grim personality is not a result of myself, but of her — the constant example that I need to, in her words, "lighten up."

I remember more than anything the day she told me something I didn't want to hear. We had finished watching Goliath get run out of Reikonos and she was off to visit her family in Pharesia, and me to mine in Termina. She teleported me to Santir, and caught my arm after I thanked her but before I could get away. "I think he loves you," she told me.

"I think you're wrong." She and I were officers together; we'd been on more than a few adventures, and yet we were no closer than any two other members of Sanctuary. "I suspect he merely feels the heat of that which he carries betwixt his legs." I was lying, deflecting what she was saying. I was warming up to Cyrus Davidon, but I was hardly ready to accept anything but sincere affection at that stage. One step at a time, I believed, was most prudent.

"That too," she said. "But it doesn't mean he's immune to the other."

"You exaggerate," I told her. "I am fond of him as well, but we've only known each other for a couple of years — "

"A veritable eternity to humans," she replied. "He feels it; you clearly feel something back. Life — even for us elves — is too short and entirely too unpredictable to continue to let it drag out." She shrugged. "Just making an observation."

Before I could tell her to keep her observations to herself, she teleported away in a gust of wind. Now that she has died, just a few months later, all I can think about was what she had said about life being too short. Even for us elves indeed.

Cyrus rubbed his eyes, turned the page, and looked at the next passage.

I can't believe he followed me. I've always suspected him of madness, but I never anticipated that he would come with me when I left. It's been days since we left Sanctuary, and now we're in Termina. Home.

Yet with father ailing, it doesn't feel like home. Mother, as usual, is on the warpath. From the moment we arrived, all she has done is spit ill-considered wattle at Cyrus. He responded finally, once we were out of sight, by rubbing his hand across a painting in the hallway. Of course, we could hear it along with his whispered admonition of, "Enjoy the smell of that, hag," and Mother knew right away what he'd done.

"I heard that," she screeched at him. "Keep your hands off my things!"

The door shut behind him, but we still heard his reply. "Yes, Mother."

She turned to me and gave an approving nod. "I like him. He's much wittier than your last."

"He's not my..." I clenched my jaw shut in frustration. "...anything."

The sound of rain cascading from the top of the tower was soothing. Cyrus flipped the page and looked to the next passage.

I stared down at my father, and he looked back at me. "You seem conflicted, my daughter."

"Is that so unusual?" I asked him, trying to hide my fears behind a smile that was as fake as Aisling's desire for anything but rutting. I couldn't believe he kissed me. I couldn't believe I kissed him back. And I couldn't decide whether I was incredibly happy or just the opposite, so I believe I might have come off somewhat stern.

He frowned. "You are never conflicted. Your sister, she wavers, uncertain of what to do. You? Never. You always knew what you wanted and never hesitated to go for it. You are like your mother in that regard."

"You make it sound like a personality flaw."

He chuckled. "Hardly. I have been in many businesses in my life, after my days as an adventurer. Especially since you came along. The lesson I learned," he said, turning serious, "is that life will only give you as much as you're willing to fight for."

"I'm not certain I have any more fight left in me." I admitted it with a trace of sadness.

"I've felt that way myself," he said. "The days came when things were hard, when nothing went right, and it had been a string of bad news

and setbacks, sometimes for months at a time. I would get down and dispirited. Your mother kept me going, even when I didn't want to. A business would be dying in my hands and she wanted me to turn it around – and believed I could."

"I don't think this is quite the same," I told him.

"It's exactly the same." His eyes glittered. "The stakes are just higher. You put your life on the line in battle to get what you want, to shape your life to your whims by taking on adventure. I'll be the first to tell you that life will hit you hard, regardless of what you do – adventurer, business person, king. No one is immune to the brutal reality that you lose people in life. That our decisions sometimes have horrible ramifications, even the innocuous ones. That people die. And that you may feel responsible, but have nothing to do with it."

"What if I had done something different?" I asked him. "This...person...who died for me might yet be alive."

"Perhaps." He shook his head. "Perhaps not. You were born into a role that you didn't ask for. Being the chosen one of your people, their last hope, was not a fair position to put you in." His eyes hid behind a veneer of pain. "Not for one so young. Not to have so much piled upon your shoulders."

"Shhh," I told him. "I'm not so young anymore."

"You are to me. You'll always be to me."

The sound of an argument made its way up the stairs and I exchanged a look with my father. We heard mother's heated words, lashing at Cyrus, and he inclined his head toward the door. "Go."

Cyrus remembered the argument and the kiss that had happened only scant minutes before it. His brow folded downward, as he recalled what had happened after, the battle for the bridge...and all else.

I stormed into my room to change, Mother on my heels. Cyrus and Isabelle had left, and I was to join him, to "take a walk" is what I had said. In truth, I cared naught for the walk. I only wanted to find a secluded place where I could kiss him. As utterly rubbish as it sounds, it is true. Me. All I wanted was to feel him against me. If we found a place private enough, I think I would even have been amenable to more.

Mother followed me into my room as I slipped on my undershirt and cloth pants. "Have you given any thought to what will happen in the future?"

"Yes, I have," I said offhand. "I think, in the next few minutes, I'll strip him naked, get astride him like a harlot, and ride him until I wring every sound of pleasure from his lips that I can."

My mother let out an elvish curse. "You think of only what will happen in the next minutes and hours and days, but not that which will fill the rest of your life. You're still a child — and you think like a child."

"Yes, well, what I'm about to do to him is distinctly inappropriate for children." I graced her with a wicked smile.

"He will die when you are barely an adult in our society," she said with anger. "He will be dust by the time your second century rolls around. You can't even be covekan with him, experience the most intimate emotional bond of our people, because he'll be dead before he reaches an age where he can experience it!"

"I don't care!" I shrieked at her. "It's MY life! Mine! Not yours! This is why I left at fourteen, to get away from you and your incessant need to tell me what to do in every instance. I don't care what elven society would have me do; I care less what you would have me do." I finished strapping on my breastplate and pulled myself up to my full height, which allowed me to look down on her. "I care about what I want to do." I didn't bother to hit her with the shoulder of my armor as I passed, but given her expression, you might have thought I did.

"If you mean to do what you say," she said with an air of haughty triumph as I reached the door, "then why are you putting on your armor?"

"Because I'm a paladin," I shot back at her. "A holy warrior of Vidara, sworn to the cause of defending those who cannot defend themselves." I took two steps back toward her and put my finger in her face. "And because the length of time to take it all off only builds the anticipation and heightens the pleasure for when the moment arrives." I shot her a dazzling, evil grin and stormed out, leaving her with a look that was distinctly...disappointed.

Cyrus's eyes skipped down the page as the same passage continued.

Of course I look back on the argument now and think about how positively over the edge I was at that moment. I never did find a secluded place with him because the dark elves burned Santir to the ground and invaded Termina. My home. My mother, dead, myself injured, and my hometown seized by the oldest enemy of our people. Add to that my father's death a few days later and I'm surprised I was still able to move.

Recovering in the palace was a gloomy affair. Cyrus hovered at a distance, afraid to embarrass me in front of Arydni or Nyad. If I had still felt the same about him as I did the day we left to take the walk, I wouldn't have cared if they were there or not, especially as I continued to mend.

But I didn't. Every time I looked at him, I thought of the argument with Mother. The last one; the worst we've had. I've disappointed her on a thousand occasions. But the last time, the very last time we had a private conversation, to have her look at me like that...

She was dead less than twelve hours later. And all I can think of now is that look...that haunted, disappointed look...and it makes me feel like I'm fourteen again, and leaving her all alone in a house that's too big for her.

He flipped a few more pages, skimming as he went, until he found one of particular significance. He clenched his hand and felt the cracking of his joints beneath the gauntlet.

We were caught. Hopelessly. Mortus stared down at us, and I knew in that moment that every one of us was dead along with any hope left for my people.

Except we weren't. Alaric was a genius, playing upon the pride of the God of Death, using flattery in a way that few can, giving him golden words that must have cured like honey poured in his ear. I thought, just for a moment, that he would let us all go.

But hope failed as he forced a choice upon us — Curatio or myself; he would only allow the rest of them to pass if one of us stayed behind.

My thoughts were dark, jumbled. I had lost everything — home, Mother, Father. Mother's words had settled in my heart, until the thought of holding Cyrus close to me was more bitter than the taste of ashes on my lips. I wanted him but I knew it was not to be and I couldn't tell him. I didn't want to tell him. All I wanted was for these overwhelming emotions to end, to give me peace, to let me sleep a full night, to not have my heart be filled with constant sorrow.

And there was Death himself. The eight-armed, four-legged representation of it, and he offered me a way out. By my death, I could buy the lives of the hundreds with me.

And I would never have to tell him.

Curatio, damn him for his nobility, spoke up first. "I have had a long and storied life. I will remain behind."

"No!" I shoved my way to him. "You can give our people hope with what you know. You're the only one who can read...it." I stared up at my end, his face horrific, and I wondered how he would finish me. "I will remain with you, God of Death, as your sacrifice." At that moment, I only hoped it would be quick.

Curatio tried to shove the parchment into my hand. "I'm not the only one who can read it," he whispered, then raised his voice. "You are young, and have so much to live for."

I shoved him away. "I do not. I am weary of this life, of living in a world that would take everything from you a piece at a time, until you have naught left." Mortus met my gaze evenly, and I could see dark amusement in the eye that faced me. "If you would have me be your sacrifice, strike swift and true. End it – and be quick about it."

"Done." Knowing he had accepted my sacrifice, I felt my head bow and my body relax. The legends said a god could destroy a mortal in one blow. I could not have asked for a swifter end.

"NOOOO!" I felt something hit me, hard, in the chest, sending me reeling to the ground. When I looked back, I saw Cyrus with his sword raised, Mortus's hand descending with the killing strike that had been meant for me. I had not the time to scream, though I felt it upon my lips, nor to cry, nor the strength to throw myself in front of him. He was going to die, for me, because everything Niamh had said was true.

He loved me. He always had. And I had felt the same, but he was out of my reach.

The God of Death hit him with enough force to kill, his palm landing on the edge of Cyrus's sword. The warrior who I loved was flung apart and I saw him covered in light as the blow landed, pulling him back together, his body landing on the field a hundred feet away. I breathed a sigh of relief when I saw him lift his head, dazed.

Then I turned back to the God of Death and I saw his hand was asunder, his black blood coursing onto the ground around him as he howled in anguish, and I knew that something was very, very wrong.

Cyrus remembered Mortus, the way he had staggered, the way he shrank as the battle had gone on. And finally, the way his crumpled body had looked in death, so pathetic that it was hard to believe he had been a god at all.

He didn't awaken me when he opened the door to my quarters. I had been awake and thinking again about all the things that had been weighing on me for so long. The emotions had once more overwhelmed me like the waves of the Torrid Sea washing over a ship until she breaks apart and drowns. I wondered if that was to happen to me, awash in these horrible feelings that I couldn't seem to control, this despair and sorrow that was unending.

He spoke quite a bit that night. The theme was the same – that my feelings would pass in time, and that he had felt pain such as this before. I tried to keep from fighting back with stinging words, but I fear I may have failed.

Finally, I told him the truth. Or at least most of it. I told him it would not work between us. I lied to him.

Because in truth, it would work fine. He would love me all the days of the rest of his life, I think, and I would love him all the rest of mine. Unfortunately, mine would last up to 5,900 years past his. I feared spending every day of them feeling about him the way I felt now.

I lost my home, my mother and my father.

My first lover stabbed me in the back, killed my friends, and left me to die.

I stabbed the man I loved more than any of them through the heart, saw the emotion wash over his face while I watched, impassive, a small voice inside me screaming what a fool I was to do it.

But I made a decision. Mother would have approved. My sorrow over losing him after a long, full life together would be worse than losing him before we had even begun. If I loved him this much now, how much worse would it get given a hundred years to compound? Putting an end to it now would hurt, certainly, but would I even notice next to all the other emotional agony I was experiencing?

He left. And I found out.

The answer was yes. Yes, I did notice.

And it made it ever so much worse.

Cyrus blinked back the tears again at her words. *She felt the same way then as I did. Dammit.* He brushed them away and turned back to the next passage, trying to keep his thoughts on what he was reading.

I watched him leave, with all the pomp and circumstance that Alaric could arrange. Cyrus rode out on that beautiful horse he always uses. I saw him go through the gate and look back. I could see him, and I could swear he was looking at me. After only a moment, he turned and rode away. I watched the formation halt a short distance from the wall, and a wizard teleportation spell swept them onward.

The next days were dark. I didn't leave my room or my bed. J'anda, Vaste and Larana kept showing up, the latter bringing food every time she appeared. She never spoke, but I saw the pity and sorrow in her eyes every time she looked upon me. I've heard it said she pines for Cyrus, and I knew every time she appeared that it was true. She would try and clean my quarters when she showed up, and she never fussed about talking, unlike the others.

After a week I found the strength to leave my quarters. All right, I was forced out of them by that relentless harridan, Erith. She stopped by and harrassed me until I finally cleaned up, put on something cloth and went down to the lounge one afternoon. It was abuzz with activity when I got there (damn Cyrus for putting that word in my mind) yet she and I found a quiet place to sit and talk. Nothing deep — mostly superficial things — but I had a cup of ale, and it was the first time I'd felt...alive...in forever.

I noticed a dark elf standing by the door. He was tall for his sort, lanky, with distant eyes but a familiar look. I saw Alaric cross the foyer and speak with him at some length, taking an envelope from him. Then the dark elf departed.

I have known Alaric for...years. Years and years. He remains mostly an enigma, even to me, but this time I knew something was wrong. His hand hung at his side, and even with his helm on, I could almost see him flinch.

I walked away from Erith in the middle of a sentence. Alaric seemed not to notice me, even as I drew close to him. He continued to stare at the words on the page. "Hello, lass," he said. "It's good to see you up and moving again."

"I could hardly stay down forever."

"No," he agreed, "you could not."

"What have you got there that has you so distressed?" I stared at him, watching for his reaction.

He forced a smile. "Good news, certainly. We only ever get good news around here. Especially of late."

"We rarely get good news around here," I said, snatching the envelope out of his grasp. To his credit, he didn't try and stop me. "Especially of late."

"Let me summarize," he said. "Terian's father has died."

I started to hand the letter back. "That's a tragedy. Are you going to send a messenger to deliver it to him?"

His eye flickered, and I caught a hint that made me stop before giving it back to him. "I think not," he said.

I don't know why, but I felt a sudden chill, perhaps from standing in front of the main door. I looked at the parchment I held in my hands, and something told me — compelled me, really — to read it.

Dearest Terian,

I am writing to inform you that your father was killed in action with the dark elven army during the invasion of Termina. He fought and died with so many of his comrades in arms, taking the Grand Span that allowed our forces to march into the center of the city. As the foremost dark knight in our country, the Sovereign immediately declared a holiday in his honor, and pronounced whoever killed him a war criminal of the worst kind, and surely marked for death.

Unfortunately, his priceless sword, the one passed through our family for generations, was lost with him...

I looked up from the parchment, looked at Alaric, and I knew he saw the despair in my eyes. "Was it you?" he asked.

"No," I replied. "I fought him, certainly. He was a beast, the strongest dark knight I've ever battled. He set upon Cyrus when he was wounded, and nearly killed him before I intervened. He almost killed me as well but Cyrus stabbed him through the back." I blinked in disbelief. "We had no idea he was Terian's father..."

"Nor could you have," Alaric said. "Terian and his father parted ways many years ago, and on less-than-agreeable terms. I know after he left us two years ago, Terian attempted a rapprochement with his father that did not go well for either party, but..." He shook his head. "I do not know how he will take this news."

"That's why you're not sending him a messenger," I said. "You're afraid of how he'll react. When he sees this letter, he'll know it was either me that killed his father..." I let my words drift off.

"Or Cyrus," Alaric said. "Or some combination of both. I would rather wait and control his reaction, to have him here, surrounded by those of us he has known for so long when he finds out, rather than have him learn of his father's death by Cyrus's hand at some ill-timed juncture, when he might be predisposed to..." Alaric paused, searching for the right words, "...reckless action."

"You mean revenge." The words were cold when I said them.

Alaric did not blink. "I mean revenge." He took the letter back from me and tucked it behind him, along with his hands. "So long as we do not inform Terian, everything should proceed apace." He shook his head. "Though I consider him a brother, the dark knight is dangerous and unpredictable at times and I will not have Cyrus or you anywhere nearby when the truth is told. By holding off, we keep him – all of you, really – safe." He folded his arms. "They will proceed on their mission without news from us. It will be better for all if we hold off on this news until they return."

Alaric is usually spot-on in his predictions. He has a keen observatory eye for the nature of us mortals, probably from long experience – or possibly some undisclosed skill that allows him to look into the heart of a person. In this case, though, he didn't misjudge a person so much as he mistook an event. After all, he couldn't have known that Aisling had brought back Terian's father's sword from Termina. He couldn't have known that Cyrus had not only shown it to Terian, but given it to him, not realizing that he'd grown up around it, and knew his father's sword when he saw it – and knew that if his father was parted from it, it wasn't willingly. Or while he was still alive.

We didn't find out until much, much later how very wrong Alaric was.

Cyrus closed the book. His mind was strained, having read for hours. He felt a throbbing behind his eye, a little pain that told him he was overwhelmed. Emotions tugged at him, he felt his breathing get ragged, and he felt himself reach for his sword in anger, then stop. Then he reached for it again and touched the hilt, felt the power surge through him, and he pulled it away only through sheer force of will.

*I can't believe she...didn't tell me...I didn't know...*Thoughts flew through his mind, whirling, driving him to distraction. A flash of anger was hot, and he turned and punched the wall behind him, cracking the stone. He punched again, this time at a bookshelf, and it broke in an explosion of wood, splinters flying everywhere. *She didn't tell me...she didn't...*Another flash of pure rage took hold of him and he threw the diary as hard as he could.

It flew across the room and hit the painting that hung above the hearth. When it impacted, the frame splintered and broke in two. The bottom half fell, bouncing off the mantle to the ground. The top half hung at a tilted angle, and the painting that the frame had sheltered fluttered down, coming to rest facedown on the floor.

Cyrus blinked. Behind the hanging vestiges of the frame was an indentation in the wall that the painting had covered. A small shelf was secreted behind it. He crossed the gap to the fireplace and stared at it. The shelf was small, recessed a few inches; just enough to hold the contents.

A book. Worn, aged and ragged, he lifted it from the shelf and opened it to the first page.

Here begins the account of Alaric Garaunt, Guildmaster of these halls, and the first of my name...

He read the next page, and a feeling ran through him—a chill as certain as if he had run through the rains outside—and he sat down once more and let the fire wash over him as he read the old knight's tale.

A Note to the Reader

If you enjoyed this book and want to know about future releases by Robert J. Crane, you can go to my website (robertJcrane.com) to sign up for my mailing list! I promise I won't spam you (I only send an email when I have a new book released) and I'll never sell your info. You can also unsubscribe at any time.

I wanted to take a moment to thank you for reading this story. As an independent author, getting my name out to build an audience is one of the biggest priorities on any given day. If you enjoyed this story and are looking forward to reading more, let someone know - post it on Amazon, on your blog, if you have one, on Goodreads.com, place it in a quick Facebook status or Tweet with a link to the page of whatever outlet you purchased it from (Amazon, Barnes & Noble, Apple, etc). Good reviews inspire people to take a chance on a new author – like me. And we new authors can use all the help we can get.

Thanks again for your time.

Robert J. Crane

About the Author

Robert J. Crane was born and raised on Florida's Space Coast before moving to the upper midwest in search of cooler climates and more palatable beer. He graduated from the University of Central Florida with a degree in English Creative Writing. He worked for a year as a substitute teacher and worked in the financial services field for seven years while writing in his spare time. He makes his home in the Twin Cities area of Minnesota.

He can be contacted in several ways:

Via email at cyrusdavidon@gmail.com
Follow him on Twitter - **@robertJcrane**
Connect on Facebook – **robertJcrane (Author)**
Website – **robertJcrane.com**
Blog – robertJcrane.blogspot.com
Become a fan on Goodreads –
http://www.goodreads.com/RobertJCrane

Cyrus Davidon Will Return in

CRUSADER
The Sanctuary Series, Volume Four

Fate and choices have placed Cyrus and Vara a world apart; Cyrus finds himself embroiled in a conflict in the land of Luukessia, defending the people against a tireless, implacable foe while suffering through his own doubts and personal struggles in the wake of Vara's decision.

Meanwhile Sanctuary faces a growing crisis as the war consuming Arkaria deepens and comes home - The Sovereign of the Dark Elves has his eye fixed on Sanctuary itself and it remains up to Vara and Alaric to keep the guild safe against the onslaught of armies.

Coming **Fourth Quarter 2012**

The Sanctuary Series
Epic Fantasy by Robert J. Crane

The world of Arkaria is a dangerous place, filled with dragons, titans, goblins and other dangers. Those who live in this world are faced with two choices: live an ordinary life or become an adventurer and seek the extraordinary.

Avenger
The Sanctuary Series, Volume Two

When a series of attacks on convoys draws suspicion that Sanctuary is involved, Cyrus Davidon must put aside his personal struggles and try to find the raiders. As the attacks worsen, Cyrus and his comrades find themselves abandoned by their allies, surrounded by enemies, facing the end of Sanctuary and a war that will consume their world.

Available Now!

Champion
The Sanctuary Series, Volume Three

As the war heats up in Arkaria, Vara is forced to flee after an ancient order of skilled assassins infiltrates Sanctuary and targets her. Cyrus Davidon accompanies her home to the elven city of Termina and the two of them become embroiled in a mystery that will shake the very foundations of the Elven Kingdom – and Arkaria.

Available Now!

Crusader
The Sanctuary Series, Volume Four

Cyrus Davidon finds himself far from his home in Sanctuary, in the land of Luukessia, a place divided and deep in turmoil. With his allies at his side, Cyrus finds himself facing off against an implacable foe in a war that will challenge all his convictions - and one he may not be able to win.

Coming Fourth Quarter 2012!

Savages
A Sanctuary Short Story

Twenty years before Cyrus Davidon joined Sanctuary, his father was killed in a war with the trolls and he has never forgiven them. Enter Vaste, a troll unlike most; courageous, loyal and an outcast. When Cyrus and Vaste become trapped in a far distant land, they are forced to overcome their suspicions and work together to get home.

Available Now!

A Familiar Face
A Sanctuary Short Story

Cyrus Davidon gets more than he bargained for when he takes a day away from Sanctuary to visit the busy markets of his hometown, Reikonos. While there, he meets a woman who seems very familiar, and appears to know him, but that he can't place.

Available Now!

Alone
The Girl in the Box, Book 1

Sienna Nealon was a 17-year-old girl who had been held prisoner in her own house by her mother for twelve years. Then one day her mother vanished, and Sienna woke up to find two strange men in her home. On the run, unsure of who to turn to and discovering she possesses mysterious powers, Sienna finds herself pursued by a shadowy agency known as the Directorate and hunted by a vicious, bloodthirsty psychopath named Wolfe, each of which is determined to capture her for their own purposes...

Available Now!

Untouched
The Girl in the Box, Book 2

Still haunted by her last encounter with Wolfe and searching for her mother, Sienna Nealon must put aside her personal struggles when a new threat emerges – Aleksandr Gavrikov, a metahuman so powerful, he could destroy entire cities – and he's focused on bringing the Directorate to its knees.

Available now!

Soulless
The Girl in the Box, Book 3

Available now!

Family
The Girl in the Box, Book 4

Coming Fourth Quarter 2012!

Trust
The Girl in the Box, Book 5

Coming Fourth Quarter 2012!

Made in the USA
Monee, IL
06 January 2022

88275404R00216